The Harlem Cycle Volume II

The Big Gold Dream
All Shot Up
The Heat's On

GW00730270

CHESTER HIMES

The Harlem Cycle Volume 2

The Big Gold Dream
All Shot Up
The Heat's On

This edition first published in 1996 by
Payback Press, an imprint of Canongate Books Ltd,
14 High Street, Edinburgh EH1 1TE

The Big Gold Dream and *All Shot Up* © Estate of Chester
Himes, 1960; *The Heat's On* © Estate of Chester Himes, 1966
'The Dilemma of the Black Writer in America' © Estate of
Chester Himes, 1948

All rights reserved

British Library Cataloguing-in-Publication Data

A catalogue record for this book is available upon request
from the British Library

ISBN 0 86241 631 0

Typeset in Minion and Serif Modular by
Palimpsest Book Production Limited,
Polmont, Stirlingshire
Print and bound in Denmark by Norhaven A/S Rotation

Contents

About the Author

That Chester Himes is not more widely known is a telling indictment of the society he grew up in and eventually left in order to gain artistic freedom. He did have a successful career as a writer but initially in a foreign land and in a language which he never wrote in. Many less resilient human beings would have simply quit.

Born in Missouri in 1909, Himes began writing fiction in jail, where he served seven-and-a-half years of a twenty-year sentence for armed robbery. His first novel, *If He Hollers Let Him Go*, was published in 1945, but was too fierce for the times. According to the author, it was prevented from becoming a bestseller by his nervous publishers who would not meet the demand for reprinting. It sounds like a bad joke. If only it were.

The other books he wrote whilst in the States met with a similarly frosty response and Himes, bitter and frustrated by this lack of an audience in his homeland, decided to move to France. The lecture which follows and which Himes delivered in Chicago in 1948, 'The Dilemma of the Black Writer in America', gives a telling insight into why he felt he had to leave. It appears he made the right decision.

It was having moved to Paris that he met Marcel Duhamel, the editor of Gallimard's Serie Noire, who persuaded Himes to try his hand at writing a detective novel for his famous crime list. The result was *La Reine des pommes* (*For Love of Imabelle*) which was later titled *A Rage in Harlem*. The novel went platinum, winning the prestigious Grand Prix de la Litterature Policière which had never before been won by a non-French author, and Himes rapidly became established as an acclaimed and consistently bestselling author.

He went on to write eight more Coffin Ed and Grave Digger novels in what came to be known as *The Harlem Cycle* although Himes himself always referred to them as his domestic thrillers. They did eventually get published both in the States and Britain but long after they should have been.

Comparisons can be made to other artists who went into self-imposed exile. Joyce and Beckett are two Irishmen who escaped the suffocating and parochial atmosphere of their native land and in the course of doing so wrote arguably their most important books. From black America, Richard Wright, James Baldwin, Bud Powell and Dexter Gordon are just four major figures who left America and found the respect and success they deserved by becoming outsiders. As George Clinton chillingly observed, 'America Eats its Young'.

Himes left America in body but never in spirit. All his work explores the inherent double-standards and hypocrisy of the Land of Liberty and in Coffin Ed and Grave Digger he created one of the most memorable and complex pairs of detectives that exist in literature. Daily they faced the paradox of being law enforcers for an unjust system while attempting to provide a modicum of justice for a race that the law continually excluded and yet victimised. Their dialogue often reflects the bitter irony of their lot and Himes uses their voices to denounce racial injustice and the American system that made and continues to make it possible.

It is easy to dwell on the serious side of Himes' writing and forget the fact that his humour was irrepressible. His genius was in managing to create page-turning thrillers that combined ferocious wit, social protest and political commentary. The result was a fiction that transcended any genre.

Chester Himes died in Spain in 1984. The body of work that he produced – eighteen novels, two volumes of autobiography and over fifty short stories – will live on forever.

The Dilemma of the Black Writer in America

In order to evaluate the problems confronting the American Black writer, we must first examine the reasons compelling all writers, of all races and nationalities, to write. The obvious answer, the one that comes first to mind, is that we write to express and perpetuate our intellectual and emotional experiences, to relate to others the processes of our thoughts and the creations of our imagining. That is the pat answer.

But in fact we have a greater motive, a nobler aim; we are impelled by the search for reality. We write not only to recount our experiences and our intellectual processes, but to interpret the meaning contained in them. We search for the nobler meaning of life in the realities of our experiences, in the realities of our dreams, our hopes, our memories. Anger and fear serve the realization of our humanity as do love and charity.

The essential necessity of humanity is to find cause for its existence. Man cannot live without some knowledge of the purpose of life. If he can find no reason for life, he creates one in the inevitability of death. We are maintained at our level of nobility by our incessant search for this cause.

The writer seeks an interpretation of the meaning of life from the sum of his experiences. When his experiences have been so brutalized, restricted, degraded, when his very soul has been so pulverized by oppression, his summations can not avoid bitterness, fear, hatred, protest; he is inclined to reveal only dwarfed, beaten personalities and life that is bereft of all meaning. But his logic insists that humanity can not exist without meaning. He must find the meaning regardless of the quality of his experiences. Then begins his slow, tortured progress toward truth.

The American Black writer, more than any other, is faced with this necessity. He must discover, as must all American Blacks, why he continues to live in a society where death has always been held preferable to oppression; he must discover within his oppressed condition some meaning to his life.

From the outset the American Black writer will be assailed by conflicts. He will be in conflict with himself, his environment and his public. The personal conflict will be the hardest. He must decide at the beginning the extent of his honesty. He will derive no pleasure from the recounting of his hurts. He will find it shattering to reveal the truth of his experience – or even to discover it. He will encounter more agony by his explorations into his own personality than American Whites can conceive. For him to delineate the degrading effects of oppression will be comparable to a self-inflicted wound; many suicides have had far less reason. He will have begun an emotional crusade that will carry him through the horrors of the damned. But he will find no valid interpretation of his experiences in terms of human values until the truth is known. And if he does not discover this truth and reveal it, his life will be forever veiled in mystery, not only to Whites but to himself; and he will be heir to all the preconceptions in existence.

And this must be his reward for his integrity: he will be reviled by many American Whites and many American Blacks alike.

The urge to submit to the pattern prescribed by oppression will be powerful. The appeal to retrench, equivocate, compromise, will be issued by friend and foe alike. The temptation to accede will be compelling; the reward coercive. The oppressor pays, and sometimes well, for the submission of the oppressed.

To escape the toll for honesty will come readily a number of rationalizations. He may say to himself: 'I must free myself of all race consciousness before I can understand the true nature of human experiences, for it is not the race problem at all, but the human problem.' Or he may call upon his African heritage, not as a source but as an escape, and say to himself: 'My heritage is African, I have no other heritage.'

But he will discover that he can not accomplish this departure; he will realize in the end that he possesses a heritage of slavery, that he is the product of American culture, that his thoughts and emotions and reactions have been fashioned by his American environment. He will discover that he cannot free himself of his race consciousness because he cannot free himself of his race. To paraphrase a statement of Joe Louis', 'He may run, but he can't hide.'

Once the Black writer's inner conflict has been resolved and he has elected the course of honesty, he immediately enters into conflict with his environment. Various factors of American life and American culture will be raised to stay his pen. The most immediate of these various conflicts is with the publisher. From a strictly commercial point of view, most publishers consider honest novels by Black writers on Blacks' experiences bad ventures. If there is nothing to alleviate the bitter truth, no glossing over her harsh facts, no compromising on the vital issues, most publishers feel that the book will not sell. And the average publisher today will not publish a book he thinks will not sell.

However, should the Black writer find a publisher guided by neither profit nor prejudice (a very rare publisher indeed), he may run into the barrier of preconception. Many truly liberal white people are strongly opinioned on the racial theme, and consider as false or overdrawn any conception that does not agree with their own. Often these people feel that their experiences with Blacks (unfortunately not as Blacks) establish them as authorities on the subject. But quite often their opinions are derived from other Blacks who have attained financial success or material security, in fact fame and great esteem, through a trenchant sort of dishonesty, an elaborate and highly convincing technique of modern kow-towing. It is unfortunate that so many white people who take an active and sympathetic interest in the solution of the American racial dilemma become indoctrinated first by such Blacks. Instead of receiving a true picture of Blacks' personalities, they are presented with comforting illusions. Should the publisher be of this group, he concludes that the honest Black writer is psychotic, that his evaluations are based on personal experiences which are no way typical of his race. This publisher does not realize that his own reasoning is self-contradictory; that any American Black's racial experience, be he psychotic or not, is typical of all Blacks' racial experiences for the simple reason that the source is not black skin but oppression.

Then there is, of course, the publisher with such a high

content of racial bias as to reject violently any work that does not present the Black as a happy contented soul. But there will be no conflict between the Black writer and this publisher; it will never begin.

Once the Black writer's work is past the printer, his inner conflict having been resolved and his publisher convinced, there begins a whole turbulent sea of conflict between the writer and his public.

If this writer, because he has prepared an honest and revealing work on Black experience, anticipates the support and encouragement of middle-class Black people, he is doomed to disappointment. He must be prepared for the hatred and antagonism of many of his own people, for attacks from his leaders, the clergy and the press: he must be ready to have his name reviled at every level, intellectual or otherwise. This is not hard to understand. The American Black seeks to hide his beaten, battered soul, his dwarfed personality, his scars of oppression. He does not want it known that he has been so badly injured for fear he will be taken out of the game. Most American Blacks' highest ambition is to be included in the stream of American life, to be permitted to 'play the game' as any other American, and he is opposed to anything he thinks will aid in his exclusion. The American Black, we must remember, is an American; the face may be the face of Africa, but the heart has the beat of Wall Street.

But Blacks will themselves oppress Blacks, given the opportunity, in as vile a manner as anyone else. The Black writer must be able to forsee this reaction. He has already expected the antagonism and opposition of the white American. These oppressors who have brutally ravaged the personality of a race dare their victims to reveal the scars thus inflicted, because the scars of those assaulted personalities are not only reminders, but affronts.

It is this guilt which, now we are all aware of and understand, that keeps the oppressor outraged and unrelenting. It is his fear that he will have to resolve a condition which is as much his heritage as slavery is our own. The guilt revolving in this fear is a condition the oppressor will not acknowledge, a fact which traps the white oppressor in his own greatest contradictions. The oppressor can not look upon the effects of his oppression without being aware of this contradiction; he does not want to be confronted with this evil, but neither can he escape it nor will he try to solve it. He will go to any extent, from the bestial to the ridiculous, to avoid confrontation with this issue.

As the late Horace Clayton wrote, in *Race Conflict in Modern Society*:

> To relieve himself of his guilt, to justify his hate, and to expel his fear, white men have erected an elaborate facade of justifications and rationalizations. The Black is a primitive, dangerous person who must be kept in subordination. Blacks do not have the same high sensibilities as do Whites and do not mind exploitation and rejection. Blacks are passive children of nature and are incapable of participating in and enjoying the higher aspects of the general American culture. Blacks would rather be by themselves. Blacks are eaten with tuberculosis and syphilis. But these rationalizations do not quell the gnawing knowledge that they, white Americans who profess to believe in Freedom and the dignity of the human personality, are actively or passively perpetuating a society which defiles all that is human in other human beings.

We already know that attacks upon the honest Black American writers will emanate from the white race. However, the tragedy is that there are Whites who themselves are guiltless of any desire to oppress, but suffer the same guilt as do the active oppressors. Because of this they abhor with equal intensity the true revelations of Blacks' experiences. Among these are truly thoughtful, sincere, sympathetic white people who will shudder in protest at the statement that all American Blacks hate all American Whites.

Of course, American Blacks hate American White people. What sort of idiocy is it that reasons American Blacks don't hate American Whites? Can you abuse, enslave, persecute, segregate and generally oppress a people, and have them love you for it? Are white people expected not to hate *their* oppressors? Could any people be expected to escape this natural reaction to oppression? Let us be sensible. To hate white people is one of the first emotions Black Americans develop when they become old enough to learn what their status is in American society. We must, of necessity, hate white people. We would not be human if we did not develop a hatred for our oppressors. At some time in the lives of every Black American there has been this hatred for white people. It could not possibly be otherwise.

To the Black writer who would plumb the depth of Black experience there is no question of whether American Blacks hate American Whites. The question is how does this hatred affect the Black's personality? How much of himself is destroyed by this necessity to hate those who oppress him? Certainly hate is a destructive emotion. In the case of Blacks, hate is doubly destructive. The American Black experiences two forms of hate. He hates first his oppressor, and then because he lives in constant fear of this hatred being discovered he hates himself because of this fear.

Yes, hate is an ugly word. It is an ugly emotion. It would be wonderful to say there is no hate; to say, we do not hate. But merely to speak the words would not make it so; it would not help us Blacks rid ourselves of hate. It would not help you, who are white, rid yourselves of hate. And it would not aid in the removal of the causes for which we hate. The question the Black writer must answer is how does the fear he feels of this hate affect his personality?

There can be no understanding of our experiences, our general behaviours, our compulsions, reactions and actions, our sexual impulses, our marital relations, our crimes, reasonings and conclusions of our thoughts: until we understand the reasonings and conclusions of our thoughts, the impact of this fear upon our personalities. It is not enough to say we are victims of a stupid myth. We must know the reasons for this stupid myth and what it does to us.

If this plumbing for the truth reveals within the Black personality a homicidal mania, lust for Whites of opposite sexes, a pathetic sense of inferiority, paradoxical anti-Semitism, arrogance, Uncle Tomism, hate and fear and self-hate, these then are some of the effects of oppression on the human personality. These are daily horrors, daily realities, the daily experiences of an oppressed minority.

And if it appears that the honest American Black writer is trying to convince his audience that the whole Black race in America, as a result of centuries of oppression, is sick at soul, the conclusion is unavoidable. It could not conceivably be otherwise.

The dilemma of the Black writer lies not so much in what he must reveal, but in the intellectual limitations of the reader which so often confine men to habit and withhold from them the nobler instruments of reason and conscience. There should be no indictment of the writer who reveals this truth, but of the conditions that have produced this truth.

American Blacks *have* written honest books and they have been published and read. That is evidence that the dominant white group in America is not entirely given over to an irrevocable course of oppression.

There is an indomitable quality within the human spirit that can not be destroyed; a facet deep within the human personality that is impregnable to all assaults. This quality, this force, exists deep within Blacks and White alike, because we are all human. It rests so deeply that neither prejudice, oppression, lynchings, riots, time or weariness can ever corrode or destroy it, otherwise during the three hundred years Blacks have lived in America as slaves and near subhumans, the whole moral fibre and personality of Blacks now living would be a total waste and their white oppressors would be drooling idiots, dangerous maniacs and raving beasts. It is that quality within all humans that cries: 'I will live!'

There is no other explanation of how so many Blacks have been able to break through the restrictions of oppression, retain their integrity, attain eminence, and make valuable contributions to our whole culture. The Black writer must not only reveal the truth, but also reveal and underline this higher quality of humanity.

My definition of this quality within the human spirit that cannot be destroyed is *growth*. Growth is the justification of human life. Children will grow from poverty and filth and oppression, and develop honor and integrity, and contribute to all mankind.

It is a long way, a hard way to grow from the hatred of the faces of men. Eventually Blacks will discover they are not alone.

Chester Himes
Chicago, 1948

The Big Gold Dream

1

'Faith is a rock! It's like a solid gold dream!'

The voice of the Sweet Prophet Brown issued from the amplifiers atop a sound truck and reverberated from the shabby brick faces of the tenement houses flanking 117th Street.

'Amen!' Alberta Wright said fervently.

Her big brown cowlike eyes cast a look of adoration across the gleaming white sea of kneeling worshipers upon Sweet Prophet's exalted black face. She felt as though he were addressing her personally, although she was only one of six hundred white-robed converts kneeling in the noonday sun on the burning hot asphalt.

'On this dream every church in all the world is built,' Sweet Prophet continued lyrically.

A moaning fervor passed over the kneeling figures like a cool breeze. Spectators and converts alike were gripped, in dead seriousness, as though cast under a spell.

Black, brown and yellow people packed the sidewalks all the way from Seventh Avenue to Lenox Avenue. They crowded into the tenement windows, jammed the smelly doorways, clung to the sides of electric light poles and stood on garbage cans to watch the performance of this fabulous man.

Sweating foot cops in wet clinging shirts and mounted cops on lathered horses surrounded Sweet Prophet's throne to keep back the mob. The street had been closed off at both ends by a police barrier. Sweet Prophet sat on a throne of red roses on a flower-draped float at one end of the block and spoke into a microphone connected to a sound truck behind him. Over his head was a sunshade of gold tinsel made in the shape of a halo. About his feet was a circle of little black girls dressed as angels.

He threw back his head and said, in a voice of indubitable sincerity, 'Faith is so powerful it will turn this dirty black pavement into gleaming gold.'

'Don't I know it!' Alberta said aloud.

Her hand closed about Sugar Stonewall's fingers like a steel vice. Dressed in a wrinkled rayon sports ensemble, he knelt on the pavement beside her. She had insisted that he be near her in this great hour of triumph, even though he had not been converted. But she did not look at him; her eyes were closed. Tears trickled down her smooth brown skin.

'Put your trust in The Lord,' Sweet Prophet said.

Suddenly Alberta was on her feet. 'I did!' she cried, arms upraised. 'I did! I put my trust in Him and He sent me a dream because I had faith.'

'Kneel down, honey,' Sugar pleaded. 'You're messing up the service.'

But his plea went unheeded. Alberta was a big, muscular woman with a flat, pretty face, now contorted in ecstasy. Clad in a tightfitting white maid's uniform, her long-fingered hands reaching toward the sky, she drew everyone's attention. Her ecstasy was contagious.

'Amen!' the converts chorused.

With the natural-born instinct of a master showman, Sweet Prophet sensed the sympathetic mood. He interrupted his dissertation and said, 'Tell us your dream, sister.'

'I dreamed I was baking three apple pies,' she said. 'And when I took them out the oven and set them on the table to cool the crusts busted open like three explosions and the whole kitchen was filled with hundred dollar bills.'

'My God!' a worshiper exclaimed.

'Money!' another cried.

'Money! Money! Money!' others chorused.

Even Sweet Prophet looked impressed. 'And did you have faith, sister?' he asked.

'I had faith!' Alberta declared.

'Hush up, honey, for Christ's sake,' Sugar Stonewall warned.

But she paid him no attention. 'I had faith!' she repeated. 'And God didn't fail me. God has set me free.'

'Amen!' the worshipers chorused with heartfelt earnestness.

Upon this note Sweet Prophet stood and raised his hands for silence. His tremendous bulk was impressive in a bright purple robe lined with yellow silk and trimmed with mink.

Beneath it he wore a black taffeta suit with white piping and silver buttons. His fingernails, untrimmed since he first claimed to have spoken with God, were more than three inches in length. They curled like strange talons, and were painted different colors. On each finger he wore a diamond ring. His smooth black face with its big buck teeth and popping eyes was ageless; but his long grizzly hair, on which he wore a black silk cap, was snow-white.

Silence descended over the multitude like night.

'I now baptize you, who have seen the glory and harkened to the call, in the name of the Father, the Son and the Holy Ghost,' he said.

Sugar Stonewall picked up the basket of lunch Alberta had prepared for the celebration afterward and beat it for the sidelines. And not a moment too soon.

At the completion of Sweet Prophet's words, fire hoses at each end of the block manned by stalwart deacons, were turned on simultaneously. Streams of water shot high into the air and came down upon white-clad figures in a veritable deluge.

Drenched by the cold holy water pouring from heaven, the converts, most of whom were women, were seized by uncontrollable ecstasy. They danced and screamed and shouted and moaned, carried away with emotion, caught up in a mass delirium. They sang and prayed, gasped and strangled in a frenzy of exultation.

A buxom woman cried, 'My skin may be black, but my soul ain't got no color.'

'Wash me as white as snow,' another screamed, tearing off her dress so that the purifying water could wash her naked skin.

'I had faith, didn't I, God?' Alberta chanted, caught up in the mass hysteria, her transfigured face turned toward heaven. Water flowed unnoticed into her nostrils, almost strangling her. 'I had faith!' she continued, sputtering. 'And you didn't fail me God.'

Finally the hoses were turned off, and Sweet Prophet's church band, arranged about the sound truck, began to play hymns in rock and roll time.

The drenched, half-drowned converts crowded about the

throne of Sweet Prophet to buy bread crumbs, which he took from the pockets of his robe. They paid from one to twenty dollars per crumb.

Waving the sheafs of greenbacks he held between his long twisted varicolored fingernails, he crooned ardently, 'Faith will reduce the Pacific Ocean to a drop of water; it will change the Rocky Mountains into a grain of sand.'

Other persons from among the multitudes of spectators had come to have their infirmities cured by the touch of Sweet Prophet's hand. Hands lifted a crippled child. A paralysed woman was wheeled forward on a stretcher. A worried-looking man extended an eviction notice. Number slips for that day's play were brushed against the throne; a pair of dice were surreptitiously rubbed against the hem of Sweet Prophet's robe.

Alberta Wright found Sugar Stonewall sitting in a crowded doorway. He gave her the bottle of drinking water from the lunch basket and told her to go and have the prophet bless it.

She fought her way to the side of the float and held the bottle aloft. Sweet Prophet recognized her, and a look passed between them. He reached forth a long-nailed hand and touched the lip of the bottle.

'Out of this water will come miracles,' he intoned.

'Amen,' a woman said.

Alberta looked dazed. As though stunned by the magnitude of her good fortune, she dug a wet $50 bill from her brassiere and thrust it toward Sweet Prophet. In return she received a bread crumb the size of a garden pea. She put the crumb into her mouth, looking heavenward, and washed it down with water from the blessed bottle, drinking long and heartily.

Everyone who looked on the scene was convinced the water had been imbued with healing powers.

Suddenly Alberta began to leap and dance in a frenzy of exultation. Her big-boned body shook like a nautch dancer. Her face shone with religious fervor.

'I got Him inside of me!' she cried. 'I got God inside of me. I can feel Him inside of my stomach.'

The spectators were caught between amusement and awe.

'I can feel Him in my bones!' Alberta screamed. 'He's in my blood.'

She was shaking in a very delirium of passion.

'Oh, where is my Sugar?' she cried. 'Sugar Stonewall!' she called. 'Where are you, Sugar?'

Suddenly the faces blurred in her vision. The sky took on the colors of the spectrum, as though the world had turned into a rainbow. Her eyes protruded from her head, and sweat beaded all over her face. She began to moan and whimper, as though the ecstasy was more than she could bear; then she staggered and reeled, fell on to the street and lay twitching on the wet pavement, from which steam had begun to rise.

'She's having a fit,' someone cried.

The crowd surged forward. Faces were distorted with excitement. People struggled frantically to get a look.

Sweet Prophet realized something unusual was happening. With quick presence of mind, he signaled his band to begin playing 'When The Saints Come Marching In', then beckoned to his top elder, Reverend Jones.

Elder Jones was on the alert, as always. Dressed in a gold-braided white uniform with colored tassels sprouting from the shoulders, like a rear admiral in the Cuban navy, he ascended the dais and bent toward the throne, cupping a hand to his ear.

'See what is happening to that woman down there,' Sweet Prophet directed.

Elder Jones descended to the street and knelt beside Alberta. His expression became grave. The spectators hemmed him in, leaning over his shoulders, and bombarded him with questions.

'Get back,' he ordered sharply. 'Give the sister air. She's had a trance. She's gone to talk with God.'

The spectators backed away with awed expressions. But still he had to conduct his examination with the utmost circumspection. He held Alberta's hand while furtively seeking her pulse – he didn't find any. He looked at her nostrils, and there was no movement. Her eyes had rolled back into her head so that only the whites showed. He stroked her face, feeling for the vein in the temple, but her skin was like cooling wax. He would have liked to put a mirror over her mouth, but couldn't risk alarming the spectators. He was so terrified he could hardly breathe, but he kept repeating, 'Glory be to Jesus,' to camouflage his fears. He requested the police to keep back the crowd, then climbed slowly to the throne dais.

Sweet Prophet gave one look at Elder Jones' black face, which had dried to the texture of wood ashes, and expected the worst. 'Well?' he asked fearfully.

'She looks dead to me,' Elder Jones reported.

Sweet Prophet's already protruding eyes bulged perilously from their sockets. 'Great God Almighty!' he whispered in a tone of consternation. 'How in God's name could that happen?'

Elder Jones' mouth felt cotton-dry, and the hot air burned inside of his nostrils. 'The only way I figure it could have happened is the water you blessed was poisoned,' he said.

'Lord in Heaven help us,' Sweet Prophet moaned. 'How could it be poisoned?'

'Only God knows,' Elder Jones said.

Sweet Prophet drew a bottle of smelling salts from somewhere beneath his robe and held it to his nose. He couldn't afford to faint in this emergency, but his head whirled in a blind panic.

He pulled a yellow silk handkerchief from his pocket and patted his forehead.

'Are you certain she's dead, Elder?' he asked with a faint remnant of hope.

'I couldn't find any pulse, and she sure looks dead,' the other affirmed.

As luck would have it, one of the little angels encircling the prophet's throne overheard the elder. Her eyes stretched, and her mouth dropped open.

'Daid? Is she really and truly daid?'

'Hush, child,' Sweet Prophet said anxiously, but it was too late.

A spectator had heard her – a big bull-voiced man wearing purple suspenders over a yellow shirt.

'Great jumping Jehoshaphat, she ain't in no trance!' he shouted in a voice that carried above the marching brass of the band. 'She is plumb dead!'

'Shut up, fool!' Elder Jones shouted. 'Do you want to panic everybody?'

But the damage was done. Word ran through the crowd like quicksilver that the converted woman who had drunk of the holy water had dropped dead.

Pandemonium broke loose. Emotions already ignited by religious fervor skyrocketed in terror. The excitable people began milling and screaming and fighting one another in animal panic.

Sweet Prophet knew he had to do something quick to avert catastrophe. It was the most desperate situation he had ever faced in his long and checkered career as a revivalist. It was worse even than the time he had been accused of raping three twelve-year-old girls.

His whole career hung in the balance. The next twenty minutes would determine the fate of his cult, which had taken him twenty years to build up. Not only his career as an evangelist, but his personal fortune was at stake. He didn't know what he was worth, but his followers, along with the press, insisted on calling him a multimillionaire. And it had been to his advantage to nurture this legend. His followers referred to his millions with personal pride. They boasted that he was richer than Father Divine, richer than Daddy Grace. Religious people love a winner, he had learned. By that they knew that God had blessed him. He rode around in a royal purple Rolls Royce with a gold plated radiator; in the winter he wore an overcoat made of ranch mink; he wore a diamond ring on each finger and diamonds in his shoes; he maintained a French-type wine cellar stocked with vintage wines and champagnes that he paraded for effect, although he never drank himself. All this might go by the board if it was discovered that the water he had blessed had poisoned one of his converts.

But he had not gotten where he was by means of a chicken heart. He had the nimble wits of a confidence man and the nerve of a bank robber. His brain worked best under pressure. 'Get the bottle, Elder, get the bottle for God's sake and hide it,' he said, then silenced the brass band with a gesture and spoke fervently into the microphone.

'Be calm! Be happy! Rejoice! Praise be to God! Let us all kneel in prayer. God is calling the holy ones.'

The face of a big black man turned ashy gray. 'I is getting the hell out of here,' he muttered.

He pushed through the crowd and started running. Others followed. Terror spread through the assemblage.

'Stay and pray!' Sweet Prophet warned. 'You can't run away from God.'

He signaled for the band to begin playing again and raised his big bass voice in song: 'Swing low, sweet chariot, coming for to carry me home ... All sing,' he commanded. 'I looked over Jordan and what did I see, coming for to carry me home ...'

Hundreds of people broke in wild flight, knocking down women and children and trampling them in the street. But the converts and the religious remained. With their drenched white dresses clinging to oversized bodies, they turned their entranced black faces toward the sky and began to sing their own individual songs.

'Oh, Jesus, I is coming ...'

'I hear you calling me ...'

'Call me, Jesus, I is ready ...'

A big powerful woman clung to her husband, who was trying desperately to get away. 'What's the matter with you? Don't you want to go to heaven?' she was screaming.

Tears streamed down a toothless old woman's stoic face. 'Hurry, God, and take me while I is pure,' she prayed.

'*Let us all kneel in prayer*,' the voice of Sweet Prophet boomed.

Automatically, as though under the influence of mass hypnotism, the multitude knelt in the street.

Sweet Prophet began praying over the loud-speakers with a steady, moving fervor:

'*The Lord giveth and the Lord taketh. Ashes to ashes and dust to dust; if God doesn't get you the devil must ...*'

No one noticed Sugar Stonewall turn the corner into Seventh Avenue and begin to run. He was a long-limbed, double-jointed man with fallen arches and flat feet. He ran as though his feet were made of beef filets and the streets were paved with broken glass, using his arms, like a windmill to keep him afloat. But he was putting his heart into it. He didn't know how much he would have to do, nor how much time he would have to do it in.

2

The colored corporal in charge of the street detail rushed to the nearest police telephone box and telephoned the Homicide Bureau.

Elder Jones, at Sweet Prophet's direction, dashed to the nearest drugstore and telephoned the police precinct station for an ambulance.

Some well-meaning person telephoned the fire department.

Someone else telephoned Harlem's great undertaker, H. Exodus Clay.

It was Sunday, and all of them were delayed; but the undertaker's hearse got there first. The regular driver, Jackson, was attending the First Baptist church with his wife, Imabelle, when the call came in, so the relief driver took it.

He was a young man without much experience, but eager to make good. Mr Clay told him to get a death certificate before bringing the body in. When he got to the scene there was no one present to give him the necessary death certificate, and he didn't have time to wait.

He grabbed the body, loaded it into the wicker basket, shoved the basket into the hearse and took off with the siren wide open before the police realized what was happening. He gripped the steering wheel in a death grip and stared at the onrushing street with a fanatical look.

The first place he went to was Harlem Hospital. They told him they couldn't give him a death certificate, but they would examine the body in the emergency receiving room and telephone the police for him.

'Hell with that!' he said. He didn't have time for all that foolishness.

From Harlem Hospital he drove furiously to Knickerbocker Hospital, also located in Harlem.

The doctors there, after listening to his request, told him he had better take the body to the morgue, where he could find an assistant medical examiner on duty who would issue the necessary certificate.

By the time the police got on the job of tracing his movements, he was heading south, down the East Side Highway at eighty-five miles an hour, making for the morgue on First Avenue at 29th Street.

Directly after the hearse had left the scene, Sweet Prophet called for his Rolls Royce, and was driven rapidly to his Temple of Wonderful Prayer around the corner on 116th Street. Anticipating all sorts of trouble from the hard-boiled Homicide police, he desired to face them on his home ground.

The others arrived consecutively:

First, two fire trucks bringing oxygen tents and inhalators;

Second, the Assistant Medical Examiner, who had been alerted by the Homicide Bureau;

And last, a big black sedan from the Homicide Bureau itself, with a uniformed driver, bearing three plain-clothes detectives, a sergeant and two corporals.

By then the body was gone, the prophet was gone, the witnesses were gone, the bottle which had contained the allegedly poisoned water was gone, and Sugar Stonewall was long gone.

Now, more than an hour had passed since Alberta Wright had swallowed the first gulps of the water from the bottle Sweet Prophet had blessed, and Sweet Prophet was sitting behind a hand-carved mahogany desk in his sumptuous 'Receiving Room' on the third-floor front of his Temple of Wonderful Prayer. Across from him, in the high-backed period chairs usually assigned to the supplicants, sat three detectives. They were enclosed, as it were, by an invisible wall, behind which the room was jammed to the walls by as many of the prophet's followers as could squeeze inside. Others jammed the outside hallways and staircases, and hundreds stood below on the street.

The temple was a four-storied apartment building, housing a modern motion picture theater, which Sweet Prophet had converted into his Church of Wonderful Prayer. His living quarters were on the top floor.

The Homicide sergeant was saying, 'Now all I want to do is get the picture straight while the Medical Examiner locates the body and determines the cause of death. There has been some confusion here.'

'The Lord shall confound the wicked,' Sweet Prophet said.

'Amen,' said the followers.

The sergeant, a tall lean hatchet-faced Irishman named Ratigan, blinked. 'As to that, we'll soon find out,' he said. 'You were baptizing these people?'

'They had answered to the call, and the Sweet Prophet was opening the gates to God's green pastures so that they may graze in faith with God's chosen flock,' Sweet Prophet said.

'Amen,' the faithful said.

'Just stick to the answers, Reverend,' Sergeant Ratigan said.

'I am a prophet,' Sweet Prophet said. 'God called to me at the corner of this very street and Lenox Avenue more than thirty-three years ago. It was a Saturday night and the street was filled with sinners – pimps and prostitutes and thieves. God touched me on the shoulder. I looked around and saw nobody. He said, "I am God. I make you my prophet on Earth. I send you forth to save these people from degradation and damnation!"'

'Praise be God and bless Sweet Prophet,' the faithful said.

'Jesus Christ, do these people have to be here?' Ratigan said, gritting his teeth. 'They are interfering with the questioning, obstructing the police and loitering, all of which is against the law.'

'They are humble, very humble,' Sweet Prophet said. He tossed a handful of bread crumbs onto the floor, touching off a mad scramble. 'See how humble we all are,' he stated to the bug-eyed detectives. 'We will even eat off the floor for Sweet Prophet.'

Many of the faithful were lapping the crumbs from the thick purple carpet.

'All right, all right, stop feeding them crumbs and let's get back to the killing,' Sergeant Ratigan said harshly.

'There was no killing,' Sweet Prophet denied. 'No killing and no death. There was a departure. A saint departed for heaven.'

'The question is, did any human dispatch her on her way?' Ratigan said.

'None! No human hand was raised against her,' Sweet Prophet said.

'Who poisoned the bottle of water?' Sergeant Ratigan asked.

'The water was not poisoned,' Sweet Prophet denied. 'I blessed it with my own hand.'

'How is it then that she died after drinking it?' Ratigan asked.

'If you think she died from drinking that water, bring me a gallon of it and I will drink it all,' Sweet Prophet said.

'What did she do for a living?' the sergeant asked.

'She was a cook for a white family in Westchester County,' Sweet Prophet said.

'What kind of woman was she?' Ratigan asked.

'An upright, God-fearing, Christian woman,' Sweet Prophet said.

'Do you have any idea why someone might want to poison her?' Ratigan asked.

'No one would have ever wanted to poison her,' Sweet Prophet stated emphatically. 'She was a great cook and a steady wage-earner. No one on God's green earth would poison that type of woman.'

'How about a jealous husband or a disgruntled lover?' the sergeant asked.

'Only the Almighty Father, who is swayed neither by the color of the skin nor the smartness of the brain, but judges only by the sincerity of the heart, would have called Sister Wright from her life on Earth to offer her a seat in heaven – as useful as she was to everybody,' Sweet Prophet said.

One of the four gilded telephones on the desk began to ring. Sweet Prophet looked at them without moving, and a sedately dressed middle-aged woman, who had been standing impassively by the wall behind him, stepped forward and miraculously picked up the right one.

'The blessed Sweet Prophet's Temple of Wonderful Prayer,' she enunciated in a well-modulated voice.

The harsh sound of a voice at the other end came into the room, but the words were indistinct.

'Very well,' the woman replied and, looking up toward the sergeant, said, 'It is for you, sir, if you are Sergeant Ratigan.'

The sergeant got to his feet and reached across the desk for the receiver.

'Ratigan,' he bellowed. 'Shoot!'

The sound of the harsh voice, metallic and indistinct, poured into the dense, listening silence, punctuated by Ratigan saying, 'Yeah ... Yeah ... Well, that's that ...'

He hung up the receiver and said to his assistants, 'Let's go.'

3

A dilapidated moving van, minus the name of the owner or any identifying inscription save for a license plate almost obliterated by dirt, drew up in front of a four-storied brick tenement on 118th Street. The block was parallel to the one on 117th Street where the baptism had taken place a short time before.

Two big overall-clad colored men, one of whom had been driving, and a small, white-haired Jew, wearing a black suit and a brown felt hat, got out.

'Hey, auntie,' the Jew called to a big black woman leaning from a first-floor window. 'What floor does Rufus Wright live on?'

The woman gave him an evil look. 'If you means Alberta Wright, she lives on the top floor.'

The Jew's eyebrows shot upward, but he didn't reply.

'If Rufus has brought in a woman, we won't touch it,' he said to his helpers as they climbed the smelly stairs.

The helpers said nothing.

On the fourth floor, a slick-looking Negro with straightened hair beckoned from the rear door and said, 'Psst.' He was wearing a pink sport shirt, a green silk suit and yellow linen shoes, and he had a wide, confidential grin.

The Jew and his helpers entered the parlor of a two-room flat.

The Negro closed the door and locked it, then said, 'All right, daddy-O, let's get on.'

The Jew looked about suspiciously. 'You're alone, ain't you?' He had been around colored people so long he talked like one.

'Ain't I always?' the Negro countered.

'You know I got to get it straight.'

'All right, set up your alibis.'

The Jew frowned. 'That's a bad word,' he said, but the Negro didn't argue the point. The Jew asked, 'Your name is Rufus Wright, ain't it?'

'Right,' Rufus said.

The helpers, standing inside the doorway, sniggered. Every time the Jew bought anything from Rufus, he went through the same act.

'This is your place, ain't it?'

'Right.'

'You own the furniture, don't you?'

'Right.'

'Who is this woman, Alberta Wright?' the Jew threw in suddenly.

'Her? She's my wife,' Rufus said, without batting an eye.

'Why didn't you stick to being a bachelor?' the Jew complained. 'That was safer.'

'Well, you see, daddy-O, this time it's different,' Rufus said. 'This time it's on her account that I got to sell my furniture.'

'What's wrong with her?'

'Nothing wrong with her. She's dead is all. That's why I got to raise some money on a Sunday. I got to pay the undertaker some money in advance so he'll go down to the morgue and get the body.'

The Jew grinned at his helpers to show he appreciated the story. 'Well, that's all right,' he conceded, relaxing. 'Now we got everything straight.' He turned again to his helpers and called them to witness. 'You boys heard what Mr Wright said?'

They nodded.

'All right, Rufus boy, let's get down to business. Is that the set you want to sell?' he asked, pointing toward a huge blond-oak television set on a gate-legged table.

'I've decided to sell all my furniture,' Rufus said. 'This funeral is going to be expensive, and I got to make a down payment of five hundred dollars.'

'For that much, you had ought to got the whole Blumstein's department store,' the Jew said drily.

'There's a lot of good stuff here,' Rufus contended.

The Jew looked over the room, and his expression went sour. The room was jammed with a motley collection of worn-out furnishings arranged about a potbellied stove like molting chickens about a mother hen: threadbare rugs; moth-eaten over-stuffed chairs and a sofa, broken-legged tables; clocks without works; ceramic statuettes that had been through the Inquisition; a stuffed pheasant with a bald patch on its back; a set of scarred antlers mounted on the wall, flanked by faded lithographs of English hunting scenes; cutout photos of Negro blues singers hanging beside reproductions of the Virgin Mother and Child, The Last Supper and The Crucifixion cut from calendars given out by undertaker H. Exodus Clay.

'Do you call this furniture?' the Jew asked.

'These are mostly antiques in this room,' Rufus said. 'But there's a brand new set of furniture in the bedroom.'

'Your wife couldn't say no to her white folks, could she?' the Jew cracked. 'She must have brought everything home that they left for the trash man.'

'She couldn't throw nothing away either,' Rufus added.

Grinning, the Jew took a notebook and stylo from his inside coat pocket and went to work. Rapidly and with scarcely a look, he itemized the furnishings, allowing $50 for the television set and $19 for everything else.

'I can't use the stove,' he said. 'Sixty-nine bucks for the lot. Okay.'

'You mean that's all you want to pay for everything in this room?' Rufus asked incredulously.

'That's more than it's worth,' the Jew said, adding with a grin, 'I wouldn't pay for it if it wasn't for your wife needing a decent funeral.'

With an abrupt motion, Rufus opened his mouth and stuck it in front of the Jew's face. 'Here, take my teeth too and have it done with,' he blubbered.

The Jew looked into his mouth with interest. 'Holy Mackerel, you got a red tongue, blue gums and white teeth,' he observed. 'If anybody calls you a Communist, you just open your mouth and show them the national colors.'

Rufus closed his mouth and looked sheepish. 'All right, sixty-nine bucks; if I got to, I got to.'

The helpers started to move the furniture but the Jew stopped them. 'Wait till I get it down legal,' he cautioned.

In the bedroom the bureau drawers and the dressing table still contained Alberta's personal effects, lingerie and toilette articles as she had left them that morning, and the bed was made up and covered with a pink rayon spread.

'Get these drawers cleaned out,' the Jew said.

Rufus began piling the contents helter-skelter in a corner of the room. The Jew went about his business of assessing the furniture without paying him the slightest attention.

When he had thrown off the bed linen to examine the mattress, the Jew said sharply, 'This has been damaged.'

The seams of the mattress on all four sides, both top and bottom, had been opened with a knife wide enough to permit a hand.

'I had to open it to put in some bug powder,' Rufus said. 'We been bothered with the bugs. But all it needs is sewing up a little and it'll look like new.'

The Jew wasn't listening. He was sticking his arm through the openings and probing the padding with his fingers. With an enraged gesture, he wheeled it over to the floor and probed the other side. His face was a study of frustration.

'The deal's off,' he choked in a furious voice. His sallow skin had turned the dull purple of a ripe fig.

'What the hell's the matter with you!' Rufus shouted, his eyes bugging in matching fury. 'You think I'm going to sell you a mattress if there was any money hidden in it?'

'It's risky, too risky,' the Jew said, half cowed by Rufus's threatening attitude. 'If money has been stolen, I won't touch it.'

'What risk is you taking?' Rufus kept raving. 'You don't never take no risk. It's me takes all the risks. The way you cover yourself up with all kinds of legal tetches, all of Congress couldn't get nothing on you.'

The Jew gave in. 'All right, all right. We don't have to fight. I just like to do my own looking, whether I find anything or not.'

'Hell, you think you're going to find a bale of money in every mattress you buy,' Rufus said scornfully.

It was rumored in Harlem that twenty years ago the Jew

had found thirty-five thousand dollars in cash hidden in a mattress he had bought for 75c from a flea-bag hotel room in which an old white beggar had died.

Rufus kept on needling. 'Us colored folks ain't got no money to hide. You Jews got it all.'

The Jew was finished with it. 'All right, drop it, boy. Twenty-seven fifty for what's in here, okay?'

'That's just what I mean,' Rufus said. 'My old lady paid two hundred seventy-five for this set less than a month ago.'

'All right, stop breaking my heart – thirty-five, okay?' the Jew said.

Rufus wiped his smooth black cold-creamed face with a white silk handkerchief. 'Okay, man, okay,' he said harshly. 'Let's get finished; I ain't got all day.'

The Jew hid a vindictive smile and went into the kitchen. He took one look at the enamel-topped table and tubular stainless steel chairs with foam-rubber plastic-covered seats and said, 'I can see that your wife was a cook.'

He sat at the table and added up the total, allowing $13 for the kitchen's contents, exclusive of the table service and utensils. It came to $117. He then wrote a receipt on a form taken from a pad that looked like a check book:

Received from A. Finkelstein $117.00 for total furnishings of apartment No. 44, 118th Street, Manhattan, New York City.

Leaving it undated, he asked Rufus to sign it.

'Man, don't you never talk to me no more about taking risks,' Rufus grumbled as he signed.

'You got to bury your wife,' the Jew needled slyly. 'I ain't got no wife.'

The helpers exchanged looks and grinned.

'No cracks,' the Jew warned. 'You just sign here as witnesses.'

Laboriously, they spelled out their signatures below.

'Okay, now you can take this junk and load it,' the Jew said, tucking the receipt carefully into a stuffed wallet and extracting a thin sheaf of banknotes.

Stolidly the helpers shuffled into the sitting room and began slamming the furniture about. The colored lady had retired from her grandstand seat in the front window when they appeared on the street with the first load, but other windows up and down the street on both sides were occupied with the customary Sunday afternoon sightseers. No significance was attached to the moving. In a number of windows only the grayish bottoms of big bare black feet resting on the sills were visible from below; and they remained stationary. A patrol car idled past, but the cops didn't give the movers a second look. Moving on Sunday was a perfectly legitimate undertaking; many people figured that was the best time to do it.

The helpers loaded the bureau and the dressing table in the van alongside the sitting room suite, then, after knocking the bed apart, brought it down in sections. One of them brought down the mattress, and the other brought down the springs. They packed the springs but left the mattress on the tailgate to be used as a buffer for the stuff from the kitchen. Before going back up, they went forward to the driver's compartment and drank heartily from a bottle of California muscatel wine.

A young man standing in the doorway of the adjoining tenement sucked on a marijuana cigarette and watched them with an expression of infantile concentration. He had a big, flat body, whose wide square shoulders gave the impression of abnormal strength. He had a small head with a round babyish face and smooth brown hairless skin. His big eyes with their drug-widened pupils looked completely senseless. Despite the heat he wore a heavy tweed jacket with thick shoulder pads, a wide-brimmed beaver hat pulled low over his forehead and skintight mustard-colored corduroy pants tucked into black and white cowboy boots. On first sight he looked like a harmless moron.

As soon as the Jew's two helpers went back upstairs, he squashed the marijuana butt, stuck it into the band of his hat and sauntered toward the truck. Without looking about to see whether or not he was being watched, he shouldered the mattress as though it were stuffed with down and began walking casually in the direction of Lenox Avenue.

A young brown-skinned woman, looking out of a window as he passed her tenement lodging, laughed melodiously.

'Hey, baby, come look at this spook with his house on his back,' she called over her shoulder.

A muscular black man, naked to the waist, appeared at her

side. 'He's probably found a new gal and he's moving in with her,' he said.

The young man turned the corner at Lenox Avenue and disappeared.

When the helpers came down with the kitchen table and chairs, they noticed the mattress was missing. They looked up and down the street. The young woman saw them and shouted, 'Ain't no need of looking, 'cause sleepy done got it.'

'Sleepy who?' one of them asked.

'How do I know who?' she replied. 'You think I knows any niggers who steals mattresses?'

The muscular man reappeared at her side, and the helpers had business back upstairs.

The Jew was sniffing about in the kitchen when they came up. Figuring he might find something good to eat, they didn't disturb him with news of the stolen mattress but hurried to get finished.

The Jew lifted the lid from a big iron pot on the stove and found it half filled with a concoction of boiled rice and squares of orange-colored meat that smelled like fish. He dished up some with his finger and tasted it. 'Mmmm, it's good,' he said. 'What is it?'

Rufus stuck his nose in the pot and tasted a bit of the bright-colored meat. 'It's alligator tails and rice,' he said. 'It's a great dish in South Carolina.' Then he added, 'That's where my wife came from.'

'Rest her soul,' the Jew said, took a plate from the cupboard and began serving himself.

When the two helpers finished they found their boss eating from a plate on the stove and Rufus from a plate on top of the icebox.

'Tails and rice,' they chorused in unison and joined the feast, putting their plates on the sink.

One stopped long enough to look for some whiskey but only found a bottle of black rum behind a stack of used paper sacks on the top shelf.

'You don't mind if us drink a little of this?' he asked Rufus.

'Help yourself,' Rufus said.

He and the Jew drank beer.

By the time they had cleaned the pot, everybody felt lovey-dovey. It wasn't until the three of them had gone downstairs and were about to enter the van that the driver remembered to tell the Jew about the stolen mattress.

The Jew looked thoughtful. He wasn't worried about the mattress, but with everybody having the same idea, he resolved to look into the stuffings of the living room suite as soon as possible.

Rufus was thinking along the same lines. Upstairs he had taken off the locked door of the clothes closet by knocking out the pins of the hinges, and was searching inside. But he didn't find anything but clothes, two empty pasteboard suitcases, a stack of shoe boxes filled with slips containing the hit numbers for the past five years and a variety of nameless junk.

He looked as though he had been taken.

After a moment he shrugged and walked out of the flat like a man trying to play the part of a good loser. He locked the door with the key that Sugar had given him, went down the stairs and hesitated for a moment in the entrance. He didn't see anyone who seemed concerned with him, so he went down the street and around the corner and got into his car parked in the shade on Lenox Avenue.

4

On the south side, Harlem is bounded by 110th Street. It extends west to the foot of Morningside Heights, on which Columbia University stands. Manhattan Avenue, a block to the east of Morningside Drive, is one of the corner streets that screen the Harlem slums from view. The slum tenements give way suddenly to trees and well-kept apartment buildings, where the big cars of the Harlem underworld are parked bumper to bumper. Only crime and vice can pay the high rents charged in such borderline areas. That's where Rufus lived.

Sugar climbed the stairs of a modern brick building at

the corner of 113th Street and knocked at the door of a second-floor apartment.

Rufus answered. He had shed his green silk jacket, but was still wearing the pants along with the pink sport shirt.

'I want to talk to you,' Sugar panted menacingly.

'I got a woman inside,' Rufus said. 'Let's go in the park.'

They went down to the street and crossed to the small triangular park formed by the converging of Morningside Drive and Manhattan Avenue at 112th Street. Across the Drive was the rocky incline of Morningside Park, filled with Sunday picnickers. They sat on a green wooden bench.

'Look here, nigger, I told you just to take the television set,' Sugar said accusingly.

'You told me she had some money hid there somewhere,' Rufus contended. 'I searched the place and I didn't find nothing.'

'Hell, do you think I didn't search it before I came for you?'

'I heard she dropped dead,' Rufus said. 'I had to get something for my trouble.'

'You didn't have no right to take the furniture – that was mine,' Sugar stated.

'If she had anything, she didn't hide it in that furniture,' Rufus said. 'You can take it from me, man; I have searched too many of these places to miss.'

'She had something hidden there, all right,' Sugar contended. 'I'll bet my life on it.'

Rufus looked skeptical. 'You know she didn't have much sense. An ignorant woman like her always hides everything in the mattress. And there wasn't nothing in that mattress.'

'She had sense enough to fool both of us so far,' Sugar reminded him.

'Then she must have hid it somewhere else,' Rufus said.

'Where else could she have hid it?' Sugar persisted.

'How in the hell would I know? I wasn't living with her. You was,' Rufus said. 'And as far as that goes, you ain't got any proof that she ever had anything.'

'Oh, I got proof enough,' Sugar said. 'Besides which, she gave herself away.'

'How?'

'Never mind how – that's my little secret.'

'You mean because she locked you out of the house last night?' Rufus asked.

'Naw, man, hell, she done that lots of times before,' Sugar admitted, but he didn't feel that it was necessary to explain to Rufus the source of his suspicions. He had the feeling that Rufus was smarter than he was, and he didn't want to give him too much to go on. 'If you knew her as well as you claim to, you would know she must have got hold of something in order to get religion suddenly,' he added.

Rufus looked thoughtful. 'Maybe you're right,' he conceded. 'I'll go through her junk again, piece by piece.'

'Where is it?' Sugar demanded.

'I ain't saying,' Rufus replied. 'You got your little secret; I got mine.'

'All right, man, just don't get yourself hurt.'

'Hell, man, I trusted you; now you got to trust me.'

'I trust you – I am just telling you, is all. It's halvers.'

'I know it's halvers, man. If I find it, you'll get your half, all right.'

'Just remember this is worth your life, man,' Sugar threatened.

'You talk like a mugger,' Rufus complained aggrievedly. 'You don't have to threaten me, man.'

'I ain't threatening you,' Sugar denied. 'I'm just advising you. Don't try nothing funny.'

Rufus stood up. 'I'm going, man, I got a chick waiting.'

'Just don't get careless and find yourself dead,' Sugar called after him.

5

For years, Third Avenue crossed the Harlem River a few blocks north of 125th Street on the tracks of the Third Avenue Elevated and continued northward through the Bronx to Fordham Road. Now, with the old El gone out of existence,

Third Avenue simply leaps from shore to shore. On one shore the address is Third Avenue, Manhattan; on the other it is Third Avenue, Bronx. In both Manhattan and the Bronx, its character is the same. It is a street of the second-hand and the down-and-out; of pawnshops, of grimy bars, of poverty and bums – a truly democratic street.

In the block between 166th and 167th Street in the Bronx there is a grimy bar owned by a Greek with a colored bartender serving a clientele of all races; an Army-Navy surplus store; a kosher meat market; a second-hand clothing store run by the United Protestant Missions; a pork store; a store front with a name protected by a heavy iron grille strong enough to serve as the gates for Alcatraz; a big wooden gate that had once been painted yellow; and a big weather-blackened brick building housing a brewery owned by the descendants of a German immigrant.

It was ten o'clock at night. Save for an intermittent bus, scattered automobiles and a few forlorn pedestrians straggling by, the street was deserted. Only the lighted window in the brewery and the fly-specked window of the bar at the opposite end showed signs of life.

Two brass locks securing the iron grille of the nameless store gleamed dully in the feeble light from the distant street lamp. Vaguely visible in the display window behind, broken furniture was stacked to the ceiling as though to form a secondary barrier. The windows of the three floors above the store were boarded shut.

The wooden gate to one side enclosed a short brick-paved driveway leading to a wooden shed with a tin roof. Protruding from the shed was the back end of a moving van.

There was a small doorway in the back of the shed that opened onto a small concrete courtyard extending across the rear of the store. Two windows, boarded up and barred, flanked a center door that was protected by a grille similar to the one in front. But light was coming from a small basement window at ground level on the far side.

Through dirt-spattered panes a basement room was visible. One corner of the basement had been partitioned off and equipped for a cabinetmaker's workshop. Workbenches were built along three walls, above which were tool racks containing all types of woodworking tools. Near the inner wall stood a band saw, a wood lathe, a planing mill and an electric drill.

What was left of Alberta's moth-eaten overstuffed parlor suite was scattered about the center of the floor in the spill of bright white light from a green-shaded drop lamp.

The Jew was kneeling beside the sofa, which was still intact. The skeletons of the two overstuffed armchairs had been pushed to one side like the bones of a carcass. The covers and overstuffing were piled in a heap between them.

He felt the sofa as though he were assaying a prime beef, poked it here and there and then caressed it with soft loving strokes.

'Marvelous,' he muttered to himself. 'Marvelous. More than a hundred years old. Made in New Orleans. Been through the Civil War. Extraordinary! What treasures these black cooks collect.'

Suddenly he picked up his tools and began stripping the sofa like a past master. All the while he talked to himself.

'That Rufus, what a fool. Trying to outwit Abie – ha ha.'

First he pried loose all the hidden tacks.

'The mattress – colored people's strongbox, ha ha.'

Then with a razor blade he ripped the seams of the outer fabric and skinned it back as though skinning an animal. Save for the sound of ripping threads and his labored breathing, it was silent as a tomb. The silence oppressed him. He talked to relieve the silence, not because the words expressed his thoughts.

'Little fortunes ... little fortunes ... from little fortunes big fortunes grow ...'

Beneath the covering was a layer of horsehair, and beneath that a layer of yellowed cotton. With immaculate care, the Jew removed each layer. His nimble fingers probed and explored every inch of padding before he laid it aside.

'He was searching for something. He thinks Abie doesn't know. He thinks he has fooled Abie. The fool – ha ha ...'

He thought he heard a sound.

'What's that!' he exclaimed.

His eyes flew to the basement window. Quick as a cat he moved toward a hidden switch beneath the projecting edge of a bench and turned off the light. The small rectangular window was outlined by the almost imperceptible light of a city night. No telltale silhouette was visible. He had been holding his breath. He breathed once and listened. Only the heavy muted sounds penetrating the thick wall of the brewery disturbed the silence.

'No one in miles,' he muttered.

But he did not switch the light back on yet. He felt an inexplicable nervousness – not a premonition, more a building up of tension. He walked through the darkness to the door leading to the stairs. Something brushed against his leg. Shock went through him like cold fire. He jumped to one side, feeling his hair rise from an ice-cold scalp. His hands clawed desperately along the tool rack for a weapon.

Then a cat mewed and moved forward to rub against his other leg. He looked down and saw twin ellipsoids of green light shining in the dark.

He sucked in his breath with a watery sound.

'Sheba!' he gasped. 'Sheba, little pussy.'

He reached down to stroke the purring black cat.

'Sheba! Little queen. You will make a corpse of old Abie yet.'

He crossed the room, turned on the light and went back to work. The kitten played around his feet.

He worked absorbedly. When the padding was removed he sounded the burlap-covered wooden frame with a small wooden mallet. His ear was cocked, listening to the sound of the wood. He worked along the back of the frame down the back legs, then around to the front legs and up the sides. The arms of the frame were seemingly solid cylinders of a light white wood. The mallet made small light sounds as it tapped against the solid wood.

'Impregnable,' the Jew muttered.

Disappointment showed in the creases of his face. The cat rubbed against his leg again, and he shoved it aside with a gesture of frustration.

He began tapping the other arm. Suddenly he bent his head to listen. There was a slight hollow sound beneath the mallet blows. His face lit slowly with an expression of uncontainable avarice.

The cat had withdrawn to a distance and sat washing her face with offended dignity.

The Jew knelt and examined the end of the cylinder in the bright light. It was identical with its mate, the grains of the wood unbroken as though cut from a solid beam. He exchanged his mallet for a small iron hammer and tapped the end gently, listening. Then he took a small wood chisel from the bench and began cutting a small circle. A few minutes later the plug sank in.

'Ingenious,' he muttered admiringly.

He speared the plug with a gimlet and worked it out from the arm. Behind was a cylindrical opening of an inch in diameter. He probed with his finger. His expression changed to astonishment. With a pair of pincers he fished a cylindrical packet, which fitted exactly, from the opening. The outer cover was yellow oiled silk in a state of perfect preservation. He sniffed it; it smelled slightly perfumed.

He went over to the workbench, switched on another light and smoothed the packet flat. It took the shape of a plain silk pouch, closed with a flap but unsealed. He opened the pouch and extracted a neat sheaf of bright green bank notes held by a paper band. He sucked in his breath. His face was a study in emotions.

'Fantastic!' he muttered. 'Brand-new.'

The notes were of one-hundred-dollar bills.

Slowly his tongue came out and slid from side to side on his bottom lip.

As he counted the notes, his eyes widened. There were 1,000 hundred-dollar bills.

Suddenly he bent double, laughing as though he had suddenly gone raving crazy. He was laughing so hard he did not hear the light sound made by a shoe sole scuffling against the pavement outside the basement window.

But the cat heard. The cat stopped washing its face and stared unblinkingly at the silhouette of a man peering through the dirty panes.

The silhouette withdrew, and the cat went back to washing its face.

The Jew finally got himself under control. He straightened up and stared at the money. Saliva trickled from the corners of his mouth. He wrung his hands as though washing them. The cat stopped washing its face again and watched him silently. He patted the money. He turned it over and looked at the other side, then held one of the notes against the light.

'Incredible,' he muttered.

The next instant his body went rigid. He froze in a listening attitude, his ear cocked. The unmistakable sound of an automobile starting reached his ear. Before his face could form an expression the motor caught and the loud hard roar of a big truck motor racing at top speed shattered the silence. There could be no mistake. Someone had started the motor of his moving van in the shed. No one but himself had keys to the gate. Someone had broken in.

The motor raced, then was cut to idle and left running.

He stacked the money, slipped it back into the pouch, and pulled open a drawer in the workbench, moving with incredible speed. He put the pouch into the drawer and withdrew a .38 calibre Colt revolver, loaded with tracer bullets, and a large black three-cell flashlight with an oversized lamp. He switched out the light over the bench and moved quickly toward the master switch beneath the other bench. His body, once put into motion, seemed to gather speed. The black-clad figure capped with yellow-gray hair armed with revolver and flashlight gave the impression of incalculable danger.

The switch clicked faintly, and the room was plunged into darkness. But the Jew moved through the darkness as though he could see. He ran lightly on tiptoes through the open door and up the stairs. One of the stairs creaked beneath his weight, and he swore silently in Yiddish.

The staircase turned at a landing and entered the back hall of the first floor, directly beside the back door. The Jew halted for a moment to peer through the grimy panes into the back courtyard. But, coming from the bright light of his workroom, his eyes had not adjusted to the darkness. He put his ear to the pane but could hear only the sound of the idling motor.

With infinite caution he unlocked the inner door. The slight sound made by the clicking of the bolt was barely perceptible above the sound of the idling motor. The door opened soundlessly.

He waited with his face pressed to the iron grille, looking and listening. There was still only the sound of the idling motor. The Jew figured it was a trap. But he didn't know whether it was a legitimate burglar or some teenage hoodlums. He had a telephone in the ground floor cubbyhole office. He could have phoned for the police, but he didn't want the police meddling into his business, poking about and asking questions.

He decided to set a trap of his own. He unlocked the grille and pushed it back on its hinges until it formed a right angle, guarding the entrance from any attack from the left. Then he backed into the shadows and waited.

Five minutes passed. The cat came up the stairs, looked outside, sniffed and walked in a dignified manner across the couryard with its tail straight up, looking neither to the right nor the left. The Jew knew that was no indication; Sheba would simply ignore anyone she didn't know.

Ten minutes passed, then fifteen. The Jew began growing impatient. He wanted to get back to his money. It could have been some pranksters. No one in their right senses would want to steal his moving van. And had anyone wanted to get into the store, they would have made a move by now. He would wait another five minutes.

He was guessing at the time; but the clock of his mind was fairly accurate. When the five minutes had ticked off in his brain, he put the revolver beneath his coat and cocked it to muffle the sound. Then, holding the heavy black flashlight extended in his left hand, thumb on the switch, and holding the heavy revolver extended in his right hand, finger on the trigger, he emerged slowly from the dark square of the doorway.

To the right of the doorway, a man plastered to the brick wall stepped out. He had outwaited the Jew.

The Jew saw the hammer descending and moved instinctively a fraction of an instant before it struck him on the bone point of his right shoulder. His gun arm went numb with the brackish taste of bone ache. The gun went off before it fell, clattering, to the pavement. Out of the roar the bullet drew a white line through the dark against the brick wall of the brewery and ricocheted upward in a series of arabesques.

The man kicked at the gun with his left foot at the same time that he swung the hammer again with his right hand.

The Jew had pressed the switch, and the light came on the instant the hammer smashed the reflector. It was as though a bolt of lightning had struck once, almost at the moment of the thunder, making the darkness blacker. The flashlight sailed from the Jew's hand and rolled across the yard. His hand and forearm were filled with pins and needles up to his elbow.

The Jew was blinded. Both arms were useless. But he kicked out viciously and caught his assailant on the shin. Grunting with pain, the assailant doubled over. The hammer blow aimed at the Jew's head struck him in the ribs. The sound of a breaking rib came like a drum beat from under water. The Jew tried to scream but didn't have the breath. His assailant swung back-handed from a one-footed stance. The blow caught the Jew over the right ear with the sound of a butcher cleaving a marrow bone. The Jew's tightly stretched mouth went instantly slack; his taut muscles went limp. He fell in a flabby heap.

The assailant bent over and rained blows on the prostrate figure. For a time there was only the rising and the falling of the hammer, the soft meaty sounds as it landed on the Jew's face and head.

Then suddenly it stopped.

The assailant dropped the hammer to the pavement, sat down and put his face in his hands. Inhuman sounds spewed from his mouth. He sounded as though he were crying with uncontrollable terror.

Suddenly the crying stopped.

The assailant rose to a squatting position and snapped on a cigarette lighter. In the flickering light the Jew appeared to be a bundle of bloody rags. The light snapped off quickly.

Quickly, in the dark, the assailant searched the Jew's body. He found nothing, no money, no wallet, no papers.

He had to go inside. His body shaking with terror, he couldn't find the switch. By aid of his cigarette lighter, he descended the stairs. Suddenly a stair squeaked beneath his weight. The cigarette lighter fell from nerveless fingers, and he had to grope for it in the darkness. His breath made a wheezing sound. Finally he found the lighter. It didn't work immediately. He groped his way to the bottom of the stairs and tried the lighter again. It burned, but the flame was more feeble than before.

Time was running out.

For a moment he stood in the door and looked over the room. Objects were barely discernible in the dim flickering light, but he made out the workbench where the Jew had last been seen standing. He crossed to it, put the lighter down and began snatching open drawers. He found it where the Jew had put it.

He held the oiled silk pouch in his hand as though it were as fragile as hope of heaven. His body was bent forward. His eyes were focused. His face held an expression of savage greed.

One hundred grand, he thought.

Suddenly he heard the loose stair creak.

His head was gripped in a vise of ice. It was the dead Jew coming for his money. Instinctively he whirled about, snatching up a wood chisel for a weapon. Only his stifled breathing was audible, but he could sense a presence on the stairs.

He put the pouch into his hip pocket and buttoned the flap, then snapped on his lighter, held it in one hand and the chisel in the other and tiptoed cautiously toward the door.

As he reached the door, he heard feet clatter down the stairs. His body collided with another. In the dark neither could see. He stabbed out with his chisel and heard a sharp cry of pain. At the same time he felt the cool, quick, almost painless slash of a knife across his cheek. Theirs was a brief but furious struggle. He stabbed out crazily, pumping the chisel with an insensate fury. He could feel the difference when it chopped into the wall and when he made contact with cloth and flesh. He couldn't see the knife, but he knew it stabbed the air about him. He felt it enter his flesh countless times. He felt no pain, but he was crazed with terror.

On both sides there were unintelligible grunts – no more. No words were spoken. No curses uttered. Two bodies weaved and ducked and stabbed blindly in the utter darkness. Then the first one broke free and ran.

He thought he was running toward the stairs until he banged into a solid object in the dark. He bounced off, tripped over something else and fell full length onto something that felt like bed springs. He could hear the other in furious pursuit, banging into furniture and grunting like an animal.

The springs seemed to have wrapped themselves about his legs. He fought them off as though they had hands, kicking and stomping. Other objects rose from the dark and struck him in all conceivable places. Something hooked into his ear and tore the lobe. Something else chopped him squarely in the mouth. Objects clutched his ankles. It was as though the broken and dilapidated furniture had taken on life to torture him like a mob of lynchers. His pursuer was undergoing the same torture but that was no consolation.

By the time he had made a tour of the basement storeroom, he had been battered unmercifully. His breath came in sobs. He still clung to the chisel, but he scarcely had the strength to use it. Finally he encountered the stairs. He dragged himself up. He could hear his unseen assailant furiously fighting the treacherous furniture and grunting unintelligible curses in the dark.

He came out in the dark courtyard sucking for breath. His mouth ballooned with vomit, and his teeth bit together. He found the body of the dead Jew where he had left it. He felt a crazy impulse to scream at the top of his voice. He knew he was bleeding from many stab wounds, but he couldn't feel them.

The sudden silence below alerted him again. He heard the loose stair squeak loudly as a foot leaped upon it. He ran toward the shed.

The motor of the moving van was still running as he had left it. Without a loss of motion he leaped into the driver's seat. He put the big old van into reverse, raced the motor and released the clutch. It backed into the gate like a battering ram. The gate broke from its hinges and sailed across the sidewalk into the middle of Third Avenue. The truck followed.

He pulled the emergency brake from force of habit and was running before he hit the ground.

Morningside Park is one of those rocky jungles on the unin-habitable eastern edge of the stone ridge forming the bluffs overlooking the Hudson River. For the most part it is over-grown with dense foliage and interlaced with steep winding stairways, upon which none but the simple-minded dare to venture after dark.

Shortly after midnight, patrol cars converged on that area of the park near the bench where Sugar had met Rufus that afternoon.

There had been an anonymous report to the precinct station that a man was heard screaming there.

But by the time the first of the patrol cars arrived, the screaming had ceased. Drops of dark blood led from a flashy green sedan parked at the curb. There were blood splotches on the back of the driver's seat and on the steering wheel. The drops grew into heavy blobs on the sidewalk leading toward the darkness of a public lavatory and the black-dark jungle of the park beyond. The lavatory was closed and locked for the night, and the trail of blood led around it into the overgrown foliage. Police flashlights stabbed the pools of darkness in the dense undergrowth.

The usual Harlem crowd had collected on the sidewalk and the street, and the cops had difficulty keeping them back.

'Here it is!' a cop announced.

It was curled deep within a clump of shrubbery where it had crawled to hide.

'Stand back! Get back!' a police corporal ordered.

'I know him; I knows that man,' a big black man in working clothes said excitedly. 'He be George Clayborne.'

'And who be you?' the corporal asked.

'I be the janitor of that there house across the street. That there is where George Clayborne lives.'

'Take his name,' the corporal ordered; he seemed to have put himself in charge. 'Get a statement; and the rest of you get some statements from these other people. We can't do no more until the Medical Examiner and the Homicide men arrive.'

'That be his car there,' the janitor informed the young cop who was taking his statement.

The cop opened the front door and found what looked like bloodstains on the steering wheel and front seat.

He shouted for the corporal.

A skinny little black girl, with ribbon-tied braids sticking out from her head at all conceivable angles, looked about carefully until she found the biggest cop. She sidled up and tugged his sleeve.

He gave a start and clawed at his pistol. All these wild-looking colored people had set his nerves on edge. When he saw who had touched him, he turned bright red.

'What do you want?' he shouted angrily.

The little girl looked up at him through big brown solemn eyes. 'I seen who done it,' she said.

The big cop gave another start. 'What?' He wasn't sure he had heard right.

'It was a white lady. I seen her with the knife.'

'White lady!' The big white cop rejected that. 'Go home and go to bed; you don't know what you're talking about.'

'I seen her with the knife,' the little girl insisted. 'It had blood all over it, and she was all in white like a ghost.'

'What's that?' the big slow-witted cop barked. 'You mean dressed in white. Then she wasn't no white lady.'

'Nawsuh, she were just dressed in white, is all,' the little girl said stolidly. 'I seen which way she went.'

'Come on, we'll get after her,' the big cop said, all for action. 'We'll go in the car and you show us which way she went.'

He pushed his way through the crowd to his car, where his partner sat behind the wheel, smoking.

'This little girl saw the murderer,' he said. 'She's going to show us where she went.'

They put the little girl between them. She pointed down 112th Street toward Eighth Avenue.

The car roared down the long block with the siren wide open and burst into Eighth Avenue at sixty miles an hour.

The little girl craned her neck and pointed suddenly toward

a white-clad figure walking rapidly down Eighth Avenue in the direction of 110th Street. 'There is she!' she cried.

The patrol car was half way across the avenue, traveling at the speed of one mile a minute. The driver stood on the brakes and wheeled the car at a sheer right angle as though piloting a supersonic jet plane in an open sky. The scream of tires blended with the scream of the siren, and a northbound car on Eighth Avenue sheered off to the left side of the street and crashed head on into a southbound car, which was sliding sidewise on locked brakes as a result of the patrol car crossing in front of it. The patrol car hit the curb broadside with the edges of its wheels, started turning over, scraped against an iron light post that knocked it back on four wheels, hit a row of garbage cans and knocked them across the wide sidewalk through the plate glass windows of a supermarket. The crash of metal on metal and tin against glass rended the night with ear-splitting sound, and people were seen to duck for cover as far away as Seventh Avenue.

Across the street the white-clad figure started to run, but the patrol car hadn't stopped moving. It slued across the street, the driver bleeding from a gash in his cheek caused by broken window glass, and shimmied to a shaky stop alongside the running woman.

The cops were out and on the street before the car stopped, and the big cop made a running tackle and brought the woman down. She landed on her right thigh, kicking back with her left heel, and caught the cop smack in the mouth. By the time the other cop had rounded the car, she was getting to her feet, and she greeted him with a backhanded blow in the eye.

She was a big strong woman, as quick as a cat, and she fought the two cops as though she had gone stark raving crazy.

The quick crowd gathered as usual, and they saw a good fight.

Finally the cops got her flat on her stomach with her hands crossed behind her. The big cop sat astride her legs and the driver knelt on her neck while they snapped on the handcuffs. Before letting her up, they searched her, to the delight of the spectators, and found two knives in her uniform pocket.

One of the knives was sticky with coagulated blood.

They released her and stood up, standing away at a respectful distance as she scrambled to her feet.

'Why did you do it?' the big cop barked.

'Do what?' she asked sullenly.

If evil looks could have killed, both cops would have dropped dead in their tracks.

'Kill him,' the big cop persisted.

'Kill who?' she said.

'This is the knife,' the driver stated.

'What knife?' she said.

'Give me the knife,' the big cop said to the driver. 'You're dripping your own blood on it.'

The driver passed him the knife. He wrapped it in his handkerchief.

Intense black faces watched this performance with profound interest.

The big cop decided on a new tactic. 'What did you run for, then?'

'Everybody was running,' she said. 'I thought the world was coming to an end.'

'Resisting arrest,' the big cop went on. 'Why did you do that if you're not guilty? The police are your friends.'

This got a well-deserved laugh from the appreciative audience, but both she and the cop were in dead earnest.

'How did I know you was the cops?' she said. 'I heard the noise and thought the Judgment Day was here; and somebody grabbed me by the legs. I thought it were the devil. You'd resist, too, if the devil had you by the legs on Judgment Day.'

'You're not that simple-minded,' the big cop said. 'Come on, let's take her in,' he said to the driver.

By then the patrol cars had moved over from Morningside Drive, and screaming people were running down the streets toward the scene of the new excitement.

'I doubt if this car will run,' the driver said.

'Here comes the wagon, anyway,' the big cop announced, pointing toward the Black Maria pushing through the crowd.

The drivers of the wrecked cars were complaining to the corporal.

'Sue the city,' he advised them.

Residents were helping themselves to provisions from the

smashed showcase of the supermarket. The stone-blind cops didn't see a thing.

'Where's that little girl who fingered this suspect?' the driver asked. 'We need her as a witness.'

The big cop looked about but didn't see her. 'Jesus Christ, why did you let her go?' he asked accusingly.

'Me let her go!' the driver exclaimed indignantly. 'You let her go as much as me.'

'I was occupied subduing this suspect,' the big cop said.

'Hell, what do you think I was doing?' the driver demanded. 'Here, look at my eye.'

'Okay, okay,' the big cop said.

They searched among the crowd for the little girl and inquired for her, but without success. So they took the woman to the station without the little witness.

Photographs had been taken of the body in the bush, and it had been dragged into the lavatory for further examination. Its clothes had been removed.

'I find nineteen stab wounds about the head, neck, shoulders and back,' the Medical Examiner said. 'We can more or less say that was the cause of death.'

The sergeant from the Homicide Bureau looked at the grim object laid out on the tiled floor and felt slightly nauseated.

'He looks as though he were beaten up, too,' he observed.

The two plain-clothes men and the uniformed cops gathered about stared silently.

The Medical Examiner wiped his hands with a cloth dampened with alcohol.

'Yes, that's the strange thing,' he admitted. 'He was severely beaten with some sort of blunt instrument at least half an hour before he was killed. But notice – all of the bruises are on the front of the body, but are not concentrated in any one area like the stab wounds. There are bruises from the shins to the forehead, as though he were beaten while lying on his back.'

'Somebody didn't like him,' the sergeant said.

'Offhand I would say that both the stab wounds and bruises were inflicted by more than one person,' the M.E. said. 'But we can judge better after the autopsy whether more than one knife was used.'

'You think it was a gang killing, then?' the sergeant asked.

'Either that, or the murderer was an exceedingly quick and powerful person.'

'Well, a woman has been found with a bloodstained knife,' the sergeant said. 'And from what I've heard of the report turned in by the arresting officers, she fills the bill as quick and powerful.'

The M.E. looked skeptical. 'In my experience with women-folk, I've never come across any that quick and powerful,' he said.

'Well, we're going to see soon,' the sergeant said.

The M.E. went toward his car, shaking his head; the sergeant went toward his car, his head on tight as a nut.

7

The sergeant was named Frick. He was a lean, black-haired man who suffered secretly from stomach ulcers. He looked now as though one of the ulcers had suddenly bitten him.

'Did you say your name was Alberta Wright?' he asked incredulously.

The woman, sitting on the stool in the cone of light that spilled from the 300-watt lamp, replied sullenly, 'Yassuh, that's what I said.'

The sergeant looked from the face of one of the colored detectives flanking him to the face of the other.

'Did you hear her?' he demanded.

'What about it?' Grave Digger Jones asked politely.

He stood like a farmer resting on his plow, his big, slack frame in the dark, wrinkled suit at a slouching ease.

'Yesterday around noon a call came into the bureau that she'd dropped dead at some kind of a religious festival,' the sergeant said.

'She looks alive enough now,' Coffin Ed Johnson remarked.

He stood on the other side of Sergeant Frick. In all but his face he was the counterpart of Grave Digger. But his acid-scarred face, the memento of an acid-throwing rumpus one night in a shanty on the Harlem River further uptown, looked like the mask of an African witch doctor.

They were both precinct detectives, but the Homicide sergeant had asked them to take part in the interrogation.

The sergeant looked down at the woman as though he expected her to take sudden flight. But she seemed attached to the stool, which was bolted to the middle of the bare floor in the sound-proof, windowless room in the Harlem precinct station known to the underworld as the Pigeon's Nest. She still wore the dirt-blackened white maid's uniform and white rubber bathing cap in which she had been baptized.

'You're giving the Homicide Bureau a hard way to go,' the sergeant said. 'Yesterday you were dead, and now here you are alive and killing someone else.'

'I ain't been dead, and I ain't killed nobody,' Alberta denied.

'All right, all right, start lying,' the sergeant said. 'Tell me all that happened.'

She talked in the flat, whining voice she reserved for white persons who questioned her.

When she had finished talking, the sergeant said, 'You took me at my word, didn't you?'

'Nawsuh, what I told you is the truth,' she maintained.

The sergeant looked again at the colored detectives. 'Do you believe that fairy tale?' he asked in the direction of the police stenographer, who had taken it all down, at his small desk in one corner.

The police stenographer said nothing.

'Some of it,' Grave Digger said.

Beneath a battered felt hat his dark, lumpy face flickered with secret amusement. He understood the art of lying.

'Take some, leave some,' Coffin Ed supplemented.

The sergeant looked as though he had been given a big dose of castor oil. He turned back to Alberta and demanded, 'Let me hear that again. Maybe I didn't hear it right the first time.'

'Hear what again?' Alberta asked. 'You mean tell you all over again what I just told you?'

'No, just tell me that part about your finding the knife,' the sergeant said. 'We'll get back to the rest when we get that clear.'

She took a deep breath and wiped the sweat out of her eyes. 'It ain't nothing to get clear,' she began apathetically. 'It were just like I said. I were sitting on a bench in Central Park—'

'Doing what?' the sergeant interrupted.

'I were resting.'

'By yourself?'

'Yassuh, by myself. And I seen this patrol car go past on a Hundred Tenth Street and turn into Manhattan Avenue.'

'What time was it?'

'I don't know. I didn't have no watch, and I weren't interested in the time. Why don't you ask them what was driving the car?'

'I have. Just answer my questions. What happened then?'

'I had a premonition.'

'Premonition of what?'

'I don't know of what. Just a premonition, is all.'

'How did you feel? Faint? In a daze? Clairvoyant? Or what?'

'I felt just like I always feel when I has a premonition – like something bad was going to happen.'

'To who?'

'I didn't have no feeling about who it was going to happen to.'

'Do you have them every time you see a police patrol car?'

'Nawsuh. I has them about lots of things. I don't know why I has them. Some folks say I got second sight.'

'You didn't have one just before the police arrested you, did you?'

'Nawsuh.'

'That's too bad for you. All right, go ahead, what happened when you had your premonition?'

'I got up and followed the patrol car.'

'You said before that you ran after it,' the sergeant corrected.

'Yassuh, I ran,' Alberta admitted. 'Wasn't no use of dallying around. Premonitions don't last forever.'

'What did you expect to happen?'

'I didn't know what to expect. Just something bad, is all. Something told me I ought to be there.'

'Be where?'

'Where it happened.'

'Why you? Why should you be there? What did you have there? Who did you know there?'

'I don't know. The ways of the Lord are mysterious. I don't question them like you does. I had a premonition and I ran after the patrol car, and that's all there is to it.'

'The way in which you keep carrying on about the Lord, I feel as if He's right here in this room,' the sergeant commented sarcastically.

'He is,' Alberta replied solemnly. 'He's right here by my side.'

'All right,' the sergeant said. 'So what happened when you got there?'

'When I got there I saw a crowd of people and policemen gathered around. I asked a woman what happened. I said some man was killed. I asked her who it were. She said she didn't know. I asked her how he were killed. She said he were stabbed to death.'

'Who did you expect it to be?' the sergeant asked abruptly.

'I didn't expect it to be nobody.'

'All right, so when you got there somebody slipped you the knife. Who was it?'

'Ain't nobody done no such thing and I ain't said nobody did,' she replied angrily. 'I stepped on something, and, when I looked down to see what it were, I seen it were a knife all covered with blood.'

'Where was that?'

'It were in the gutter.'

'Exactly where?'

'In front of the playground.'

'And you tried to conceal it because you knew who had used it,' the sergeant charged harshly.

But Alberta was not intimidated. 'Nawsuh, I didn't do no such thing,' she contradicted heatedly. 'It were just like I said before – suddenly the Lord tapped me on the shoulder and told me to take the knife and throw it into the pond in Central Park and I would save an innocent man's life.'

'How?'

'By throwing the knife in the pond, that's how.'

'All right, who was the innocent man?'

'The Lord didn't say.'

'Well, ask Him, then,' the sergeant snapped. 'You say He's right there by your side.'

'Yassuh,' she replied imperturbably, and turned and spoke to the emptiness. 'Lord, who were it?'

The stenographer stopped writing and looked up sharply. For a space of time no one spoke.

Then the sergeant asked sarcastically, 'What did He say?'

'He said He weren't going to tell,' Alberta replied stolidly.

The police stenographer giggled, but the faces of Grave Digger and Coffin Ed remained impassive.

Sergeant Frick looked at them and rubbed the palm of his hand violently across his forehead. Every time he came to Harlem on a case he got a violent headache.

'What is it you believe about this fairy tale?' he asked the colored detectives.

'What she said she did is probably true,' Grave Digger replied. 'Why she did it is another story.'

'Do you mean to say you believe anybody is stupid enough to try to hide a murder weapon from the police without even knowing who the murderer is?' the sergeant said incredulously.

'Sure,' Coffin said. 'I believe it. Not that this woman is doing that, but there are people in Harlem who will.'

'Why, for Christ's sake?'

'Most people in Harlem consider the police as public enemies,' Grave Digger elaborated. 'But no doubt this woman has a good notion of who the murderer is.'

'That's what I think,' the sergeant said, then turned back to Alberta and shot the question. 'When was the last time you saw George Clayborne?'

'I ain't never heard of him,' she denied.

'He was a crony of your husband's,' the sergeant ventured.

'He were?' she said unconcernedly, ignoring the bait. 'Do tell!'

The sergeant colored.

'What did you say your husband's name was?'

'I didn't say, but, if you wants to know, he's named Rufus Wright.'

'Where does he work?'

'I don't know and I don't care. I ain't seen him in nearmost a year, and what he do don't interest me.'

'Who is your man?' Grave Digger asked.

'My man! He named Sugar Stonewall.'

'What was he doing at Clayborne's house?' the sergeant slipped in cleverly.

'He ain't been there,' Alberta maintained doggedly. 'He left for Detroit on the nine-fifteen, like I said.'

'No, he didn't,' the sergeant said. 'He was waiting for Clayborne in front of Clayborne's house when Clayborne came home. He had some business to transact with Clayborne. You were waiting in the park for Stonewall to come and tell you the outcome of the business. When you saw the patrol car pass you knew something had gone wrong. You rushed to the scene. When you found out that Clayborne had been killed, you knew Stonewall had killed him. You found the knife Stonewall had thrown away. You recognized it. You knew it could be traced to Stonewall. That's why you were going to throw it into the lagoon. All right, why did Stonewall kill him?'

'If you know all that what you asking me for?' Alberta said stubbornly.

'I'm just trying to make it easy for you,' the sergeant said. 'I sympathize with you,' he went on, looking as sympathetic as an executioner. 'I don't want to see you take the rap for a no-good man who runs away leaving you holding the bag.'

'He ain't left me holding nothing,' she contradicted doggedly. 'Sugar Stonewall wouldn't kill a fly.'

'Why weren't you at home?' Coffin Ed asked.

'I told you why. I were lonesome with Stonewall gone. I just walked down to the park and watched the young folks boating in the pond. I had just set down to rest when I seen the patrol car pass.'

'Alberta, I am damn tired of listening to your lies,' the sergeant said. 'I am going to book you on suspicion of murder and keep you in solitary confinement until you decide to tell the truth.'

'The Lord will be with me,' she said defiantly.

'I am going to put out a reader for this man, Sugar Stonewall,' the sergeant informed the colored detectives. 'And

I will wire the Detroit police, too. I want you fellows to check this woman's story.'

'Right,' Grave Digger said. He waited until the police stenographer had followed the sergeant from the room, then turned to Alberta and said invitingly, 'Now that we are all colored folks here, you can tell us the story and let's get it over with.'

'I done told all there is,' she maintained stubbornly.

'Okay, we'll find out,' he said roughly. 'Where are the keys to your flat?'

'How do I know,' she muttered. 'They took them at the desk.'

'Let's lock her up,' Coffin Ed grated. 'She's getting on my nerves.'

'Get up,' Grave Digger said.

They took her out and turned her over to the matron.

8

Half an hour later they had searched her flat and found it empty. They started to leave the building, on their way back to question her again.

'Pssst!' the big fat lady who lived on the first floor of the tenement on 118th Street hissed from her front window.

It was past one o'clock, and the street was deserted. Not a window was lit. Only the rats were in evidence, scavenging among the loaded garbage cans; and the hunting cats watching them from dark corners with baleful eyes.

Grave Digger jerked his thumb toward a vaguely visible outline of a female half filling the lower part of a black-dark window. Coffin Ed nodded.

'Come inside,' the woman whispered. 'I got something to tell you.'

They turned and re-entered the dimly lit hall.

'Never look a stool pigeon in the mouth,' Grave Digger said in a low voice.

Coffin Ed loosened his long-barreled, nickel-plated .38 caliber revolver in its oiled shoulder holster. Grave Digger noticed the gesture and thought, *A burned child fears fire.* He tightened with trepidation. He wondered if Coffin Ed would ever get over the memory of the acid splashing into his face. It had left him trigger-happy; and a trigger-happy detective was as dangerous as a blind rattlesnake.

To the right, a door opened cautiously a crack and then opened fully into a black-dark room.

'Get some light on,' Coffin Ed grated, the revolver flashing suddenly in his hand.

'Easy does it,' Grave Digger said.

A gasp was heard from the darkness, and a light came on suddenly. 'Lord God, you scared me,' the big fat black woman moaned. 'I just didn't want nobody to see me talking to the cops.'

They stepped inside, and Coffin Ed kicked the door shut behind him, holding the revolver loosely at his side. The fat lady rushed to the front window and drew the shades.

They were standing in the parlor. She offered them whiskey, which they declined.

She said with an air of secrecy, 'I saw you when you came, and I knew you were going up to Alberta Wright's.'

'What's happened up there?' Grave Digger asked.

The fat lady's eyes widened. 'Don't you know? Her furniture was stolen while she was away at the baptism.'

The detectives became suddenly alert.

'I bet you were sitting in your window with a grandstand seat,' Coffin Ed said.

'I didn't see them take it away, but I saw them when they come with the moving van,' she admitted.

'All right, let's have it,' Grave Digger said. 'And, if you are a friend of Alberta's, you'll give it to us straight.'

'Lord, that child is just like a daughter to me,' she said, then went on to tell with great relish the events leading up to the theft of the furniture.

'What did this Rufus Wright look like?' Grave Digger asked.

She described him as though she had been his valet.

'And Alberta knew who he was when you told her?'

'Oh, she knew him all right,' the fat lady said. 'Do you reckon they is relations?' She licked her lips as though it tasted good. 'Maybe he's her husband; I know that other nigger ain't.'

'Maybe,' Grave Digger said. 'You keep on watching, and if you see anything else, you call the precinct station and ask for one of us. You know who we are, don't you?'

'Lord, if I didn't know, I could guess,' she said, watching Coffin Ed slip the long-barreled revolver back into its oiled shoulder holster.

She was back in her front window before the small, battered, black sedan, with Grave Digger at the wheel and Coffin Ed beside him, pulled away from the curb.

They returned to the precinct station and got on the telephones.

Coffin Ed called the morgue and got a description of the corpse and the clothes it had been wearing at the time of death. He then called the downtown Homicide Bureau, got Sergeant Frick on the phone and asked him to send up a photograph of the corpse; but he knew he wouldn't need it. Now he knew the corpse's other name was Rufus Wright.

Grave Digger telephoned the Bronx police to get a line on the location of the Jew's warehouse. He got more than he had expected.

After they had pooled their information, they reached an unspoken accord.

'We had better slip her out the back way,' Coffin Ed said. 'The lieutenant won't like it.'

Grave Digger smiled. 'Her and her private God.'

They drove, with Alberta between them, crosstown toward the Harlem River. In that section of Park Avenue in back of the 125th Street Station, prostitutes and muggers lurked in the dark shadows of the stanchions of the railway trestle, waiting to take some sucker's money – or his life.

'Where are you taking me?' Alberta asked finally.

'To get your furniture that Rufus stole,' Grave Digger replied.

She didn't say another word.

They crossed over on the Ellis Street Bridge and picked up Third Avenue in the Bronx at the subway junction at 149th Street.

When they came to the Jew's warehouse, the moving van was parked at the curb and the wooden gate had been leaned against the iron grille of the store front.

Two uniformed cops were on duty, and a patrol car was parked across the street.

'We're from Harlem,' Grave Digger said.

'Yeah, the inspector telephoned us you were coming,' one of the harness bulls said.

They took Alberta round to the back door and down into the basement room.

'There was more than this,' she said.

'Look around,' Coffin Ed suggested.

They turned on all the lights and watched her search the basement, then the whole main floor. She seemed more interested in mattresses than in anything else. When she had finished she asked, 'Ain't there no place else?'

'This is all,' Grave Digger said.

Tears welled up in her eyes.

'What is it you're looking for?' Coffin Ed asked.

But she didn't say. All she said was, 'The Lord is going to make them pay for this.'

'If they haven't paid now, they never will,' Grave Digger said, 'The Jew has been murdered, too.'

Her dark face turned slowly gray.

'The Lord struck them dead,' she said.

'Not the Lord,' Grave Digger corrected. 'Somebody down here. Do you want to tell us about it now?'

'I want to talk to my preacher,' she said.

'Well, you had better have him get in touch with your friend, The Lord,' Grave Digger suggested. 'You are going to need Him.'

They took her back to the precinct station and had her transferred downtown to the city jail.

9

Sugar stood beside a felt-covered kidney-shaped table in a room back of a grocery store on Lenox Avenue near 118th Street, watching the stud poker game.

'What time is it?' he asked the game keeper.

The game keeper pulled out an old-fashioned Elgin watch.

'Twenty-eight minutes and fifty-seven seconds past two o'clock,' he replied, gold crowns flashing as he talked.

'I got to go,' Sugar said.

'What's stopping you?' the game keeper asked.

Sugar picked his way through the dark store, and the door keeper let him out into the street.

He hurried back toward Eighth Avenue, warily approaching the scene where Alberta had been arrested. The crowds had disappeared, and the dark street was practically deserted.

The wrecked cars had been pushed to the curb, and a lone patrolman guarded the supermarket. Otherwise the coast was clear. He found a colored man who had witnessed the rumpus sitting on a tenement stoop, as though waiting for something else to happen. The man told him the cops had found the murder knife on the lady they arrested.

Sugar couldn't figure that one. He knew she hadn't killed him, but what was she doing with the knife? He couldn't think of a single reason. But that could wait. Whatever she was doing with it didn't make any difference now. It spelled trouble, big trouble with a capital T.

He felt in his pocket for a cigarette. He didn't have any. He was hungry, but he didn't have the price of a feed. He didn't know anybody he could borrow so much as half a dollar from. The jokers he played tonk with didn't have any more than he had ordinarily, and that was only what their women gave them; and he knew they wouldn't lend him any if they had. He didn't have anything valuable enough to sell. He didn't have the talent to pick pockets, if there had been anybody's pocket to pick. He didn't have the nerve to rob anybody. He wasn't strong enough to mug. He hadn't made any connections with other women since he had had Alberta; he had been too lazy. He was a naturally lazy man.

And now he didn't even have any place to sleep, as tired and worn out as he was, having been up all the night before and running around all day long.

That was when he came to realize how much Alberta meant to him.

There was no need now of thinking about ways and means of stealing her money.

The main thing now was to get his woman back. Let her do the worrying. She'd find them some place to stay and something to eat. She might even find her money back. She was a strong, resourceful woman. He could depend on her.

But it would take money to get her out on bail.

He thought of Cassie. She was another kitchen slave, like Alberta. If she could afford to keep that Dummy in chips, maybe she had something cached away. And she and Alberta were such good friends maybe she would dig some of it up.

He went over to Cassie's on 112th Street, but nobody answered.

He stood in the street, feeling low and disgusted. Harlem was rough, he thought. If you didn't have money, you didn't have friends. He thought of the time he had been in jail down South. He had seen a hungry rat lapping up red pepper and sitting in a pan of water to keep its stomach cool.

He saw a man coming from the direction of Seventh Avenue. As the man came nearer Sugar saw that he was big, and wearing an old cap and clean starched overalls. But Sugar's eyes lit on the lunch pail the man was carrying. If he had had a knife, he would have tried to mug the man for his lunch. But he hadn't been able to borrow a knife. No one had been willing to lend him a knife. It wasn't what he might have done with it; it was just that nobody wanted to be without a knife. It wasn't that people wanted to use their knives on other people; it was just that they wanted to have their knives in case other people started cutting on them.

The big workman passed, keeping at a distance, his free hand in his pocket gripping his knife. Not that he suspected Sugar of any bad intentions; he just wanted to be prepared.

Sugar's feet started moving him in the direction of home. It was empty; the furniture was gone; the door was locked; his woman was in jail; and what was more the home didn't belong to him, and he didn't have the key. But it was home, the only one he had.

'Pssst!'

He came near jumping out of his skin.

The big fat black lady was invisible in the dark window.

'Who that?' he asked in a frightened whisper.

She came closer, and he could make out the whites of her eyes in the dim light from the distant street lamp.

'It's me – Miz Teabone.'

'Hell,' Sugar said evilly. 'Why don't you go to bed.'

'The police been here looking for you,' she informed him in a stage whisper.

'Looking for me?' He was ready to light out and run a crooked mile.

'Grave Digger and Coffin Ed,' she whispered theatrically. 'Where's your woman?'

'She's in jail.'

'I knowed it,' Mrs Teabone said triumphantly. 'When I heard over the radio that a Jew-man named Abie had been killed up in the Bronx, I knowed she done it. I got second sight.'

'The Jew!' Sugar exclaimed. 'He dead?'

'He ain't alive,' she said juicily. 'She beat his head in with a hammer.'

'She didn't do it,' he said loyally. 'It must have been somebody else.'

'You is the only other somebody else,' she said.

Again his feet got the message before it arrived at his brain. He was running. He didn't know where he was going, but he was on his way.

Something came up fast behind him and grabbed him by the sleeve. It sounded like a winded animal. His scalp rolled. It was late at night, he was alone on the street and he didn't have a knife. He tried to put on speed. He was afraid to look around.

'Let go!' he gasped in terror.

The thing tightened its grip and pulled up beside him. They turned the corner into Lenox Avenue, neck and neck. The thing grunted urgently. He looked about and saw a gaping mouth circled with even white teeth in a broad flat face. But behind the teeth was a gaping black hole where normally a tongue should have been.

'Dummy!' he exclaimed, panting.

He stopped and sucked in air.

'Jesus Christ, man, don't scare me like that,' he complained.

Dummy kept grunting. His soft brown eyes, peering out from beneath knobs of scar tissue, were urgent.

'Man, stop making those noises,' Sugar said.

Dummy clutched his hand and stuck a dirty scrap of writing paper in it.

Sugar took it and turned to let the light fall over his shoulder.

He read: *the mens wants you/lay low/go to mammy stormy/she safe.*

He looked up.

Dummy's head jerked anxiously up and down.

He nodded and said, 'Okay.'

Dummy grinned, and his mouth looked like an exhibit of dental plates.

He was a short, heavy-set Hawaiian-looking man with thick, gray-shot, curly hair. His coarse, lumpy face was interlaced with tiny scars. He had cauliflowers for ears and pile hammers for hands. Muscles bulged from his dark brown T-shirt, but fat put him in the heavyweight division. He might have been any age from thirty to fifty.

He made an *O* with his right thumb and forefinger and turned down Lenox toward 116th Street. Sugar watched him for a moment. He had the half-sliding, bent-over gait of a full-grown gorilla.

Sugar wondered how he knew the police were looking for him. Where did he come into the story? What was his pitch? Did he know about the money?

On sudden impulse he decided to follow Dummy. But it wasn't easy. Dummy kept looking to both sides and over his shoulder with the instinctive caution of a man who can't hear. Sugar stepped into a doorway and let Dummy turn the corner into 116th Street. Then he ran after him in his high-kneed, churning, double-jointed gait.

He rounded the corner just in time to see Dummy disappear into the shadows beneath the entrance to Sweet Prophet's Temple of Wonderful Prayer.

Mammy Stormy's was over on Seventh Avenue near 115th Street. If Dummy saw him walking down 116th Street, he would naturally figure he was on his way to Mammy Stormy's. But if Dummy had gone into the Temple, he would soon know.

Above a narrow entrance, wedged between a dismal grocery

store and a curtained hair-dressing parlor, was a small sign hanging in a glass box with the faintly discernible word: *Hotel.* At night the hotel entrance served the resident prostitutes as a sentry box and transient drunks as a water closet. During the day dogs dropped in to find out what the neighboring dogs had been eating.

As Sugar approached, a teenage girl came down the steep flight of stairs. Her cotton dress was rumpled and torn, and her straightened hair was mussed and stuck out from her skull like a mangled cactus plant. She was a thin girl, with small breasts, and her thin black face was wet with tears and ugly from crying.

Dummy came quickly from the entrance to the Temple and trotted across the street. Sugar kept coming toward them, trying to look as though it wasn't any business of his.

'He Georgiaed me,' the girl told Dummy hysterically. 'He sent me to Georgia.'

Sugar couldn't help but hear her. He knew she meant that a man she had taken to her room had shown her some money, but afterwards had refused to pay her. He was surprised to learn that Dummy was trying to pimp.

Dummy told the girl to shut up with sign language, but she didn't understand. She thought he didn't understand what she was trying to tell him. She tried to demonstrate with gestures how the man had used her and put her out of the room without paying her.

'You ought to lay for him and rob him,' she said. 'He got a big roll of money; I saw it.'

Dummy grabbed her and shook her, trying to make her hush. He didn't want Sugar to know what was happening. But the girl thought he was going to beat her because she had let herself be cheated.

'Don't beat me,' she begged. 'I'll help you. We can both rob him easy; he ain't got nothing but a knife.'

Dummy pushed her back into the hotel entrance. She fell on the stairs and didn't try to get up. In his excitement he was trying to talk. The sounds made Sugar's flesh crawl.

Dummy took a dirty scratch pad and a pencil stub from his hip pocket and scrawled hurriedly: *git goin man / the gunmens be here soon,* and gave it to Sugar.

'How do you know the cops is looking for me if you been here all night with this chippy whore?' Sugar asked suspiciously.

Dummy wrote, *they found the knife you throwed away on alburda*.

Sugar's eyes popped. 'The knife I throwed away! What knife?'

Dummy wrote: *the one you stabbed rufus with*.

'Man, Jesus Christ, look here,' Sugar began, but Dummy grabbed him by the arm and pointed.

At the end of the block the dim lights of a small black sedan were turning slowly into 116th Street. It was now close to four o'clock.

A gargling sound issued from Dummy's mouth as he tried desperately to talk. But Sugar got the message anyway. From that distance he couldn't recognize the car nor see the faces of its occupants. But only Grave Digger Jones and Coffin Ed Johnson could raise that look on Dummy's face.

The only way to go without being seen was up the stairs. Sugar leaped over the huddled figure of the little prostitute and started quickly up the steep flights of stairs. Dummy stuck a foot inside and kicked the girl, and she jumped to her feet and followed Sugar.

'Ain't you coming, too?' Sugar called softly down the stairs.

But Dummy sprinted across the street and vanished in the shadows of the entrance to the Temple.

10

Grave Digger and Coffin Ed had what they called their 'stool pigeon route,' which took them through the congested slum area of Harlem known as The Valley. Whenever possible they covered this route in the early hours of morning, shortly before going off duty, and contacted their stool pigeons.

Each stool pigeon had a place of contact and a time. They were not expected to show up every night, because neither did the detectives; but, if they missed three nights straight running, it was their little hip pockets, as they say in Harlem, which meant they were in trouble. Care was taken that no stool pigeon ever got to know another stool pigeon.

When they showed in their battered black sedan, idling slowly along the street, the stool pigeon at his post would give the signal. The signal was for him to cut whatever he was doing and duck into the nearest doorway, as though he were ducking the cops. After which the detectives would turn into the first dark street and park unobtrusively in the shadows with the lights cut. Then wait. Sometimes the stool pigeon could make it in a few minutes. Sometimes it took more than a half hour. The stool pigeon had to be given time to shake his companions and make a clean getaway. There was no sense in having a stool pigeon who was known to be a stool pigeon.

After returning from the Bronx with Alberta Wright, the detectives got on their route. They needed information about Rufus and the Jew. The Medical Examiner's report, photographs, fingerprints, the findings of the criminal laboratory and all the results of modern police techniques – including police theories – were generally useless in solving murders in Harlem. Interrogations helped but little because the criminal and lower-class elements of Harlem were for the most part natural-born and highly talented liars. Third-degree methods were useful, but they couldn't beat the truth out of everybody. If there were no eyewitness accounts, the detectives had to depend on stool pigeons.

On this case, they didn't know where to start. The Jew had been killed for robbery. That was the only reason that particular Jew would ever be killed, they reasoned. Rufus might have got his from Alberta, but they didn't believe it. With the number of stab wounds he had on him, she should have had at least some bloodstains on her white uniform – which she hadn't.

Grave Digger summed it up by saying, 'There is no need of thinking about this business until we get more to think about.'

'Such as what did the Jew find in this poor domestic worker's furniture of sufficient value to make somebody knock him off,' Coffin Ed added.

'And why did Rufus get croaked after he had already completed his part of the deal,' Grave Digger threw in.

'Let's find somebody with a roll of fresh money and work back from that,' Coffin Ed said, 'Our folks will kill one another for damn near anything, but whenever they kill a Jew it's for money.'

'Right,' Grave Digger said. They were on the second lap of their route when they got the first message of interest. A small-time hoofer from The Celebrity Club on 125th Street told them about a punk who had shown up an hour earlier flashing a roll for the benefit of the chorus girls, trying to score. The hoofer sat in the back seat while the detectives cross-examined him.

'What was his name?' Coffin Ed asked.

'I didn't get it, boss; he's a stranger around here.'

'What does he do?'

'I don't know, boss.'

'You could tell his pitch from the way he looked.'

'I didn't see him, boss. Just heard the girls talking about him. They said he looked like a starker, a real down home mugger. Blowing gage and talking underneath their clothes like as if they were hustlers. They didn't like it.'

'What size roll?' Grave Digger asked.

'They didn't count it, boss.'

'They saw it.'

'Just the edges, boss. He kept it gripped tight in his fist and just flashed the edges.'

Grave Digger and Coffin Ed exchanged looks.

'Did he score with any other chippy?' Coffin Ed asked.

'Didn't nobody say, boss. Anyway, he left.'

'You're not much good,' Coffin said harshly.

'I do the best I can, boss.'

'Yeah, if you get caught peddling marijuana to teenagers, you get life under the new Federal law,' Grave Digger said. 'You know that, don't you?'

'I knows it, boss, but I ain't peddling no weed.'

'All right, get out – you stink,' Colin Ed said.

The stoolie got from the car as though it had caught on fire.

Grave Digger and Coffin Ed looked at one another.

'What do you make of it?' Grave Digger asked.

'From here it looks like some punk found some stage money and is trying to have a ball on it,' Coffin Ed said.

'Yeah, but that's such an old gag for a town like Harlem.'

'You know, Digger, Harlem's full of squares,' Coffin Ed said.

'Maybe this punk is a square himself,' Grave Digger mused. 'But we should look into the play just the same – when we get time.'

'Right now I want to hear somebody talk about a Jew,' Coffin Ed said.

'Right,' Grave Digger said, and started up the car.

The next message was a blank. It came from a slap-happy wino whose claim to fame was that once he had fought on the card at Madison Square Garden as a heavyweight. True, he had only been a four-rounder in the prelims and nobody had ever heard of him before or since, but he had been there.

He started out of the Braddock Bar over on Eighth Avenue, saw the dicks' car coming and ducked back in.

'Shall we pass him?' asked Grave Digger, who was driving.

'We haven't got much time,' Coffin Ed admitted. 'But sometimes out of the mouths of fools comes the solid tip.'

Grave Digger smiled to himself.

They waited for the wino. He didn't keep them waiting. He approached their car as if he didn't care who saw him, opened the back door without waiting for Coffin Ed and crawled up on the seat. His foul breath filled the car with the smell of stockyards.

'Spit it out and scram,' Coffin Ed said brutally. 'You are suffocating us.'

'You want to know who stuck up that United Cigar store?' the wino asked.

'Who?' Coffin Ed grated.

'Me,' the wino said jubilantly, and started laughing like hell.

Coffin Ed was out of the car, big feet planted on the pavement; he had his gun club-fashion in his hand, the back door open; he reached in, grabbed the ex-pug by the collar of his shirt and was yanking him bodily through the door before Grave Digger realized what was happening.

'Don't hurt him, Ed!' Grave Digger cried. 'Don't hurt him – he's simple-minded.'

Coffin Ed's burn-scarred face was diabolical with fury. But he caught the descending gun butt before it crashed against the wino's skull. He pushed the wino back against the car and slapped him across the mouth.

'You're not funny,' he said in a voice so dangerous it sent cold shivers down Grave Digger's spine.

The ex-pug fainted from terror.

Coffin Ed pushed him to one side with his foot.

'Where is your sense of humor, Ed?' Grave Digger asked.

'I haven't got any,' Coffin Ed admitted as he holstered his revolver and got back into the car. 'They burned it out of me.'

Grave Digger started the car, but Coffin Ed halted him by a touch of the arm.

'What do we do with this punk?'

'Leave him there,' Grave Digger said. 'If he stuck up that cigar store, I'm Cupid.'

Coffin Ed grunted.

'It takes all kinds to make the world, Ed,' Grave Digger added philosophically.

'Yeah? Some of the funny ones are going to quit work,' Coffin Ed said.

They had practically covered their route before they got the last message.

It came from Dummy.

When they saw Dummy duck into the entrance to Sweet Prophet's temple, Grave Digger pulled the battered sedan over the curb and off the street into the exit way beside a chain movie theater. On one side were the double iron doors of the movie house, on the other the brick side wall of the adjoining building.

After a while Dummy showed himself on the sidewalk, walked in that direction – looking on all sides, as was his habit – and suddenly disappeared.

Coffin Ed looked from the darkened car and saw two eyes gleaming beside him in the dark. He opened the back door and Dummy got in.

'What's new?' he asked.

'He can't see in here,' Grave Digger said. 'Let's take him to the station.'

Dummy was squirming about in the back seat, digging out his dirty scratch pad and stub of pencil.

Coffin Ed got into the back seat with him, and Grave Digger backed the car into the street. When they pulled up before the green lights of the precinct station, Dummy scribbled in alarm: *is a pinch?*

Coffin Ed got his face into the light and said, 'No pinch, just some questions.'

Dummy relaxed and grinned.

They took him to the Pigeon's Nest. He sat on the stool in the spill of white light and imagined he was back in the ring. He looked as happy as a kid with a new toy.

'He'd still fight if they let him,' Grave Digger remarked.

Dummy read his lips and nodded vigorously. He jumped to his feet and began shadowboxing, his gaze pinned on the floor, watching his imaginary opponent's feet.

'Sit down,' Coffin Ed said, but Dummy wasn't watching his lips, and Coffin Ed had to push him back onto the stool.

Grave Digger brought the two straight backed chairs from the corner desk and they sat facing Dummy in the light.

'Get your paper and pencil out,' he said.

Dummy wet the stub in his tongueless mouth and poised the scratch pad on his knee.

'Who killed Rufus?' Grave Digger asked, taking a shot in the dark. He didn't expect an answer, but Dummy was a night bird, and there was always a chance he might know something.

mugger, Dummy wrote without hesitation.

Grave Digger took the pad and passed it to Coffin Ed. They exchanged looks. Grave Digger handed back the pad and asked, 'Did you see it?'

Dummy nodded.

'Know him?' Coffin Ed asked.

Dummy shook his head. He drew a circle about his face with his index finger and shook his head again.

'You didn't see his face?'

Dummy nodded.

'Tell us what you saw,' Grave Digger said.

Dummy wrote: *rufus drove up / mugger braced him in car / pulled him out / put knife on throat / pushed him toward outhouse / rufus try to run / mugger stab him in back / keep stabbin / rufus down on hands and knees / crawl into the bush / mugger follow / i didn see nobody come out.*

The detectives read the scrawled words in amazement.

'Where were you?' Grave Digger asked.

Dummy reached for the pad and wrote: *i was hidin in bushes.*

'Doing what?' Coffin Ed asked, but Grave Digger held up his hand and said, 'We'll get back to that. Let's find out what the killer looked like.'

Dummy shook his head earnestly.

'All right – you didn't see his face, but you saw his back,' Grave Digger said.

Dummy wrote quickly: *i saw his arm risin and fallin with the blade.*

'You saw more than that,' Coffin Ed said. 'What did he look like? What was he wearing? What size was he?'

Dummy scribbled frantically: *big man built like a heavyweight had on a tan jumper and longbill army cap he was young strong fast all I saw.*

'Was there anyone else in sight?' Grave Digger asked.

i didn see nobody.

As Dummy filled the pages with his answers, Grave Digger tore them from the pad and stuffed them into his pocket.

'What did you do?' he asked.

i ran up the hill i couldn call the cops i didn want tangle with big strong starker and his knife i couldn tell nobody what i saw i wait to tell you.

'You know Sugar Stonewall?' Coffin Ed asked.

Dummy nodded.

'Was it him?'

Dummy shook his head.

'We'd better get the lieutenant in on this,' Grave Digger said.

Dummy's mouth flew open, and choking sounds issued from the gruesome cavity.

'It's all right,' Grave Digger reassured him. 'Take it easy. We have to take a statement.'

Beads of sweat came out suddenly on Dummy's scarred, knotty face.

'Who around here talks sign language?' Grave Digger asked his partner.

'The lieutenant, I think,' Coffin Ed said. 'I've seen him playing with it.'

'All right, Dummy, you just sit and take it easy,' Grave Digger said, getting to his feet. 'We're not going to hold you unless we have to.'

Coffin Ed followed, and they went out and locked the door.

Lieutenant Anderson was in command of the night shift. He was a student of dactylology. He took over the questioning of Dummy, translating Dummy's replies for the detectives and a police stenographer, who sat at the desk and recorded the interrogation in shorthand.

Dummy stated that Alberta Wright had visited Cassie in her flat on 112th Street at about ten-thirty o'clock the previous night. She had come alone. He had been absent when she arrived. When he returned home Alberta was sitting at the kitchen table across from Cassie. Cassie was eating watermelon seasoned with black pepper and drinking salted beer.

'Where had you been?' Anderson interrupted to ask.

'I was watching out for my girls,' Dummy replied.

'Your girls?'

'He's got two chippy whores,' Grave Digger explained. 'He's trying to teach them how to hustle. He wants to be a pimp.'

Lieutenant Anderson had been on night duty in Harlem for over a year. During that time he had come to know his two ace colored detectives well, and he depended on them. He knew they had their own personal interpretation of law enforcement. Some people they never touched – such as madames of orderly houses of prostitution, operators of orderly gambling games, people connected with the numbers racket, streetwalkers who stayed in their district. But they were rough on criminals of violence and confidence men. And he had always thought they were rough on dope peddlers and pimps, too. So Grave Digger's casual explanation of Dummy's pimping surprised him.

'And you let him go about breaking in young girls to hustle?' he asked.

'If he didn't do that he would do something worse,' Grave Digger said. 'He would be a mugger or a cat burglar or a stick-up man. He can't talk and he can't hear. He probably could get a job as a porter or a dishwasher; but he won't do that. He has been in the chips, and he figures those jobs are degrading. He used to be one of the greatest welterweights in the business, but the racketeers who owned him sent him to the tank so often he got both his eardrums burst. When he was no longer useful to them, they kicked him out of the profession. Then the do-gooders got hold of him and primed him to spill before the state committee investigating boxing, and the gangsters kidnapped him one night and cut his tongue out. They unloaded him from a car in Foley Square in front of the state building where the investigation was being conducted and it was just luck a patrol car passed in time to get him to hospital to save his life. Since then he has tried his hand at the usual occupations of an ex-pug – writing numbers, gambling, bodyguarding. Some big boxer gave him some money to open a shoe-shine parlor, but he used it to buy a new Cadillac, and the first night he had it he got it smashed up because he couldn't hear the horn of a truck. Now he's trying to pimp. If these chippies don't work for him, they will work for some other pimp. At least he treats them better than most pimps would; he protects them and doesn't beat them up. And when a chippy makes up her mind to be a whore, there is no stopping her. So we let him go. What would you do?'

'God knows,' Lieutenant Anderson said. 'Let's get back to the story. You live with this woman, Cassie?'

Dummy nodded. 'She's my old lady,' he said.

'She lets him stay in her house and does what she can to take care of him,' Grave Digger explained once more. 'But she's just a cook and a liquor-head to boot, so she doesn't have much money. He doesn't make much pimping either, but it keeps him in small change.'

'Yeah,' the lieutenant said. Then to Dummy, 'What did you go home for?'

'To get ten bucks,' Dummy confessed. 'Tricks weren't walking.'

'And Alberta Wright was there when you arrived?'

'Yes, sir,' Dummy said.

He told them that Alberta had told Cassie that Rufus had stolen her furniture while she was in a religious trance. She had stopped by to see if she could find out where Rufus lived from Dummy. She and Rufus had worked together for five years after their marriage as a domestic couple – he as the butler-chauffeur and she as the maid-cook. Then he had stolen their savings and had run away with another woman. She hadn't seen him for more than two years, and didn't know where he lived or what name he had taken.

When Dummy came, he had told Alberta the setup. Rufus had been working with the Jew for more than a year in a furniture-stealing racket. Abie had an outlet second-hand furniture store on Third Avenue near 125th Street in Harlem, and another place on Third Avenue in the Bronx, where he kept the hot stuff to cool off. Rufus entered apartments of people who were out of town on visits or business and sold the furnishings to the Jew in the role of proprietor. The Jew was covered; he demanded a statement of ownership from Rufus and gave a signed and witnessed receipt.

Dummy had told Alberta that if she wanted her furniture back, the Jew would return it for what he had paid Rufus, plus twenty per cent handling charges, and ten dollars an hour for its removal and return – no questions asked on either side.

'A slick little racket,' Lieutenant Anderson commented.

'I saw her furniture,' Grave Digger put in. 'It wasn't worth that kind of deal.'

'That's what Cassie said,' Dummy told them. 'I told Alberta I would handle it for her, but she just wanted to find Rufus.'

'All right, Dummy, quit beating around the bush,' Grave Digger said. 'What did she have hidden in her furniture that made it worth while to steal?'

'She said it was just mojos and potions and charms,' Dummy said. 'African and Haitian stuff. Witch doctor bones that had been dried on the equator and special voodoos from the West Indies; hearts' blood from Mexico and dried snake bites from East India. All kinds of magic stuff, she said.'

Grave Digger and Coffin Ed looked at one another and then at Lieutenant Anderson. The lieutenant looked nonplussed.

'Let's get this straight,' the lieutenant said. 'She told you she had this stuff hidden in her furniture.'

'Yes, sir, that's what she said.'

'And you believed it?'

'No, sir, but that's what she said.'

Grave Digger chuckled, 'Can you imagine the Jew going to all that trouble stripping her furniture looking for a handful of mojos?'

'What would she want with mojos if she had just got religion?' Coffin Ed said.

'I'm just telling you what she said,' Dummy repeated.

'You think it was something else?' Lieutenant Anderson asked the detectives.

'In order to bring the Jew into it, there had to be money,' Grave Digger said. 'Or else they thought there was money.'

'What did you think it was, Dummy?' the lieutenant asked.

'I thought she was just mad at Rufus. He had done stole her money once, and I thought she figured him stealing her furniture was the lick that killed Dick.'

'What do you think now?' Coffin Ed asked. 'You know the Jew has been killed, too?'

Dummy nodded, 'I think it was something else,' he admitted.

'What?' Coffin Ed persisted.

'Something she stole,' Dummy said. 'Some jewelry.'

'We can check that soon enough with her employers.'

'Maybe she got it from somebody else.'

'All right,' Anderson said. 'You told her where Rufus lived?'

'No, sir,' Dummy said. 'I told her I would see if I could find out where he lived, and she promised to give me ten dollars if I did.'

'And you found out where he lived and told her?'

'No, sir, I knew where he lived,' Dummy said. 'I left her with Cassie and went to see what I could get out of Rufus. He wasn't at home, and I waited across the street. That's how come I saw him when he drove up.'

'You left her with Cassie, and Cassie gave her Rufus's address,' the lieutenant said.

'No, sir, Cassie didn't know it,' Dummy said. 'And she wouldn't have told her nohow.'

'We'll soon find out,' the lieutenant said. 'I'm going to have her brought in.'

'It won't do no good,' Dummy said. 'By now she's stone drunk.'

'We'll see,' the lieutenant said. He ordered the stenographer to transcribe the notes and have the statement typed, and told the detectives to lock Dummy up until they questioned Cassie.

But Cassie was too drunk to be moved other than in an ambulance, and they figured it best to let her sober up at home.

It was broad daylight by the time the statement was ready for Dummy to sign.

Grave Digger had one last question. 'Have you seen Sugar Stonewall?'

Lieutenant Anderson had gone home, and Dummy had to use his pad and pencil to reply. He wrote: *no sir i aint seen sugar in a week.*

Coffin Ed asked his question. 'Who's carrying a fresh roll about town?'

nobody i know of, Dummy wrote.

They let him sign the statement and drove him back to where they had picked him up. Then they drove back to Lenox Avenue, found an all-night greasy spoon, sat on the counter stools and had coffee and doughnuts.

11

'Let's wake up Sweet Prophet,' Grave Digger said.

'He ain't going to like it,' Coffin Ed said.

'That's for sure,' Grave Digger agreed.

Sweet Prophet received the detectives in the sitting room adjoining his bedroom on the top floor of the building housing his Temple and reception room.

The housekeeper had opened the curtains and raised the windows looking down on the busy shopping area of 116th Street. Motor sounds and loud voices came in with motor exhaust smell and the stink of hot dirty pavement.

The room had a north light and was furnished like a corner of the lobby of the Paramount Theater. Fat, complacent gold and silver cherubs chased coffee-brown angels about the sunrise-pink wall paper, while the appropriately sky-blue ceiling was filled with more golden stars than in the Milky Way, whirling dizzily about a silver moon containing the vague outline of a face with a startling resemblance to that of Sweet Prophet.

'If this ain't heaven, it will have to do until the real heaven comes along,' Coffin Ed remarked.

'Shhh,' Grave Digger cautioned. 'Here's the Prophet.'

Sweet Prophet looked both mad and sleepy. His eyes popped from a scowling countenance. His yellow silk pyjamas, peeping from beneath a dressing gown with candy stripes of red and white, gave the impression of a carnival on the loose. His big feet were encased in bright red Turkish slippers trimmed in gold; and his long kinky white hair was topped with a Fez of matching red with a golden tassel falling from the crown.

He greeted them in a vexed manner. 'Gentlemen, I got the best lawyers east of the Mississippi River.'

'Okay, throw us out,' Grave Digger said.

'Since you're here, sit down, sit down,' he said, plumping himself on a high-backed gilded chair that resembled a throne. 'We're all colored folks, ain't we? You don't have to stand on ceremony with me. I am a humble man.'

The detectives pulled up chairs that put them two feet lower than the Prophet.

'We hate to trouble you at this hour, Prophet,' Grave Digger said, 'but it's important.'

Sweet Prophet folded his hands across his stomach. He was wearing all of his diamond rings, but his long fingernails were encased in protective hard-rubber fingers of matching colors.

It must be hell when he's got to scratch himself, Coffin Ed thought.

'Important!' Sweet Prophet echoed. 'More important than a good night's sleep?'

'It's about one of your recent converts,' Grave Digger elaborated.

'My God, don't tell me another one has dropped dead –

took off – departed, I mean,' Sweet Prophet said, searching for the appropriate expression. 'That would be the bitter end.'

Grave Digger carefully laid his battered hat on the bright green-carpeted floor. He and Coffin Ed had uncovered their heads in deference to the great man.

'No, it's about Alberta Wright,' Grave Digger said. 'We want to ask you a few questions about her.'

'Gentlemen, let the dead rest in peace, I beg you,' he said piously. 'That poor woman deserves it, as hard as she has worked all of her life.'

'That's the point, Prophet,' Grave Digger said. 'She's not dead.'

'What! Not dead!' Sweet Prophet exclaimed in bug-eyed amazement. 'Do you mean that woman is still alive? Or has she risen from the dead?'

'Pull yourself together, Prophet,' Grave Digger said drily, 'She never was dead.'

'Good God, man, I saw her die myself,' Sweet Prophet snapped.

'She was just unconscious.'

'In a trance, you mean.' Sweet Prophet fished his yellow silk handkerchief from his candy-striped dressing gown pocket and wiped his dark, sweating brow. 'I never thought of that. You startled me.'

'And what we're trying to do,' Grave Digger went on calmly, 'is get her story.'

'That woman's story can be told in two lines,' Sweet Prophet said. 'Born like a fool, and worked like a mule.'

'That might be so,' Grave Digger said. 'But we want to know what happened at the baptism.'

'God only knows, gentlemen. I blessed the bottle of water – I presume it was water – and she drank it and flopped. I thought she was dead, but you say she went into a trance, and that's all right with me. I'll have to remember it.'

'All right, a trance,' Grave Digger said. 'That is as good as any explanation for the present. How long had she been a follower of yours?'

'Bless my soul, gentlemen, she was not strictly a follower of mine, as you put it. Just a new recruit. I never saw the woman before she came to me yesterday morning to confess her sins and request to be baptized.'

'You mean you baptize people without knowing anything about them?' Coffin Ed put in finally.

'Gentlemen, you didn't have to see that woman but once to know everything there was to know about her, like I said before,' Sweet Prophet declared. 'She was a born kitchen mechanic.'

'Okay, be that as it may,' Grave Digger said. 'What prompted her to get religion all of a sudden?'

'Who knows?' Sweet Prophet said, gesturing with his elongated hands. 'Women of that type get religion for ten thousand reasons – some have just murdered their husbands, other have had nightmares.'

'She must have given some reason,' Grave Digger persisted.

'If she did, I didn't listen,' Sweet Prophet said. 'Women always lie about the reason they get religion. If I harkened to them, I couldn't last.'

'Okay, let's skip it,' Grave Digger said. 'Just tell me what she might have owned that someone would go to the trouble of stealing.'

Sweet Prophet's eyebrows went up an inch, and his eyeballs extended precariously. 'You mean to say someone stole something from her?' he asked in an incredulous voice. 'Gentlemen, that would be the miracle.'

'Her furniture was stolen while she was unconscious, and two people have been killed about it,' Grave Digger informed him.

His eyeballs came out so far they seemed on the verge of rolling down his cheeks. 'She killed them,' he stated more than asked.

'We don't think so,' Grave Digger said.

'Look, brothers,' Sweet Prophet began, wiping his face with the big yellow handkerchief. 'We are more or less in the same business, collaring the sinners. Let us level with each other. Nobody has been killed about that sister's furniture, unless she killed them. I looked on that sister's face and listened to her confession. She has never owned anything in her life that the white folks didn't give her. And they haven't given that sister anything that anybody else would want. She was that kind of woman – is, rather.'

'Would you be breaking any kind of vows or such if you told us what sins she confessed to?' Grave Digger asked.

'Nothing worth repeating,' Sweet Prophet assured him. 'She was just a poor woman living in adultery and working like a dog to pay for it – like any other thousands of poor simple-minded colored women in Harlem. Nothing to make the Lord skin back His ears.'

'She had something,' Coffin Ed stated.

Sweet Prophet looked at him from his popping eyes. 'The only thing that sister had was faith,' he said. 'And between you and me, gentlemen, her faith were not worth stealing.'

'Well, let's try to get some facts,' Grave Digger said. 'What happened to her after she seemed to drop dead?'

'I never found out,' Sweet Prophet confessed. 'Until you told me better, I thought the sister at rest with her Maker. Brother Clay's hearse came and took her away, and afterwards the downtown policemen asked me some questions. But one of them got a phone call, and they dropped it without any explanations.'

'You didn't make any effort to find out what had happened to her?' Grave Digger asked.

'No, with death the work of Sweet Prophet ends and the Lord takes charge,' Sweet Prophet said. 'You might ask undertaker Clay.'

'We will,' Grave Digger said.

He and Coffin Ed stood up.

'Thank you for your cooperation, Prophet,' he added. 'We hope we haven't disturbed you too much.'

'I am always glad to be of service to our colored police,' Sweet Prophet declared. 'As long as you don't come to arrest me.'

'I may as well tell you that Alberta Wright wants to see you, if you haven't already got the message,' Coffin Ed said before leaving.

'Don't they all,' Sweet Prophet said.

Mr H. Exodus Clay had just come down from his living quarters on the top floor of the old brownstone mansion on 134th Street, where he had his undertaking parlor. He looked more than ever like a body dressed for burial, with his parchment-colored skin still half dead from sleep and his long white dried-out kinky hair freshly combed and brushed.

He received them in his office, the front room that had the light in the window that never went out.

They went straight to the point.

'We're trying to find out what happened to the woman one of your drivers picked up for dead at Sweet Prophet's baptism yesterday,' Grave Digger said.

Mr Clay adjusted his pince-nez. 'You mean the body that came to life,' he said in his dry, impersonal voice. 'Just a minute – I will send for the driver.'

'It was like this, Mr Clay,' the young man who drove the hearse explained. 'They-all sent me to the morgue to get the death certificate. But when I got there the man said I had to bring the body inside so he could look at it before he could give me the certificate, but I couldn't handle it alone and he helped me. We carried it into a big white room and laid it on a long white table, then the man began messing around with a lot of instruments and things and kept on talking about what a fine specimen it was. I asked him if it was dead, and he asked me where I got it from. I told him, and he said it would take him about an hour to finish his examination and for me to go outside and come back in an hour. Then I asked him if it was going to take a whole hour just to find out if it was dead, and he said it wasn't dead but it would take him that much time to find out what was wrong with it. So I figured there wasn't any need of me waiting a whole hour for it if it wasn't dead. So I just came on back here and put the hearse away and wiped it good and clean.'

Mr Clay turned to the detectives and asked, without batting an eye, 'Does that answer your question?'

Grave Digger put on his hat, and Coffin Ed did like-wise.

'It does indeed,' he said.

They went next to the morgue.

The morgue attendant who was on duty Sundays was off on Mondays, and the one on duty didn't know anything about the case.

'You think we ought to rouse him at his house?' Coffin Ed asked.

Grave Digger looked at his watch. 'Not this morning. It's already nine o'clock, and my wife has probably begun to worry.'

'Mine, too,' Coffin Ed said. 'So let's call it a day.'

'Right,' Grave Digger said. 'As long as we keep the woman locked up, nothing is going to happen.'

12

The three steep flights of stairs led to a long dimly lit hall with eight flanking doors. It was the fourth floor, and that was as high as the stairway went.

Sugar ran to the grimy front window and looked down on the street. Dummy was nowhere in sight. The detectives' car had disappeared, too. He walked slowly back to the other end and joined the girl, who was huddling in the corner. There was something screwy about this business, he was thinking. It was moving too fast. Too much was happening for Alberta's money to have been a secret.

'He lives in there,' the girl whispered, pointing toward a warped door showing yellow light about the edges.

Sugar smelt the sharp scent of marijuana coming through the cracks.

'Who?'

'The man I was talking about with all the money.'

The door had been fitted with a staple and hasp; it had shrunk so much that the cheap Warder lock was useless.

'If anyone with a lot of money lives in there, he ought to have his head examined,' Sugar said absently.

'It ain't his,' she said. 'He stole it.'

'Shut up and let me think,' Sugar said.

The only way it made sense was for Dummy to be looking for the money, too, he thought; or how would he know so much about what had happened? And then, as he chewed over that, the whole picture clicked suddenly in his mind.

It all hung on the murder of the Jew. If the Jew hadn't been killed, it might have figured that whoever killed Rufus got the money. But it stood to reason that whoever killed the Jew had already sounded Rufus and was convinced he didn't have it. So he figured the Jew must have it. Because whoever it was must have been someone who had heard Alberta blabbing about her dream at the baptism. All kinds of hustlers hung around Sweet Prophet's activities, hoping some of the Prophet's money would fall off. And then this joker, whoever he was, would have found out where Alberta lived and beat it over there to burglarize the house. But he, Sugar, had got there first; then, after he had left, Rufus had come; and the Jew had arrived while Rufus was still there and had moved all the furniture. So this joker must have been watching from the street, waiting for a chance to break in, and when he saw the furniture being moved he knew somebody had already got the money. So the logical thing had been to sound Rufus first.

But after he had killed the Jew and hadn't found the money, he figured that Rufus had outsmarted him. So he laid for Rufus.

But by that time Rufus had been warned by the killer's first approach, and he wouldn't be carrying the money around on him. It was ten to one he had hidden it in his own flat, Sugar realized. He had very likely already found it by the time the Jew arrived. Suddenly Sugar understood the reason Rufus decided to sell all the furniture to the Jew – he had already found the money and used that stupid play to cover it up. Rufus must have been laughing at Sugar when they met yesterday afternoon. Yeah, he had been so cute he had gotten himself killed, Sugar thought maliciously.

And now the fact that Dummy had begun to look for it, too, meant that it hadn't been found. Dummy wasn't the kind to waste his efforts on wild-goose chases. It would be just like Dummy to know who killed Rufus and why he was killed – if he hadn't done it himself.

'Come on,' he said to the girl.

'Where you going?' she asked.

'What do you care,' he said. 'You ain't got no other place to go, have you?'

She followed him docilely, relieved at being told what to

do. She had never done anything on her own initiative in her life.

He paused in the entrance of the hotel to look up and down the street. No one in sight.

'Where did Dummy go?' he asked.

'How do I know?' she replied stolidly.

'Come on.'

She started to walk along with him, but he stopped her.

'You're subject to get arrested for prostitution walking with me,' he said. 'And I don't want to get picked up, either. So you go ahead, turn down Seventh to a Hundred Twelfth Street and go over to Eighth Avenue. Wait for me on the corner.'

She started off without a word. He followed at a distance, but when she turned into the dark side street he kept on down Seventh Avenue to a once pretentious apartment house in the middle of the block.

Mammy Stormy had a six-room apartment on the top floor, where she gave parties for domestic workers every weekend. They began Saturday night and ended Monday morning. She sold food and drinks, and cut the blackjack game. She called them 'house rent' parties because, supposedly, they were for the purpose of paying her rent, but she lived from them.

Back during the depression of the 1930's, everyone who had a house threw these parties to pay their rent. However, most had quit the practice as industrial jobs opened to colored people and the pay for domestic work increased. But Mammy Stormy had kept right on; she hadn't missed one for the past twenty-eight years.

She never left the apartment. She weighed close to four hundred pounds, and she didn't trust elevators and couldn't navigate the stairs. She hadn't worn anything but nightgowns and felt slippers for a decade.

Sugar found her sitting in an ancient armchair in the kitchen, fanning herself with an undertaker's fan. Sweat flowed like a waterfall down her smooth black face. A pot of white beans and chitterlings simmered on the coal-burning stove. Dirty dishes were stacked everywhere; empty bottles were strewn about the floor.

A blackjack game was in progress in the dining room, but the players were just marking time. Other half-drunk, satiated, sleepy people wandered about the other rooms, waiting for daylight and time to go to work.

The smell of food made Sugar's stomach crawl, but he didn't have the price of a dish.

'Dummy sent me,' he told Mammy Stormy.

'What do he want now?' she asked.

'His ears hurt him; he wants you to send him some sweet oil,' Sugar said.

'Lord, why don't he do something about his ears,' she said.

'Do what?' he asked.

That stumped her.

'Look in the bathroom in the medicine cabinet and you'll find the sweet oil,' she said. 'And tell him don't bring none of his chippy whores into my house.'

'I'll tell him,' he said.

He found the bottle marked sweet oil, but while he was there he noticed one of her rose-colored nylon nightgowns hanging up to dry. That gave him an idea. He took down the nightgown, took a yellow-orange-and-white-striped bath towel from the rack, rolled them into a bundle and hid them beneath his coat. He left the house by way of the parlor, and didn't see Mammy Stormy again.

It was dawn when he came out onto the street. The girl was waiting on the corner where he had told her to wait. They went toward Manhattan Avenue.

In the middle of the block he stopped in a tenement hallway, removed the label from the bottle of sweet oil and slipped the nightgown over his clothes. Then he tied the towel about his head like a turban. The girl stared at him open-mouthed. She was either too tired or too stupid to laugh.

'What is that for?' she asked.

'Never mind,' he told her. 'You just keep your mouth shut no matter what I do, and don't laugh.'

But the garish ensemble was too much even for Harlem. The crew of a garbage truck making its last round froze in open-mouthed amazement as he approached.

'Great God Almighty, another prophet!' one of them ejaculated.

The girl started to giggle, but Sugar snapped at her. 'Shut up!'

They found the janitor of the apartment where Rufus had lived taking in the garbage cans. He put the empty can down and wiped his hand across his eyes. His lips moved as he mumbled something to himself.

He was a big, slow-motioned man with a dark leathery face. Short kinky hair fringed a bald head decorated with a crescent-shaped scar. He wore faded blue denim overalls and a hickory-striped shirt, all neatly washed and pressed. His big misshapen feet were encased in dirt-splotched canvas sneakers. His faded brown eyes gave the impression of a mind that was even slower than his body.

'I'm looking for a gentleman by the name of Mister George Clayborne,' Sugar said.

The janitor stared at him stupidly. 'What you want him for?' he asked with unconscious rudeness.

'I have an appointment with him,' Sugar said.

'Is that so,' the janitor said, scratching the scar on his head. 'Who is you?'

'I'm a doctor,' Sugar said. 'This is my daughter and assistant.'

The janitor looked at the skinny anemic girl with the cheap torn dress, then back at Sugar's outlandish garb.

'A doctor,' he echoed with disbelief. 'I ain't never seen a doctor what looks like you, nor an assistant what looks like her, neither.'

'I am an African doctor,' Sugar said with dignity.

'Oh,' the janitor said, looking relieved. 'I wondered where you came from wearing them night clothes.' He appeared satisfied by the explanation, but he wanted it clarified. 'I suppose you is one of them witch doctors.'

Sugar drew himself up and gave the impression of being offended. 'I am not a witch doctor,' he rebuked. 'There are other kinds of doctors in Africa besides witch doctors. I am a baby doctor.'

'Oh,' the janitor said, looking suspicious again. 'Mr Clayborne didn't have no babies.'

'I know he doesn't,' Sugar said. 'That's why he wants me to treat him.'

'I don't get that,' the janitor said frankly. 'You is a baby doctor and a man wants you to treat him who ain't got no babies.'

'I treat people so they can get babies,' Sugar explained patiently. 'If a man has lost his potency and can't make any babies, I give him massages with my magic oil. One massage is enough to start him going.' Reaching down through the décolleté of the nightgown, he extracted the bottle of sweet oil from his jacket pocket.

'You got on regular clothes underneath,' the janitor observed, his diminishing suspicions increasing again.

'Of course I have on regular clothes,' Sugar said. 'This gown is my doctor's uniform.'

'Oh,' the janitor said. That appeared to satisfy him.

'This oil,' Sugar went on to explain, 'is made from the fat of the tails of bull kangaroos mixed with the essence of the productive organs of lions. It will make you hop like a kangaroo and roar like a lion. After three massages any man of any age will become a father.'

The janitor's eyes popped with interest and amazement.

Sugar pinned a stare on him. 'Are you a father?' he demanded.

'I got grown children,' the janitor stammered guiltily. 'I'm sixty-four years old. But my wife, she got two young kids by her first husband.'

'You are an old man,' Sugar said, tapping him on the chest with his forefinger to drive home the point. 'You got a young wife. You are in trouble mister.'

'You telling me, doctor,' the janitor said. 'You don't know what trouble is.'

Sugar poked him in the ribs. 'After you have had three massages with this magic oil, your troubles will be over. She won't look at another man. You will have her eating out of your hand.'

The janitor giggled gleefully. 'He he. Wouldn't that be something?'

Sugar looked sympathetic but said regretfully, 'I'm afraid I won't have time for you this morning, as much as I would like to help you.'

'Oh,' the janitor said, wilting disappointedly.

'I have to treat Mr Clayborne, and I have other patients,' Sugar explained.

'You don't have to worry about Mr Clayborne,' the janitor said with rising spirits. 'He's dead.'

'Dead!' Sugar exclaimed in amazement. 'When did he die? How did it happen? I talked to him just yesterday, and he looked in fine health, other than he couldn't make babies.'

'He was stabbed to death last night,' the janitor informed him. 'Right over there in them bushes,' he added, pointing toward the park.

Sugar glanced at the clump of bushes in the park and shuddered. 'It's a pity,' he said. 'Such a fine man. He would have made a good father.' Sighing, he added, 'Well, in that case I will take you in his place.'

The janitor hesitated. 'The only thing is I got to get my morning chores done first, and that takes some time. If you don't mind waiting, I will pay you—'

Sugar cut him off with an impatient gesture. 'I do not charge for my services,' he said with asperity. 'My patients give me whatever they can afford. But I cannot give you a treatment later on. This magic only works during the first hour of the day, and tomorrow I am going on to Philadelphia.' He turned to the girl and said, 'Come on, Mamba, we can't keep our other patients waiting.'

'Wait a minute, doctor,' the janitor begged. 'I'll just leave those chores if you'll give me a treatment.'

Sugar hesitated with reluctance. 'Well,' he finally conceded. 'If there is no delay.'

'Oh, there won't be no delay,' the janitor promised eagerly. 'If you-all will just follow me.'

He led them along the alley beside the building and through a side doorway into a whitewashed basement corridor. Overhead were asbestos-covered steam pipes, and on each side were freshly painted green doors to the various basement rooms.

Before one of the doors he said, 'Can you-all wait here a minute, doctor, while I get the keys? I don't want my wife to know about it.'

He went around a corner, and they heard him opening the door to his living quarters. A woman's sleepy voice said crossly, 'Is you just got to make so much noise and wake up the children?' They heard a door close softly, and he reappeared with a brass ring the size of a knitting hoop, containing all the master keys.

He unlocked the door, and they entered a storeroom filled with trunks, packing cases and a few odd items of furniture belonging to the tenants.

'Make a place to lie down,' Sugar directed.

The janitor put two steamer trunks end to end and dusted them off.

'Remove your overalls and underwear,' Sugar directed.

'You mean take them off?' the janitor asked.

'How do you expect me to massage you with them on?' Sugar asked.

The janitor looked embarrassed. 'With her here?'

'She's seen a lot of bare backsides,' Sugar said.

Giggling with embarrassment, the janitor slipped off the shoulder braces of his overalls and let them fall to his ankles. He was wearing boxer-type shorts with red roses on a purple background. He let these fall to his ankles also, keeping his back turned to the girl; then he lay on his stomach across the trunks.

The girl watched these proceedings in a stolid, unsmiling, unblinking amazement.

Sugar poured oil on the leathery skin and began massaging. He mumbled sounds, which the janitor believed to be magic words of an African language.

The janitor had placed the key ring on the dusty top of a nearby dressing table.

After a few minutes, Sugar said, 'My assistant will continue while I go wash my hands. Where is there a wash basin I can use?'

'Hand me my keys, doc,' the janitor said without moving. He separated one and gave the ring back to Sugar. 'This is for the boiler room; it's the third door to the right. You'll find everything you want there.'

Sugar took the keys and motioned for the girl to begin massaging the janitor's back. She took over and began rubbing stolidly back and forth like a Spanish peasant washing clothes on a stone slab.

Sugar left the room. He was grateful to the janitor for giving him the keys; otherwise he would have had to take them. He found the door to the boiler room, unlocked it and entered. He stayed long enough to take off the nightgown and towel and put them in the furnace. Then he found his way up to the ground floor and continued up to the second floor by means of the front stairs. He took his time trying the various keys until he found one that unlocked the door to the apartment formerly occupied by Rufus. The door opened on a small hallway that connected the two front rooms and a bathroom to one side. Rufus had done well by himself, Sugar thought.

He went through the sitting room, opened the front window and looked up and down the street. A few early risers were up and about; but it didn't take long to catch a moment when the street was clear. He tossed the keys so that they fell directly in front of the entrance. Then he closed the window and drew the curtains.

He wondered how long it would take the janitor to discover he'd been tricked. As for the girl, if no one stopped her she would keep on rubbing until the skin came off.

He began to search.

13

The keys were lying in the street.

It's a trap, Dummy thought automatically. Nobody could go to a joint looking for some way to get in and find the keys lying at his feet. Life wasn't that easy.

But if the police thought he would fall into their trap, they didn't know Dummy. He looked quickly up and down the street, trying to spot the stake-out. But he didn't see anyone who looked like a dick. Two women who couldn't be anything but housemaids were trudging toward the bus-stop; a late worker was hurrying toward the subway kiosk on 110th Street.

Dummy didn't believe that Grave Digger and Coffin Ed would be that crude; so it must be the Homicide men playing around. Well, he would play around, too.

He kept on walking like an ordinary man on his way down the street, going about his business. He didn't see the keys. It was by the merest accident that his foot kicked the ring. He picked them up and went looking for the janitor like an honest man, holding them openly in his hand. He looked into the vestibule, then came back to the sidewalk. He went over and peered down the alleyway beside the building. He came back and stood in the vestibule. There was a button beside the mail boxes marked *Super*, but he didn't see it. If he had, he would have rung it, and, when someone answered it, he would have given them the keys.

He was making up the story as he went along, and making himself believe it.

He tiptoed up the stairs, walking on the balls of his feet. Every nerve in his body was alert. His hands hung free and his shoulders were loose, ready to throw a punch with either hand from any angle. He didn't find the janitor on the second floor as he expected. Someone – he supposed it was one of the tenants on his way to work – had told him he had seen the janitor on the second floor cleaning out the apartment of the man who had been killed the night before.

But the door to that apartment was closed. He didn't try the knob. Instead, he rang the bell.

Sugar was inside of the hall closet to the left of the entrance when the bell rang. It sounded right over his head. He was going through the pockets of Rufus's clothes. He jumped so violently he struck his head against the shelf above the clothes rack. Luckily, it didn't make much of a sound, but it raised a knot. After that he was afraid to move. He held his breath, while ice-cold chills ran up and down his spine. He strained his ears, trying to catch the sound of movement outside, meanwhile keeping his nerves braced against another ring. But the bell didn't ring any more, and for a time he didn't hear a sound.

Dummy had taken out his scratch pad and pencil. He wrote, *janitor I found your keys*, on a page and tore it from the pad.

Sugar heard the sound of paper tearing. It shattered his nerves more than a hammering on the door would have done. He couldn't figure it out. Then he saw the edge of a piece of paper pushed underneath the door. There was little more than an inch of the paper showing and nothing was written on that part. He stared at it as though it were a time bomb. Hackles rose on the back of his neck. What did it mean?

Dummy had inserted the paper so that the greater part still remained outside. Then he tiptoed to the staircase and stood back out of sight from the door, only the edge of his face showing as he peeped around the corner to see if anyone would draw the paper inside.

Sugar felt instinctively that it was a trap. But he couldn't be sure. It might be a warning. No, that was out; it couldn't be a warning – not for himself, at any rate. But it might be a message to Rufus by someone who didn't know yet that Rufus was dead. It might have something to do with the money; it might be the key to the whole thing.

He got down on his hands and knees and tried to look underneath the door. He couldn't see anything. He stared at the strip of paper. There must be something written on the part he couldn't see, he thought. But he was afraid to touch it. The odds were too great that it might be a trap. Someone was trying to find out if anyone was in the flat. If it were the police, they would have simply come on in. They would not have rung the bell. The only person who would set that kind of trap was the person who had killed Rufus, he concluded.

He heard a key being inserted in the lock.

Dummy had satisfied himself that there was no one within the flat. If the police had a stake-out, he must be in another apartment. Dummy decided he'd have to risk it. There was always the possibility that the janitor had dropped his ring of keys. And if the police did catch him, he could claim that he found the keys in the door.

Sugar scuttled away from the door, crawling on all fours like a frightened crab. He needed a weapon – a good solid club. The killer was a knife-man, and Sugar's only hope was to knock him out before he got a chance to use it.

He had been through the sitting room and bedroom before, and he didn't remember having seen anything sufficiently substantial. So he made for the kitchen. His first choice was the kitchen stool, but then he noticed a heavy iron skillet with a grip handle that was just the thing.

He snatched it from the hook and rushed back to the door, stationing himself on the opening side so he'd be behind the door when the intruder entered.

The fourth key worked. Dummy had the door open and the key extracted and was stepping into the room, holding the key ring in his right hand, when his sixth sense sounded the alarm. He ducked backwards with the automatic instinct of the ring, and the heavy iron skillet passed by his head so close he felt the backwash. He circled out of the ducking motion like a piston on a cam shaft and came back with a shoulder smash against the door that knocked Sugar off his feet. Dummy was through the door, and had kicked it shut behind him, while Sugar was still clawing the air. It was over in a second. He led with a left to the ribs and crossed a right to Sugar's solar plexus. Sugar sat on the floor, and the lights dancing before his eyes kept him from breathing.

Dummy was surprised to find out it was Sugar. He wondered how much Sugar knew. Alberta had given him the impression that Sugar didn't know about the money; or why hadn't she asked Sugar to find out where Rufus lived instead of coming to him? But it looked now as though Sugar knew as much as he did – which wasn't much of anything, he admitted to himself. In fact, Sugar might know more. His eyes narrowed with suspicion.

Sugar kept gasping until his vision returned. He saw Dummy standing over him.

'It was you,' he gasped.

Dummy continued to stare at him.

Sugar remained in his sitting position on the floor.

'You killed him,' he said gaspingly.

Dummy took out his stub of pencil and scratch pad and wrote: *I saw you kill him but I didn't tell.*

Sugar read it and got to his feet. He was scared. 'Look here, man, if you're thinking of trying to frame me, I can prove I didn't do it. How about you?'

Dummy showed him a tongueless grin and wrote the question: *what you doin here?*

'What are you doing here yourself?' Sugar countered.

Dummy wrote: *quit playin dumb i am lookin for the money like you is.*

'It's Alberta's money,' Sugar said. 'I'm going to see that she gets it back.'

Dummy wrote: *not if i find it first.*

'All right, we'll go halvers,' Sugar bargained.

Dummy wrote: *just if we find it in here outside dont count.*

Sugar nodded. There would be time enough to work out what to do after they found it. The main thing was to keep a close watch and protect himself, because if Dummy had killed Rufus, he wouldn't hesitate about killing him, too.

Dummy wrote: *we search together.*

Sugar nodded. 'That's the best way,' he agreed.

It was not a difficult place to search. The two rooms and kitchen had been furnished from Blumstein's department store on 125th Street. The sitting room furniture was of modernistic oak veneer, was known as the King Cole suite, and had been manufactured in the Bronx. In the bedroom was a Deluxe bridal suite in bland maple from Grand Rapids, Michigan. The television set bore the stamp of one of the big Jersey City dealers, who advertised over the local radios that he would deliver, install and have working, within one hour of receiving an order by telephone, any size television set to any of New York City's five boroughs at any time of the day or night.

Before starting, Sugar had gone into the kitchen for a glass of water. Dummy had followed quickly, but not before Sugar had snatched the plastic pepper shaker from the kitchen table and slipped it into his side pants pocket. He managed to unscrew the top while they went over the furnishings and through all of the various drawers.

Neither let the other get out of sight. Chiefly, they watched one another's hands. Every now and then they stared at each other with secret speculation. It was Sugar's intention, if Dummy found the money, to dash the pepper into his eyes, snatch the money and run. Dummy's plan was not so subtle; he merely intended to knock Sugar unconscious and walk out with the money, leaving him there.

But they didn't find anything except the worldly possessions of Rufus Wright, which weren't worth talking about.

Dummy wrote: *somebody beat us to it.*

'It didn't have to be here,' Sugar said.

Dummy wrote: *where else.*

Sugar shook his head. He wasn't giving Dummy any leads.

Before leaving, they went to the window to case the street. There was the customary array of downtown porters and domestic workers on their way to work. They didn't spot anyone who looked like a detective. But while they were watching they saw the girl come from the alleyway, carrying a pair of overall pants, and start highballing in the direction of 114th Street. A moment later the janitor appeared in his hickory-striped shirt and flowered shorts and took out after her. They disappeared around the corner.

Dummy looked at Sugar and wrote the question, *you bring my girl here?*'

Sugar nodded, without offering any further explanations.

Dummy didn't ask for any; he wrote: *you owe me.*

'I'll pay you,' Sugar said, thinking it was no more than right.

'I ain't got it now, but I'll pay you later.'

They shook hands to seal the agreement.

Sugar left first, whistling nonchalantly as he walked rapidly in the direction of 110th Street.

Dummy remained long enough to give the flat another quick going over; then he paused for a moment in the downstairs vestibule to search the street with his roving gaze. Satisfied, he placed the ring of keys on the sidewalk where he had found them and headed in the opposite direction. He had both hands in his pockets, and he shuffled along looking as innocent as a five-year-old English bulldog who had just killed the neighbor's pedigreed cat.

14

'What time is it?' the bus driver asked the roving checker at the bus stop at 111th Street.

The checker consulted his watch. 'Seventeen minutes and thirteen seconds past seven o'clock,' he said.

The driver synchronized his watch and put the bus in gear.

Sugar had been standing with the people waiting for the bus, but he hadn't got on board. He had been watching to see Dummy leave the building up the street. He had seen him come out, place the keys back on the sidewalk and walk off, but a moment later a woman jostled him, and, when he got the street in focus again, Dummy had vanished. However, he was satisfied that Dummy had gone about his business.

He hastened back toward the house, but a woman tenant on her way to work had beaten him to the keys. She was ringing the super's bell when he arrived.

Dummy watched him from the doorway up the street where he had ducked. He grinned to himself. He figured that Sugar had doubled back to search the flat again; perhaps Sugar had found a likely hiding place and had saved it for a private search. But Dummy was satisfied that the money wasn't there.

He waited until Sugar re-entered the building. Then he kept on his way, this time without hesitating or looking back.

Sugar made as if to pass the woman, then stopped and looked inquiringly at the keys.

'You want to return the super's keys?' he asked.

'I found them in the street,' she said defensively.

'He must have dropped them,' Sugar said. 'I'm just going downstairs. I'll take them to him.'

The woman looked at him suspiciously, but she was late and didn't have time to argue. She handed him the ring grudgingly, saying, 'I hope I'm doing right; I hope you ain't no burglar.' He was about to protest, but she salved her conscience by adding, 'Anyway, I have rung the bell.'

Without replying, Sugar hastened through the basement doorway and descended the stairs. He hadn't seen the janitor return, but it was a risky business.

He found the janitor's wife standing in the open door to their quarters, looking up and down the corridor. She was what he had expected, a loose, ripe, high-yellow woman with cowlike eyes and a petulant expression. Smooth fat arms and mounts of cream-colored flesh showed above the décolleté blue rayon nightgown, and black hair hung in long greasy curls about her shoulders.

When she saw it was a man she became coy, more from

habit than desire, and asked in a simpering voice, 'Did you ring my bell?'

'Yes, ma'am,' he said politely, letting his gaze rove approvingly over her padded figure. 'I found these keys on the sidewalk out front.'

Her expression changed instantly to one of suspicion. 'Where's he at?'

'The last I saw of him he was chasing some young girl,' Sugar said.

The next instant her face darkened with an evil look. 'I'll fix him,' she threatened. 'Around here chippy-chasing at this hour of the morning.'

'Can I come in?' Sugar asked. 'I want to ask you some questions.'

'Come right on,' she said, merely turning her body to let him pass.

She took up most of the doorway, and in passing he rubbed against her body. It was a pleasure.

At seven-forty-four, Alberta was taken by a matron from the cell that she occupied with two other colored women into the small reception room, where lawyers interviewed their clients and detectives re-examined suspects.

She still wore the maid's uniform, but now it was gray all over, and streaked with black. She had removed the bathing cap, and her straightened hair stuck out in all directions. She looked bone-tired, and her expression was sullen.

The shyster waiting for her knew his way around. He had a degree in law from a colored university in Washington, DC, and a license to practice in New York State. Most of his business was making bail for prostitutes and racketeers and pleading them guilty if the fine was right. His youthful, grinning black face inspired confidence in most people, but it had the opposite effect on Alberta.

'Slick sent me,' he said.

'Who is you?' she asked.

'I'm his lawyer,' he said.

'What he want?' she asked.

'He said if you will tell him where it is and go halvers, he will get you out when he gets it,' he said.

'I wouldn't be surprised but what he ain't already got it himself,' she said.

'What would he want to make a deal for if he already had it?' he asked.

'Because if he's got it, he's got two murder charges to go along with it,' she said.

'That's just the point,' he said. 'He ain't got it, and you got the two murder charges instead.'

'How can he get me out?' she asked.

'He's got somebody tapped for the killings,' he said.

'What killing?' she asked.

'Both of them,' he said.

'Then he knows who done them,' she said.

'I didn't say that,' he denied. 'I said he can give somebody to the police to satisfy them so they will let you go.'

'I don't want him to do that if the person he's going to accuse ain't guilty,' she said.

'All right then, let's say the person is guilty. Does that satisfy you?' he asked.

'Is it somebody I know?' she asked.

He hesitated. 'He don't know if it's anybody you know or not. He don't know who you know. It's not your man, if that's what you want to know,' he said.

'All right – I'll give him half when I get out if he tells the police who did it,' she bargained slyly.

'You've got to tell him where it is first,' he said.

'You've got to give me time to think,' she said, stalling.

He looked at his watch. 'Listen, woman, you ain't got no time to think,' he said. 'I got to be out of here by eight o'clock, and I'm not coming back, and your case is coming up at ten o'clock.'

'You go back and tell Slick he had better watch himself,' she said. 'God is going to strike him dead like He done those other two.'

He jumped up in exasperation. 'You are a religious fanatic, woman,' he charged. 'I don't want to talk to you any more. You're crazy.'

'He's the crazy one,' she said, 'if he thinks I'm going to split half with him because I'm here in jail for something I ain't never done.'

He snatched up his cream-colored straw hat with the fancy red-and-blue polka dot band and left.

The matron took her back to her cell.

At eight-three, Sugar reappeared in front of the house by way of the main entrance just as the janitor was turning into the alleyway beside the house. They saw each other at the same instant. Sugar noticed that the janitor was again decently clad in his overalls. Then he took off, running.

The janitor turned and gave chase.

After they had run about half a block, the janitor called, 'Hey, doc! Hey, doc!' They ran another half block and the janitor shouted again, 'It worked, doc! It worked!'

Sugar couldn't figure that out. If the janitor hadn't discovered he had been tricked, then why had he chased the girl? That took some deep figuring. But he didn't have the time for it. And what was more, he wasn't taking any chances on stopping and demanding an explanation. He turned the corner into 112th Street running on the edges of his soles and ducked into the first tenement doorway. He hid on the stairs, looking around the banister, and saw the janitor run past. But he didn't leave until he saw the janitor come walking back.

Then he slipped from the building and kept on over to Eighth Avenue, went up to 117th Street, turned back toward Manhattan Avenue and entered a building in the middle of the block. It was a walk-up in fairly good repair; the tiled floors were clean, and the walls were painted.

He walked up to the third-floor front and pushed a buzzer beside a bright red lacquered door. A respectable-looking buxom brown-skinned woman wearing gold-rimmed glasses opened the door onto a chain and asked through the crack, 'Who you want to see?'

'Mabel,' he said.

The woman smoothed her gray-streaked hair and looked at him appraisingly.

'She ain't in,' she decided to say.

'When will she be in?' he asked.

'It's hard to tell,' she said. 'Who shall I tell her called?'

'She don't know me,' he said. 'Just tell her I've come from Rufus and I'll be back.'

'You say you come from Rufus!' she echoed. Her eyes popped behind the glittering spectacles. 'And you say you is coming back. Naw, you ain't, neither!' she concluded, and slammed the door in his face.

'I shouldn't have told her that,' he admitted to himself. 'She must know that Rufus is dead.'

It was eight-twenty-nine.

'Well, well,' Sergeant Ratigan from Homicide said. 'You are the woman who started all this business. And it looks from here as if you finished it off, too.'

Alberta remained silent and sullen.

He was questioning her in the same room where the shyster had propositioned her less than an hour previously.

'Tell me,' he said. 'Just between us friends, why were you playing dead?'

'I wasn't playing dead,' she denied stolidly.

He crossed his legs and strapped his hands about one of his bony knees. 'What were you doing then?' he asked. 'Playing a joke?'

'I don't know what I was doing,' she said.

'Just so,' he said, and took time out to reread the long report turned in by Grave Digger and Coffin Ed.

'Everyone is convinced you are not guilty, it seems,' he said on finishing. He showed her the front rows of his tobacco-stained teeth in what he thought was a sympathetic grin, inviting confidence. 'Now! All you have to do is tell me who did it and you can go.'

'Go home?' she asked.

'Right,' he said.

'I don't know who did it, and that's the God's truth,' she said.

He sighed and took a cheap cigar from his pocket. He cut the cellophane band with a small penknife, snipped off the end of the cigar and punctured it with the point of the knife. He lit it with a paper match, spinning it between thumb and forefinger until it was burning evenly.

'All right, Alberta, you can't get away with playing stupid,' he said. 'Now I want you to tell me what happened from the time you drank the water at the baptism until you were arrested with the bloodstained knife.'

'The last thing I remember was feeling the Spirit creeping all through me after I had drunk the water Sweet Prophet blessed and then seeing visions—'

'What kind of visions?' he interrupted with quickened interest.

'Visions of heaven,' she said.

His interest faded.

'The air looked like it was full of stars and bubbles, and then it seemed like I fell down and all around me was the faces of angels,' she went on.

'What kind of angels?'

'Colored angels. They looked just like ordinary people, but I knew they were angels. I thought I was dying and going straight to heaven. I was that happy!' she stated.

'The prophet said you had a religious trance,' he informed her. 'Do you believe that?'

'He's a prophet – he ought to know,' she said. Then suddenly she was struck by the realization of what he had said. 'Oh, you mean a *religious trance!*' The weariness and sullenness were wiped from her face, and her smooth, dark, immature features lit with ecstasy. 'A religious trance,' she echoed wonderingly. 'Me, Alberta Peavine Wright. I had myself a religious trance. What do you know about that!'

'All I know about it is what I'm told,' he said drily, and then suddenly asked, 'What did the water taste like?'

'Taste like?' she repeated. 'It tasted just like holy water.'

'What does holy water taste like? I have never tasted any.'

'It tastes just like water what has been made holy,' she said. 'What do you want me to say?'

'I just want you to say what is true.'

'Well, that is true.'

'That you drank the water and went into a religious trance?'

'Yassuh.' Not the slightest hint of a doubt showed in her face. 'Ain't I the lucky one,' she exulted. 'I'm going to write home and tell Ma so she can tell Reverend Tree, who is always bellyaching about us living in sin up here in Harlem.'

'All right, come down to Earth and let the Lord rest for a moment,' he said peevishly. 'You were taken to the morgue by a mistake, and you were still there when you regained consciousness. You know all about that?'

'Yassuh.'

'You were released from the morgue at four-twenty-six o'clock – so the record states. What did you do?'

'I went home,' she said.

'Just that?' he persisted.

'Well, I didn't know then that I had had a religious trance,' she elaborated. 'The man in the morgue said I had fainted probably from a sunstroke or else being too excited. So I just caught a bus and went home. When I found my furniture had been stolen, I went downstairs and asked Miz Teabone had she seen anybody suspicious about the house. She lives on the first floor and has a window on the street, and she sees nearmost everything that happens around there—'

'I don't doubt it,' he muttered.

'She told me what she had seen, and I knew it was some of Rufus's doings,' she continued.

He pounced on her. 'How did you know it was Rufus?'

'How did I know it were him?' she repeated. 'For one thing she described him, and I knew right away it was him because wouldn't anybody else be mean enough to me to steal my furniture. He's always stealing something from me,' she added.

'So you started searching for Rufus. With a knife,' he said.

'Nawsuh, that ain't so,' she said. 'I first started looking for Sugar Stonewall. I hadn't seen him since just before it happened and—'

'Just before what happened?' he cut in.

'My religious trance,' she replied doggedly. 'I didn't know where he had gone or what had happened to him, and I needed him to help me look for Rufus, so I started looking for him first.'

He looked at the report again and conjectured. 'You must have gotten home at about five o'clock.'

'Nawsuh, not that soon. It were Sunday and the buses were slow, and it was nearer six o'clock when I got home. And then, after I found my furniture gone, it took me some time to get myself together. I had just got religion, and I didn't want to go and lose it the first thing. Then it must have taken me an hour to talk to Miz Teabone – she asked that many questions. So it must have been seven-thirty or eight o'clock when I started looking for Sugar.'

'And it was around ten-thirty when you wound up at Cassie's. You spent three hours looking for Sugar.'

'Yassuh. It took every bit of that long. I went everywhere I thought he might be at.'

'Where would all those places be?'

'Oh, around and about,' she said. 'If you don't know Harlem, it wouldn't be no use of telling you.'

'This is quite different from what you told before,' he pointed out.

'Yassuh, I'm telling the truth now,' she said.

'All right, when did you leave Cassie's?' he asked.

'I don't know exactly. I left there right after Dummy left. I happened to remember that Rufus was on the H.'

'Heroin?'

'Yassuh. And I asked Cassie where people bought that stuff. She told me there was a place in a house on 110th Street called Esther's, and I went there and sat on a bench in the park across the street where I could watch the door. I figured that after he had got the money for my furniture he would be going there sooner or later to buy some dope. And after that it were just like I said – I saw the patrol car pass and turn into Manhattan Avenue, and I had a premonition.'

'You needn't go into that again,' he said. 'It is all written down here.'

'It is?' she asked in surprise.

'Yes, everything you said has been taken down,' he told her. 'Now, tell me, just exactly what were these people looking for?' he asked. 'Had you come by some money recently?'

'Nawsuh,' she denied stolidly.

'Jewelry?'

'Nawsuh.'

'You mean to sit there and tell me that these two smart people went to all that trouble and got themselves killed just to get hold of your worn out furniture?'

'It weren't worn out,' she denied.

'Worn out or not,' he snapped. 'Do you want me to believe that was all they were after?'

'It looks like it,' she replied evasively.

'It doesn't look like it to me,' he said.

'Unless they had some other reasons I didn't know nothing about,' she added.

'Listen, Alberta, if you play square with me, I will play square with you,' he promised.

'Yassuh,' she said noncommittally.

'What did you have?'

'I done told you,' she said. 'I didn't have nothing but my furniture.'

'All right,' he said wearily. 'That's your story.'

She didn't say anything.

'Who were Rufus's friends?' he asked, trying another tactic.

'I didn't know them,' she said.

'Who was his girl friend? You would know that. He was your husband. You would certainly be curious enough to know who his girl friend was.'

'Nawsuh. I didn't care nothing about him nor his girl friend, nor about anything he did – long as he left me alone,' she said.

'He stole your savings and ran away with a woman and you don't know who she is,' he said incredulously.

'Nawsuh, I never knew,' she said.

'And you didn't do anything about it,' he said sarcastically.

'Oh, I would have cut his throat at the time, if I could have found him,' she confessed. 'But he left town so I couldn't find him and I got over it. That was what first turned me to Jesus.'

'That I believe,' he said. 'Now this is the last time I am going to ask you,' he went on. 'What did you have that was so valuable that two smart men got killed for stealing it?'

'They must have got killed for something else,' she said doggedly.

He wiped his face with the palm of his hand. 'Be reasonable, Alberta,' he pleaded with her. 'We have got to establish the motive.'

'I done told you all I know,' she maintained stubbornly.

'Well, since you won't tell me, you are going to have to tell the Grand Jury,' he said, getting to his feet.

15

At nine-thirteen o'clock Dummy was sitting on a stool behind a dilapidated wooden pushcart, watching the entrance of the hotel on 116th Street across from Sweet Prophet's Temple Of Wonderful Prayer.

His friend, the pushcart proprietor, was carefully quartering watermelons and arranging the quarters on cracked ice in the bed of the pushcart, beneath the strip of faded tan canvas that would protect them from the sun.

Dummy saw the young man pause in the hotel entrance beneath the faded sign and case the street in both directions. But the young man did not see Dummy.

This young man was lucky that he was not wearing a tan jumper and a long-billed army cap, because all young men of his size and age wearing tan jumpers and long-billed army caps were being picked up by the police that morning.

Instead the young man was wearing a heavy tweed jacket with thick shoulder pads, a wide-brimmed beaver hat pulled low over his forehead and skintight mustard-colored corduroy pants tucked into black and white cowboy boots.

Dummy's little prostitute could have identified him as the one who had cheated her much earlier that morning, but she was not there.

Two dark buxom housewives in cotton shifts, carrying shopping bags loaded with assorted groceries, passed the hotel entrance. The young man raised his beaver hat and grinned at them with a suddenness that was startling. The women stiffened with offended dignity, passed him without a word and then, a few paces farther on, looked at one another and giggled.

Dummy knew instantly that the young man was sky high on marijuana. He grinned to himself. That was going to make it easy.

The young man stepped to the sidewalk and turned in the direction of Seventh Avenue. Dummy got from his stool and followed at about a ten-yard distance. The pushcart proprietor continued to fiddle with his watermelon display without giving him a glance.

The young man walked with an exaggerated swagger, tipping his beaver hat indiscriminately to all the women he passed. Beneath the padded coat his shoulders looked as wide as a team of yoked oxen.

Dummy followed in the shuffling, half-crouching gait of a prize fighter stalking his opponent. He looked constantly to both sides and over his shoulder, using his eyes in place of ears.

The young man joined the people waiting for the bus around the corner. He puffed his cigarette rapidly, made erratic, meaningless gestures and stared into the women's faces.

Dummy loitered in front of a jewelry store next to the corner. The window was filled with watches, atop price tags giving the credit terms. He saw the reflection of the bus when it approached 116th Street.

It was a green Fifth Avenue bus, a Number Two. It came up Fifth Avenue to the north end of Central Park, turned over to Seventh Avenue, and passed through the middle of Harlem.

Dummy waited until it had almost finished loading, then dashed around the corner and hopped aboard.

The young man had stayed up front. Dummy took a seat in the back and looked out of the window.

The Theresa Hotel Grill looked busy, but the hotel entrance was dead; not even the doorman was on duty, and the sports who held up the walls later in the day had not yet awakened. The big two-faced clock on the opposite corner in front of the credit jeweler's said six minutes after nine.

Along the way the RKO movie theater was closed, the churches were closed, the bars were closed, the pool rooms were closed, the undertakers were closed. Hotel entrances looked dead; a trickle of shoppers patronized the various food stores. Only the greasy spoons were doing good business.

Across 145th Street, Seventh Avenue passed between two housing developments, the Rockefeller-built Dunbar Apartments and the slum clearance Federal Housing Project. They looked dead, too.

At 155th Street the bus turned west onto the end of the bridge over the Harlem River and passed high above one of Father Divine's Heavens on the roof of which, in giant white letters, was the word *peace*. Then it turned north into the winding strip of Edgecombe Drive, overlooking the flats along the river bank.

Dummy heard the bell ring, and, as the bus slowed down for the stop at 157th Street, he saw the young man go down the stairs. He let the young man alight; then, just before the door closed, he jumped up to follow as though he'd forgotten his stop. The young man recognized him; Dummy was known to everyone in the Harlem underworld.

But Dummy didn't give the young man a glance. He waited for the bus to drive on and cut across the street.

Only one side of the Drive was built up; the other was a steep rocky park descending to the flats, on which were built the Polo Grounds and a new housing development.

Without hesitating, Dummy entered the ornate lobby of the Roger Morris Apartment House, better known as 555. In its day it had been a very pretentious apartment dwelling for upper income whites, but now it was occupied for the most part by successful colored racketeers, jazz musicians, madames and current prize fighters.

He knew that, when the young man had come this far, he was coming here. And he knew there would be nothing to arouse the young man's suspicions in his coming here, too. He stood in the hall, talking in sign language to the dumb porter, whose hero he was. The young man came in and saw them talking. His face burst into its sudden moronic grin, and he made some eccentric gestures with his hands as though to join in the conversation. The two mutes ignored him.

He went back to the elevators and went upstairs.

Dummy and the porter talked about prize fighting. The porter leaned on his mop and let the water stand on the floor. A young woman, passing as a model or a showgirl, came from the elevator and had to walk through the dirty soapy water in her fragile pink shoes. She complained with shocking vulgarity, and the porter told her with gestures what she could do. Dummy went on saying that with a few weeks training he'd be in shape to take on the Cuban Kid.

The young man came down accompanied by a middle-aged man equally as tall but slimmer, with a pale tan ascetic-looking face. He was dressed in a tropical worsted suit of slate blue, black and white shoes, a dull ivory-colored shirt and a tie and matching display handkerchief the color of tarnished silver.

'Who are they?' Dummy asked his friend.

'The slick is a payoff man for the Tia Juana numbers house,' the porter said. 'I haven't seen the starker before.' Then he added, 'The slick is called Slick.'

With his hands Dummy said, 'I'll be hearing you,' and moved off.

Outside, Slick and the starker separated. Slick got into an olive green Chrysler New Yorker hardtop and drove off south. The starker walked down to the corner and stood waiting for the bus.

Dummy walked the short block up the incline to St Nicholas Avenue and caught the faster Number Three Fifth Avenue bus and was down on 116th Street waiting for the starker. He had resumed his seat on the stool behind the pushcart watermelon stand, and was watching a customer sink his grinning teeth into a quarter of bright red, black-seeded, ice-cold watermelon, when the starker walked rapidly from Seventh Avenue and re-entered the hotel.

Then suddenly Dummy's roving gaze picked up the debonair figure of Slick lounging before the entrance to Sweet Prophet's Temple across the street. Dummy got up, crossed the street and sat on the front stool of a lunch counter, where he could command a view of the whole sidewalk. He pointed to a grill-plate covered with roasting hot dogs. The counter-girl served him one off the front, put it in a bun and slid him the mustard. He then pointed to a shiny nickel-plated juice machine, and the girl drew him a glass of pale yellow liquid called lemon squeeze. He sat there, munching his hot dog in his tongueless mouth and sipping the cold chemical-tasting drink, while watching Slick out of the corners of his eyes.

He noticed that Slick was watching the entrance of the hotel across the street under the pretense of being interested in Sweet Prophet's press clippings, which were on display under glass in the Temple entrance.

Following Slick's gaze, Dummy saw that the starker had

reappeared in the hotel entrance, smoking a cigarette. From the way he held the cigarette, pinched between the thumb and forefinger of the right hand, and sucked at it, Dummy knew it was a marijuana cigarette. The starker was watching the entrance to the stairs that led to Sweet Prophet's private quarters, while Slick watched him. There was an intentness about both of them that caused Dummy to wonder.

Suddenly the starker tipped his beaver hat to nothing. Slick stepped quickly from the shadowed entrance of the Temple into the bright sunshine. As he passed the entrance to Sweet Prophet's quarters, a legal size Manila envelope slipped from beneath his coat and fluttered to the sidewalk. He walked a few steps further and paused with his left hand on the handle of a parked car while he fumbled in his pockets with his right hand, as though searching for the keys. No one was close by at the moment, and seemingly no one but Dummy noticed the lost envelope. Nevertheless, the starker kept his gaze riveted on it.

At that moment a buxom colored woman emerged from Sweet Prophet's entrance and stepped from the sidewalk. She stopped for a moment to adjust her tight-fitting cotton print dress more sedately over her corseted figure. She looked like a sister who would say 'Amen' at the drop of a hat. The pious expression on her face fought a losing battle with a flaunting pride; her soul was saved, and she knew it. Beneath the bare ham-sized, full black arm she carried a flat, black, narrow attaché case. Her hostile gaze roved over the street scene disapprovingly; then she got astride her dignity and started off.

Her sharp eye lit on the Manila envelope. She started to pass it, but something she saw written on it made her hesitate. She peered with drawn brows, her lips moving slightly as she read. Then suddenly her whole demeanor underwent a complete change. Greed replaced the pious expression on her face. Her dignity gave way to stealth. She looked about furtively to see if she was being watched, then bent over quickly to adjust her shoe. In doing so, the attaché case slipped from beneath her arm and fell directly on top of the envelope, completely hiding it. When she had finished adjusting her shoe and had straightened up with the case, the envelope had disappeared.

Once more the starker tipped his hat to the bright hot sunshine.

Slick turned quickly away from the parked car and approached the woman from the rear.

'I beg your pardon, madame, but I just dropped that envelope,' he said politely. 'It must have slipped from my pocket while I was putting away my wallet.'

The woman looked as offended as though he had said, 'Hi, baby, how about a date?' She drew up to her full fat height and said sharply, 'What envelope? What are you talking about?'

They were standing in profile, and Dummy could read their lips. He swallowed with a sound like a dog gulping meat.

A slight frown creased Slick's forehead. 'The one you just picked up, madame?'

'I didn't pick up any envelope,' she said harshly, trying to move off. 'And if you don't let me alone, I'll call that policeman.'

A uniformed cop was standing down at the corner, twirling his white billy.

But Slick put his hand on her arm, nevertheless, and detained her.

'Now, madame, there is no need of creating a scene,' he said smoothly. 'I happened to see your reflection in the window of my car when you stooped to pick up the envelope. You are holding it on the other side of that attaché case.'

The woman looked suddenly embarrassed. 'Oh, *that* envelope!' she exclaimed with a laugh. Then, as she looked him over more carefully, her eyes got small and hard with suspicion. 'How do I know it belongs to you?'

'How would I know you had picked it up if I hadn't dropped it?' he countered indulgently.

The woman thought that over, and wasn't satisfied. 'All right, if it's yours, then describe it,' she demanded.

Slick lost his confident expression. He cleared his throat and said hesitatingly. 'It's a brown bank envelope.'

The woman pounced on him. 'What bank?'

'The Corn Exchange,' he said, as though guessing at random.

The woman turned her back and slipped the edge of the envelope from beneath the attaché case far enough to read the return address. Nothing else was written on it.

'Hah!' she exclaimed triumphantly, turning back to confront him. 'You didn't see as good as you thought; it's from the Manufacturer's Trust Company.'

'That's what I meant,' Slick said, putting on a bright smile. 'I have money in several banks, and it slipped my mind which bank I had been to this morning.'

'It slipped your mind, right enough,' she sneered. 'Because it don't belong to you, slicker. You just figured I was an ignorant woman and you could beat me out of it, but you figured wrong, mister man.'

'Well, it doesn't belong to you either,' Slick said, losing philosophically. 'And my only purpose in accosting you was to see that it is returned to its owner. No one up here in Harlem can afford to lose that much money.'

Her eyes narrowed. 'How do you know how much money is in it?' she demanded, her cupidity getting the better of her logic.

'Let's count it and see,' he suggested reasonably.

'What for?' she asked with growing resentment.

'So we can divide it,' he said frankly.

'I'm a law-abiding, religious woman,' she said, getting on her high horse. 'I'm not going to have anything to do with you.'

'Then I'll call the policeman on the corner and tell him what you found,' he said indifferently.

'Wait a minute,' she said hastily. 'Let's see how much there is, first.'

She turned her back and drew forth the envelope, but he demanded, 'Let me see, too.'

Reluctantly, she allowed him to watch her while she opened the flap and looked at the contents. A sheaf of bright green bank notes tied with a paper band peeped out of them.

She started to pull it out but he stopped her quickly. 'Watch out – don't show it. Somebody will see and get suspicious. Just leaf back the edges.'

They both looked about and up and down the street, then moved closer together to form a screen. She slid the edges of the notes out far enough to show the hundred-dollar marker. She gasped. Her lips moved slightly as she leafed the notes back one by one. Her hand trembled. 'My God,' she whispered. 'Twenty thousand dollars.'

'Put them back,' he cautioned.

She pushed the notes back into the envelope.

'Ten thousand apiece,' he breathed. Taking a Manila envelope of similar shape and size from his inner pocket, he said, 'You give me the envelope and keep your eye on the policeman while I take out my half.'

Sight of the similar envelope combined with the artfulness of his request reawakened her suspicion.

'Naw you don't,' she said in a strident voice, clinging to the envelope and drawing away from him. 'You must take me for a square. I know all about you slick con men switching envelopes.'

A look of extreme disgust contorted his features. 'Here, woman,' he said, handing her the envelope. 'You divide it. I never saw anyone so suspicious.'

But his ready acquiescence inspired her with cunning. Her face took on a look of sanctimonious concern. 'We had better wait,' she suggested in an earnest voice. 'Maybe Sweet Prophet lost it. He's the only person around these parts who ever has that much money, and I don't want to take nothing of him. I had better take it upstairs and ask him.'

'I'll go with you,' he said quickly.

'No, you had better not,' she said. 'He'll get suspicious if he sees me bringing in a stranger, and he'll take it away from both of us and turn it over to the police.'

'Listen, woman,' he said, getting tough. 'Do you think I'm going to trust you out of my sight with my ten thousand dollars?'

She thought for a moment, and her eyes got small as ball bearings. She thrust the attaché case toward him and said, 'Here, you keep this bagful of money if you don't trust me. It's Sweet Prophet's weekend take, which I was taking to the bank. I'll bet there's more money in there than there is in this envelope anyway.'

Reluctantly, he accepted the case. 'All right, I'm going to trust you this time,' he said. 'But don't you try to double-cross me, because, if you do, I'll keep the money in this bag.'

'Oh, you can trust me,' she lilted triumphantly as she turned away. 'I believe in what is right.'

He watched her pass through the entrance and start up

the stairs. Then he turned and walked quickly toward his own car parked farther down the street, passing in back of Dummy without noticing him. At the same time the starker quit his post in the hotel entrance across the street, hastened down the opposite sidewalk and cut across the street to pile quickly into the back of Slick's car. The car started, and they drove off.

Dummy jumped from his stool and sprinted down the street. He turned in past the exit doorways of the theater where he had met the detectives earlier, and came out into an alley between the two streets. He was in time to see the big dark woman in the print dress come stealthily from the back entrance of Sweet Prophet's house. She turned toward Seventh Avenue, hurrying along. He followed her.

She caught a Number Three Fifth Avenue bus at 110th Street, and he just managed to get in behind her. She got off at 145th Street and Convent Avenue and walked over to Broadway. He was right behind her. She entered a branch of the Chase National Bank and stopped at the window of a receiving teller. When her turn came, the teller smiled and greeted her. 'Good morning, Sister Hopeful, how is Sweet Prophet?'

'Fine and dandy,' she said happily. 'He wants to put three thousand dollars in the bank.'

She passed him the deposit slip, already made out, and thirty bright green, brand-new hundred-dollar bills.

He looked at the top note, and his eyes widened in incredulity. Quickly he thumbed them back, staring at each in turn, his eyes becoming wider and wider. Then, very much as the Jew had done, he doubled over and began to laugh. He couldn't help it; he knew the cashier would give him hell, but what could he do?

Finally he said in a strangled voice, 'You are ninety-four years late and in a different country.'

She continued to grin; she didn't know what he meant.

'This is Confederate money,' he explained.

'Confederate money,' she echoed stupidly.

'Money issued by the Confederate states – the South – during the Civil War. It is not legal tender any more, I'm afraid.'

Numb with shock, she reached over slowly and picked it

up and stared at it. 'It do look different, don't it?' she said stupidly. 'And you say it ain't worth nothing?'

'Well,' he said hesitantly, 'It's valuable as a souvenir – if you're from the South.'

All of a sudden, her eyes popped from their sockets as though they had exploded. Her face turned gray. Her mouth opened wide. Sound came from it – a lot of sound.

'I been robbed!' she screamed. 'I been swindled. That black son of a bitch has done beat me out of all my Christian money!'

It required the efforts of two bank guards to subdue her and send her to the police station to tell her story.

Dummy stole quietly away.

16

At ten o'clock, Alberta was arraigned before the Municipal Court and bound over to the Grand Jury. Her bail was set at $2,500. No one was there to go her bail.

She was transferred downstairs from the city prison to the county prison. They are both in the same building, because Manhattan is a county as well as one of the boroughs of New York City.

She was mugged and fingerprinted, and her Bertillon measurements were taken. Then she was put in a cell with a light yellow sloppy-looking woman serving a year and a day for shoplifting.

'The top bunk, dearie,' the yellow woman said. Alberta climbed up into the top bunk and lay down.

'What's your rap, dearie?' the yellow woman asked.

'I ain't got any rap,' Alberta muttered.

'What are you down for, then?'

'I ain't down for nothing.'

'That ain't going to get you nowhere, dearie, acting like that. You've got your mouth stuck out a country mile.'

'What if I is,' Alberta said.

The yellow woman laughed maliciously. 'You'll get used to

it, dearie. I've been down so long that down don't worry me.'

'I want to see my preacher,' Alberta said.

'Who is your preacher, dearie?'

'Sweet Prophet.'

'That old hustler.'

'Don't talk like that about my preacher,' Alberta said.

'He ain't no preacher,' the yellow woman said. 'He's a pimp.'

Alberta got down from her bunk and stood over the yellow woman. Her face was pulled up, and she looked threatening.

'You take that back,' she demanded.

The yellow woman sized her up. 'All right, dearie. I was wrong,' she said. 'Have you got any money?'

'I got fifty dollars,' Alberta said.

'You have, honey!' the yellow woman exclaimed in a sugary voice. 'You got fifty bucks. Why, honey, you just give me half of it and I'll get word to your preacher.'

'How are you going to do that?' Alberta asked suspiciously.

'It's easy. You just got to grease the right palm. What's the old – er – prophet's phone number?'

'I don't know.'

'Well, it don't make any difference, if he's in the book. You just give me the money and relax.'

'I ain't got nothing but ten-dollar bills,' Alberta said.

'Well, just give me thirty dollars,' the yellow woman said. 'It ain't going to break you.'

Alberta fished three ten-dollar bills from her brassiere and handed them to the yellow woman.

'If he don't come, I want my money back,' she said.

'I can't do no business like that, honey,' the yellow woman said as she stuffed the bills into the toe of her shoe. 'Use your head. All I can do is to get word to him; if he don't come, it won't be my fault.'

Alberta gave in. 'All right. Maybe he won't have time to come, but just tell him to get me out of here.'

'I'll sure tell him that, honey,' the yellow woman promised.

She raked her tin cup across the bars, then lay on the floor and writhed and screamed.

Shortly, a big Irish matron appeared.

'I got the cramps,' the yellow woman gasped. 'I feel like I'm dying.'

'All right, just relax,' the Irish matron said. 'If you ain't died yet from the cramps, you won't die now. I'll call Mrs Ball to take you to surgery.'

When the matron left, the yellow woman winked at Alberta and said, 'You got to learn that if you're in here for any length of time. The only thing they'll take you to surgery for right away is the cramps. After you get there, you can make any connections you want.'

'I just want to see my preacher,' Alberta said. 'He'll tell me what to do.'

17

Sugar Stonewall was in the courtroom when Alberta was bound over. It was safe enough. Half of the spectators were colored people who looked just like him. Still, he was tense.

He had begged his subway fare downtown. Now he stopped a colored woman in the corridor and asked, 'Lady, can you give me fifteen cents to get uptown? I just ain't got no money.'

She fished a subway token from her purse and handed it to him without looking up.

He stopped on the way out and drank from the fountain. Water wouldn't nourish him, he knew, but it helped to weight his empty stomach down.

He walked over to Broadway and caught the A express train, transferred to a local at 125th Street and rode back to 116th Street.

It was about eleven o'clock when he arrived at the tenement on 118th Street where Alberta had her flat.

The big black woman hanging out of the front window on the ground floor was beginning to show signs of wear. The sun was on that side of the street, and her eyes blinked sleepily in the sunshine, but she was still hanging on with grim determination.

Sugar tried to slip past her, but she opened her eyes and caught him.

'I thought you'd be in jail by now,' she said by way of greeting.

'Why don't you leave me alone, woman,' he muttered.

'I ain't doing nothing to you,' she said, taking offense. 'It ain't none of my business what you people do.'

He entered the hall without replying. He kept going, up to the roof, and paused for a moment at the top of the fire escape to case the windows on the other side of the back court. Most of the windows were wide open, and housewives were visible doing their Monday morning chores. The weekly washings were strung on pulley lines from one building to another, crisscrossing one below the other down the narrow pit to the bottom. The graveled tar of the flat, burning hot roof was soft beneath his feet.

Finally he relaxed. He was on familiar ground. The heat bubbling from the tarred roof, the smell of cooking collard greens and pork and the jarring clash of colors on the lines of Monday wash put him at his ease.

He went down the fire escape and tried the window. A woman watched him from the kitchen window across the courtyard, but she had seen him in the flat often enough to know him. The shades were drawn and the window was locked, but he had long before prepared for such an emergency. A tiny hole was chipped in the window glass just above the catch, and a rusty tenpenny nail was wedged in the corner between the window frame and sill, where he had left it.

He opened the latch, raised the window and went inside, slipping beneath the shade. The woman across the way lost interest and returned to her chores when she didn't hear any sounds of fighting.

He discarded his sweat-stained rayon jacket and dirty straw hat and went to work. He searched every nook and cranny in the three rooms, going about it methodically. He examined every board in the floor, the baseboards, probed all the rat holes. He even pried loose the tin can tops nailed over the larger rat holes and speared in the openings with a fork. He went through the closet and the cupboards, moving the dishes and the utensils, and the cans, boxes, cartons and stacks of old paper sacks to look underneath them. He emptied the containers of salt and flour, sugar and corn meal, dried peas and hominy grits, and refilled them one by one. He searched the fire-box of the potbellied stove in the sitting room, the oven of the gas stove in the kitchen, inside the electric refrigerator and underneath.

Then he dumped the shoe box containing the policy slips and studied them. They didn't give him any clue.

Two hours later he was convinced the money wasn't there. He was beginning to doubt whether there had been any money. The only thing left to do was to go back and try to find Mabel. It wasn't likely that Rufus had given her any large sum of money to keep for him, but she might know something. The trouble was getting in to see her.

From the kitchen window he could see the people in the various kitchens across the courtyard sitting down to eat. He figured this would be a good time to call on Mabel. But he was so tired and hungry his wits were blunted. He figured he ought to eat first. He had seen food in the refrigerator but had not paid it any attention.

Now he explored it again. He found three pork chops, two eggs, a saucepan half-filled with cold hominy grits and a serving dish containing dandelion greens and okra that had been boiled with pigs' feet. The pigs' feet had already been eaten.

He got out the big iron skillet, poured in some half rancid drippings from the lard can on the back of the stove and put the chops on to fry. While they were frying, he pried the hominy grits from the saucepan in one piece, and cut it into slices an inch thick.

When the chops were done he added more drippings, fried the hominy grits a rich brown, stacked them alongside the chops and fried eggs country style. He put the fried eggs on top of the grits and dumped the greens and okra into the pan, bringing it just to a boil.

He left everything on top of the stove and ate, standing, until it was all gone. By then he was so sleepy he couldn't keep his eyes open.

He went into the bedroom, stretched out on the floor with his head on the pile of Alberta's lingerie and went to sleep.

Twenty minutes later he was snoring loud and steadily. When he exhaled, his snores sounded like a herd of buffalos drinking water; when he inhaled they sounded like a round saw cutting through a fat pine knot. His mouth was open, and a bottle fly was crawling about the crater as though trying to get up nerve to take the plunge. Every now and then Sugar would strike at it limply with his right hand, but he only succeeded in knocking his bottom lip out of shape.

He didn't wake up when the window was slowly raised by someone on the fire escape. He didn't see the man slide cautiously underneath the shade and enter the room.

The man had an open knife in his hand. It had a heavy, brutal-looking blade about seven inches long. The man approached on tiptoe and looked down at his face. He chased the fly with his shoe, but Sugar didn't stir.

The man tiptoed to the door and looked into the kitchen; then he tiptoed to the other door and looked into the sitting room. Then he went back, stood over Sugar and watched him sleeping. He looked as though he were trying to make up his mind about something.

After a while he knelt down beside Sugar and placed the knife on the floor within easy reach. He took his time searching all of Sugar's pockets.

All this didn't even cause a break in Sugar's snoring.

The man did not even smile. Obviously he had no sense of humor.

He picked up the knife and stood up. Still holding the knife open and ready, he scrounged out of the window backwards and went up the fire escape, leaving the window open.

18

A short time after Sugar arrived at the tenement on 118th Street, Dummy arrived back on 116th Street.

The clock in the window of the credit jeweler's said: 11.27.

Dummy kept along that side of the street until he came to the hotel. After looking about in all directions, he entered the hotel like a minister ducking into a house of prostitution. He climbed the smelly stairs to the fourth floor.

It was hot and airless beneath the low, flat, tarred roof, and the heat brought out stinks from the half-rotten floor that had been buried for decades.

A heavy brass padlock hung from the staples screwed to the door frame, but the wood where the hinge of the hasp was screwed to the door looked weakened by previous screw holes. Dummy could have broken through the flimsy door with his shoulder, but it was too risky at that time of the day. He hadn't brought along anything to pry loose the hasp because he had been expecting to find a simple warded lock.

In exasperation he snatched at the big brass lock, and it came open in his hand. His mouth gaped open in a grunting laugh. Ninety-nine people out of a hundred confronted with that lock would have attempted to break open the door, he thought; and hardly anyone would spot that it was a phony. Not a bad idea if you couldn't afford a lock that worked, he thought.

He removed the lock, pushed the door open and walked in. The occupant hadn't taken the trouble to bother with the warded lock.

The room stank with the scent of stale reefer fumes and the rank body odors that collect in stagnant air. A green window shade was drawn over the single tightly closed window, but sunlight filtered through the cracks in it to form an abstract pattern on the dirt-gray sheet that covered the three-quarter bed. A corner was curtained off for a clothes closet by a sleazy curtain, faded with age. In another corner was a wash basin the size of a bird bath; the single tap dripped cold water that left an indelible rust stain on the white enamel. Dirt encrusted the linoleum floor.

Dummy closed the door and snapped up the shade, flooding the room with hard bright sunlight. The light couldn't hurt it.

Dummy looked beneath the bed. He found the remains of a cotton mattress that had been split down the middle and the padding pulled out and stuffed back in. He began grunting with excitement, making a sound like a hog guzzling swill.

He left the mattress where it was and gave his attention to

a warped, scarred pasteboard suitcase lying flat on the floor against the inside wall. The lock didn't work, and the snaps weren't fastened. He lifted the lid and poked about in an accumulation of dirty cotton socks and underwear, holding his nose with his other hand. He didn't bother to close the suitcase. He crossed the room, drew open the sleazy curtain and examined the few soiled garments draped over wire hangers hanging from a sawed-off broomstick. The clothes took more of his time than anything else. But, even so, he was finished in under five minutes.

He was relieved to get out of the room, but his muscles didn't relax until he had quit the hotel and put a block's distance in between.

Around the corner on Lenox Avenue, a smooth-looking curly-haired young man sat in a two-toned Buick hardtop parked at the curb. Colored men and women approached him at the rate of one every ten seconds and handed him a canvas bag of money and a rubber-bound scratch pad, the size of a playing card, filled with pages of numbers.

He was a pickup man for a numbers house. Two hard-faced, oversized colored men sat in a black Mercury sedan parked directly behind him. They were the bodyguards hired by the house.

Dummy stopped to write in his scratch pad. He tore out the sheet and approached the pickup man. Before he got there, one of the big colored men in the Mercury opened the door and hit the pavement. No sooner had Dummy passed the written sheet to the pickup man than the bodyguard clutched the back of his neck.

'It's just Dummy,' the pickup man said.

'I know it's Dummy,' the bodyguard man said. 'Since when did he get to be one of our writers?'

'He wants to know where we're drawing today,' the pickup man said.

Since the police had tightened up on gambling, the lottery was floated to a different place every day.

'Don't tell him nothing,' the bodyguard said. 'He's a stool pigeon.'

A writer squeezed ahead with his bag of money and play slips and the pickup man said, 'Woodbine.'

The bodyguard gave Dummy a push, and the pickup man didn't look at him again. Dummy gave no sign that it mattered.

Fifteen minutes later he got out of a taxi in front of a hotel way uptown in the Harlem Heights on St Nicholas Avenue near 154th Street. The sign over the entrance read *Hotel Woodbine*. Dummy paid the driver and went inside.

Two men came in with heavy luggage and were sent to a suite reserved in advance. Two women followed with modernistic cases that might have been sound recorders and were sent to the same suite. They came in taxis, two at a time, well-dressed men and women, until the entire staff of sixteen had arrived.

Four bodyguards took seats about the lobby, one of them in the chair beside Dummy. He leaned over and whispered through his cupped hand, 'Don't dig your grave, stoolie.'

Dummy got up and moved to another chair. He knew the setup, and he was not interfering. Upstairs in the two-room suite, the office staff would set up four adding machines and an electric addressograph. There were eight pickup men, who collected the play slips and money from two hundred number writers. The pickup men turned in the books to the women operating the adding machines. The totals were tabulated and checked against the money turned in.

While this was taking place, two men set up the drawing machine. It was a small felt-lined keg with a sliding door, mounted on a winch and turned by a crank. Small black balls made of gutta-percha, lettered in luminous white paint from 0 to 9 – three of each number, making thirty figures altogether – were put into the keg, and the door securely closed. The crank was turned over ten times, the door was opened and a blindfolded man put his hand in the keg and drew out one ball. This was repeated three times, and the three numbers thus drawn, in the order in which they were drawn, comprised the winning number for that day.

The blindfolded man who drew the number was not a member of the staff. A different man was picked each day from among the two hundred writers or from the regular players.

When the number was drawn the play slips were rapidly checked and the winning slips put aside for the payoff.

Then the addressograph was set with the name of the house and the winning number:

Tia Juana
321

As many slips – called hit-slips – were printed as time would allow.

The winning play slips were paid off and assembled in eight collections. The equipment was repacked. The office staff, the man who drew and the eight pickup men left hurriedly. The operator and his two lieutenants remained to wait for the eight payoff men, who took the place of the pickup men. The payoff men arrived, collected the payoffs and left. The operator and his lieutenants came out last with the take.

Dummy watched them come and go. He knew that, in addition to the four bodyguards in the lobby, there were two more in the Mercury sedan outside and probably others stationed out of sight. He didn't make any sudden moves, but he timed his movements so that he was just leaving as Slick came down and started out the door.

He slipped Slick a sheet of paper from his scratch pad on which was written: *the punk is doublecrossin you.*

Slick glanced at it, looked up quickly at Dummy and said, 'Come on,' with the quick, sure decision of a man who knew the score. The pale yellow eyes sent a chill down Dummy's spine. He obeyed automatically.

They went down the stairs, and Slick nodded in the direction of 154th Street. He walked a little apart from Dummy, on the right side and a little apart. The two guards in the Mercury sedan never took their eyes from them. Nothing was said.

They walked in silence to the corner, and Dummy glanced at Slick for directions. Slick bent his head in the direction of his car, parked two doors up the street.

They arrived at the Chrysler hardtop, and Slick said in a low, controlled voice, 'Stand still a moment.'

Dummy had his back turned and was facing the car. He didn't see the motion of Slick's lips, and he had taken it for granted that Slick wanted him to get into the car. He put his hand on the door handle and he had started to open the door when suddenly he felt a hand grip his shoulder and his body spun violently around.

Up the street a motor roared, and a car sped down the incline and cut in front of the Chrysler with dragging brakes. A big scar-faced Negro in a red sport shirt and a Panama straw was out of the door and in the street with a snub-barreled .38 revolver in his hand before the car stopped skidding.

Dummy felt his guts shrink.

'I'll handle it,' Slick said coldly to the gunman. 'It's a private matter.'

'You're new here, son, so I'll tell you,' the gunman said in a flat Southern voice. 'There ain't no private matter when you're carryin' the house money.'

Slick ignored him. 'You're a dummy, eh?' he said to Dummy.

Dummy nodded.

'You can read lips, though.'

Again Dummy nodded.

'Put your fingertips on your shoulders and your elbows out,' Slick ordered.

Dummy did as he was ordered.

Slick frisked him with quick, sure movements.

'He's clean,' he said to the gunman.

'Watch out for him,' the gunman said, getting back into the car. 'He might be a stoolie.'

Slick gave him a thin, cold smile.

Two colored men were passing on the opposite side of the street. They made as though they hadn't seen a thing.

The front car backed up and pulled up by the corner.

Slick went around and got behind the wheel of his Chrysler and turned south on Saint Nicholas Avenue. Far down the incline of the black-topped avenue, stretching toward the east, rooftops in the Valley of Harlem could be seen.

Slick turned toward Dummy as they purred past the basement entrance to Bucky's Cabaret and asked, 'What makes you think so?'

Dummy made motions like writing and pointed toward his pocket. He wasn't taking any chances. Slick smiled thinly and nodded. Dummy fished out his stub of pencil and dirty scratch pad.

He wrote: *he got the mattress in his room all cutup money was in it,* and held it up for Slick to read.

'How do you know that?' Slick asked.

i seen it Dummy wrote.

'No, I mean the money,' Slick said.

it figgers the money was gone before the jew got there, Dummy wrote.

Slick pulled up for a red light at 145th Street. A real cool black chick in a beige blouse and aqua slacks gave him the eye. But he had business on his mind.

'How do you figure that?' he asked Dummy as he started up again.

Dummy wrote rapidly: *nobody aint found it he didn get mattress from the jew must got it afore the jew got there rufus didn get it that for sure.*

'It ain't for sure he got it, either,' Slick said. 'The bitch might have hid it somewhere else. She might still have it – how do you know?'

Dummy began grunting with excitement, *no she aint got it she looking for it.*

'How do you know she's looking for it?' Slick asked. 'She's in jail. Can you read minds?'

Dummy made sounds like a stopped-up drain. He started to write, but he didn't have space on that sheet and tore it off. Slick reached for it, drew it from his fingers and slipped it into his side coat pocket.

Dummy wrote on the clean sheet: *i seen her fore she got rested she come see my cassie looking for rufus she say i know better she looking for money.*

Slick's face didn't show any signs of heightened interest, but his hands tightened on the steering wheel.

'Did she tell your woman she had hid the money in the mattress?' he asked.

she didn tell nothin but we knew had to be sumthin sides just her furniter the way she look, Dummy wrote.

'That still don't figure absolutely that he got it,' Slick said.

somebody got it and he the only one could of, Dummy wrote.

'Why hasn't he cut out if he's got it?' Slick asked. 'What's he hanging around for?'

what he got the civil war money for, Dummy countered.

Slick laughed. 'You're doing the talking,' he said.

he trying to con you to thinkin he aint got it, Dummy wrote.

Slick's face got cold and hard. 'That's easier said than done,' he concluded, reached over, tore the sheet from Dummy's pad and put it into his pocket with the other sheet. 'Now just sit here and be still,' he ordered. 'I got work to do.'

They were approaching 125th Street, and Slick became alert to his surroundings. He was the payoff man for the district between 125th Street and 116th Street, bound on the west by Manhattan Avenue and on the east by Lenox Avenue.

'And if you spot any snoopers, point them out,' he added. 'If you're a stool pigeon like they say, you ought to know them all.'

Dummy made as if he were looking somewhere else and didn't get it.

Slick wore a money belt divided into pockets, in which he carried the payoff money, the winning slips and hit-slips. He stopped off at the numbers drops in barber shops, pool rooms, tobacco stores and shoe-shine parlors along the way, and met the roving writers in hallways and parked cars or in their flats. He kept five per cent of the payoff for his end on the small, everyday hits, but on the big hits, which he had to deliver in person to the winner, he kept ten per cent. The writers delivered the small payoffs and kept ten per cent for their end. Only the office staff, the pickup men and the guards were on salaries; the others took their commissions out of the winnings.

It was two-seventeen by the clock in the window of the credit jeweler's on 116th Street when Slick finished his rounds. He pulled up on the opposite side of the street, a half block's entrance from Sweet Prophet's Temple of Wonderful Prayer, and parked. He wasn't concerned about the woman they had beat earlier. She would be looking for a man in a black Buick sedan, the car beside which he had been standing when she first saw him. The way he thought about it, if he had to hide from all the squares he had beat, he could never show himself on the street.

Dummy saw the starker when he turned in from Seventh Avenue. He was wearing the same ensemble – beaver hat, tweed jacket, mustard-colored corduroy pants and cowboy boots.

Slick saw him, too, in the rear-view mirror.

The starker crossed the street, jaywalking through the traffic, and rounded the Chrysler to get into the front seat beside Slick. Then he saw Dummy and seemed to freeze.

'Get in the back seat,' Slick said.

He got into the back seat.

'Dummy, this is Susie,' Slick said. 'Susie, this is Dummy.'

Neither moved or made a sound to acknowledge the introduction.

'We're going uptown to my pad and have a little talk about a matter of interest to us all,' Slick said, and put the ignition key in the lock, starting the motor.

Susie took a marijuana butt from behind his ear and lit it.

Dummy sat with his hands on his knees and his head moving continuously from one side to the other.

Slick accelerated the car slowly and slid into the stream of traffic.

19

A woman let them in to the third-floor apartment in Roger Morris. Dummy's hope of catching sight of his deaf porter friend in the vestibule hadn't borne fruit. He would have signaled him a message, if no more than to say 'Watch out.'

He experienced an infinite dread of going unarmed to a strange apartment with Slick and Susie. The woman did nothing to allay it.

Dummy thought that she was a very strange woman. Ordinarily she would have looked like any other sepia-colored well-kept women, of which there were millions. But her hair was dyed bright yellow and pulled so tightly in a severe bun at the nape of her neck that it stretched the skin about her eyes, making the lids slant like an Oriental's. She wore a high-necked, tight-fitting Chinese gown of deep purple silk.

She was thin, but she didn't look anemic. Her nostrils had a pale pinched look, and the pupils of her brown eyes were so distended her eyes looked almost black. She carried her head unnaturally high, and she didn't speak. Silently she led them down a close-smelling, almost pitch-dark hall, past several closed doors, to the front sitting room.

It was a big room with three windows overlooking Edge-combe Drive and the rocky clifflike park dropping to the flats bordering Harlem River; in the distance the streets of West Bronx could be seen, rising like a terraced landscape fashioned of bricks.

In the brighter light Dummy saw at a glance that she was a junky; that she sniffed cocaine; that she had been sniffing it for so long she didn't know what life was without it and couldn't live such a life for one full day. That didn't worry him; but her silence did. That and something else about her that he couldn't figure. She never looked directly at anyone.

'Sit down,' Slick ordered the two of them, and sprawled onto a chaise longue flanked by a glass-topped cocktail table. To the woman he said, 'Fix my pipe and bring my rod.'

The woman moved, as though flowing, through another door into another room.

Susie and Dummy found chairs on opposite sides of Slick, as far apart from each other as possible. Dummy sat on the edge of his seat with his feet drawn back and his leg muscles tense, as though prepared to leap in any direction the occasion demanded. But Susie sat sprawled out in his seat – his legs extended, his cowboy boots crossed and the brim of the beaver hat pulled down over his eyes, as though to give the impression he had been there before and was not impressed.

However, it was an impressive room. The furniture didn't match and didn't fit, but every piece was expensive and unusual. Everything, including the curtains and drapes – with the exception of the console radio-record player-television set – had been stolen at one time or another, and Slick had bought it hot.

Dummy's gaze roved from one piece to another. The furniture seemed to be trying to tell him something, but he didn't know what.

No one spoke. The silence oppressed Dummy and put his nerves on a screaming edge. Susie lit a fresh stick of marijuana, took out his knife and began strapping the blade on his boot. Slick didn't seem to be bothered at all.

The woman returned, moving so silently across the carpeted floor that no one saw her until she stood beside the cocktail table flanking Slick's chair. She placed a round, ivory-coloured plastic tray on the glass top. The tray held a small nickel-plated alcohol lamp and a water-cooled pipe. The metal bowl rested on the alcohol lamp, and the bit was stuck into a coil of transparent tubing like the head of a sleeping snake. Nestled among the rest was a flat, vicious looking, blued-steel eleven-shot .38 caliber Colt automatic pistol.

The gazes of both Susie and Dummy focused on the pistol and didn't leave it.

The woman took the opium pill from her pocket, kneaded it skillfully with slim, delicate fingers and shaped it into a tiny ball. She fitted the ball into the shallow cavity of the metal bowl and lighted the alcohol lamp, and at the first bubbling of the pill she picked up the bit, unfurling the tube, and placed it between Slick's lips.

Four puffs and it was finished.

The woman cleaned up and removed the tray, leaving the pistol on the glass top. She flowed silently from the room without having once looked directly at anyone.

Slick lay back with his eyes half closed and seemed lost to the world. The silence ran on. He didn't give the impression of having any intention of breaking it.

Dummy swallowed nervously, making a sound like a baby burping. Susie gave a violent start and jerked up the knife. Slick looked over at Dummy sleepily.

'Don't make so much noise,' he said in a slow lazy voice.

They sat waiting. The silence got on Susie's nerves. The windows were closed against the heat, and the room was in the shade. But the air was motionless, and a haze of marijuana smoke collected about Susie's head.

Dummy could sense the silence, although he couldn't hear it. His eyes rolled in their sockets, and his head turned slowly from side to side as though controlled by an eccentric gear. He looked at the knife in Susie's hand; his gaze traveled upward to

Susie's face, then turned and ran along the wall, passed over pieces of furniture and focused for a time on Slick's face; it traveled down the length of Slick's reclining body, then slowly returned over the same orbit.

Slick gave himself twenty minutes for the hop to settle comfortably in his head. Then he came suddenly to life.

'Now,' he said briskly, sitting up.

He picked up the automatic pistol, ejected the clip, saw that it was fully loaded, looked at the cartridge in the chamber and reinserted the clip. The safety was on; he snapped it off and laid the pistol back atop the table within easy reach.

'What d'you think of this?' he asked in a conversational tone of voice, took the first of the three pages from Dummy's scratch pad and held it out toward Susie.

Susie stared at it. His babyish face did not change expression. No intelligence showed in his dilated eyes.

The play took Dummy by surprise. He hadn't expected that development. He had overplayed his hand. Now he was caught running a bluff, facing two armed men – and all he had were his fists. The fists of a prize fighter are considered lethal weapons in New York, but they won't stand up to a gun and a knife.

His body froze and his intestines knotted into a hard lump of gristle. Except for his gaze jerking back and forth from the sheet of paper to Susie's face, he might have been petrified. Now was the time when he needed all his wits, but his brain felt frozen, too.

'Here, rockhead, take it and read it,' Slick said to Susie. 'And get your brains thawed out; you're going to need them.'

Susie stood up slowly, stepped over to Slick and took the paper in his left hand. He looked vaguely puzzled. The dead marijuana butt was glued to his bottom lip like a shred of stained paper, and he held the open knife in his right hand like a riding crop. From a sitting position he looked bigger than he actually was; his shoulders looked a mile wide, and his legs resembled building piles.

His lips moved as his slow, drugged mind spelled out the words: *the punk is doublecrossin you.*

He frowned and looked down at Slick. The cold, repelling expression on Slick's face made him blink. It was obvious that he didn't get it. He read the line again.

'Do it mean me?' he asked incredulously.

Slick didn't answer.

Susie's gaze swung to Dummy. He pointed with the fore-finger of the hand in which he held the note as though aiming a pistol. 'He wrote it,' he said thickly.

All of a sudden he went berserk. His babyish face contorted with insensate rage. He leaped at Dummy and cut at his face with a slashing motion. It went so fast no one was prepared. The big brutal blade moved faster than sight.

A hair-raising noise issued from Dummy's tongueless mouth, sounding like a wild horse screaming in terror. But his body moved automatically from an instinct born in the ring. He gripped the arms of the chair and pushed back with both feet, shifting his full weight to his shoulder blades braced against the back of the chair, and kicked out with his feet tight together. The canvas sneakers didn't carry the impact that hard-soled shoes would have, but the pushing power did the trick. They caught Susie at the top of the thighs and sent him crashing backward into the television set as the arc of the slashing blade passed within a fraction of an inch of Dummy's eyes.

With the same motion, Dummy came down on his feet as Susie bounced from the heavy television set as though his flesh were made of rubber. Susie came in, stabbing sideways in strictly an amateur's thrust, and Dummy wove beneath it and right-handed him in the solar plexus. Spit-drenched air spewed from Susie's stretched mouth in a rush of whining sound, and his eyes bugged out.

'Cut it out,' Slick said in a level voice as he picked up the automatic pistol.

Dummy didn't see him, and Susie didn't hear him. Susie moved in a rage that didn't need breath and stabbed back-handed at Dummy's crouching figure. It was a desperate, unbalanced, half-aimed thrust, but it would have caught Dummy in the back of the neck if he hadn't made a blind, headlong dive. He dove into the cocktail table and smashed to the floor, landing, belly flat, on top of the broken glass.

'Cut it out, I said,' Slick repeated without moving from his seat. He acted as though he had seen a lot of fights and had command of the situation.

But still Susie didn't hear him. The blood was beating in

his ears, and his vision was blurred. He doubled to the floor, retching, his neck muscles swollen and corded from his effort to get his breath.

For a moment the tableau held.

At that moment the woman opened the door and took one step into the room. Her gaze darted about as though to locate the source of the commotion, but she didn't look at anyone in particular.

A sudden pool of silence dropped into the room like an air pocket in a raging storm, and she said in an anxious voice, 'Honey, you all right?'

Lying on his belly, Dummy read her lips and felt his hair rise.

Susie got his breath with a sound like hissing steam and straightened up. He saw Dummy and started toward him. Dummy pushed to his feet and ran, doubled over, past the woman and through the door. She didn't look at him, but when he ran past her she screamed.

'I'll kill you,' Slick said in a flat, absolute voice.

Susie pulled up as though he had run full tilt into an invisible wall.

'Put that knife away and sit down,' Slick ordered. Then he said to the woman. 'It's all right, baby.'

Susie folded the knife, stuck it into the watch pocket of his corduroy pants, went back to his chair and sat down. But he wasn't looking at Slick; he was looking at the woman and frowning.

'The other one,' the woman said hesitantly.

'He's all right,' Slick said, adding as though by way of explanation, 'he's a dummy.'

'Oh,' the woman said.

Dummy could be heard working with the locks on the outside door.

The woman returned through the door she had entered and closed it behind her. She lay on the bed, reached over to the bed table and turned up the small gilt radio she had been listening to. Dummy had passed through the room to the hall, but he couldn't get the outside door open.

Finally Slick got up from his seat and went through the other door and down the hall, carrying the pistol loosely at his side.

He touched Dummy on the shoulder and said, 'You can't get out without a key.'

It was too dark in the hall for Dummy to read his lips, but Dummy knew what he wanted. He turned, walked docilely ahead of Slick back to the front room and resumed his seat.

Slick returned to the chaise longue, ignoring the broken table.

'Let's don't have any more of that,' he said. 'It disturbs baby.' He placed the automatic on the floor beside him, then took the other two pages from Dummy's pad and held them out toward Susie.

'Now read these and let's talk about it,' he said.

Susie got up, took the pages, sat down and read them, his lips moving as he spelled out the words.

'Well, what about it?' Slick demanded.

'About what?' Susie muttered sullenly.

'Where's the money?'

'I ain't talking in front of this dummy,' Susie said. 'He's a stool pigeon.'

'So what?'

Susie began to puff up; his neck began swelling as though he were choking, and his cheeks puffed out. 'Look man, what is you trying to do?' he challenged. 'You and him ain't trying nothing like a frame on me, is you?'

'Not me,' said Slick indifferently. 'I just want the money.'

'Because if you is,' Susie went on, 'you're going to have to use that rod 'stead of just waving it 'round.'

Slick nodded toward Dummy. 'Ask him what he's trying to do.'

Both of them turned and stared at Dummy. He sat forward on the edge of his seat, gripping his knees with his hand, and looked from one to the other.

'What you want?' Susie asked in a threatening tone of voice.

Dummy shrugged and made a V with the thumb and forefinger of his right hand.

'What's that mean?' Susie asked.

Slick turned his stare back to Susie. 'You're not very bright, rockhead,' he said. 'He wants to cut himself a slice of our pie.'

'He's going to get more slices than he's looking for,' Susie threatened.

'You worry too much,' Slick said. 'I know what I'm doing.'

'Maybe you does, but I don't,' Susie said.

'Let him alone,' Slick said. 'We might need him.'

'Need a stool pigeon?' Susie echoed.

'Why not? If he's really a stool pigeon, it's a damn good thing we got hold of him in time, with what he already knows,' Slick pointed out.

'I just ask you, don't oversport yourself,' Susie said. 'I ain't nobody to play with.'

'We got that settled,' Slick said coldly. 'Now where's the money?'

'Listen, I told you what was what,' Susie flared.

Again Slick nodded in the direction of Dummy. 'He doesn't believe you.'

Susie turned and looked at Dummy again. 'You're going to be sorry you ever messed in my business,' he promised.

'I'm getting tired of this,' Slick said in his flat, deadly voice. 'I asked you where was the money.'

'I ain't got it,' Susie said, giving him a straight answer.

'Okay – I hope you're leveling,' Slick said.

'I'm leveling,' Susie said.

'Okay, you haven't got it. Let's start from there. What did you find in her joint?'

'Nothing. Her joker had already searched it again before I got there, and if anything was hid there he'd been sure to find it,' Susie said.

'How do you know he didn't?' Slick asked.

'He didn't,' Susie said. 'I found him asleep on the floor, and I looked around and saw he'd searched the joint; then I searched him. He didn't even wake up. You can bet if he'd had anything worth stealing, he'd been wide awake.'

'Let's get back to the mattress,' Slick said.

'I has told you, there wasn't nothing in that mattress,' Susie flared angrily.

'So you did,' Slick said. 'You also said you saw her put it there.'

Susie corrected him. 'I said I seen her sewing the mattress up. And I took it for granted that would be the only reason she'd be sewing up a mattress in the middle of the night.'

'Too bad you didn't get it then,' Slick said.

Neither of them noticed Dummy leaning forward with his eyes stretched.

'I couldn't have with her joker hanging 'round,' Susie said.

'And it wasn't in the mattress when you got it,' Slick said.

'It weren't there, and the side of the mattress had been cut open again,' Susie said. 'One of them beat me to it,' he added. 'But I don't know which one.'

Grunting sounds issuing from Dummy's mouth drew their attention. He had gotten out his scratch pad and was writing in it. He got up and showed Slick what he had written.

Slick looked up at Susie. 'He says neither of them got it.'

Susie's face swelled with sudden rage. 'If he keeps on trying to frame me, I'm going to stick him,' he threatened again.

Dummy moved away from the broken table so it wouldn't be in his way if he had to protect himself.

Slick reached out a foot and touched him on the leg. 'How do you know neither of them got it?' he asked.

Dummy wrote in his pad: *i know alright.*

'He just says he knows,' Slick told Susie.

'He knows more than what's good for him,' Susie said.

maybe she still got it on her, Dummy wrote in his pad and showed it to Slick.

'Not in jail, she hasn't,' Slick said. 'And it was you who said she didn't know where it was.'

Dummy shrugged.

'Maybe she took it out the mattress and hid it somewhere else,' Susie said.

Dummy shook his head in the negative.

'I got a feeling that we ain't being very smart,' Slick said.

'You're supposed to be the brains,' Susie reminded him.

'That's right,' Slick acknowledged. 'And I'm going to start using them.'

20

Between eight and nine o'clock on weekday evenings Sweet Prophet received in private such of his followers who had problems or wished to make confession and new recruits who wished to arrange for baptisms at some future date.

He sat behind the hand-carved mahogany desk in his sumptuous receiving room on the third floor of his Temple of Wonderful Prayer, while his supplicants sat in the high-backed period chairs across from him.

Attired in a Geneva gown of canary-yellow silk and a sequined headpiece similar to that seen on the statues of Krishna, he looked like the rising sun. The diamonds in the rings on all his fingers sparkled whenever he gestured, and his long twisted fingernails of rainbow hue squirmed as though alive.

Elder Jones stood at his right side, wearing a fresh white uniform.

His private secretary – a quiet, middle-aged woman of culture – sedately dressed in a freshly laundered black linen frock, stood at his left.

The assistant secretary, who had been entrusted with the weekend income to take to the bank, was still downtown in the Fingerprint Bureau of the Central Police Department examining photos of colored confidence men, trying to pick out the one who had swindled her that morning. She had looked at the mugs of criminals until her head swam, but still she stayed on, afraid to report to the Prophet that his money was lost.

Outside, seen through the open front windows, the day was dying. The street lights were on, and the lights in the show windows of stores and in the hot-box apartments; and the sign lights and automobile lights lit up the many-colored faces of the people crowded on the burning hot sidewalks.

Sweet Prophet's hour of consolation was almost over. He was glad of it; other folks' problems had never seemed so distasteful. Strain showed in his face; his bulging eyes looked worried and harassed. It had been a long day for him; he hadn't been able to sleep again after the detectives' pre-dawn visit.

'Who else is there?' he asked.

'Sister Alberta Wright,' Elder Jones replied.

Sweet Prophet looked startled. He hesitated. Finally he sighed and said. 'Send the sister in.'

Alberta paused just inside the door and stared at Sweet

Prophet. She looked downcast and bedraggled in the now-filthy garments in which she had been baptized; but her eyes were wide and alight with hope. Sitting there in his brilliant garb, Sweet Prophet appeared to her as a great shining light that had come into this dark moment of her life.

She fished the last ten dollars from her brassiere, went forward and laid it on the desk in front of him. Wearily, he found a crumb of bread for her in the pocket of his gown and pocketed the money. She put the crumb in her mouth and knelt on the floor.

'Arise, my child,' he said.

She got up from her knees and sat forward on the edge of the chair.

'What is troubling you, my child?' he asked.

'I hate to keep bothering you after you have been so good to get me out of jail,' she said. 'But I'm in big trouble.'

'Tell me about it, my child,' he said.

'It began with my dream,' she confessed. 'When I dreamt about those three pies exploding with hundred dollar bills, I knew The Lord had sent me a message. So I went and played twenty dollars on the *money row* in the three biggest houses in Harlem. That was all the money I had, sixty dollars, but I knowed The Lord had sent me a message, and I had faith. And just like I believed, my number popped out like it were sent for, and I hit for thirty-six thousand dollars.'

'Thirty-six thousand dollars,' Sweet Prophet echoed. 'That is a lot of money, child.'

'Yes, Sweet Prophet, it sure was,' she admitted.

'So the houses have gone back to paying six hundred to one,' he remarked.

'Yes, Sweet Prophet, they pays off good if you got the message,' she said.

'And you had twenty-nine thousand, four hundred dollars left after paying off the commissions?'

'Yes, Sweet Prophet. I had to give the writers the ten per cent which they collects on a hit, and then I had to give the payoff men from each of the houses a thousand dollars for bringing me my money safely. But how did you know?'

'My child, a prophet must know all the workings of sin in order to combat it,' he said.

'But I didn't figure it was no sin if The Lord himself sent me the message,' she argued.

'No, my child, the sin was that you took this money which The Lord sent to you for the expiation of your sins and hid it for your own self, instead of bringing it to Sweet Prophet, who would have taken a share for The Lord, and returned you the rest in safety.'

'How did you know I hid it?' Alberta asked in surprise.

'My child, a prophet knows everything,' he said.

'Then where is it now?' she asked.

'We ain't come to that part yet,' he said testily. 'You ain't finished your confession.'

'I didn't intend to keep it hid, Sweet Prophet,' she resumed. 'I honestly intended to bring it to you for you to take out The Lord's share; but I hadn't got religion then, and I figured I ought to get religion first and get myself baptized so I could come to you in my purity and place the money at your feet for you to give me back in your bounty what you figured I should have. And besides that, Sweet Prophet, my man was away from home when they paid me off, and I figured it would be no greater sin to put temptation in his way. So I hid the money in my mattress, figuring you wouldn't want to deal with the money of a sinner anyway. And so that's why I came to you early Sunday morning and give you the five hundred dollars—'

'You gave to The Lord through me,' Sweet Prophet corrected, to keep the record straight in case of an inquiry by the income tax collectors.

'Yes, Sweet Prophet, gave to The Lord through you,' Alberta parroted, 'the five hundred dollars for to pay to get baptized.'

'And afterwards you dilly-dallied around for so long before performing this duty to The Lord that the money was stolen,' he said.

'I weren't dilly-dallying around,' she protested. 'It was stolen whilst I was in my trance.'

'The Lord will forgive you,' he consoled her. 'The Lord wouldn't be expecting you to guard your money while you were in a trance.'

'Yes, Sweet Prophet, I believe The Lord will forgive me,' she said. 'But The Lord ain't done it yet. All The Lord has done so far is chastise me. And that's what I can't understand. Why would The Lord want to chastise me by letting my money be stolen whilst I was setting in heaven at His feet?'

'You haven't told me all that happened as yet, Sister Wright,' Sweet Prophet said. 'I can't explain The Lord's actions until I know what you have been up to.'

Alberta recounted in detail everything that had happened to her since her release from the morgue.

'Now they are saying I beat out the Jew-man's brains with a hammer and cut my husband's throat with a knife,' she concluded.

'If they have charged you with that, you are really in big trouble, Sister Wright,' Sweet Prophet admitted. 'But you didn't do it?'

'No, Sweet Prophet, I didn't do it,' she wailed. 'You've got to believe me, Sweet Prophet. I ain't never in all my life hit nobody in the head with a hammer hard enough to kill him, and I didn't cut my husband's throat neither, as much as he deserved it.'

'Then why do they think you did it, Sister Wright?' he asked.

'It was because of the knife,' she said. 'They caught me trying to get rid of the knife I found. They said it was the knife that Rufus had been killed with, and, when I saw it lying there, I thought so, too. I didn't know what had happened. All kinds of thoughts ran through my head. I hadn't seen Sugar, and it came to me all of a sudden he might have found out that Rufus had stole my furniture, and I could see them getting into a fight. I figured maybe Sugar might have stabbed Rufus in self-defense, because it would be just like Sugar to throw away the knife and run.'

'If that is what happened, all you have to do is tell the police, and they will arrest Sugar and drop the charges against you,' Sweet Prophet said.

'But he didn't do it,' she declared. 'I'd bet my life he didn't do it. He's so tenderhearted he won't even cut off a chicken's head, and I know he wouldn't have stabbed Rufus all those times.'

'Well, there is one good thing that has come out of it,' Sweet Prophet consoled her. 'The Lord has saved you the trouble and expense of getting a divorce; He has made it possible for you to go and sin no more.'

'Well, that much He sure has done,' Alberta admitted glumly.

'Do the police know about the money you had hidden?' Sweet Prophet asked her, his thoughts taking another tack.

'I didn't tell them,' she said. 'I wanted to ask you first whether I ought to.'

'No, Sister Wright. If you are innocent, don't tell them about the money,' he advised. 'If they learn about the money, they will believe for sure that you are guilty.'

'But what am I going to do, Sweet Prophet?'

'Are you dead sure you left the money in your mattress?' he asked.

'As sure as I'm sure that I'm setting here and you is setting there,' she said.

'Did anyone see you when you hid it?'

'Not unless they got eyes that can see through walls,' she contended. 'The door was locked and the shades were drawn, and I had put Sugar out of the house for the night.'

'How did you know he didn't go back and steal it while you were in your religious trance?' he asked.

'He wouldn't have stole all of it,' she declared. 'I know my Sugar. He would have been too scared of me to steal all of it. That's why I love him. If I got to work to support him, the least he can do is be scared of me. Besides which, why did Rufus and the Jew-man steal my furniture if they weren't looking for the money? I got sense enough to know my furniture weren't worth nothing to nobody but me.'

'How would your estranged husband and the Judaist know about the money if you haven't told anybody, Sister Wright?'

'I don't know, Sweet Prophet. You is the only one I have told, and that's the truth,' she said.

'Somebody knew you had it,' he persisted.

'I don't know who it could have been,' she maintained.

'The man who delivered it knew it,' he pointed out.

'But there were three different payoff men, one from each of the houses,' she argued.

'One of them must have known that you hit in the two other houses,' he stated.

'He didn't find it out from me,' she said. 'I didn't tell nobody.'

'They delivered the money to your home?' he asked.

'Yes, Sweet Prophet, they sent it as soon as the drawings were over.'

'But not at the same time?'

'No, Sweet Prophet. The Dollar house sent theirs first. They were drawing in Harlem on Saturday and didn't have far to come. A man called Buddy brought it. Then the Monte Carlo house sent theirs next. They were drawing in the Bronx and had farther to come. A man called Bunch Boy brought theirs. And the Tia Juana house sent theirs last because they were drawing away over in Brooklyn. They got a new man called Slick Jenkins who brought theirs.'

'And this Slick Jenkins was the last one to come?' Sweet Prophet asked.

'Yes, Sweet Prophet, but he didn't know I had hit in the other two houses,' Alberta said.

'It stands to reason that he found it out in some way, came back and stole your money, child,' Sweet Prophet declared.

'I don't see how he could have found out,' Alberta contradicted. 'He didn't see the other money because I hid it as soon as I got it, and I didn't tell him nothing.'

'You must have given yourself away in some manner,' Sweet Prophet persisted. 'If this Slick Jenkins is accustomed to paying off big hits, then he is accustomed to the winners hiding their money, and he would know just where to look. You probably left your mattress uncovered when you hid the other money.'

'That's just it, Sweet Prophet, I didn't hide the money in my mattress at first. I cleaned out a lard can and put the money in that and hid it in the refrigerator. I didn't put it in the mattress until after Sugar had come home and I had put him out. I got to thinking it would be safer if I slept on it; but there weren't nobody around when I hid it, and it was still there when I got up yesterday morning because I took out the five hundred dollars to pay for my baptism, and it was there then.'

'Of course, child,' Sweet Prophet said. 'Slick didn't have a chance to steal it until after you had left for the baptism.'

'But what about Rufus and the Jew-man stealing my furniture?' she argued stubbornly. 'What did they do that for if Slick had already stole my money.'

'Just think about one thing at the time,' Sweet Prophet said angrily.

'I'm thinking about it,' she muttered. 'And it don't seem right. He'd be scared to steal the money. The houses wouldn't have no payoff man who stole back the hits; they'd kill him.'

'You said he was a new man.'

'He's just new in Harlem. He was doing the same thing for a house in Chicago before he came here, and he'd know better,' she contended.

Sweet Prophet lost patience. 'Can't you get it through your thick head that he stole your money, woman?' he said angrily. 'There is no other way it could have happened.'

'If you say he stole it, he stole it,' Alberta said, quailing.

'You go to him and tell him to give you your money back,' Sweet Prophet commanded her. 'You tell him that I said so. Tell him that I said I will call down the wrath of heaven on his head if he doesn't give you back your money. Do you know where he lives?'

'Yes, Sweet Prophet, he lives at Five Fifty-five.'

'Then you go up there and get your money back,' he concluded.

'Yes, Sweet Prophet,' she said docilely.

21

'We should have thought of that before,' Grave Digger said.

'It was the Jew who threw us,' Coffin Ed reflected. 'Taking that furniture apart.'

'He's still throwing us,' Grave Digger admitted. 'But first things first.'

'Let's go find her then and lock her up again,' Coffin Ed suggested.

'And fast, before somebody gets hurt,' Grave Digger said.

Fifteen minutes after Alberta had left Sweet Prophet, the detectives' small battered black sedan pulled up before the entrance.

Sweet Prophet was still sitting behind his desk. He still

looked like the rising sun. But the lines of weariness on his pop-eyed countenance had been replaced with a look of fury. He was drinking ice-cold lemonade from a frosted silver pitcher in a cut champagne glass, but the way he gulped it, it didn't seem cold enough to satisfy him.

He greeted the detectives irritably. 'It took you long enough to get here.'

'How did you know we were coming?' Coffin Ed demanded.

Sweet Prophet wiped his face with his yellow silk handkerchief. 'I telephoned for you,' he said.

'We didn't get your call, but here we are,' Grave Digger said. 'What's the beef?'

'My secretary was swindled out of three thousand dollars this morning by a confidence man, right outside of my door, and he hasn't been caught.'

The detectives stood in front of his desk with their hats pushed back on their heads. They stared down at him.

Another woman – the gullible secretary – had been added to the scene since Alberta's departure.

'And I was just trying to help him,' she said.

Grave Digger addressed Sweet Prophet, ignoring her. 'You reported it, didn't you? This morning, I mean.'

'I did,' the secretary said.

'She reported it,' Sweet Prophet hastened to sustain. 'She went to the police right after it happened, but I have just now found out about it.'

'Then you have done all you can do,' Grave Digger said unsympathetically. 'We're after another matter. Why did you go Alberta Wright's bail?'

'That woman! She's the plague of my life!' Sweet Prophet exclaimed in exasperation. 'I did not go her bail. I would not have gone her bail. I do not know how she got out of jail. She thinks I went her bail, and I couldn't very well disillusion her. But whoever did go her bail did not do me any favor.'

The detectives tensed. Coffin Ed's acid-burned face became grimmer, and a vein began throbbing in Grave Digger's temple. Before it had been necessary to find her; now it was urgent.

'That makes it a horse of another color,' Grave Digger said. 'You know she's been robbed?'

'Yes, I know all about it,' Sweet Prophet admitted. 'She came here straight from jail and told me everything.'

'She told you that she hit the numbers for thirty-six thousand dollars.'

'Yes, and you can take it from me that she is as innocent of those killings as I am,' Sweet Prophet said.

'Anybody would be innocent to you with that much money,' Coffin Ed remarked.

'That's for later,' Grave Digger said roughly. 'Where is she now?'

'My God, how do I know?' Sweet Prophet snapped. 'I would imagine she's trying to get her money back, if she's got any sense. After what she told me about the payoff, it was as plain as the nose on your face that one of the payoff men named Slick Jenkins stole her money. I sent her to his house to get it back.'

'You sent her,' Coffin Ed echoed.

The detectives stared at Sweet Prophet incredulously.

'You mean to say you sent her out alone to demand her money from a hoodlum you don't even know, knowing that two men have already been killed about it?' Grave Digger asked, the jugular vein swelling in his neck like corded rope.

'No one is going to hurt that woman,' Sweet Prophet said callously. 'God takes care of children and fools.'

'People will recrucify Jesus Christ for thirty-six grand,' Coffin Ed said harshly.

'You're getting alarmed over nothing,' Sweet Prophet said.

'Leave off!' Grave Digger grated. 'Did she say where Jenkins lives?'

'In the Roger Morris,' Elder Jones volunteered.

'Let's go,' Grave Digger said, striding toward the door, but just before leaving he turned and called to Sweet Prophet. 'I don't think much of your Christianity, buddy.'

It was forty-four city blocks to the house on Edgecombe Drive, and the streets were filled with traffic. They went up Seventh Avenue with the siren open, scattering cars like ninepins, and turned over to the Drive on the 155th Street Bridge.

The elevator was occupied. They took the stairs two at a time.

The woman in the Chinese gown answered their ring. They stood flanking the door. Coffin Ed had eased his pistol loose in its holster and stood with his hand resting on the butt.

'Yes?' the woman said, opening the door onto a heavy burglar-proof chain. She looked through the crack, but not directly at either of them.

Grave Digger flashed his shield. She didn't look at it.

'Yes?' she asked again, impatiently.

'We want to talk to Jenkins,' Grave Digger said.

'Who are you?' she asked.

Both of them looked at her sharply.

'Are you trying to be cute?' Coffin Ed challenged.

'Leave off,' Grave Digger said, and told the woman. 'We're detectives. Do you want to see our identifications?'

'That's not necessary,' she said. 'Slick isn't in.'

'May we come in and look around?' Grave Digger asked.

'No,' she said. 'I said he wasn't in.'

'You're making life hard for yourself,' Coffin Ed said.

'Slick left at a quarter to eight,' she said. 'He hasn't been back.'

She closed the door. They heard keys turning and bolts locking.

Coffin Ed looked at the locks as though he might enjoy shooting them off.

'I don't quite dig her,' Grave Digger said.

They went down to the lobby and found the doorman, a tall, slender man with a winged mustache and a thin rusty-brown face beneath a yachting cap. His gold-braided purple uniform had been pressed so often it shone like waxed paper.

'We're the men,' Grave Digger said, flashing his shield.

'You don't have to tell me, boss,' the doorman said.

'When did Slick Jenkins leave?'

'Before eight, boss.'

Grave Digger and Coffin Ed exchanged glances.

'Alone?' Grave Digger asked.

'No, boss, he had a mugger with him what's been hanging on to him for the past few days.'

'Mugger!' Grave Digger echoed. 'Give us a rundown.'

The doorman gave a pinpoint description of Susie, then for good measure threw in a description of Slick, of Slick's car, and the license number. He conducted a little business on the side peddling marijuana cigarettes, and he figured every little bit he did for the police would help him if he got into a jam.

Grave Digger described Alberta and asked if she'd been there.

'I ain't seen nobody like her, boss, and if I'd seen her I sure wouldn't have forgot her.'

'Okay, boy, when Jenkins turns up I want you to telephone the 126th Street Precinct Station and leave word,' Grave Digger ordered.

'Right, boss. My name is Sam. Don't forget old Sam, boss.'

'What's your racket?' Coffin Ed asked.

'I ain't got no racket, boss; I'm just a peace-loving boy.'

'Damn right,' Coffin Ed said. 'Peace at what price?'

They went back to their car.

'We're either too late or too early,' Grave Digger said.

He got the precinct station on the radio telephone and asked Lieutenant Anderson to put out a pickup for Slick Jenkins, giving a description of his car and the license number.

Lieutenant Anderson said that Sweet Prophet had telephoned in to say that Alberta Wright's man, Sugar Stonewall, was there at the Temple.

'Off again, on again,' Grave Digger muttered.

They did the forty-four blocks back to 116th Street with the siren blaring.

Sweet Prophet was sitting as though he hadn't moved.

He greeted them with, 'He left. I couldn't hold him.'

'We've got to get a new car,' Grave Digger said, then asked, 'What did he want, did he say?'

'He wanted me to go his woman's bail because I had baptized her, but I told him that someone had beat me to it.'

'Yeah, somebody wants her out bad,' Grave Digger said. Slowly his voice was getting thick. 'Did he say where he was going?'

'I sent him up to see Slick Jenkins,' Sweet Prophet said. 'I told him that I had sent his woman up there, and that was where he was most likely to find her. After that I couldn't hold him.'

'You're sitting there trying to play God with these little people,' Grave Digger said in a voice that sounded as though his mouth were stuffed with cotton. 'And all you're doing is shilling for Clay, the undertaker.'

'I'm a busy man,' Sweet Prophet said defensively.

'Yeah, but not so busy as you would be breaking up rocks,' Grave Digger said, then asked, 'What does Stonewall look like, if you weren't too busy to have looked.'

Sweet Prophet kept an offended silence, but the two women and Elder Jones gave a composite description.

'Gone again, John again,' Grave Digger muttered as he climbed behind the wheel.

They went back up the way they had come; but traffic had thinned considerably on Seventh Avenue, and everyone with a guilty conscience had got in off the street.

In answer to their questions, Sam the doorman said, 'Ain't nobody looked like him been through this door, boss, or I would have seen him, and I ain't blind.'

'All right, stand out on the sidewalk where we can watch you,' Coffin Ed ordered.

'I ain't going to try to tip nobody off,' Sam said aggrievedly.

'I don't want to have to worry about it,' Coffin Ed said. 'I got other things to worry about.'

The doorman came out, stood in the center of the sidewalk and didn't move to open the door when the tenants came in and out.

Grave Digger got into their car and eased it to the curb between the racketeers' big shiny cars. It looked out of place. He sat behind the wheel, watching the people pass. He looked out of place. Coffin Ed took up his station on the other side of the entrance, leaning with one hand propped against the top of another big shiny car. He didn't look as though he went with the car, but the people who passed acted as though they didn't notice.

Grave Digger talked to Lieutenant Anderson again, but nothing new had come in.

There was nothing to do but wait. Half of a detective's working time was spent in waiting and watching. They waited and watched.

Twenty minutes later they saw Sugar Stonewall alight from a Fifth Avenue bus and cross the street. Coffin Ed intercepted him and took him by the arm.

'I'm the man,' he said.

'First time I was ever glad to see the man,' Sugar confessed.

Coffin Ed took him to the car and frisked him. Sugar was as docile as a lamb. They put him on the back seat and Coffin Ed sat with him while they drove down to the precinct.

Sugar spoke only once, to ask, 'You got a cigarette, chief?'

'Afterwards,' Coffin Ed grunted.

They took him into the Pigeon's Nest and installed him on the wooden stool, beneath the glaring light.

'Talk fast and straight,' Grave Digger ordered.

'Yassuh, boss, where do you want me to begin?' Sugar asked.

'You look like a bright boy,' Grave Digger said. 'Just lead up to it slowly, so we can get the picture. Everything is needed now.'

Sugar didn't need any further prompting. Sweat flowed from the creases of his face, and the smell of animal fear emanated from his skin. He talked fast and eagerly.

'It began like this, boss – me and Alberta has been shacking up together for about eight months. Most times when she came home from work at about eight o'clock, I'd be there waiting for her. Weekdays she'd start drinking as soon as she got in – she liked to drink, but she weren't no lush. She'd just sip enough to knock herself out by ten o'clock and I'd help her get to bed. But shucks, I'd just be getting wide awake myself, so I'd go down to the corner and play tonk, and, if I didn't get home 'til three or four the next morning, it wouldn't make any difference to her because she'd be so dead asleep couldn't nothing wake her—'

'You slept all day,' Coffin Ed cut in with an outburst of contempt.

'You see, boss, I been sick,' Sugar explained.

'For eight months?'

'Let him get to the point,' Grave Digger said.

'Well, last Saturday night I got held up in a poker game and didn't get home until after ten o'clock. I figured she was going to be mad all right, because that's when we generally got together, but I didn't expect her to grab me by the collar and throw me out of the house. That's what first made me suspicious, but all I suspected at first was she'd got herself another man. That worried me—'

'I'll bet it did,' Coffin Ed cut in again.

'Yassuh, it sure did,' Sugar admitted. 'So I went down to the bar and thought about it, and the more I thought about it the madder I got. So after a while I crept up on the roof and started to come down the fire escape to sort of spy through the bedroom window. I had made me a little peephole in the window shade in case I was ever going to need it, and I figgered I needed it then. But, when I started to come down from the roof, I saw some joker on the fire escape spying through her window, too. I started to holler at him, but I didn't want—'

'Wait a minute,' Grave Digger said. 'You saw a man looking through her bedroom window?'

'Trying to, anyway. But he saw me 'bout the same time I saw him, and he took off down—'

'Hold on. You saw this man?'

'Yassuh, but I didn't see him good. The fire escape is in the back, and he was gone on down to the bottom 'fore I could get close to him. I would have chased him, but—'

'Hold on, hold on!' Grave Digger grated. 'What did he look like?'

'Like I said, boss, I didn't see him plain but—'

'Big man or little?'

'Big. Rough-looking. Looked like he was young, the way he went down them rungs.'

'How was he dressed?'

'I didn't notice too plain, boss. He was wearing a big hat and a coat like everybody else. He was a colored man, that's for sure.'

Grave Digger and Coffin Ed looked at one another in silence.

'You think he's lying?' Coffin Ed suggested.

'Let him go on. If he's lying, we'll find out,' Grave Digger said.

'And, if you are, it's going to be rough,' Coffin Ed promised.

'I ain't lying, boss, I swear before God,' Sugar said, knuckling the sweat out of his eyes. 'And I couldn't be mistaken, 'cause I seen him again.'

'You saw him again?' Grave Digger echoed.

'Yassuh, when I come down the second time I found him in

the same place, and he run down to the bottom again like he done before.'

'And you didn't see him any better?'

'I forgot to tell you. I seen he had on boots – cowboy boots.'

'Boots!' Grave Digger said.

'Yes suh, black and white cowboy boots. I wondered if he belonged to a gang, but I hadn't heard of no gang what wears cowboy boots.'

Grave Digger and Coffin Ed exchanged looks again.

'Sounds a little like him,' Coffin Ed said.

'Could be,' Grave Digger admitted. 'It begins to figure.' He turned back to Sugar. 'How did you figure it?'

Sugar looked puzzled. 'Him, you mean? I didn't think nothing of it. Just another prowler – that neighborhood is full of prowlers. She didn't have nothing for him to steal –' He broke off. His eyes bucked suddenly, and his jaw dropped open. 'Christ almighty, I bet he was after her money!' he exclaimed.

'You just now thought of that?' Grave Digger asked incredulously.

'Well, boss, I admit I've been thinking like a square,' Sugar said. 'But I hadn't figgered out when I first seen him that she had any money. I was looking for another joker in her bed. So I just figgered he was another prowler, and I didn't give him no more thought.'

'All right, all right – if you're lying, we're going to find it out,' Grave Digger said. 'So when did you figger out she had some money?'

'Well, when I seen she didn't have no other joker in her bed, I figgered she must have got hold of some money, because that's the only reason she'd have for throwing me out the house – to keep me from finding out. Then when I seen her praying—'

'Praying!' Coffin Ed exclaimed.

'Yassuh, boss, she was kneeling beside the bed with her arms hanging down, praying. I figgered right away then she had hit the numbers for a big stake. It figgered. She hadn't had nothing before worth praying about.'

'All right, it figured,' Grave Digger conceded. 'What did you do then?'

'I stayed there, watching all night so she wouldn't get away, but after she turned out the light she didn't get up again. When it got day I had to leave because the people in the windows across the way began watching me suspiciously. I went across the street and watched the door, and when she came out I followed her. When I seen her go into Sweet Prophet's house, I figgered she was giving him the money to keep, so I kissed it goodbye, went to the bar and had some drinks. But after a while I figgered I ought to go back – I was getting tired and hungry by then. And that's when I found her getting ready for the baptism and the picnic. I fell in and went along with her because there wasn't nothing else to do. But when I knowed she hadn't given any money to Sweet Prophet was when she told about her dream—'

'Her dream?' Coffin Ed echoed.

'Yassuh, she jumped up right in the middle of the ceremony and said she had dreamed she was baking three pies and when she took them out the oven they exploded with hundred-dollar bills. I knew then she had played the money row in all three houses and had hit; and I knew she hadn't given the money to Sweet Prophet from the way he licked his chops and his eyes bugged out. I could see it was the first he had heard of it, and I knew she still had the money hidden somewhere. So when she was getting herself baptized, I dropped a little mickey into her bottle of drinking water.'

'You had the mickey ready beforehand,' Grave Digger said.

'I always carry a mickey,' Sugar confessed. 'Other folks has their knives and pistols, but I ain't no fighter. And I has to have some kind of way to protect myself. So I just carrys me a little Mickey Finn. But I didn't figger she was going to take the bottle to Sweet Prophet to get it blessed and then start drinking it right away. I figgered she'd drink it while we were having our picnic lunch, and then the other sisters would take her and lay her out somewhere and it would give me a chance to search the house. I didn't have no idea it would cause such a big rumpus. When the people started running and screaming, thinking she'd dropped dead, I beat it before somebody connected me with her and had me held. I had a key to her place what she didn't know about, so I beat it around there and searched it.'

'Then you were there before Rufus and the Jew got there?' Grave Digger said.

'It was me that got them there,' Sugar confessed. 'When I didn't find nothing in the mattress, I remembered that Rufus and the Jew worked this furniture racket, and I made a deal with Rufus to sell the Jew the television set and have him take it away. The way I had it planned was that I'd go get Alberta and bring her home, and when she found the set missing she'd get so scared for her money she'd rush right away to see if it was safe, and I'd find out where it was at. But when I went back to get Alberta, I found out they had taken her away in a hearse and didn't nobody know where she was. So I went back to her place to see if she'd come home but didn't nobody answer. I'd given Rufus my key, so I snuck down the fire escape again and spied through the window. That's when I found out they'd taken all of her furniture.'

'You went after Rufus,' Grave Digger interjected.

'Yassuh, but not with no knife,' Sugar denied. 'Rufus claimed he hadn't found the money and that's why he sold all the furniture, but he promised to take another look.'

'Then it was Rufus who went to the Jew's warehouse looking for the money,' Grave Digger said.

'I don't know, boss, I'm just telling you what he said.'

'And you went with him,' Coffin Ed put in.

'Nawsuh, boss, I didn't even know where it was at.'

'The Bronx police figure there were two men there when the Jew was killed,' Coffin Ed persisted.

'It sure weren't me,' Sugar denied.

'Let him get on,' Grave Digger said. 'Time is getting short.' He asked Sugar, 'What were you doing all this time?'

'All I was doing was hanging around outside of Rufus's house watching to see what he would do,' Sugar confessed. 'He didn't come out until after it got dark – it must have been about nine-thirty – then he got in his car and drove off. I didn't want to be seen hanging around so much in the street, so I went over to Eighth Avenue and hung out in a bar. I was there when I heard the patrol cars passing, and I knew something had happened. When I got back to Manhattan Avenue, I saw the people crowding in the street and the police looking at Rufus's car; and, when I seen the blood on the seat and all over the sidewalk, I knew it was Rufus who'd been stabbed, even before they found him. I didn't want to get caught there, so I moseyed on back to Eighth. And the next thing I knew I saw the cops arresting Alberta, and I figgered they'd be looking for me next so I beat it. I didn't know the Jew had been killed till I went to Alberta's house and the woman there in the window told me. I was scared to stay there; then the next thing I knew Dummy caught up with me on the street and told me the cops was looking for me – as if I didn't know.'

'Dummy!' Grave Digger echoed. 'What was Dummy doing there?'

'I don't know, boss. I figgered he must have been looking for the money, too.'

When he had finished telling the part he had seen Dummy take in the search, he became terrified at the detectives' anger.

'I was just trying to get it back for her,' he whined.

'You and Dummy teamed up,' Coffin Ed accused.

'Nawsuh, boss, he went his way and I went mine,' Sugar denied. 'I went back to Alberta's place, got in through the window and searched it again. Then I just went to sleep, boss. I was beat. But somebody else came here whilst I was sleeping, 'cause they left the window open – but I don't know whether it was Dummy or not; I didn't wake up.'

'It figures close enough,' Grave Digger said. 'Only it doesn't leave us much time.'

'All I'm scared of is somebody might hurt her,' Sugar said.

Coffin Ed knocked him off the stool and started to kick him in the face, but Grave Digger restrained him.

'Easy, Ed, he'll keep,' he said.

They didn't wait to cross-examine him. They didn't have time. Where before it had been urgent, now it was desperate. They booked him on suspicion and left the station running.

'Dummy first?' Coffin Ed suggested.

'Later,' Grave Digger said. 'We got to find the woman before they kill her. Let the money go for the time being.'

22

Grave Digger turned off the lights before turning the corner and cut off the motor before reaching the entrance. The car coasted to a stop in front of the entrance to the tenement on 118th Street.

'Let's just hope we're right,' he said.

They got from the car fast, but with a minimum of sound, and approached the door like grim reapers.

'Pssst!' the big fat black window-watcher called to them.

She looked as though she hadn't left her post. In the shadow she resembled a melted lump of wax.

'If you looking for her, she ain't come back,' she said.

Grave Digger felt his heart sink. Coffin Ed grunted as though he had been punched in the stomach. But neither of them hesitated.

The entrance door was closed. Grave Digger gripped the knob and pushed. The door didn't give.

The woman was leaning over the sill, trying to see what he was doing.

'This door is locked,' he said.

'Locked!' the woman croaked in amazement. 'That door ain't been locked since I lived here, and that's been six years.'

'It's locked now. Who has a key?'

Coffin Ed had his pistol out. The long nickel-plated barrel gleamed in the dim light.

'Move over,' he said. 'I'll blow it open.'

'Easy does it,' Grave Digger cautioned. 'Let's don't risk any noise.'

'I got a key,' the woman said, groaning as she got from her chair. 'But I ain't never used it, and I don't know exactly where it is.'

Coffin Ed pushed at the edge of the door. 'It ought to break easy enough,' he said.

'Take it easy,' Grave Digger said tightly. 'We don't want to make any graves.'

'I found it,' the woman called from the window in a stage whisper.

'Give it here,' Grave Digger said, leaning over to take it.

'It won't work from the outside,' the woman said.

'Then go open it, woman,' Grave Digger said savagely. 'What's wrong with you?'

They heard her door open softly and padded feet slither

across the hall floor. The key was inserted with a slight grating sound, and the rusty bolt creaked as it moved.

They entered the front hall. In the dim light the woman looked about to cave in from exhaustion. The skin of her face had shrunken and turned gray, and lines like spider webs had formed about her eyes, which were as red as live coals.

'I been watching just like you told me,' she croaked.

Neither of them answered. With drawn pistols they started up the stairs, taking them three at a time, Grave Digger leading and Coffin Ed at his heels. Their pistols swung in gleaming arcs like the swords of warriors of old.

At the top, they slowed down and moved cautiously. Making as little sound as possible, they bent, their heads together, and listened at the panel of Alberta's door. They did not hear a sound.

Coffin Ed took out his pocket flashlight and held it in his free hand. Grave Digger gripped the knob, tightened it with a slow pull, turned it silently and pushed. The door didn't budge. He took out his own flashlight.

They looked at one another. Grave Digger nodded. They drew back, angled their shoulders and hit the door simultaneously.

The lock broke, and the door was flung back to the wall. They went through the opening side by side and leaped far apart. Their flashlights raked the darkness; their pistols swung in arcs.

The room was empty. The door to the bedroom was closed. In the next flat a man laughed and a woman's voice was heard distinctly through the thin wall: 'I tole him his eyes may shine and his teeth may grit . . .' From below, the bass notes from a jazz recording came up through the floor as though someone were hammering on the ceiling with the meaty part of their fist.

They crossed the room on tiptoe and flung open the bedroom door. The drawn shade rustled suddenly in the current of air from the open window, and the muzzles of their pistols leveled in that direction at the height of a man's heart.

The room was empty. They released their breath in a soft sigh and looked at each other again.

'Where do we go from here?' Coffin Ed asked.

Grave Digger nodded toward the kitchen door.

They crossed the room, and Grave Digger opened the door without caution. Their lights focused suddenly on a body lying on the floor.

'Too late,' Grave Digger said in a thick cottony voice. 'Too late,' he repeated bitterly.

'Maybe not,' Coffin Ed said.

She lay doubled up on her side on the linoleum floor. She still wore the same uniform in which she had been baptized, but now it was black with dirt. Her hands were tied behind her with a cotton clothesline, which had been run down between her feet and wrapped about her ankles. Her feet had been drawn up to the level of her hands. She was gagged with a yellow bath towel, which was knotted at the back of her head. There was a large red stain on the underside, where blood had soaked into it from the corner of her mouth. Blood, seeping slowly from her greasy matted hair, came from a wound in the top of her head. Her eyes were closed, and her face looked peaceful. She looked like she was asleep.

Coffin Ed switched on the overhead light, and both detectives holstered their pistols. Grave Digger knelt beside the body and felt for the pulse. Coffin Ed unknotted the gag. She moaned suddenly when the gag was removed and swallowed her tongue. Coffin Ed reached two fingers down her throat and pulled it up, and blood that had collected there poured from her mouth. Grave Digger found a serving spoon in the cupboard drawer and bent the handle to form a hook. Coffin Ed eased his fingers from her mouth while Grave Digger inserted the spoon to hold her tongue in place and hooked the handle over her upper lip.

They found two small burns on each side of her mouth. There were cigarette butts and the stems of burned paper matches on the floor.

'I'll go and call for the ambulance,' Coffin Ed said, whispering.

'No need for silence now,' Grave Digger said.

He heard Coffin Ed thundering down the stairs as he cut the cotton rope binding her hands and feet and gently straightened out her legs. He found more of the small round burns on the back of her hand. His neck was swollen and corded until the flesh bulged over his collar, and he seemed to have difficulty with his breathing. He lifted her head slightly and inserted a flat pan under her so that it lay level. He didn't turn her over. He didn't touch the wound.

He poked at the cigarette butts with his fingertips. One was the butt of a marijuana cigarette. He didn't bother to pick them up. Finally he got to his feet and looked around, but there was nothing to see.

Coffin Ed returned.

'They're rushing an ambulance from Harlem Hospital,' he said, then after a moment added, 'Anderson said he'd telephone the Homicide Bureau to see what they wanted done.'

'They didn't get anything out of her, so they knocked her in the head,' Grave Digger said in a thick, cottony voice.

'They must have had a lookout staked and saw us coming,' Coffin Ed surmised.

'I don't dig this business,' Grave Digger admitted.

While waiting for the ambulance, they went over the apartment briefly. They saw the signs where Sugar had searched, but nothing to indicate that money had been hidden there. They raised the shade, went out through the bedroom window and climbed the fire escape to the roof. They saw nothing that told them anything. It was easy enough to get down to the street in a dozen places from the flat, adjoining roofs on both 118th and 119th Streets.

'Poking around like this is the long way,' Grave Digger said.

'Then it might not lead anywhere,' Coffin Ed agreed.

They went back into the kitchen and looked at the woman on the floor.

'Either Slick and his muscle boy, or Dummy alone, or all three together,' Coffin Ed said. 'Or else somebody we don't know about.'

Grave Digger didn't reply.

The sound of a siren came through the night.

'If they were hanging around, they're gone now,' Coffin Ed said.

Nothing more was said.

They heard the ambulance draw to a stop down on the street. Steps sounded on the stairs. Two white-clad colored interns came briskly through the front room, one carrying an instrument case. They were followed by a uniformed white driver carrying a rolled-up canvas stretcher.

The interns glanced once at the detectives, then knelt beside the woman and made a quick, cursory examination without opening the instrument case. One pressed the skull gently beside the wound. Alberta moaned.

'Is it bad?' Coffin Ed asked.

'Can't say with concussion,' the intern replied without looking up. 'Only the X-rays will tell. Stretcher,' he said to the driver.

The driver unrolled the stretcher and laid it on the floor parallel to the body, and the interns worked the edge underneath her side. Then, while one intern held her head, the driver and the other intern rolled her over gently on her back onto the stretcher.

'You want something?' the intern asked Coffin Ed.

'Just get her to talk,' Grave Digger said in his thick, cottony voice.

'Talking is not good for a concussion case,' the intern said.

'Good or not,' Grave Digger said brutally.

All three of the ambulance crew looked at him.

The first intern said dispassionately, 'All you cops are heartless bastards.'

Grave Digger let out his breath. 'It's hard to say who's heartless and who isn't,' he said. 'There's a woman hurt, and there's a killer loose. She can tell us who he is before someone else gets it.'

No one answered him.

The driver and one of the interns picked up the stretcher and the other intern, carrying the instrument case, led the way out. The detectives followed.

With the arrival of the ambulance, the tenement had come alive. Tenants crowded into the hallways and peered from open doors.

'Get back into your holes and thank God it isn't you,' Coffin Ed said to a group of them.

The window-watcher was waiting in her doorway. Her red eyes peered from a gray face, on which there was a look of consternation.

'I don't see how she could have got in without me seeing

her,' she said, clutching at Grave Digger's sleeve. 'I hardly left the window at all.'

He shook her off and passed without replying.

The ambulance was rolling when they got into their car.

'I got a hunch we're just getting started on this thing,' Grave Digger said as he unhooked the radio telephone and dialed the precinct station.

'We're going uptown to Five Fifty-five Edgecombe Drive, Slick Jenkins' apartment,' he told Lieutenant Anderson. 'If anything comes in, you know where to reach us.'

'No, wait where you are for the sergeant from Homicide,' Anderson directed. 'He wants to work this out.'

'There isn't time,' Grave Digger said.

'Wait anyway,' Anderson ordered.

Grave Digger cradled the telephone and started the motor.

'Heartless,' he repeated to himself as though it worried him.

23

'Is Slick back?' Grave Digger asked Sam, the doorman.

'Yassuh, boss, he come back about fifteen minutes ago, and I phoned the precinct station like you said,' Sam replied.

'Alone?'

'Nawsuh, he got the same boy with him.'

'All right, just don't try to play both sides of the street,' Grave Digger warned him, and he and Coffin Ed brushed past.

They took the elevator along with two ladies of the night. A rigid silence was maintained. Coffin Ed's grim, acid-burned face was enough to scare the devil out of hell.

The sepia-colored woman with the dyed yellow hair, dressed in the same tight-fitting purple silk Chinese gown, answered their ring again. She opened the door onto the safety chain.

'Yes?'

'We're the police – we're back again,' Grave Digger said.

'Slick hasn't come back,' she said, beginning to close the door.

'We have a search warrant,' Grave Digger said, causing her to hesitate.

'And we don't want to have to shoot open the door,' Coffin Ed added.

'May I see it?' she asked resignedly.

Grave Digger took a legal size envelope from his inside coat pocket. It bore the return address of an insurance company. From it he extracted a typewritten letter suggesting that he examine their new life premiums. He unfolded the letter and held it out toward her.

Both detectives had their gazes pinned on her slanting brown eyes. Her eyes looked down in the direction of the letter, but when she reached for it her hand went aside. Grave Digger moved the paper within her grasp. She took it and then instantly returned it.

'I see,' she said in a low voice. 'Then I will have to let you in.'

She had to close the door to unlatch the chain. Both detectives drew their pistols. The chain made a slight rattling sound, followed immediately by the distant sound of a door being opened. A muted voice asked sharply, 'Who is it?' They heard her say, 'It's two policemen; they have a search warrant,' and then the muted voice, lowered to a whisper, saying, 'Hold them a minute.' There was an almost imperceptible sound of a door closing and a lock clicking shut.

Keys turned inside the entrance door, and bolts moved. She drew the door inward.

'Come in, please.'

Holding their pistols in their right hands and their flashlights in their left, they entered a pitch-dark hall.

She closed and locked the door, and turned toward the front of the building.

'Follow me, please.'

They tried the doors as they passed. Three opened into darkness, and the fourth was locked. From behind it came the sound of tense whispering, and then a sound like painful retching. Coffin Ed flattened himself against the wall beside the door, while Grave Digger followed the woman through the doorway at the end of the hall into the front sitting room. It was lit by a floor lamp and a table lamp, and through the three front windows the terraced lights of the Bronx were visible.

From behind the other door to the locked room Grave Digger heard a sharp gasp and the muffled sound of scuffling. Then a key was being turned.

The thick, enraged voice of an imbecile shouted, '*He's gittin' away!*'

Grave Digger was already moving toward the closed door, but the woman blocked the way. He reached out to push her aside, but the motion was arrested by the sight of Dummy coming through the opened door. Blood was coming from his mouth, and he was mewling like a cat.

'He's hurt my cat!' the woman cried hysterically.

Grave Digger felt the hair rise on his head.

The heavy thunder of two shots from an automatic gun crashed, one after another. They were followed almost simultaneously by the hard, deafening impact of Coffin Ed's .38 as he shot through the lock in the hall door.

A big broad-shouldered man wearing cowboy boots and a beaver hat staggered after Dummy through the open door. Dummy took four steps into the room and fell face downward on the carpet. The big man fell like a log right behind him. His hat flew off, and his face smashed into the sole of Dummy's canvas sneaker.

Then from the room came the low grating sound of Coffin Ed's voice, saying, 'Drop it,' sounding as dangerous as a rattlesnake's rattle.

Grave Digger leaped over the big man's body, knocking the woman to her knees, and went into the room with his pistol ready.

The room was a bedroom, with twin beds covered with green chenille spreads. Beyond the second bed Slick stood motionless, looking straight ahead. He wore a pink flannel smoking jacket with a blue velvet collar, and in the soft light from the single bed table lamp his thin, ascetic face was expressionless. The blued steel .38 caliber automatic lay on the bedspread in front of him.

Coffin Ed stood just inside the hall door with its shattered lock. His .38 caliber revolver hung motionless at his side. From the muzzle of its long nickel-plated barrel came a lingering wisp of smoke, adding to the tingling smell of cordite in the room.

Grave Digger lowered his pistol and let out his breath.

'All right, bring him in here,' he said, turning to re-enter the sitting room.

The woman was on her hands and knees, rocking from side to side.

Dummy lay on his belly with his arms spread out and his face turned to one side. The handle of the knife Susie had been sharpening on his boot earlier in the day protruded from the center of his back, between the shoulder blades. He was breathing in soft shallow gasps, and shaking his head almost imperceptibly. His brown eyes peered from beneath the lumps of scar tissue with the pleading look of a sick dog.

'Don't worry, I won't pull out the knife,' Grave Digger assured him, and gave his attention to the other man.

Susie had two bullet holes in the back of his heavy tweed coat, from one of which the heavy pumping of blood was beginning to ebb. He had the absolutely motionless, relaxed, gone-for-good look of the brand-new dead.

'Straight through the ticker,' Grave Digger muttered.

He stood aside as Coffin Ed ushered Slick into the room.

Without looking at the body, Slick stepped over it. He stepped past the woman without looking at her either, and stood with his hands raised shoulder high. He didn't move while Coffin Ed frisked him.

'He killed my cat,' the woman said suddenly, and began to cry hysterically.

'Jesus Christ!' Grave Digger said.

Holstering his gun, he put his hands beneath the woman's arms and lifted her gently to her feet.

'Your cat is all right,' he said. 'This man called Dummy was stabbed, and your husband shot his partner in the back.'

She seemed reassured. He helped her to the chaise longue and laid her down. Then he turned and looked at Slick.

'Now I know why they call you Slick,' he said.

Slick didn't answer.

Grave Digger found a telephone on a table near the door. He telephoned Harlem Hospital for an ambulance and then contacted Lieutenant Anderson at the Precinct Station.

'Hold everything,' Anderson ordered. 'Sergeant Frick from the Homicide Bureau is on his way up there now.'

'Right,' Grave Digger said.

'I don't know anything about these people,' Slick said. 'They've been trying to proposition me into helping them rob some woman, but I nixed them off. They came here tonight to try again. When you people came, each one accused the other of stooling. I had to shoot the big guy, Susie, to keep him from killing the little dummy.'

The detectives stared at him. Neither bothered to answer.

After a moment Slick added sardonically, 'I got a soft heart.'

Grave Digger slapped him with the open palm of his right hand with such force that he spun three feet, straight into Coffin Ed's short right to his belly. They beat him until the doorbell rang, one slapping and the other punching – not hard enough to bruise, just hard enough to hurt.

The room was beginning to empty. For a time it had been crowded.

The ambulance had come and taken Dummy.

An assistant Medical Examiner had arrived and examined the body. He had written on the tag that was later tied to the right big toe:

NAME: *Susie Green*
AGE: *apprx.* 26
NATIONALITY: *colored*
ADDRESS: *unknown*
DIED: *murdered by two gunshot wounds penetrating the back of the thorax, one penetrating the heart*

The body had begun its lonely journey to the morgue.

Sergeant Frick had arrived with two assistant detectives. They remained.

A table had been dragged to the center of the floor, and Sergeant Frick sat behind it. One of the detectives sat beside him with a pad and stylo to take down the preliminary statements.

'I'll talk to the woman first and get her out of the way,' Frick said.

'I had better tell you, she's blind,' Grave Digger said.

The woman pulled her knees beneath her and hunched forward on the chaise longue.

'I'm blind, but I can hear,' she said.

The five policeman stared at her with varying emotions.

Slick, sprawled in an armchair against the inner wall, said menacingly, 'Just keep your mouth shut, bitch.'

His face was swollen, as though he had run into a nest of hornets, and his discolored eyes were almost shut.

Coffin Ed reached over and slapped him across the mouth. Slick didn't move.

'No more of that,' Sergeant Frick said sharply.

Grave Digger leaned against the wall, looking into the distance.

'I want to make a statement,' the woman said in a tired, dead voice. 'Slick killed the Jew.'

Grave Digger pushed from the wall, and his body tensed. The other four policemen froze.

Slick sat forward in his chair. 'Bitch, if you try to frame me, I'll kill you, if it takes all my life to do it,' he threatened in a deadly voice.

'Take him out,' Frick said.

Grave Digger reached down, clamped Slick back of the neck and yanked him to his feet. Coffin Ed took him by the arm.

'Let Haines take him – I want you two here,' Frick said.

The second white detective from the Homicide Bureau hand-cuffed Slick's hands behind him and marched him down the hall toward the kitchen.

'Go on,' Frick told the woman.

'Slick knew that a woman named Alberta Wright hit the numbers for thirty-six thousand dollars,' the woman said.

The detective scratched rapidly on his pad.

'He propositioned Susie to rob her on a half-and-half basis,' she went on. 'He told Susie where she lived and gave him the setup. Susie went down to rob her, but he didn't get a chance. Her man was hanging around outside her window all night. But Susie got a chance to see her hide the money in her mattress before he was chased away. When he got back on Sunday and looked through the window, he saw Rufus there. He went down the street to wait for Rufus to leave, but the Jew came with his moving van and started taking away all of her furniture. So he stole the mattress from the van. But the money wasn't in the mattress.

'He came here Sunday afternoon and told Slick what had happened. Slick thought that either Rufus or the Jew had found the money; he didn't know which. He and Susie left the house and were gone for about an hour. I heard them talking when they came back. They had found out where Rufus lived, but they weren't sure he had found the money, and they didn't know where the Jew had taken the furniture. Slick decided he'd watch Rufus. He told Susie to wait here for a telephone call in case he would need him. He telephoned here Sunday night, sometime between ten-thirty and eleven o'clock. When I heard the phone ring I went to the kitchen and listened in on the extension.

'Slick told Susie that the Jew had searched the furniture and had found the money. He said he had followed Rufus to the Jew's place in the Bronx and had seen the Jew find the money. He said he had trapped the Jew and killed him; he didn't say how he had done it; but he said the Jew had given the money to Rufus and that Rufus had got away. Susie asked him how he had let Rufus get away, and he said Rufus had stabbed him in the shoulder. He told Susie to go to Rufus's place on Manhattan Avenue and get the money from him before he could get into his house and hide it.

'When Slick came home he gave me the clothes he was wearing and told me to get rid of them. Then he went into the bathroom, and bandaged his shoulder and had me fix him three pipes of opium. Before he went to sleep, he told me to wake him up when Susie called. Susie didn't call at all that night, and it was morning when Slick woke up. He thought that Susie had double-crossed him. He had dressed and had started out to look for Susie when Susie came here. Susie told him he had got the money from Rufus, but it was only Confederate money. Slick didn't believe him.

'Susie had some plan of using the money for a confidence game to beat Sweet Prophet, and Slick agreed. They went out together and came back a couple of hours later with the money they had made. But Slick wasn't satisfied; he still thought Susie was trying to trick him. They left again when Slick went to work

– he was a payoff man for the Tia Juana house – and when they came back they brought Dummy. There was a fight, and Slick drew his pistol on Dummy.

'Later on Slick called up a bail-bondsman and had him go Alberta Wright's bail. When the bondsman phoned around eight o'clock to say that Alberta Wright was out, they left the house. They got back a few minutes before the policemen arrived.'

She stopped talking suddenly and waited for someone else to speak.

Frick looked from Grave Digger to Coffin Ed.

'Do you believe it?' he asked them.

The detectives exchanged looks.

'I believe it,' Grave Digger said. 'It figures all around.'

'It's just her word,' Frick said. 'She hasn't offered any substantiating evidence.'

'You'll find the clothes he was wearing in my overnight case in the bedroom clothes closet,' she said. 'There's a pocketbook in one of the pockets that might mean something. And you ought to be able to find some kind of evidence in his car – maybe he stepped in some blood or something.'

'Get the bag,' Frick said, but Coffin Ed had already moved.

It contained the suit, with the blood splotch around a small cut on the left shoulder, just as she had said. In the inside coat pocket was an old worn billfold with half a dozen cellophane card holders containing licenses and identifications made out to Abraham Finkelstein.

'This might do it,' Frick said. 'But, as his wife, she won't be allowed to testify against him, and we will need her statement to make it stick.'

'I'm not his wife,' she said in that tired, dead voice. 'I'm just a woman he blinded, beating me with his fists.'

During the embarrassed silence that followed, no one looked at anybody else.

'Did you believe her?' Coffin Ed asked as they drove leisurely down Seventh Avenue, returning to the station to write up their report.

'Hell, no,' Grave Digger said with an almost inaudible chuckle.

'It's more likely that Rufus killed the Jew.'

'Sure it was Rufus.'

'And it was Susie who attacked Rufus, trying to get the money,' Coffin Ed surmised.

'That's the way I have it figured too,' Grave Digger agreed. 'Susie had Slick's car and followed Rufus to the Bronx then beat him back home and killed him.'

'But she'll make it stick,' Coffin Ed said.

'Yeah, she'll pay him off,' Grave Digger confirmed.

Dummy never reported the tan jumper with the bloodstained shoulder he had found in Susie's hotel room, and the police never discovered it. It stayed like the woman said.

24

For six days Alberta lay in bed in a ward with nine other women. Her head was swathed in bandages; her flat, pretty, brown-skinned face was sullen.

Police came to see her; friends came to see her; Sugar Stonewall came to see her; Dummy came in a wheel chair from another ward to see her. She did not speak a single word to anyone. She lay there with her mouth shut tight and wouldn't even say hello.

During that time sympathetic attendants washed her uniform and cleaned her once-white shoes.

On the seventh day, another Monday, she ate her breakfast in dead silence, as usual.

Then the nurse brought her clothes and gave her permission to get up and walk about the ward.

She got dressed in her clean white uniform and wrapped her pink-checked hand towel about the bandages on her head. She walked up and down the ward two or three times, then went out into the corridor. No one stopped her; no one seemed to notice her.

As though by instinct, she went downstairs to the kitchen. It was a big kitchen with a lot of people working in it, all of them clad in white uniforms. The head cook thought she was a new helper and put her to work peeling potatoes.

She got a long sharp paring knife and sat down on a wooden stool before a five-gallon can of spuds and went to work. By ten-thirty o'clock she had finished with that can. She quit, stuck the paring knife into the pocket of her uniform, got up and walked out.

Instinctively, she found the service exit. The guard on duty gave her scarcely a glance as she passed on her way out of the building; to him she looked like any number of hospital workers.

It was not far down Lenox Avenue to 116th Street. No one on the street paid her the slightest attention.

She turned over on 116th Street to the Temple of Wonderful Prayer and went upstairs to Sweet Prophet's reception room.

Elder Jones congratulated her on being well again, and told her to wait and he would see if Sweet Prophet could give her an audience.

Sweet Prophet sat behind his desk, clad in the same shining garments he had worn the previous Monday, when she had last seen him. Evidently it was his Monday outfit.

When Elder Jones informed him that Alberta Wright wished to see him, he exclaimed, 'That woman again! My God, she's got more lives than a cat!'

But he was prevailed upon to give her an audience.

He looked more than ever like the rising sun as she came into the room. She walked toward his desk with her hands in her pockets. The secretary, standing behind the Prophet, looked at her compassionately.

Sweet Prophet was searching in his pocket for the crumb he expected her to buy. He looked up with a patient expression and said, 'My child, what's troubling you this time?'

She leaned one hand on the desk, whipped the paring knife out of her pocket with the other hand and plunged it into the left side of his chest with such force that only the handle protruded.

He gasped and dropped forward over the desk like a stone.

Twenty minutes later, it was announced to the people crowded in the street that word had come from Harlem Hospital that he would live.

The blade had penetrated the left pleura, but had missed the aorta by a hair's breadth.

By that time Alberta was in the booking room of the Harlem Precinct Station, surrounded by bug-eyed cops.

Finally Sergeant Ratigan, the day man from the Homicide Bureau, who had been on the case from the beginning, arrived. He had brought along his own stenographer, and he took over the precinct captain's office for the interrogation. The captain sat in, as did several precinct detectives.

Alberta sat in a straight-backed chair, looking composed and resigned as she faced the battery of officers behind the desk.

'Why did you do it, Alberta?' Ratigan asked in what he mistakenly thought was a kindly tone of voice.

'He stole my money,' Alberta replied in the whining Southern voice she employed when talking to white people.

Ratigan's eyes popped in amazement, but he controlled his voice.

'How did he steal your money?' he asked, as though reasoning with a child.

'I gave it to him,' she said.

'Oh,' Ratigan said. 'But that doesn't mean he stole it.'

'Nawsuh, but he didn't give it back.'

'All right, let's get this straight,' Ratigan said. 'You gave him the money, and he didn't give it back. Did you ask him for it?'

'Nawsuh. I forgot I gave it to him.'

Slowly, and at first unnoticeably, she began to cry.

'All right,' Ratigan said. 'Don't get upset. Take your time and tell me just what happened.'

She swallowed. 'I went to him Sunday morning to pay for to get baptized,' she said, 'and I told him I needed to get religion because I had won all that money on the numbers.'

'It was thirty-six thousand, wasn't it?' Ratigan asked.

'Yassuh, but I didn't have but twenty-nine thousand, four hundred left,' she said.

'Yes, go on,' Ratigan prompted.

Everyone in the room was staring at her unblinkingly, their mouths half open as though their breathing were suspended.

'He told me to look him straight in the eye,' she said. 'I kept looking him in the eyes until my head seemed to get empty of everything but just his eyes. Then he said, "You will do exactly as I say." And I said, "Yes, Sweet Prophet." He said, "Go back to your house and get all the money from where it is hidden and bring it to me." I said, "Yes Sweet Prophet."'

'And I went and got the money and brought it back and gave it to him. He took it and put it away, and then he looked me in the eye again and said, "You will forget everything you have done since you came into this room." And I said, "Yes Sweet Prophet."'

'And the next thing I knew I was sitting there talking to him about getting baptized, and I had forgotten everything else. I had no idea where my money had gone until I came to in the hospital after I had got knocked on the head. Then I remembered everything. He knowed I was looking for my money, and he wouldn't give it back.'

She started crying out loud. Her big-boned body was racked by uncontrollable paroxysms.

The hard-boiled cops stared at her in awe.

'He thought I didn't know anything about hypnotism,' she wailed. 'He thought I was just a big simple fool. He didn't have to go and hypnotize me and take my money and then try to keep it,' she blubbered. 'I would have given it all to him if he had just come right out and asked for it.'

Ratigan stared at her in speechless amazement. 'You mean you would have given that charlatan all of that huge sum of money that you won if he had asked for it? Good God, woman, why?'

'Because I believed in him,' she said, crying almost hysterically now. 'That's why. If you is a black woman like me, you got to believe in something.'

Sergeant Ratigan had intended to ask her, during the course of the interrogation, why she had gone with Slick and Susie up to her empty flat where they had tortured her and struck her in the head, but now he didn't have the heart.

'The chances are the court is going to let you off if the prophet pulls through, and it looks as though he will,' Ratigan said. 'Now don't you go and stab your man Sugar, next, because you might kill him, and that will be serious.'

She looked up puzzled. 'What's he done?'

Ratigan was flustered. 'Oh, I thought you knew that he was trying to steal your money, too.'

A tiny smile peeped through her tears. 'Oh, I ain't mad at him for that,' she said. 'He was just doing what comes natural.'

Ratigan called it a finish. A matron came and locked her up until the wagon came to take her downtown again for arraignment next morning.

No sooner had the key turned in the lock than she was singing:

> *I'm blue*
> *But I won't be blue always*
> *'Cause the sun's going to shine in my back door*
> *Some day.*

Some days later, when Sweet Prophet was asked by members of the colored press why he had taken her money, he replied,

'I needed it. It takes a lot of money to be a prophet these days. It's the high cost of living.'

All Shot Up

1

It was eleven-thirty at night on ground-hog day in Harlem. It was bitter cold, and the Harlem ground hogs, as the warm-blooded Harlem citizens are called during the cold winter months, were sung in their holes.

All except one.

On the dark crosstown street off Convent Avenue, bordering the estate of the convent from which the avenue derives its name, a man was taking a wheel from a car parked in the shadow of the convent wall. He was wearing dark-brown coveralls, a woolen-lined army fatigue jacket and a fur-lined, dark-plaid hunter's cap.

He had the inside wheel jacked up on the slanting street, making the car tilt dangerously. But he was unconcerned. He worked swiftly, without light. In the almost black dark, his face was imperceptible. At certain angles the whites of his eyes twinkled like luminous crescents stirred by the wind. His breath made pale white geysers, coming from his unseen face.

He leaned the wheel against the side of the car, lowered the axle to the pavement, glanced briefly up and down the street and began jacking up the outside wheel.

He had the wheel jacked up and the dust cap off and was fitting his wrench to a lug, when the lights of a car, turning into the street from Convent Avenue, caused him to jump back into the shadows.

The car approached and passed, not going fast, not going slow.

His eyes popped. He knew he was sober. He hadn't been drinking any whiskey and he hadn't been smoking any weed. But he didn't believe what he saw. It was a mirage; but this was not the desert, and he was not dying of thirst. In fact he was cold enough for his guts to freeze; and the only thing he wanted to drink was hot rum and lemon.

He saw a Cadillac pass, the likes of which he had never seen. And his business was cars.

This Cadillac looked as though it were made of solid gold. All except the top, which was some kind of light, shining fabric. It looked big enough to cross the ocean, if it could swim. It lit up the black-dark street like a passing bonfire.

The instrument panel gave off strange blue light. It was just strong enough to illuminate the three persons occupying the front seat.

The man driving wore a coonskin Davy Crockett cap, with a big bushy tail. Beside him sat the beauty queen of Africa with eyes like frostbitten plums and a smile showing blue-dyed teeth in a black-painted skeleton's head.

The joker's heart gave a lurch. There was something shockingly familiar about that face. But it was impossible for his own true Sassafras to be riding about in a brand-new Caddy with two strange men at this hour of the night. So his gaze switched quickly to the third party, who was wearing a black Homburg and a white silk scarf and had a small, bearded face like some kind of amateur magician.

In the soft, blue-tinted light they looked like things that couldn't happen, not even in Harlem on ground-hog night.

He looked at the license of the big gold car to steady himself. It was a dealer's license. He felt a momentary reassurance. Must be a publicity gag.

All of a sudden a woman came out of nowhere. He had just time enough to see that she was an old woman dressed in solid black, her silver-white hair shining briefly in the headlights before she was hit by the golden Cadillac and knocked down.

He felt his scalp crawl and his kinky hair stand straight up beneath his fur-lined cap. He wondered if he was dreaming.

But the Cadillac took on speed. That was no dream. That was the thing to do. Just what he would have done if he had run over an old woman on a dark, deserted street.

He hadn't seen the Cadillac actually run over the old woman. But there she lay and there it went. So it must have run over her. It made sense.

Anyway, he wasn't flipping his lid. Now the question was – should he get this other wheel or should he scram with the one he had? He had an order for two. He needed the money. That little chippie he was so crazy about had told him the palm needed greasing. She didn't say palm, but it meant the same thing: money – the one lubrication for love.

If the old lady wasn't dead, she was past caring. And it wouldn't take him but ninety seconds to have this wheel off ... He was starting to bend over to his task when the next sight froze him. The old lady had moved. He noticed it at first out of the corners of his eyes; then his head jerked up.

She was getting up. She had her two hands on the pavement and one knee up, and she was pushing to her feet. He could hear her laughing to herself. He felt the goose pimples breaking out down his back, and his scalp began to crawl like a battlefield of lice. If this kept up, his black kinky hair was going to turn out white as bleached cotton and straight as the beard of Jesus Christ.

He was watching the old lady, his brain trying to absorb the impact of what his eyes were registering, when the second car turned the corner. He didn't see it until it went past.

It was a big black sedan with the lights off, traveling at a hip-tightening clip, and it made a sound like someone blowing suddenly in his ear.

The old lady had got both feet planted and was standing bent over, bear-fashion, with all four feet and hands on the ground, just about to straighten up, when the big black sedan hit her in the rump.

He never knew how he saw it; the street was black dark, the old lady was dressed in black, the car was black. But he saw it. Either with his eyes or with his mind.

He saw the old lady flying through the air, arms and legs spread out, black garments spread out in the wind like a nuclear-powered vampire full of fresh virgin's blood. She was flying in an oblique line to the left; the black car was streaking straight ahead; and her snow-white hair was flying off to the right and rising, like a homing pigeon headed for the nest.

Furthermore, in the front seat of the black sedan were the dark silhouettes of three uniformed cops.

Now this joker had seen the face of violence in many makeups. The quick, insensate leap across the river Styx was no news to him. He was not naive about the grisly jokes of death.

But what he saw now scrambled his brains. His head was running in all four directions; but his feet were just standing there like a yokel in a carnival harem. He turned around a couple of times as though he were looking for something. For what he didn't know.

Then he saw the car wheel leaning against the side of the jacked-up car. The wheel had a whitewall tire.

He grabbed the wheel and started running toward Convent Avenue. But the wheel was too heavy, so he put it down and began rolling it like a kid does a hoop.

That stretch of Convent Avenue goes down a steep hill toward 125th Street. When he came into Convent Avenue he turned the wheel down the hill. The wheel bounced over the curb and increased speed as it went down the hill. He kept up with it until it came to the next crossing. The wheel dropped from the curb and crossed the street. He stumbled slightly, and the wheel gained on him. When the wheel hit the next curb it bounced high in the air, and when it came down it went away like a super-charged sports car.

He looked down the hill and saw two cops standing beneath a street lamp at the intersection of 126th or 127th Street. He put on the brakes and skidded to a stop, made a circle and went up the cross street he had passed. He disappeared into the night.

The wheel kept on down the street and knocked the legs out from underneath the two cops, knocked down a lady coming from the supermarket with a bag full of groceries, swerved out into the street, passed through the traffic of 125th Street without touching a thing, bounced over the sidewalk and crashed through the street-level door of a tenement facing the start of Convent Avenue.

A heavy-set, middle-aged man wearing a felt skull cap, old mended sweater, corduroy pants and felt slippers, was emerging from the back apartment when the wheel crashed into the back wall of the hallway. He gave it a look, then did a double take. He looked about quickly, and, seeing no one, grabbed it, ducked back into his apartment and locked the door. It wasn't every day manna fell from heaven.

2

Roman Hill was driving the Cadillac. His thick, muscular shoulders, developed from handling a two-mule plough in the Alabama cotton fields, were hunched inside of his greasy leather jacket as though he were reining the four horsemen of the Apocalypse of St John the Divine.

'Watch out!' Sassafras screamed. It was enough to raise the dead.

'Huh!' Air gushed from his mouth, and he gripped the wheel in his big, horny hands hard enough to break it.

He didn't see the old lady. It was the scream that did it. When he first saw the old lady she was caught in the left headlamp as though she had come out of the ground. His cocked gray eyes tried to leave his head in opposite directions.

'Look out!' he shouted as he tromped on the brake.

His two passengers sailed forward against the instrument panel, and he bumped his chest against the steering wheel.

The old lady disappeared.

'My God, where she at?' he asked in a panic-stricken voice.

'You hit her!' Sassafras exclaimed.

'Step on it!' Mister Baron cried.

'Huh?' Roman's slack, tan face looked stupid from shock.

'Let's go, for God's sake,' Mister Baron urged. 'You've killed her. You don't want to stay here and get caught, do you?'

'Bleeding Jesus!' Roman muttered stupidly, and stepped on the gas.

The Cadillac took off as though it had been spurred in the cylinders.

'Stop!' Sassafras screamed again. 'You ain't done nothing.'

The Cadillac slowed.

'Don't listen to this woman, fool,' Mister Baron shouted. 'You'll get one to twenty years in jail.'

'Why come?' Sassafras argued in a high keening voice.

She had a long, oval face with under-developed features and coal-black skin; and her sloe eyes glittered like glass. 'She walked right out in front of him; I'll swear to it.'

'You're crazy, woman,' Mister Baron hissed. 'He hasn't got any driver's license; he hasn't got any insurance; he hasn't even got the car registered. They'd put him in jail just for driving it; and, for running over a woman and killing her, they'll lock him in Sing Sing and throw away the key.'

'Of all the mother-raping luck,' Roman said hoarsely as realization began penetrating his shock. 'Here I is, ain't driven my new car a half hour, and done already run over some woman and killed her stone dead.'

His forehead knotted in a tight frown and he sounded as though he might cry. But the Cadillac took off again with determination.

'Let's go back and see,' Sassafras begged. 'I didn't feel no bump.'

'You wouldn't feel any bump in this car,' Mister Baron said. 'It could run over a railroad tie and you wouldn't feel it.'

'He's right, honey,' Roman agreed. 'Ain't nothing but to high-tail it now.'

The big black Buick without lights cut in front of the Cadillac and a cop yelled out the open window: 'Pull up!'

Roman had a notion to try to cut around the Buick and escape, but Mister Baron shrieked, 'Stop – don't dent the fenders.'

Sassafras gave him a scornful look.

All three cops piled out of the Buick and converged on the Cadillac with drawn pistols. One of the cops was white; he and one of the colored cops swung short-barreled .38 caliber police specials; the other had a long flat .38 Colt automatic.

'Get out with your hands up,' one of the colored cops ordered in a hard, hurried voice.

'Right,' the white cop echoed.

'What is this all about, officer?' Mister Baron said haughtily, assuming an indignant attitude.

'Manslaughter,' the colored cop said harshly.

'Hit and run,' the white cop echoed.

'We ain't hit nobody,' Sassafras protested in her keening, nerve-scraping voice.

'Tell it to the judge,' the colored cop said.

The white cop opened the outside door of the Cadillac and jerked Mister Baron from his seat. He handled him roughly, gripping the lapels of his Chesterfield coat.

Roman had got out on the other side and was standing holding his hands level with his shoulders.

The white cop jerked Mister Baron out of the way so Sassafras could alight.

'Listen to me for a moment,' Mister Baron said in a low persuasive voice. 'There hasn't anything happened that can't be settled between the few of us. The woman's not hurt bad. I could see in the rear view mirror that she was getting up.'

Mister Baron was small and effeminate with unusually expressive eyes for a man. They were a strange shade of light brown, fringed with long, black, curling lashes. But they fitted his girlish, heart-shaped face. His only masculine feature was the small fuzzy mustache and the bebop goatee that looked as though it might have been stuck on his chin with paste.

He was using his eyes now for all they were worth.

'If you want to be reasonable, this doesn't have to go to court. And,' he added, fluttering his lashes, 'you can benefit in more ways than one – if you know what I mean.'

The three cops exchanged glances.

Sassafras shook herself and looked at Mister Baron with infinite scorn. A small-boned, doll-like girl with a bottom like a duck's, she was wearing a gray imitation fur coat and a red knitted cap which might have belonged to one of the seven dwarfs.

'If you're including me, you're barking up the wrong tree,' she said.

'What's unusual about you, dear,' Mister Baron said cattily.

'How much?' the white cop asked.

Mister Baron hesitated, appraising the cop. 'Five hundred,' he offered tentatively.

'Well, what about the old lady, if she ain't dead,' Sassafras put in. 'What you going to give her?'

'Let her lump it,' Mister Baron said brutally.

'Put these two squares in the car,' the white cop said.

One of the colored cops took Sassafras by the arm and steered her to the Buick.

Roman went docilely, still holding his hands shoulder-high. He looked like a joker who's bet his fortune on a sure thing and lost.

The cop hadn't troubled to search him. He didn't search him now. 'Get in the back,' he ordered.

Roman began to plead. 'If you-all will give me just one more chance—'

The cop cut him off. 'I ain't your mammy.'

Roman got in and sat dejectedly, shoulders drooping, head so bowed his chin rested on his chest. Sassafras came in from the other side. She took one look at him and burst out crying.

The cops ignored them and turned toward Mister Baron who stood confronting the white cop in the beam from the Cadillac's lamps.

'Douse those lights,' the white cop said.

A colored cop walked over and turned off the lights.

The white cop cased the street. On the south side, old-fashioned residences with high stone steps, which had been converted into rooming houses or cut up into kitchenettes, were squeezed between apartment houses built for the over-flowing white population in the 1920s, all taken over now by Ham's and Hagar's children.

On the north side was the high, crumbling stone wall of the convent, topped by the skeletons of trees. None of the convent buildings were visible from the street.

Aside from themselves, there was not a person in sight. Nothing moved but grit in the ice-cold wind.

'Five hundred all you got?' the white cop asked Mister Baron.

Mister Baron licked his lips, and his voice began to lilt. 'You and me could talk business,' he whispered.

'Come here,' the white cop said.

Mister Baron walked up close to the white cop as though he were going to nestle in his arms.

The white cop turned him around and closed his windpipe with a half nelson while twisting his right arm behind his back. Mister Baron beat at him futilely with his left hand.

A colored cop closed in and drew a plaited leather sap. The other cop lifted Mister Baron's Homburg, and the first cop sapped him back of the ear. Mister Baron gave a low soft sigh and went liquid. The white cop lowered him to the street, and the colored cop put the Homburg over Mister Baron's face.

The white cop went through Mister Baron's pockets with rapid efficiency. He found two scented white silk handkerchiefs, a case of miscellaneous keys, a diamond engagement ring stuck tightly about a plastic tube of lipstick, an ivory comb containing strands of Mister Baron's long wavy hair, a black rubber object shaped like a banana attached to an elastic band, and a package of one-hundred-dollar bills wrapped in greasy brown paper.

He grunted. The colored cops watched him with silent concentration. He put the package of bills into his side coat pocket and stuffed the remaining items back into Mister Baron's side overcoat pocket.

'Leave him here?' a colored cop asked.

'Naw, let's put him in the car,' the white cop said.

'We'd better get going,' the other cop urged. 'We're wasting too much time.'

'No need to hurry now,' the white cop said. 'We got it made.'

Without replying, the two colored cops picked up Mister Baron and carried him toward the Buick, while the white cop held the back door open.

Neither Roman nor Sassafras had seen a thing.

'What's happened to him?' Sassafras stopped crying long enough to ask.

'He fainted,' the white cop said. 'Get over.'

She moved toward the middle, and they propped Mister Baron in the corner of the seat.

'Hey, boy,' the white cop called to Roman.

Roman looked around.

'I'm going to impound your car, and my partners are going to stay here until the ambulance comes and then bring you to the station. And I don't want any trouble out of you folks; you understand?'

'Yassuh,' Roman said dully, as though the world had come to an end.

'All right,' the white cop said. 'Just let this be a lesson; you can't buy justice.'

'It weren't him,' Sassafras said.

'You just keep him quiet if you know what's good for you,' the cop said, and slammed the door.

He walked unhurriedly back to the Cadillac. One of the colored cops was sitting behind the wheel, the other sitting beside him. The white cop sat on the outside and slammed the door.

The cop driving started the motor and began easing off without turning on the lights. The big golden Cadillac crept silently around the back end of the Buick and had started past before Sassafras noticed it.

'Look, they is taking our car,' she cried.

Roman was too dejected to look up. 'He's impounding it,' he muttered.

'It ain't just him; it's all of them,' she said.

Roman's cocked eyes came up in a startled face. 'Why you reckon they is doing that?' he asked stupidly.

'I bet my life they is stealing it,' she said.

Roman jumped as though a time bomb had gone off in his pants. 'Stealing my car!' he shouted, his hard, cable-like muscles coming into violent life.

He had the door open and was out on the pavement and pursuing the golden Cadillac before she could start screaming. She opened her mouth and let loose a scream that caused windows to pop open all up and down the street.

Roman was the only one who didn't hear her. His big, muscle-bound body was rolling as he ran, as though the sloping black pavement were the deck of a ship caught in a storm at sea. He was tugging at something stuck down his pants leg, beneath his leather jacket. Finally he came out with a big, rusty .45 caliber revolver, but before he had a chance to fire it the Cadillac had turned the corner and disappeared from sight.

A joker on a motorcycle with a sidecar was pulling out from the curb when the big Cadillac suddenly bore down on him and the driver switched on the lights. He did a quick turn back toward the curb. From the corners of his eyes he saw a golden Cadillac pass at a blinding speed. The silhouettes of three cops occupying the front seat flashed briefly across his vision. His brain did a double take and flipped.

This joker had seen this Cadillac a short time before. At that time the occupants had been two civilians and a woman. There couldn't be but one Cadillac like that in Harlem, he was sure. If there was such a Cadillac. If he wasn't just blowing his top.

This joker was wearing dark-brown coveralls, a woolen-lined army fatigue jacket and a fur-lined, dark-plaid hunter's cap. There wasn't but one joker looking like this outside on this bitter cold night.

'No, it ain't true,' the joker said to himself. 'Either I ain't me or what I seen ain't that.'

While he was trying to figure out which was which a big black sedan screamed around the corner with its bright lights splitting open the black-dark night.

It was a Buick sedan, and it looked familiar. But not nearly so familiar as the woman he'd seen a short time before in the golden Cadillac. However, now the freak with the coonskin cap who had been driving the Cadillac was driving the Buick.

All of it was so crazy it was reassuring. He bent over the handlebars of his motorcycle, and began laughing as though he had gone crazy himself.

'Haw haw haw.' He laughed, and then began talking to himself. 'Whatever it is I is dreaming, one thing is for sure – ain't none of it true.'

3

The switchboard in the precinct station was jammed.

The switchboard sergeant relayed the reports to Desk Lieutenant Anderson in a bored, monotonous voice: 'There's a woman who lives across the street from the convent says murder and rape taking place in the street . . .'

Lieutenant Anderson yawned. 'Every time a man beats his wife some busybody calls in and says she's being raped and murdered – the wife, I mean. And God knows some of them could use a little of it – the busybodies, I mean.'

'. . . another woman from the same vicinity. Says someone is torturing a dog . . .'

'Tell her we're sending an officer over right away,' Anderson said. 'Tell her dogs are our best friends.'

'She hung up. But here's another one. Claims the nuns are having an orgy.'

'Something's going on,' Anderson conceded. 'Send Joe Abrams and his partner over to take a look.'

The sergeant switched on the radio. 'Come in, Joe Abrams.'

Joe Abrams came in.

'Take a look along the south side of the convent.'

'Right,' Joe Abrams said.

'Patrolman Stick calling from a box on 125th Street,' the sergeant said to Anderson. 'Claims he and his partner, Sam Price were attacked and unfooted by a flying saucer someone has released in the neighborhood.'

'Order them to report here before going off duty for an alcohol test,' Anderson said sternly.

The sergeant chuckled as he relayed the order. Then he plugged in another call, and his face went grim.

'Man giving his name as Benjamin Zazuly, calling from the Paris Bar on 125th Street, reporting a double murder. Says two men dead on the sidewalk in front of the bar. One a white man. A third man unconscious. Thinks he's Casper Holmes . . .'

Anderson's fist came down on the desk, and his lean, hard face went bitter. 'Goddammit, everything happens to me,' he said, but the moment he had said it he regretted it.

'Get the other two cars over there,' he directed in a steady voice. The veins throbbed in his temples, and his pale-blue eyes looked remote.

He waited until the sergeant had contacted the two prowl cars and dispatched them to the scene. Then he said, 'Get Jones and Johnson.'

While the sergeant was calling for Jones and Johnson to come in, Anderson said anxiously, 'Let us hope nothing has happened to Holmes.'

The sergeant couldn't get Jones and Johnson.

Anderson stood up. 'Keep trying,' he ordered. 'I'm going to run over and take a quick look for myself.'

The reason the sergeant couldn't get Grave Digger Jones and Coffin Ed Johnson was that they were in the back room of Mammy Louise's pork store eating hot 'chicken feetsy', a Geechy dish of stewed chicken feet, rice, okra and red chili peppers. On a cold night like this it kept a warm fire burning in the stomach, and the white, tender gristle of the chicken feet gave a solid packing to the guts.

There were three wooden tables covered with oilcloth of such a bilious color that only the adhesive consistency of Mammy Louise's Geechy stews could hold the food in the stomach. Against the side wall was a coal-burning stove flanked by copper water tanks. Pots of cooking foods bubbled on the hot lids, giving the small, close room the steamy, luxurious feeling of a Turkish bath.

Grave Digger and Coffin Ed were sitting at the table farthest from the stove, their coats draped over the backs of wooden chairs. Their beat-up black hats hung above their overcoats on nails in the outside wall. Sweat beaded on their skulls underneath their short-cropped, kinky hair and streamed down their dark, intent faces. Coffin Ed's hair was peppered with gray. He had a crescent-shaped scar on the right-side top of his skull, where Grave Digger had hit him with his pistol barrel, the time he had gone berserk after being blinded by acid thrown into his face. That had been more than three years ago, and the acid scars had been covered by skin grafted from his thigh. But the new skin was a shade or so lighter than his natural face skin and it had been grafted on in pieces. The result was that Coffin Ed's face looked as though it had been made up in Hollywood for the role of the Frankenstein monster. Grave Digger's rough, lumpy face could have belonged to any number of hard, Harlem characters.

Grave Digger sucked the gristle from his last chicken foot and spat the small white bones onto the pile on his plate.

'I'll bet you a bottle he don't make it,' he said in a low voice, barely audible.

Coffin Ed looked at his wrist watch. 'What kind of bet is

that,' he replied in a similar tone of voice. 'It's already five minutes to twelve, and she got off at eleven-thirty. You think she's waiting for him.'

'Naw, but he thinks so.'

They glanced surreptitiously at a man sitting in a worn wooden armchair in the corner beside the stove. He was a short, fat, bald-headed man with the round, black, mobile face of a natural-born comedian. Except for an overcoat, he was dressed for the street. He was staring across at them with a pleading look.

He was Mister Louise, Mammy's husband. He had been picking up a hot little brownskin waitress at the Fischer Cafeteria next to the 125th Street railroad station every Saturday night since the new year began.

But Mammy Louise had got a bulldog. It was a six-year-old bulldog of a dirty white color with a mouth big enough to let in full-grown cats. It sat on its haunches directly in front of Mister Louise's shinily shod feet and stared up into his desperate face with a lidded, unblinking look. Its pink mouth was wide open as it panted in the steamy heat; its red tongue hung down its chest. There was a big wet spot on the floor where it had been drooling as though it would like nothing better than a hunk of Mister Louise's fat black meat.

'He wants us to help him,' Coffin Ed whispered.

'And get ourselves chawed up by that dog instead of him.'

Mammy Louise looked up from the stove where she had been stirring a pot. She was fatter than Mister Louise, but not quite as tall. She wore an old woolen bathrobe over an old jersey dress, under which were layers of warm woolen underclothing. Over the bathrobe she wore a black knitted shawl; her head was protected by a man's beaver hat with a turned-up brim, and her feet were encased in fur-lined woodsmen's boots.

She was a Geechy, born and raised in the swamps south of Tater Patch, South Carolina. Geechies are a mélange of runaway African slaves and Seminole Indians, native to the Carolinas and Florida. Their mother tongue is a mixture of African dialects and the Seminole language; and she spoke English with a strange, indefinable accent that sounded somewhat similar to a conference of crows.

'What you two p'licemens whispering about so seriously?' she asked suspiciously.

It took a moment before they could piece together what she said.

'We got a bet,' Grave Digger replied with a straight face.

'Naw we haven't,' Coffin Ed denied.

'You p'licemens,' she said scornfully. 'Gamblin' an' carryin' on an' whippin' innocent folkses' heads with your big pistols.'

'Not if they're innocent,' Grave Digger contradicted.

'Don't tell me,' she said argumentatively. 'I has seen you.' She curled her thick, sensuous lips. 'Whippin' grown men about as if they was children. Mister Louise wouldn't stand for it,' she added, looking slyly from her husband's desperate face to the slobbering bulldog. 'Get up, Mister Louise, and show these p'licemens how you captured them train robbers that time.'

Mister Louise looked at her gratefully and started to his feet. The bulldog raised up and growled a warning. Mister Louise slumped back into his seat.

Mammy Louise winked her off eye at the detectives. 'Mister Louise ain't so pokey tonight,' she explained. 'He just want to set here and keep me company.'

'So we noticed,' Coffin Ed said.

Mister Louise stared longingly at the long-barreled, nickel-plated .38 caliber revolvers sticking from the two detectives' shoulder holsters.

They heard the front door to the store open and bang shut. Feet stamped. A whisky-thick voice called, 'Hey, Mammy Louise, come out here and give me a pot of them frozen chitterlings.'

She waddled through the curtained doorway leading to the store. They heard her opening a five-gallon milk can and shuffling about, and the customer protesting, 'I don't wants them loose chitterlings; I wants some frozen chitterlings,' and her sharp reply, 'If you wants to eat 'em frozen just take 'em outside and freeze 'em; hit's cold enough.'

Grave Digger said, 'Mammy Louise can't stand this Northern climate.'

'She got enough fat to keep her warm at the North Pole,' Coffin Ed replied.

'The trouble is, her fat gets cold.'

Mister Louise begged in a piteous voice, 'One of you gennelmens shoot him for me, won't you.' He glanced toward the curtained doorway and added, 'I'll pay you.'

'It wouldn't kill him,' Coffin Ed replied solemnly.

'Bullets would just bounce off his head,' Grave Digger supplemented.

Mammy Louise came back and looked at her husband suspiciously. Then she said to the detectives, 'Your car is talking.'

'I'll get it,' Grave Digger said, getting to his feet before he'd finished saying it.

He slipped an arm through his jacket, grabbed his hat from the peg and pushed through the curtains as he poked his second arm into its sleeve.

The bulldog rolled its pink eyes at his receding figure and looked at Mammy Louise for instructions. But she paid it no attention. She was half moaning to herself. 'Trouble, always trouble in dis wicked city. Whar Ah comes from—'

'There ain't no law,' Coffin Ed cut her off as he put on his jacket. 'Folks cut one another's throats and go on about their business.'

'It's better than getting kilt by the law,' she argued. 'You can't pay for one death by another one. Salvation ain't the swapping market.'

Coffin Ed jammed his hat on his head, turned up the brim and slipped into his overcoat.

'Tell it to the voters, Mammy,' he said absently as he took down Grave Digger's overcoat and straightened out a sleeve. 'I didn't make these laws.'

'I'll tell it to everybody,' she said.

Grave Digger came back in a hurry. His face was set.

'Hell's broke loose on the street,' he said, poking his arm into the coat Coffin Ed held for him.

'We'd better hop it then,' Coffin Ed said.

Unnoticed by anyone but Mister Louise, the bulldog had moved over to block the curtained doorway. When Grave Digger moved toward it, the dog planted its feet and growled.

Grave Digger's long, gleaming, nickel-plated revolver came out in his hand like a feat of legerdemain, but Mammy Louise swooped down on the dog and dragged it off before he did it injury.

'Not dem, Lawd Jim, mah God, dawg,' she cried. 'You can't stop dem from goin' nowhere. Them is de *mens*.'

4

The small, battered black sedan parked at the curb in front of Mammy Louise's *Hog Store: open day & night* was still talking when they came out on the street. Grave Digger slid beneath the wheel, and Coffin Ed went around and climbed in from the other side.

The store was on 124th Street between Seventh and Eighth Avenues, and the car was pointing toward Seventh.

The Paris Bar was due north as the bird flies on 125th Street, midway between the Apollo Bar and the Palm Café and across the street from Blumstein's Department Store.

It was ten minutes by foot, if you were on your way to church, about two and a half minutes if your old lady was chasing you with a razor.

Coffin Ed checked his watch when Grave Digger mashed the starter. The little car might have looked like a bow-legged turtle, but it ran like an antelope.

It passed the Theresa Hotel, going up the wrong side of the street, bright lights on and siren screaming. Jokers in the lobby staring out the windows scattered like a hurricane had passed. They made it in thirty-three seconds.

Two prowl cars and Lieutenant Anderson's black sedan were parked in front of the Paris Bar, taking up all the available space. Save for the cops standing about in clusters, the street was deserted.

'One's a white man,' Grave Digger said.

'What else?' Coffin Ed replied.

What he meant was what else could keep the black citizens away from the circus provided by a killing.

'Butts going to jump,' Grave Digger added as he made a

sharp-angled turn and squeezed between the front car and a fireplug, jumping the curb.

Before he had dragged to a stop, crosswise the sidewalk, just short of banging into the grilled front of a drugstore adjacent to the Paris Bar, they saw the three prone figures on the sidewalk.

The one nearest wore a belted trench coat and a dark snap-brim hat that was still clinging to his head. He lay flat on his belly, his legs spread and his feet resting on his toes. His left arm was folded down beside him with the palm turned up; his right arm was flung out at an angle, still gripping a short-barreled revolver. Street light shone on the soles of his shoes, showing runover rubber heels and recent toecaps. The top part of his face was shaded by his hat brim, but orange light from the neon bar sign lit the lower part, showing the tip of a hooked nose and a long, pointed chin and leaving the thin, compressed lips invisible, so that the face seemed to lack a mouth.

One glance was enough to tell that he was dead.

The Paris Bar had a stainless-steel front framing the two big plate-glass windows that flanked the doorway. The left-side steel baseboard directly behind the stiff was punctured with bullet holes.

With the second stiff, it was different. He lay piled up like a wet towel directly in front of the door. His smooth, handsome black face peered from folds of gay-colored clothes with a look of infinite surprise. He didn't look so much dead from gunshot as from shock; but the small, round, purple-lipped hole above his right temple told the story.

The third figure was encircled by cops.

Grave Digger and Coffin Ed alighted and converged on the first stiff.

'Two hits through the top of the hat,' Grave Digger observed, his gaze roving. 'He was lying on his belly and they nailed the hat on tighter.'

'Two in the right shoulder and one in the left neck,' said Coffin Ed. 'Somebody sure wanted this son dead.'

'No one man scored five hits on this guy and him with a gun in his hand,' Grave Digger stated.

'The way I see it, two or more guns were shooting from

down there where Casper is lying, and a third gun cross-fired from a car parked at the curb.'

'Yeah,' Grave Digger agreed, counting the bullet holes in the stainless-steel baseboard. 'Somebody was using an automatic in the car and missed all ten times.'

'This guy was lying flat, and the gun in the car was shooting over him, but it gave the ones in front a chance to ice him.'

Grave Digger nodded. 'This guy knew his business, but he was outgunned.'

'Over here!' Lieutenant Anderson called.

He and a white precinct detective named Haggerty and two prowl-car cops were standing about an unconscious colored man stretched out on the sidewalk.

Grave Digger and Coffin Ed glanced briefly at the second stiff as they ambled past.

'Know him?' Grave Digger asked.

'One of the girl-boys,' Coffin Ed said.

Detective Haggerty skinned back his teeth when they approached. 'Every time I see you big fellows I think of two hog farmers lost in the city,' he greeted.

Grave Digger flipped him a look. 'The office wit.'

Coffin Ed ignored him.

Both of them stared down at the unconscious figure. He had been turned over onto his back, and his bowler placed beneath his head for a pillow. His hands were folded across his chest, and his eyes were closed. But for the labored breathing, he might have been dead.

He was wearing a navy-blue cashmere coat with handstitched lapels and patch pockets. His shirt was hidden by a black silk scarf looped at the throat. The trousers were of a dark-blue flannel with a soft chalk stripe. Black calfskin shoes, practically new, finished the ensemble.

He had a broad, smooth-shaven face with a square, aggressive-looking chin. The black skin had a creamy, massaged look, and the short, carefully clipped kinky hair was snow-white. His appearance was impressive.

'Casper looks natural,' Coffin Ed said with a straight face.

'He was sapped behind the left ear,' Lieutenant Anderson stated.

'How do you figure it?' Grave Digger asked.

'It seems as though Holmes was robbed, but the rest doesn't figure,' Anderson confessed.

'Laughing-boy yonder must have stepped out the bar to watch the bullets passing,' Haggerty cracked, amused by his own humor.

'One he didn't see,' a white cop added, grinning.

Anderson wiped off the grin with a look.

'Who's the gunman?' Coffin Ed asked.

'We haven't made him,' Anderson said. 'Haven't touched him. We're waiting for the M.E. and the crew from Homicide.'

'What do the witnesses say?'

'Witnesses?'

'Somebody in the bar must have seen the whole caper.'

'Yeah, but we haven't got any of them to admit it,' Anderson said. 'You know how it is when a white man gets killed. No one wants to get involved. I've sent for the wagon, and I'm going to take them all in.'

'Let me talk to them first,' Coffin Ed said.

'Okay, give it a try.'

Coffin Ed ambled toward the entrance to the bar, which was being guarded by a white patrolman.

Grave Digger looked inquiringly at a white civilian who had edged into the group.

'This is Mr Zazuly,' Anderson said. 'He got here right after the shooting and telephoned the station.'

'What did he see?' Grave Digger asked.

'When I got here the street was overrun with people,' Mr Zazuly said, his magnified eyes blinking rapidly behind the thick lenses of his horn-rimmed spectacles. 'The two men were lying there just as you see them, and not an officer in sight.'

'He's an accountant for Blumstein's,' Anderson explained.

'Did he hear the shooting?'

'Of course I heard the shooting. It sounded like the Second World War. And not a policeman in sight.' His round, owlish face glared from a mohair muffler with a look of extreme outrage. 'Gang wars on a main thoroughfare like this. Right out in the broad open,' he went on indignantly. 'Where were the police, I ask you?'

Grave Digger looked sheepish.

No one answered him.

'I'm going to write a complaint to the Commissioner,' he threatened.

The sound of a siren grew quickly in the night.

'Here comes the ambulance,' Anderson said with relief.

The red eye of the ambulance was coming up 125th Street fast, from the direction of Lenox Avenue.

Grave Digger addressed Mr Zazuly directly. 'And that's all you saw?'

'What did you expect him to see?' Haggerty cracked. 'Look at those specs.'

The ambulance double-parked beside a prowl car, and the cops stood by silently while the intern made a cursory examination.

'Can you give him something to bring him to?' Anderson asked him.

'Give him what?' the intern replied.

'Well, when will he be able to talk?'

'Can't say, Inspector, he might have concussion.'

'I see you're going to get ahead fast,' Anderson commented.

Nothing more was said while Casper Holmes was rolled onto the stretcher and moved.

Anderson glanced at his watch. 'Homicide ought to be getting here,' he said anxiously.

'The stiffs won't spoil in this weather,' Haggerty said, turning up the collar of his overcoat and putting his back to the ice-cold, dust-laden wind.

'I'm going to see how Ed's making out,' Grave Digger said, and strolled toward the entrance to the Paris Bar.

When Coffin Ed entered the Paris Bar, not one person looked in his direction.

It was a long, narrow room, with the bar running the length of the left side, taking up half the space. Customers sat on bar stools or stood; there were no tables.

The usual Saturday night crowd was gathered, bitchy young men wearing peacock clothes with bright-colored caps, blue and silver and gold and purple, perched atop greasy curls straight from the barbershops at seven dollars a treatment. And the big, strong, rough-looking men who made life wonderful for them. But there was not a woman present.

Coffin Ed was not a moralist. But their cliquish quality of freezing up on an outsider grated on his nerves.

'Don't everybody talk at once,' he shouted from the doorway.

No one said a word.

To a man, they were staring into their drinks as though competing in a contest of three wise monkeys: See nothing; hear nothing; say nothing. The contest was progressing toward a dead heat.

The three bartenders were rinsing glasses with an industriousness that would have gotten them all blacklisted by the bartenders' union.

Coffin Ed began swelling at the gills. His gaze flickered dangerously down the line, seeking a likely candidate to begin with. But they were all equally engrossed in silence.

'Don't try to give me that silent treatment,' he warned. 'We're all colored folks together.'

Someone in back giggled softly.

The uniformed white cop guarding the rear door stared at him with a dead-pan expression.

Coffin Ed's temper flared, and the grafted patches on his face began to twitch.

He spoke to the back of the joker on the first stool. 'All right, buddy boy, let's start with you. Which way did they go?'

The girlish young man continued to stare into his drink as though he were stone-deaf. The indirect lighting from the bar gave his smooth brown face a bemused look. His luminescent silver cap gleamed faintly like swamp-fire.

He was drinking a tall frappé highball of dark rum with a streak of grenadine, running down the center, called a 'Josephine Baker'. If La Baker herself had been reclining stark nude in the bottom of his glass, he could not have given her any more attention.

Coffin Ed took him roughly by the shoulder and turned him about.

'Which way did they go?' he repeated in a rasping voice.

The young man looked at him from big, brown, bedroom eyes that seemed incapable of comprehending anything but love.

'Go, sir? Who go?' he lisped.

Face jumping in a sudden flash of rage, Coffin Ed slapped him left-handed from the bar stool. The young man crashed against the wall and crumpled in a lump.

Eyes pivoted in his direction and pivoted away. He wasn't hurt so much as stunned. He thought it best just to lie there.

Coffin Ed looked at the next joker in line. He was an older man, dressed conservatively. Answers gushed from his mouth without his being questioned.

'They went west, that is down 125th Street, I don't mean to California.'

Coffin Ed's face looked so macabre the man had to swallow before he could continue.

'They was in a black Buick. There was three of 'em. One was driving and the other two pulled off the heist.'

He ran out of breath.

'Did you get the license?'

'License!' He looked as though Coffin Ed had abused his mother. 'What would I be doing getting their license? They looked like straight cops when they drove up, and for all I know they might just as well be straight cops.'

'Cops!' Coffin Ed stiffened.

'And when they took off I was lying on the floor like everybody else.'

'You said they were cops!'

'I don't mean they actually was cops,' the joker amended hastily. 'I figure you would know if they was real sure enough cops. All I means is they looked like cops.'

'In uniform?' Coffin Ed was taut as a crane cable, and his voice came in a rasping whisper.

'How else would I know if they looked like cops. I don't mean you, suh,' the joker hastened to add with an ingratiating smile. 'Everybody around here knows you is the *man*, no matter what you wears. All I means is these cops was dressed in cops' uniforms. Of course I ain't had no way of knowing whether they was cops or not. Naturally I wasn't

going to ask to see their shields. All I know is what I seen,
and they—'

Coffin Ed was thinking fast. He cut the joker off. 'Colored
men?'

'Two of 'em was. One was a white man.'

Heistmen impersonating cops. He was trying to remember
when was the last time that was worked in Harlem. Generally
that was a big-time deal.

'What did he look like?'

'Look like? Who look like?'

He had been concentrating so hard on trying to put the
puzzle together that he had forgotten the joker. His gaze came
back in hard focus.

'The white man. Don't start getting cute.'

'It was just like I say, boss, he looked like a cop. You know
how it is, boss,' he added slyly, giving Coffin Ed a confidential
wink. 'All these white cops look just alike.'

Under ordinary circumstances Coffin Ed would have passed
that one by; the color angle worked just about the same on
the force as it did in private life. He had played the 'all us is
black folks together' line himself on entering. But he wasn't
in the mood for comic patter.

'Listen, punk, this ain't funny, this is murder,' he said.

'Don't look at me, boss, I ain't done it,' the joker said,
throwing up his hands in comic pantomine as though to ward
off a blow.

He didn't really expect a blow, but he got one. Coffin
Ed's fists parted his hands and popped him in the left eye,
and he sailed off the stool to join the other joker on the
floor.

The customers began to mutter. He was getting their full
attention now, and they were squirming into life.

The next joker in line was standing up. He was a big,
rough-looking black man in a leather jacket and a cowskin
fez. But suddenly he felt too big for the situation and was
trying unsuccessfully to make himself smaller.

Coffin Ed measured him with bloodshot eyes. 'Do you
belong to the league, too?' he asked through gritted teeth.

'League? Nawsuh, boss. I mean if it's the wrong league I
sure don't belong to it.'

'The know-nothing league.'

'Not me, boss.' The big joker showed Coffin Ed a mouthful of teeth as proof that he didn't belong to any league, unless it was the dentists' league. 'I ain't scairt to tell the truth. I'll tell you everything I seen, I swear 'fore God. 'Course, that ain't much, but—'

'You saw two men get shot to death.'

'Heard it, boss. I wasn't in no position to see.'

'Three men masqueraded as cops—'

'I ain't seen but two, boss.'

'Robbed a man in broad view right outside of this joint—'

'I couldn't swear to it, boss; I didn't see that.'

'What did they get?'

'*Get?*' The joker acted as though he were unfamiliar with the word.

'Take?'

'Take? If they took anything, boss, I ain't seen it. I thought they was just a mess of cops doing their dirty work.'

Coffin Ed flipped.

He looped a right hook to the big joker's solar plexus, saw his mouth balloon with air. The cowskin fez flew from the big joker's head as he jackknifed forward. Coffin Ed caught him back of the neck with a loose, pulling grip, jerked his head down and uppercut him in the face with his right knee. It was a good gimmick; the knee was supposed to smash the joker's nose and fill his head with shooting stars. It worked nine times out of ten. But the big joker had his mouth open from the solar plexus punch, and his teeth crashed into Coffin Ed's kneecap like the jaws of a bear trap.

Coffin Ed grunted with pain as his leg went stiff and clutched the back of the big joker's leather jacket to keep from going down. The big joker butted him in the belly in a blind panic, trying to escape. Coffin Ed went down on his back, clinging to the leather jacket; and the big joker plunged forward over him, headed for the door. Coffin Ed pulled at the leather jacket in a choking rage. The jacket turned wrong side out, imprisoning the joker's arm and halting the forward plunge of his shoulders. But the rest of him kept on going, and he turned in a somersault and landed on his back. Coffin Ed reared up on his shoulders, made a half spin and kicked the big joker on the side of the jaw from topside down. The big joker shuddered and passed out.

Coffin Ed clutched the rim of the bar and pulled to his feet, favoring his game leg. He looked about for the next man in line. But there wasn't any line.

The customers had crowded to the back of the room and were beginning to panic. Knives flashed, and they were pushing and threatening one another.

The white cop at the back door was shouting, 'Get back! Get away from me or I'll shoot!'

Slowly and deliberately, Coffin Ed drew the long-barreled, nickel-plated .38 revolver from its shoulder holster.

'Now I want some straight answers from you minstrel-show comedians,' he said in a voice that grated on the nerves.

Someone let out a womanish scream.

Grave Digger came in from the street. Without taking a second look he opened his big mouth and shouted at the top of his voice: 'Straighten up!' Before his big voice bounced from the walls he had his big nickel-plated revolver, the twin of Coffin Ed's, out in his hand, in plain sight of everyone arrested by his voice.

Coffin Ed relaxed. A grim smile played about the edges of his scarred lips.

'Count off!' he bellowed in a voice to match Grave Digger's.

For good measure they fired four shots into the newly decorated ceiling.

Everybody froze. Not a whisper was heard. No one dared breathe.

Coffin Ed had killed a man for breaking wind. Grave Digger had shot both eyes out of a man who was holding a loaded automatic. The story was in Harlem that these two black detectives would kill a dead man in his coffin if he so much as moved.

The next moment cops of all descriptions erupted from the street. The Homicide crew had arrived and they invaded in force; a lieutenant and two detectives with their pistols out, a third detective with a submachine gun. The precinct lieutenant, Anderson, followed, with Haggerty at his heels and two uniformed cops bringing up the rear.

'What's this? What's happening? What gives?' the Homicide lieutenant shouted harshly.

'Just them two cowboys from the Harlem Q. ranch rounding up a passel of rustlers,' Haggerty cracked.

'Jesus Christ,' Anderson said, as though gasping. 'Use a little discretion, men. With what's already happened you'll have us filling our pants.'

'We're just trying to get some sense out of these people,' Grave Digger said.

The lieutenant from Homicide stared at him in popeyed amazement. 'You – you mean all you're trying to do is make these witnesses talk?'

'It works,' Grave Digger said.

'It quiets them,' Coffin Ed added. 'You'll notice it has a soothing effect on their nerves.'

All eyes turned toward the quiet, passive people crowded toward the rear.

'Well, I'll be God-damned,' the Homicide lieutenant said. 'Now I've seen everything.'

'Naw you ain't,' Haggerty said. 'You ain't seen nothing yet.'

'The wagon's here. We're going to take these people to the station for questioning,' Anderson said.

'Give us fifteen minutes with them first,' Grave Digger requested.

In the brief silence that followed, the head bartender said, 'Don't let 'em close us up, Chief – I'll tell you all about it.'

Eyes swung in his direction. He was a well-fed, intelligent-looking man of about thirty-five, who could have been palmed off as a Baptist preacher from one of the poorer congregations.

'See what I mean?' Haggerty said.

'Come on,' Anderson said. 'Your wit needs oiling.'

5

'It began with Snake Hips,' the bartender said, polishing a glass to occupy his hands.

'Snake Hips,' Grave Digger said incredulously. 'He's the female impersonator at the Down Beat Club up the street.'

'The *danseur*,' the bartender corrected with a straight face.

'What did he have to do with it?' Coffin Ed asked.

'Nothing. He was just dancing. He danced outside and we were watching him, and that's how we saw it happen.'

'Without a coat or hat? By himself? He left here and went outside to dance in this weather without a hat or coat – by himself?' Disbelief was written all over Grave Digger's face.

'He was just bitching off,' the bartender explained. He held the glass up to the light, blew on it and began polishing again. 'He had got himself a new lover, and he was just low-rating the man who used to be his lover before. You know how these people are; when they get mad at you, they get out in the street and start scandalizing you.'

'Who is the man?' Coffin Ed asked.

'Sir?'

'The man who was his former lover.'

The bartender looked for a place to hang his gaze. Finally he settled on the glass he was polishing. If his skin had been lighter, the blush would have showed. Finally he whispered. 'It was me, sir.'

Grave Digger brushed it off. 'All right, let's finish with Snake Hips. Who is his current lover?'

'I'm not sure, sir – you know how these things are with these people—' He choked a little, but they let it pass. 'I mean, one never really knows. He's been going around with a person called Black Beauty.'

They didn't ask him if this person was a man, and he didn't elaborate.

'But Black Beauty's been seen around town with a man named Baron; and I know for a fact Baron's been hanging around with a white man – I don't know his name.'

'You ever see him – the white man?' Coffin Ed asked.

'Yes, sir.'

They avoided asking him where.

'Was he one of the trio – the heistmen?' Grave Digger asked.

'Oh no, sir. He wasn't anything like that. He was a

sort of a gentleman type – you find on Broadway,' he amended.

'All right, that does for Snake Hips,' Grave Digger said as they stored away the information against future use. 'You know Casper Holmes by sight?'

'Yes, sir, he's a customer here.'

'What?'

The bartender shrugged slightly, spreading his hands, holding the glass in one and the towel in the other.

'Sometimes. Not a regular. It's just near his office, which is upstairs, and he drops by sometimes for a short one.'

'Did he pass by the front here?' Coffin Ed asked.

'Yes, sir. He must have just come from his office. But he didn't stop in here. Snake Hips was dancing, and he passed right by him as if he didn't see him – like he had something on his mind.'

'Does he know Snake Hips?'

The bartender lowered his eyes. 'It's possible, sir. Mr Holmes gets around.'

'Could Snake Hips' dancing act have been a tip-off?'

'Oh, I'm sure it wasn't that. He was just trying to drag me. You see I got a wife and two children—'

'And you still got time for these boys?'

'Well, that was it. I didn't—'

'Let him go on,' Grave Digger said harshly. 'So Casper didn't see him, or rather didn't acknowledge him.'

'It was more that. He must have seen him. But he was walking in a hurry, looking straight ahead and carrying a pigskin bag—'

Both detectives stiffened to alert.

'Brief case?' Grave Digger asked in an urgent whisper.

'Why, yes, sir. A pigskin brief case with a handle. It looked new. He was going toward Seventh Avenue, and I figured he was going to take a taxi.'

'Let us do the guessing.'

'Well, he usually parks his car out front. It wasn't there, so I figured—' Grave Digger's look cut him off. 'Well, anyway, he was just past the doorway when a black Buick sedan pulled to the curb—'

'There was parking space?'

'Yes, sir – it so happened that two cars had just pulled off.'

'You know whose they were?'

'The cars? No, sir. I think the drivers came from – or rather the passengers, there was a party of 'em – came from the Palm Café.'

'Casper notice it?'

'He didn't act like it. He kept on walking. Then two cops – or rather men dressed in cops' uniforms – got out and another one stayed behind the wheel. My first thought was that Mr Holmes was carrying valuables and the cops were a bodyguard. But Mr Holmes tried to walk past them – between them rather, because they sort of separated when he tried to pass them—'

'Where was the white man?'

'He was on Mr Holmes' right, toward the street. Mr Holmes was carrying the brief case on that side. Then they took him by the arms; one took hold of each arm. Mr Holmes seemed surprised, then mad.'

'You couldn't see his face from here.'

'No, sir. But his back stiffened, and he looked like he was mad, and I know he was saying something because I could see the side of his face working. It was lit by the sign light, and it seemed as if he was shouting, but of course I couldn't hear him.'

'Well, go on,' Grave Digger urged. 'We haven't got all night.'

'Well, sir, that was the first I figured there was something wrong. Then the next thing I knew I saw the white man knock Mr Holmes' hat off; he sort of flicked it off from behind so that it fell in front of Mr Holmes. And at the same time the colored cop – man – sapped Mr Holmes behind the left ear; he was on Mr Holmes' left side.'

'Did you see the sap?'

'Not too well. It looked like an ordinary leather-bound sap with a whalebone handle to me.'

'Did he hit him again?'

'No sir, once was enough. Mr Holmes went down like he was sitting, and the white man took the pigskin bag out of his hand.'

'Who else in the bar here saw this happen?'

'I don't think anybody else saw it. You see, the customers face this way and only us bartenders face in that direction, and the other bartenders was busy. It wasn't like they had made any noise. I saw it, but I couldn't hear a sound.'

'What about Snake Hips? Didn't he see what was happening, or was he too far gone?'

'He hadn't been banging, if that's what you mean. But he was dancing in a slow circle, doing a sort of shake dance, and he had his back to them.'

'But they must have seen him.'

'Must have. But they didn't pay him no attention. As far as they were concerned, he was harmless as a lamppost.'

'Why didn't you telephone the police?' Grave Digger asked.

'I didn't have time. I was going to, but the next thing I knew I heard a shot. A man appeared right outside of this window like he had come from nowhere. When I first heard the shot my first thought was they'd shot Snake Hips – the silly fool – then I saw this man standing there with one of those short bulldog-looking pistols held straight out in his right hand. Then I heard him say in a hard, dry voice, "Get 'em up!"'

'You heard him?'

'Yes, sir. You see, he didn't speak until after he had shot; and at the sound of the shot everybody inside of here went stone quiet.'

'That's when the two heistmen started shooting,' Coffin Ed surmised.

'No, sir. I don't know what they did because I wasn't looking at them no more. But they didn't start shooting with that man pointing that gun at them. But the cop – man – in the car started shooting. It was dark inside the car, and I could see the orange flashes.'

He ceased polishing the glass for the moment, and his brown face went ashy at the memory.

'Of course the man wasn't shooting at me, but the gun was pointing this way, and it seemed like I was looking down the barrel. I was scared enough to drop six babies, because it looked like he never was going to stop shooting.' He wiped sweat drops from his ashy face with the polishing towel.

'Eleven-shot automatic,' Coffin Ed said.

'It sounded like more than eleven shots to me,' the bartender contended.

'That's when you ducked,' Grave Digger said disappointedly, figuring the account was finished.

'That's when I should have ducked,' the bartender admitted. 'Everybody else ducked. But I ran to the front of the bar, trying to get Snake Hips' attention and call him inside, as if he hadn't heard all that shooting more than I did. But you don't know what you're thinking at a time like that. So I stood there waving my arms while the man in the car ducked out of sight. The white man had fell flat on his stomach when the shooting started, and I don't think he was hit then. I wasn't really looking, although I could see him from where I stood; but I was looking at the car, and he must have shot back at the man in the car because I saw two bullet holes suddenly appear in the right front window.'

'Now we're getting somewhere,' Coffin Ed said.

'Check,' Grave Digger echoed.

'I was still trying to get Snake Hips' attention,' the bartender admitted. 'But he was scared blind. He was just standing there with his arms straight up and his hands shaking like leaves. He was trembling all over and his coat was open, and I knew he must have been cold. I think he was saying – begging rather – for them not to shoot him—'

'Leave Snake Hips,' Coffin Ed said brutally. 'What about the other two?'

'Well, they must have begun shooting when the man in the car finished. Maybe they took advantage to get out their guns. When the shooting from the car stopped more shooting was still going on, and I looked over and saw flashes coming from both of their guns. Their pistols looked like the same kind of snubnosed pistol the man had on the ground. One of them was shooting from his right hand and the other from his left—'

'The white man the lefty?'

'No, sir, it was the colored man. He had his sap in his right hand, and was shooting from his hip—'

'From his hip?' Grave Digger said.

'Yes, sir, like a real Western gunman—'

'Hollywood style,' Coffin Ed said scornfully.

'Let him go on,' Grave Digger snapped.

'The white man had the brief case in his left hand, and he was shooting with his right hand held straight out in front of him like the man on the ground had done—'

'He's the son,' Coffin Ed muttered.

'Was either of them hit?' Grave Digger asked.

'I don't think so. I don't think the man on the ground ever got a chance to shoot at them. After the man in the car had finished shooting they opened up; or they might have even opened up before he finished shooting. Anyway, the man on the ground never had a chance.'

'And you were standing there watching all the time?' Grave Digger asked.

'Yes, sir, like a fool. I saw when Snake Hips was hit. At least I knew he was hit because he went straight down. He didn't fall like they do in the motion pictures; he just collapsed. I don't know who shot him, of course; but it was one of them up there beside Mr Holmes, because the man in the car had quit shooting by then. I figure it was the white man who shot him, because he was the one who was holding his pistol so high.'

'Don't you believe it,' Coffin Ed said. 'That son wasn't throwing bullets that wide apart.'

'His number came up, and that's that,' Grave Digger said. 'And you didn't see the man on the ground catch his.'

'Next time I noticed him he was just lying there like he had gone to sleep on his stomach, but to tell you the truth, sir, I wasn't paying no attention especially. I was waiting for the three cops – heistmen I mean – to leave so I could go out and get Snake Hips. Then when they did leave I thought what was the use – he was dead; I knew he was dead when he went down; then I remembered I wasn't supposed to move a dead body. So I just stood there.'

'And even then you didn't call the police,' Coffin Ed accused.

'No, sir.'

'What in the hell were you doing then? Hiding when it was all over?'

The bartender lowered his eyes. When his voice came it

was so low they had to lean forward to hear it. 'I was crying,' he confessed.

For a moment neither Grave Digger nor Coffin Ed had anywhere to look.

Then Grave Digger asked, in a voice unnecessarily harsh, 'Did you see the license of the Buick, by any chance?'

The bartender got himself under control. 'I didn't exactly look at it, I mean make a point of it – looking at it, I mean; then I couldn't see it too well; but it clicked in the back of my mind that it was a Yonkers number.'

'How did you notice that?'

'I live in Yonkers, and I was thinking it was fate that the car carrying the murderers of Snake Hips came from the place where I live.'

'Goddammit, let's bury Snake Hips,' Coffin Ed said roughly. 'Give us a description of the two men who got out of the car.'

'You're asking me more than I can do, sir. I really didn't look at their faces. Then the orange neon light from the bar sign was shining on them, and that makes faces look different from what they actually are; so I hardly ever look at faces outside. All I know is one man was black—'

'Not half black?'

'No sir, all black. And the other one was white.'

'Foreign.'

'It didn't strike me that way. I'd say Southern. Something about him reminded me of one of those Southern deputy sheriffs – sort of slouching when he moved, but moving faster than what it looked, and strong. Something sort of mean-looking about him, sadistic, I'd say. The kind of man who thinks just being white is everything.'

'Not the kind who'd be welcome in here,' Grave Digger said.

'No, sir. The fellows would be scared of him.'

'But not whores?'

'Whores, too. But they'd take his money just the same. And he might be the kind who'd spend it on cheap whores.'

'All right, describe the car.'

'It was just a plain black Buick. About three years old, I'd say offhand. Plain black tires. Just the ordinary lights, as far as I saw. I wouldn't have noticed it if it hadn't been for them.'

'And they drove off toward Eighth Avenue?'

'Yes, sir. Then people came from everywhere. A man came in here from Blumstein's and telephoned the police. And that's all I know.'

'It's been like pulling teeth,' Grave Digger said.

'All right, get on your coat and hat – you're going to the station,' Coffin Ed said.

The bartender looked shocked. 'But I thought—'

'And you can put down that glass before you wear it out.'

'But I thought if I told you everything I saw – I mean – you're not arresting me, are you?'

'No, son, you're not being arrested, but you got to repeat your story for the Homicide officers and for the record,' Grave Digger said.

Outside, the experts had itemized the material clues. The Assistant Medical Examiner had been and gone. He hadn't disclosed anything that wasn't obvious.

An examination of the white stiff's clothes had revealed that he was an operative for the Pinkerton Detective Agency.

'It won't take long to check with the New York office and find out his assignment. That will tell us something,' the Homicide lieutenant said. 'What did you boys find out?'

'Just what could be seen without knowing what it meant,' Grave Digger said. 'This is the bartender; he saw it all.'

'Fine. We'll get it down. Too bad you didn't have a stenographer with you.'

'We might not have got what we did,' Coffin Ed said. 'No one talks freely when it's being taken down.'

'Anyway, you got it in your heads, if I know you two,' the Homicide lieutenant said. 'As soon as they move these stiffs, we'll all get together in the precinct station and correlate what we got.' He turned to the precinct lieutenant, Anderson. 'What about those bar jockeys? You want any more of them?'

'I'm having a man take their names and addresses,' Anderson said. 'I'll go along with Jones and Johnson on the witness they picked.'

'Right,' the lieutenant said, beating the cold from his gloved hands and looking up and down the street. 'What's happening to those dead wagons?'

6

On his radio, Anderson got a call to come in. The bored voice of the switchboard sergeant informed him that the prowl car sent up to the convent reported a corpse, and asked what he wanted done.

Anderson told him to order the car to stay put and he'd send the Homicide crew up there.

The Homicide lieutenant ordered one of his detectives to call the Assistant Medical Examiner again.

Haggerty said, 'Old Doc Fullhouse ain't going to like spending his nights in Harlem with bodies as cold as these.'

Anderson said, 'You go along with Jones and Johnson; I'll take the witness back to the station in my car.'

Grave Digger and Coffin Ed, with Haggerty in back, led the Homicide car down 125th Street to Convent Avenue and up the hill to the south side of the convent grounds.

The prowl car was parked by the convent wall in the middle of the block. There was not a pedestrian in sight.

The three cops were sitting inside their car to keep warm, but they jumped out and looked alert when the Homicide car drew up.

'There it is,' one of them said, pointing toward the convent wall. 'We haven't touched anything.'

The corpse was flattened against the wall in an upright position, with its arms hanging straight down and its feet raised several inches from the pavement. It was entirely covered, except for the head, by a long, black, shapeless coat, threadbare and slightly greenish, with a moth-eaten, rabbit-fur collar. The hands were encased in black, knitted mittens; the feet in old-fashioned, high-buttoned shoes that had recently been cleaned with liquid polish. The face seemed to be buried in the solid concrete, so that only the back of the head was visible. Glossy waves of black, oily hair gleamed in the dim light.

'Holy Mary! What happened here?' the Homicide lieutenant exclaimed as the group of detectives pressed close.

Flashlights came into play, lighting the grotesque figure.

'What is it?' a hardened Homicide detective asked.

'How does it stick there?' another wondered.

'It's a bad joke,' Haggerty said. 'It's just a dummy, frozen to the wall.'

Grave Digger groped at a leg through folds of garments. 'It ain't no dummy,' he said.

'Don't touch it until the M.E. gets here,' the Homicide lieutenant cautioned. 'It might fall.'

'It looks like it might be garroted,' one of the cops from the prowl car offered.

The Homicide lieutenant turned on him with a face suddenly gone beet-red. 'Garroted! From within the convent? By who, the nuns?'

The cop backtracked hastily. 'I didn't mean by the nuns. A gang of niggers might have done it.'

Grave Digger and Coffin Ed turned to look at him.

'It's just a way of speaking,' the cop said defensively.

'I'll take a look,' Grave Digger said.

He stood on tiptoe and peered down the back of the fur collar.

'Nothing around its neck,' he said.

While still on tiptoe, he sniffed the wavy hair. Then he blew into it softly. Strands of silky hair floated outward. He dropped to his feet.

The lieutenant looked at him questioningly.

'Anyway, she's no grandma,' Grave Digger said. 'Her hair looks like a job from the Rose Meta beauty parlors.'

'Well, let's see what's keeping her up,' the lieutenant said.

They discovered an iron bar protruding from the wall at a point about six feet high. Below and above it there were deep cracks in the cement; and, at one point above, the crack had been dug out to form a long, oblong hole. The face of the corpse had been thrust into this hole with sufficient force to clamp it, and the end of the bar was caught between the legs, holding it aloft.

'Jesus Christ, it looks like it's been hammered in there,' the lieutenant said.

'There're no signs of bruises on the back of the head,' Grave Digger pointed out.

'One thing is for sure,' Heggerty cracked. 'She didn't get there by herself.'

'You're going to be a senator someday,' the lieutenant said.

'Maybe she was hit by a car,' a harness cop suggested.

'I'll buy that,' Coffin Ed said.

'Hit by a car!' the lieutenant exclaimed. 'Goddammit, she'd have to be hit by a car traveling like a jet plane to get rammed into that wall like that.'

'Not necessarily,' Grave Digger said.

The flip cop said, 'Oh, I forgot – there's a wig in the gutter across the street.'

The lieutenant gave him a reproving look, but didn't say the words.

In a group, they trudged across the street. The cold east wind whipped at them, and their mouths gave off steam like little locomotives.

It was a cheap wig of gray hair, fashioned in a bun at the back, and it was weighted down by a car jack.

'Was the jack with it?' the lieutenant asked.

'No sir – I put the jack on it to keep the wind from blowing it away,' the cop replied.

The lieutenant moved the jack with his foot and picked up the wig. A detective held a light.

'All I can say about it is it looks like hair,' the lieutenant said.

'Looks like real nigger hair,' the flip cop said.

'If you use that word again I'll kick your teeth down your throat,' Coffin Ed said.

The cop bristled. 'Knock whose teeth—'

He never got to finish. Coffin Ed planted a left hook in his stomach and crossed an overhand right to the jaw. The cop went down on his hips; his head leaned slowly forward until it stopped between his knees.

No one said anything. It was a delicate situation. Coffin Ed was due a reprimand, but the lieutenant from Homicide was the ranking officer, and the cop had already riled him with the crack about the nuns.

'He asked for it,' he muttered to himself, then turned to the other prowl car cop. 'Take him back to the station.'

'Yes, sir,' the cop said with a dead-pan expression, giving Coffin Ed a threatening look.

Grave Digger put a hand on Coffin Ed's arm. 'Easy, man,' he murmured.

The cop helped his partner to his feet. He could stand, but he was groggy. They got in the prowl car and drove off.

The others recrossed the street and stared at the corpse. The lieutenant stuck the wig into his overcoat pocket.

'How old would you say she was?' he asked Grave Digger.

'Young,' Grave Digger said. 'Middle twenties.'

'What beats me is *why* would a young woman masquerade as an old woman?'

'Maybe she was trying to impersonate a nun,' a Homicide detective ventured.

The lieutenant began to turn red. 'You mean so she could get into the convent?'

'Not necessarily – maybe she had a racket.'

'What kind of racket?' The lieutenant looked at Grave Digger as though he had all the answers.

'Don't ask me,' Grave Digger said. 'Folks up here are dreaming up new rackets every day. They got the time and the imagination, and all they need is a racket to make the money.'

'Well, all we can do now is leave her for Doc Fullhouse,' the lieutenant said. 'Let's go over the ground and see what it tells.'

Grave Digger got a heavy flashlight from the glove compartment of their car, and he and Coffin Ed walked back to the intersection.

The others covered the area nearer to the corpse. No tire marks were evident where a car might have braked suddenly; they found no broken glass.

Coming up the street from Convent Avenue, playing the light from right to left, Grave Digger noticed two small black marks on the gray-black asphalt, and they knelt in the street to study them.

'Somebody gunned a car here,' he concluded.

'I'd say a big car with a used tread, but we'll leave it for the experts.'

Coffin Ed noticed a car with a wheel jacked up. On closer inspection they noticed that the opposite wheel was missing. They looked at one another.

'That's the money,' Grave Digger said.

'For this one,' Coffin Ed agreed. 'Some local tire thief witnessed the kill.'

'What he saw made him broom like the devil was after him.'

'If he wasn't seen and taken away.'

'Not that son. He had presence of mind enough to get away with his wheel,' Grave Digger said.

'He oughtn't to be hard to find. Any son out tire-thieving on a night like this has got some pretty hot skirt to support.'

The lieutenant listened to their findings with interest but no particular concern.

'What I want to know is how this woman got killed,' he said. Then we'll know what to look for.'

A car turned in from Convent Avenue, and Coffin Ed said, 'We ought to soon know; that looks like Doc's struggle-buggy.'

Doctor Fullhouse was bundled up as though on an expedition to the South Pole. He was an old, slow-moving man, and what could be seen of his face between an astrakhan cap and a thick yellow-cashmere muffler made one think of a laughing mummy.

His spectacles steamed over the instant he stepped from his overheated car, and he had to take them off. He peered about from watery blue eyes, searching for the body.

'Where's the cadaver?' he asked in a querulous voice.

The lieutenant pointed. 'Stuck to the wall.'

'You didn't tell me it was a vampire bat,' he complained.

The lieutenant laughed dutifully.

'Well, get it down,' Doc said. 'You don't expect me to climb up there and examine it.'

Grave Digger clutched one arm, Coffin Ed the other; the two detectives from Homicide took a leg apiece. The body was stiff as a plaster cast. They tried to move it gently, but the face was firmly stuck. They tugged, and suddenly the body fell.

They laid the corpse on its back. The black skin of the cheeks framing the cockscomb of frozen blood had turned a strange powdery gray. Drops of frozen blood clung to the staring eye-balls.

'My God!' one of the Homicide detectives muttered, stepped to the curb and vomited.

The others swallowed hard.

Doc got a lamp from his car with a long extension cord and focused the light on the body. He looked at it without emotion.

'That's death for you,' he said. 'She was probably a good-looking woman.'

No one said anything. Even Haggerty's tongue had dried up.

'All right, give me a hand,' Doc said. 'We got to undress her.'

Grave Digger lifted her shoulders, and Doc peeled off the coat. The other detectives got off her gloves and shoes. Doc cut open the thick black dress with a pair of shears. Underneath she wore only a black uplift bra, and lace-trimmed nylon panties. Her limbs were smooth, and well-rounded, but muscular. Falsies came off with the bra, revealing a smooth, flat, mannish chest. Underneath the nylon panties was a heavily padded, yellow satin loincloth.

Grave Digger and Coffin Ed exchanged a quick, knowing glance. But the others didn't get it until the loincloth had been cut and stripped from the hard narrow hips.

'Well, I'll be God-damned!' the Homicide lieutenant exclaimed. 'She's a man!'

'There ain't any doubt about that,' Haggerty said, finding his voice at last.

Doc turned the body over. Across the back, at the base of the spine, was a tremendous welt, colored dark grape-purple.

'Well, that's what did it,' Doc said. 'He was struck here by great force and catapulted into the wall.'

'By what, for chrissake?' the lieutenant asked.

'Certainly not by a baseball bat,' Haggerty said.

'My conjecture is that he was hit by an automobile from

behind,' Doc ventured. 'I couldn't say positively until after the autopsy; and maybe not then.'

The lieutenant looked from the street to the convent wall. 'Frankly, Doc, I don't believe he was knocked from the street against that wall in the position that we found him,' he said. 'Isn't there a possibility that he was run over and then stuck up there afterwards?'

Doc made a bundle of the clothes, covered the body with its coat and stood up.

'Everything is possible,' he said. 'If you can imagine a driver running over him, then stopping his car and getting out and propping the body against the wall, and pushing its face into that crevice until it was stuck, then—'

The lieutenant cut him off. 'Well, goddammit, I can imagine that better than I can imagine the body being knocked up there from the street, no matter what hit it. Besides which, people have been known to do things worse than that.'

Doc patted him on the shoulder, smiling indulgently. 'Don't try to make your job any harder than it is,' he said. 'Look for a hit-and-run driver, and leave the maniacs to Bellevue's psychiatrists.'

7

It was past two o'clock Sunday morning. Sand-fine sleet was peppering the windshield of the small black sedan as it hustled down the East Side Drive. There was just enough heat from the defroster to make the windshield sticky, and a coating of ice was forming across Grave Digger's vision.

'This heater only works in the blazing hot summer,' he complained. 'In this kind of weather it just makes ice.'

'Turn it off,' Coffin Ed said.

The car skidded on a glazed spot on the asphalt, and from the back seat Detective Tombs from Homicide Bureau yelled, 'Watch it, man! Can't you drive without skidding?'

Grave Digger chuckled. 'You work with murder every day, and here you are – scared of getting scratched.'

'I just don't want to wind up in East River with a car on my back,' Tombs said.

The witness giggled.

That settled it. Conversation ceased. They didn't want outsiders horning in on their own private horseplay.

When they drew up before the morgue downtown on 29th Street, they all looked grim and half-frozen.

An attendant sitting at a desk in the entrance foyer checked them in, recording their names and badge numbers.

The barman from the Paris Bar gave his name as Alfonso Marcus and his address as 217 Formosa Street, Yonkers, N.Y.

They walked through corridors and downstairs to the 'cold room'. Another attendant opened a door and turned on a switch.

He grinned. 'A little chilly, eh?' he said, getting off his standard joke.

'You ain't been outside, son,' Coffin Ed said.

'We want to see the victim of a hit-and-run-driver from Harlem,' Grave Digger said.

'Oh yes, the colored man,' the attendant said.

He led them down the long, bare room, lit by cold, white light, and glanced at a card on what looked like the drawer of a huge filing cabinet.

'Unidentified,' he said, pulling out the drawer.

It rolled out smoothly and soundlessly. He removed a coarse white sheet covering the body.

'It hasn't been autopsied yet,' he said, adding with a grin, 'got to take its turn like everybody else. It's been a busy night – two asphyxiations from Brooklyn; one ice pick stabbing, also from Brooklyn; three poisonings, one by lye—'

Grave Digger cut him off. 'You're holding us spellbound.'

Coffin Ed took the bartender by the arm and shoved him close.

'My God,' the bartender whimpered, covering his face with his hands.

'Look at it, goddammit!' Coffin Ed flared. 'What the hell you think we brought you down here for – to start gagging at sight of a stiff?'

Despite his horror, the bartender giggled.

Grave Digger reached over and pulled his hands from his face.

'Who is he?' he asked in a flat, emotionless voice.

'Oh, I couldn't say.' The bartender looked as though he might burst out crying. 'Jesus Christ in heaven, look at his face.'

'Who is he?' Grave Digger repeated flatly.

'How can I tell? I can't see his face. It's all covered with blood.'

'If you come back in an hour or two they'll have it all cleaned up,' the morgue attendant said.

Grave Digger gripped the bartender by the back of his neck and pushed his head toward the nude body.

'Goddammit, you don't need to see his face to recognize him,' he said. 'Who is he? And I ain't going to ask you no more.'

'He's Black Beauty,' the bartender whispered. 'What's left of him.'

Grave Digger released him and let him straighten up.

The bartender shuddered.

'Get yourself together,' Grave Digger said.

The bartender looked at him from big, pleading eyes.

'What's his square moniker?' Grave Digger asked.

The bartender shook his head.

'I'm giving you a chance,' Grave Digger told him.

'I really don't know,' the bartender said.

'The hell you don't!'

'No, sir, I swear. If I knew I'd tell you.'

The morgue attendant looked at the bartender with compassion. He turned toward Grave Digger and said indignantly, 'You can't third-degree a prisoner in here.'

'You can't help him,' Grave Digger replied. 'Even if you are a member of the club.'

'What club?'

'Let's take him out of here,' Coffin Ed said.

Detective Tombs listened to the byplay with fascination.

They took the witness outside to their car and put him in the back seat beside Detective Tombs.

'Who's Mister Baron?' Grave Digger asked.

The bartender turned pleadingly to the white detective. 'If I knew, sir, I'd tell them.'

'Don't appeal to me,' Tombs said. 'Half of this is Greek to me.'

'Listen, son,' Coffin Ed said to the bartender. 'Don't make it hard on yourself.'

'But I just know these people from the bar, sir,' the bartender contended. 'I don't know what they do.'

'It's going to be just too bad,' Grave Digger said. 'What you don't know is going to hang you.'

Again the bartender appealed to the white detective. 'Please, sir, I don't want to get mixed up in all this bad business. I've got a wife and family.'

The windows of the small, crowded car had steamed over. The face of the detective couldn't be seen, but his embarrassment was tangible. 'Don't cry to me,' he said harshly. 'I didn't tell you to get married.'

Suddenly the bartender giggled. Emotions exploded. The white detective cursed. Grave Digger banged the meat edge of his hand against the steering wheel. The muscles in Coffin Ed's face jumped like salt on a fresh wound as he reached across the back of the seat and double-slapped the bartender with his left hand.

Grave Digger rolled down a window.

'We need some air in here,' he said.

The bartender began to cry.

'Give me a fill-in,' the white detective said.

'The one who got killed in the heist and the one we just saw are newlyweds,' Grave Digger said. 'This one—' He nodded toward the bartender – 'is Snake Hips' used-to-be.'

'How did you dig that?'

'Just guessing. They're all just one big club. But you got to know it. It's like when I was in Paris at the end of the war. All of us colored soldiers, no matter what rank or from what army or division, belonged to the same set. We all hung out at the same joints, ate the same food, told the same jokes, laid the same poules. There wasn't anything that one of us could do that the whole God-damned shooting party didn't know about.'

'I see what you mean. But what's the angle here?'

'We haven't guessed that far,' Grave Digger admitted. 'Probably none. We're just trying to get all these people in position. And this one is going to help us. Or he's going to get something even he can't handle.'

'Not before I get done with him,' the detective said. 'My boss man wants him to look at some pictures in the gallery. Maybe he can identify the heistmen – one of them at least.'

'How long do you think that will take?' Coffin Ed asked.

'A few hours, maybe, or a few days. We can't employ your techniques; all we can do is keep him looking until he goes blind.'

Grave Digger mashed the starter. 'We'll take you down to Centre Street.'

The detective and his witness got out in front of the Headquarters Annex, a loft building across the street from the domed headquarters building.

Coffin Ed leaned out of the window and said, 'We'll be waiting for you, lover.'

By the time they got back uptown, the windshield was frosted over with a quarter-inch coating of ice. Approaching headlights resembled hazy spectrums coming out of the sea.

They had a new dent in their right fender and a claim against their insurance company from the irate owner of a chauffeur-driven Rolls Royce whom they had attempted to pass on a stretch of slick ice just north of the U.N. Building.

Coffin Ed chuckled. 'He was mad, wasn't he?'

'Can you blame him?' Grave Digger said. 'He felt the same as Queen Elizabeth would if we tramped into Buckingham Palace with muddy feet.'

'Why don't you turn off that heater? You've said yourself it don't make nothing but ice.'

'What, and catch pneumonia!'

They had been tippling a bottle of bourbon, and Grave Digger felt sort of witty.

'Anyway, you might slow down if you can't see,' Coffin Ed said.

'It's nights like this that cause wars,' Grave Digger philosophized without slacking speed.

'How so?'

'Increases the population. Then when you get enough prime males they start fighting to kill them off.'

'Look out for that garbage truck!' Coffin Ed cried as they turned on two wheels into 125th Street.

'Is that what that was?' Grave Digger asked.

It was past three o'clock. They worked a special detail from eight until four, and this was the hour they usually contacted stool pigeons.

But tonight even stool pigeons had gone under cover. The 125th Street railroad station was closed and locked, and next door the all-night cafeteria was roped off except for a few tables at the front, occupied by the bums clinging to bone-dry coffee cups and keeping one foot moving to prove they weren't asleep.

'Going back to the case, or rather cases – the trouble with these people is they lie for kicks,' Grave Digger said seriously.

'They want to be treated rough; brings out the female in them,' Coffin Ed agreed.

'But not too rough; they don't want to lose any teeth.'

'That's how we're going to get them,' Coffin Ed summed up.

Lieutenant Anderson was waiting for them. He had taken over the captain's office, and was mulling over reports.

He greeted them, as they came in bunched up and ashy from cold, with: 'We got a line on the private eye who was killed, Paul Zalkin.'

Coffin Ed backed up against the radiator, and Grave Digger perched a ham on the edge of the desk. The rough whiskey humor was knocked out of them, and they looked serious and intent.

'Casper talk?' Grave Digger asked.

'No, he's still in a coma. But Lieutenant Brogan got through to the Pinkerton Agency and got a fill-in on Zalkin's assignment. The secretary of the national committee of Holmes' party stopped by his office earlier last night and left him fifty grand in cash, for organizational expenses for the presidential election this fall. Holmes hinted that he might take the money home with him rather than leave it in his office safe over the weekend. You know he lives in one of those old apartment houses on 110th Street, overlooking Central Park.'

'We know where he lives,' Coffin Ed said.

'Well, the secretary got to thinking about it after he had left, so he called the Pinkerton Agency and asked them to send a man up to cover Holmes on his way home. But he didn't want Holmes to think he was spying on him, so he asked that the man keep out of sight. That's how come Zalkin was there when the heist was staged.'

'How long was it before the secretary left Casper?' Grave Digger asked, frowning with an idea.

'The agency got the call at ten-twenty o'clock.'

'Then somebody knew about the payoff beforehand,' Grave Digger said. 'You can't organize a heist like that in that length of time.'

'Not even in a day,' Coffin Ed said. 'These men were pros; and you can't get pros like ordering groceries. They might have had their uniforms, but they'd have to lift a car—'

'It hasn't even been reported as stolen yet,' Anderson cut in.

'I got a notion these guns were from out of town,' Coffin Ed went on. 'No local hoods would choose 125th Street for a caper like that. Not that block of 125th Street. They couldn't depend on the weather to drive the ground-hogs in their holes; and normally on a Saturday night that block, with all its bars, and restaurants, would be jumping with pedestrians. They had to be somebody who didn't know this.'

'That doesn't help us much,' Anderson said. 'If they're from out of town, they're long gone by now.'

'Maybe,' Grave Digger said. 'Maybe not. If it wasn't for this hit-and-run business, I might buy it.'

Anderson gave him a startled look.

'What the hell, Jones; you can't think there's a tie-in.'

Coffin Ed grunted.

'Who knows,' Grave Digger said. 'There is something specially vicious about both those capers, and there ain't that many vicious people running loose in Harlem on a night as cold as this.'

'My God, man, you can't think that hit-and-run was done deliberately.'

'And then in both instances pansies were croaked,' Grave Digger went on. 'Accidents just don't happen to those people like that.'

'The hit-and-run driver couldn't have possibly known his victim was a man,' Anderson argued.

'Not unless he knew who he was and what racket he was pulling,' Grave Digger said.

'What racket was he pulling?'

'Don't ask me. It's just a feeling I got.'

'Hell, man, you're going mystical on me,' Anderson said. 'How about you, Johnson. Do you go along with that?'

'Yep,' Coffin Ed said. 'Me and Digger have been drinking out the same bottle.'

'Well, before you get too drunk with that mysticism, let me fill you in with the latest facts. The two patrolmen, Stick and Price, who thought it was a joke to report they'd been knocked down by a homemade flying saucer, have admitted they were hit by a run-away automobile wheel coming down Convent Avenue. Does that give you any ideas?'

Grave Digger looked at his watch. It said five minutes to four.

'Not any that won't keep until tomorrow,' he said. 'If I start talking to my old lady about automobile tires, as fat as she's getting, I'm subject to losing my happy home.'

8

When Roman came to the castle standing in the fork, where St Nicholas Place branches off from St Nicholas Avenue, he stood on the brake.

Sassafras sailed headfirst into the windshield, and Mister Baron's unconscious figure rolled off the back seat and plumped onto the floor.

'Which way did they go?' Roman asked, reaching for the .45 revolver that lay on the seat between them.

Sassafras straightened up, rubbing her forehead, and turned

on him angrily. 'You asking me? I ain't seen which way they went. They might have went downtown for all I know.'

'I seen them turn uptown,' he argued, his cocked gray eyes seeming to peer down both streets at once.

'Well, make up your mind,' she said in her high, keening voice. 'They didn't go into the castle, that's for sure. And you can't set here in the middle of the street all night.'

'I wish I had the mother-raper who built that castle there in the middle of Harlem,' Roman said as though it were responsible for his losing sight of the Cadillac.

'Well, you ain't got him and you better get out the middle of the street before someone comes along and claims you has stolen this Buick.'

'We has, ain't we?' Roman said.

The bump had revived Mister Baron, and they could hear him groaning down on the floor behind them. 'Oh God . . . Oh Jesus Christ . . . Those dirty bastards . . .'

Roman slipped the car in gear and drove slowly down between the rows of brick-fronted apartment buildings on St Nicholas Place.

The castle, somebody's brainstorm at the turn of the century, stood at 149th Street; above were the better-class residences for the colored people of Harlem. Roman was unfamiliar with this part of town, and he didn't know which way to turn.

Mister Baron gripped the back of the front seat and pulled himself to his knees. His long, wavy hair hung down over his forehead; his eyes rolled loosely in their sockets.

'Let me out,' he said, moaning. 'I'm going to be sick.'

Roman stopped the car in front of a red brick building with a fluted façade. Big new cars lined the curbs.

'Shut up!' he said. 'If it hadn't been for you, I never would have run off after hitting that old lady.'

Mister Baron's mouth ballooned, but he held it back. 'I'm going to be sick in the car,' he blubbered.

'Let him out,' Sassafras said. 'If you'd listened to me, none of this would have happened.'

'Get out, man,' Roman shouted. 'You want me to lift you?'

Mister Baron opened the curbside door and pulled to his

feet. He staggered groggily toward a lamppost. Roman jumped from the other side and followed him.

Mister Baron clung to the post and heaved. Steam rose as though he were spouting boiling water. Roman backed away.

'Jesus Christ in heaven,' Mister Baron moaned.

Roman let him finish and clutched him by the arm. Mister Baron tried weakly to free himself.

'Let me go – I got to make a phone call,' he said.

'You ain't going nowhere until I find my car,' Roman muttered, pushing him toward the Buick.

Mister Baron pulled back, but he could scarcely stand. His head was filled with shooting pains, and his vision wouldn't focus. 'Fool, how can I help you find your car if you won't let me telephone? I want to call the police and report that it's been stolen.' His voice sounded desperate.

'Naw, you don't; you ain't telling the police nothing,' Roman said, pushing him into the back of the car and slamming the door. He went around the car and climbed back beneath the wheel. 'You think I want to get arrested?'

'Those weren't real police, you idiot,' Mister Baron said.

'I know they weren't police. You think I'm a fool? But what am I going to tell the sure enough police about hitting that old lady?'

'You didn't hurt that old lady. I looked back once when you were driving off and saw her getting up.'

Roman stared at Mister Baron while that sunk in. Sassafras turned about to look at Mister Baron, too. The two of them, suddenly staring and immobile – he with his Davy Crockett coonskin cap and she with the tasseled red knitted cap topping her long, black face – looked like people from another world.

'You knew I didn't hurt her, and you kept egging me to run away.' Roman's thick Southern voice sounded dangerous.

Mister Baron fidgeted nervously. 'I was going to stop you, but before I could say anything those bandits drove up and took advantage of the situation.'

'How do I know you ain't in with 'em?'

'What for?'

'They stole my car. How do I know you ain't had 'em do it?'

'You're a fool,' Mister Baron cried.

'He ain't such a fool,' Sassafras said.

'Fool or not, I'm going to hold onto you until I find my car,' Roman told Mister Baron. 'And, if I don't find it, I'm going to take my money 'way from you.'

Mister Baron started laughing hysterically. 'Go ahead and take it. Search me. Beat me up. You're big and strong.'

'I worked a whole year for that money.'

'You worked a whole year. And you saved up sixty-five hundred dollars—'

'That's nearmost every penny I made. I went without eating to save that money.'

'So you could buy a Cadillac. You weren't satisfied with an ordinary Cadillac. You had to buy a solid gold Cadillac. And I'm the – the – I'm the one who sold it to you. For a thousand dollars less than list price. Ha ha ha! You had it twenty minutes and let somebody steal it—'

'What's the matter with you, man? You going crazy?'

'Now you want your money back from me. Ha ha ha! Go ahead and start hitting me. Take it out of my skin. If that don't satisfy you, throw me down and rape me.'

'Look out now, I don't go for that stuff.'

'You don't go for that stuff. You goddam chicken-crap square.'

'You're going to make me hit you.'

'Hit me! Come on and hit me.' Mister Baron thrust his womanish face toward Roman's lowering scowl. 'See if you can knock sixty-five hundred dollars out of me.'

'I don't have to. I can just throw you down and take it.'

'Throw me down and take it! Wouldn't I love that!'

Sassafras put in her bit. 'You ain't going to love what he's going to take 'cause it's just going to be money.'

'Goddammit, where were you two squares when those two bandits knocked me out and robbed me?' Mister Baron asked.

'Knocked you out?' Roman said stupidly.

'Is that what was the matter with you?' Sassafras echoed.

'And they robbed you? Of my money?'

'It was my money,' Mister Baron corrected. 'The car was yours, and the money was mine.'

'Jesus Christ,' Roman said. 'They took the car and the money.'

'That's right, square. Are you going to let me go and make that phone call now?'

'Naw, I ain't. I going to take you out and search you. I might be a square, but I ain't trusted you from the start.'

'That's fine,' Mister Baron said, and started to get out onto the sidewalk.

But Roman reached back, grabbed him and forced him out into the street. Then he got out and started shaking him down.

'Be careful, Roman,' Sassafras said. 'Somebody might come by here and think you is robbing him.'

'Let 'em think what they want,' Roman said, turning Mister Baron's pockets inside out.

'Do you want me to undress?' Mister Baron asked. Roman finished with his pockets and felt through his clothes; then ran his hands over Mister Baron's body, up and down his legs and underneath his arms.

'He ain't got it on him,' he conceded.

But he wasn't satisfied. He searched the back of the Buick.

'It ain't there, either.' He took off his coonskin cap and rubbed his short, curly hair back and forth. 'If I catch those mother-rapers I going to kill 'em,' he said.

'Let him telephone,' Sassafras said. 'He said you ain't hurt the old lady, and I is ready to swear you ain't even hit her.'

Roman stood in the street, thinking it over. Mister Baron stood beside him, watching his expression.

'All right, get in the car,' Roman said.

Mister Baron got back into the car.

Roman began talking through the window. 'You know this neighborhood—'

'Get in the car yourself,' Sassafras said.

He got back into the front seat and continued addressing Mister Baron. 'Where would they likely go with my car? It ain't like as if they could hide it.'

'God only knows,' Mister Baron said. 'Let the police find it; that's what they get paid for.'

'Let me give it some thought,' Roman said.

'How much thought you going to give it?' Sassafras said.

'I tell you what,' Roman said. 'You go and phone the police and tell 'em it's your car. Then, if they find it, I'll show 'em my bill of sale.'

'That's fine,' Mister Baron said. 'Can I get out now?'

'Naw, you can't get out now. I'm going to take you to a telephone, and when you get through talking to the police we're going to keep on looking ourselves. And I ain't going to let you go until somebody finds it.'

'All right,' Mister Baron said. 'Just as you say.'

'Where is there a telephone?'

'Drive down the street to Bowman's Bar.'

He drove down to the end of St Nicholas Place. Edgecombe Drive circles in along the ridge of the embankment overlooking Broadhurst Avenue and the Harlem River valley, and cuts off St Nicholas Place at the 155th Street Bridge. Below, to one side of the bridge, is the old abandoned Heaven of Father Divine with the faded white letters of the word PEACE on both sides of the gabled roof. Beyond, on the river bank, is the shack where the hood threw acid into Coffin Ed's face that night three years ago, when he and Grave Digger closed in on their gold-mine pitch.

One side of Bowman's was a bar, the other a restaurant. Next to the restaurant was a barbershop; up over the bar was a dance hall. All of them were open; a crap game was going in back of the barbershop, a club dance in the hall upstairs. But not a soul was in sight. There was nothing in the street but the cold, dark air.

Roman double-parked before the plate-glass front of the bar. Venetian blinds closed off the interior.

'You go with him, Sassy,' he said. 'Don't let him try to get away with nothing.'

'Get away with what?' Mister Baron said.

'Anything,' Roman said.

Sassafras accompanied Mister Brown into the bar. Roman couldn't tell which one of them swished the more. He was looking through the right side window, watching them, when suddenly he noticed two bullet holes in the window. He had been in the Korean war, and learned the meaning of the sudden appearance of bullet holes. He thought someone was shooting at him, and he ducked on the seat and grabbed his pistol. He lay there for a moment, listening. He didn't hear anything, so he peered cautiously over the ledge of the door. No one was in sight. He straightened up slowly, holding the pistol ready to shoot if an enemy appeared. None appeared. He looked at the bullet holes more closely and decided they had been there all along. He felt sheepish.

It occurred to him that someone in the car had been in a gunfight. No doubt those phony cops. He turned about to examine the other side to see where the bullets had gone. There were two holes about a foot apart in the ceiling fabric above his head. He got out and looked at the top. The bullets had dented it but hadn't penetrated. They must be in the lining of the ceiling, he thought.

He turned on the inside light and looked about the floor. He found seven shiny brass jackets of .38 caliber cartridges sprinkled over the matting.

It had been some fight, he thought. But the full meaning didn't strike him right away. All he could think of at the moment was how those bastards had taken his car.

He put his pistol back on the seat beside him and sat there picking his nose.

Two cops in a prowl car with the lights out slipped quietly up beside him. They were on the lookout for that particular car. But when they saw him, sitting there in his coonskin cap, looking as unconcerned as though he were fishing for eels underneath the bridge, they didn't give the car a second glance.

'One of the Crocketts,' the driver said.

'Don't wake him,' the other replied.

The car slipped noiselessly past. He didn't see it until it had pulled ahead.

Trying to catch some whore hustling, he thought. Mother-rapers come along and steal my car and all these cops can do is chase whores.

*   *   *

The bar ran lengthwise, facing a row of booths. It was crowded. People were standing two and three deep.

Sassafras went ahead of Mister Baron, elbowing through the jam. She stopped and turned around.

'Where is the phones?'

'In the restaurant,' Mister Baron said. 'We have to go all the way to the back.'

'You go ahead,' she said, pulling aside so he could pass.

A joker on a bar stool reached out and tugged the tassels of her cap.

'Little Red Riding Hood,' he cooed. 'How about you?'

She snatched her cap from his hand and said, 'How about your baby sister?'

The man drew back in mock affront. 'I don't play that.'

'Then pat your feet,' she said.

The man grinned. 'What you drinking, baby?'

Her glance had caught the smoky oil paintings of two brown-skin amazon nudes reclining on Elysian fields above the mirror behind the bar. She tried not to laugh, but she couldn't help it.

The man followed her glance. 'Hell, baby, you don't need much as what they got.'

She gave herself a shake. 'At least what I got moves,' she said.

Suddenly she remembered Mister Baron. She started off. The man grabbed her by the arm.

'What's the rush, baby?'

She tore herself loose and squeezed hurriedly to the rear. Glass doors opened into the restaurant, and she bumped into a waitress going through. The phone booth was to the rear on the left. The door was closed. She snatched it open. A man was phoning, but it wasn't Mister Baron.

''Scuse me,' she said.

'Come on in,' the man said, grabbing at her.

She jerked away and looked about wildly. Mister Baron was nowhere in sight.

She stopped the waitress coming back.

'Did you see a little prissy man with wavy hair come through here?' she asked.

The waitress looked her over from head to feet.

'You that hard up, baby?'

'Oh shoo you!' she cried and dashed through the swinging doors into the kitchen.

'Did a man come through here?' she asked.

The big, sweating, bald-headed cook was up a tree.

'Git out of here, whore!' he shouted in a rage.

The dishwasher grinned. 'Come 'round to the back door,' he said.

The cook grabbed a skillet and advanced on her, and she backed through the doorway. She looked through the dining room and bar again, but Mister Baron had disappeared.

She went outside and told Roman, 'He's gone.'

'Gone where?'

'I don't know. He got away.'

'Where in the hell was you?'

'I was watching him all the time, but he just disappeared.' She looked like she was about to cry.

'Get in the car,' he said. 'I'll look for him.'

She took her turn sitting in the hottest car in all of New York State while he searched the bar and restaurant for Mister Baron. He didn't have any better luck with the cook.

'He must have got out through the kitchen,' he said when he returned to the car.

'The cook would have seen him.'

'It'd take a shotgun to talk to that evil man.'

He climbed in behind the wheel and sat there looking dejected. 'You let him get away, now what us going to do?' he said accusingly.

'It ain't my fault that we is in this mess,' she flared. 'If you hadn't been acting such a fool right from the start might not none of this happened.'

'I knew what I was doing. If he'd tried to pull off something crooked, I was trying to trick him by making him think I was a square.'

'Well, you sure made him,' she said. 'Asking do it use much gas and then looking at the oil stick and saying you guessed the motor was all right.'

He defended himself. 'I wanted all those people who was watching us to know I was buying the car so they could be witnesses in case anything happened.'

'Well, where is they now? Or has some more got to happen?'

'Ain't no need of us arguing between ourselves,' he said. 'We got to do something.'

'Well, let's go see a fortune teller,' she said. 'I know one who tells folks where to find things they has lost.'

'Let's hurry then,' he said. 'We got to get rid of this car 'fore daylight. It's hotter than a West Virginia coke oven.'

9

Grave Digger and Coffin Ed were buttoning up their coats when the telephone rang in the captain's office.

Lieutenant Anderson took the call and looked up. 'It's for one of you.'

'I'll take it,' Grave Digger said and picked up the receiver. 'Jones speaking.'

The voice at the other end said, 'It's me, Lady Gypsy, Digger.'

He waited.

'You're looking for a certain car, ain't you? A black Buick with Yonkers plates?'

'How do you know that?'

'I'm a fortune teller, ain't I?'

Grave Digger signaled Coffin Ed to cut in, and jiggled the hook.

Coffin Ed picked up one of the extensions on the desk and Lieutenant Anderson the other. The switchboard operator knew what to do.

'Where is it?' Grave Digger asked.

'It's sitting as big as life down on the street in front of my place,' Lady Gypsy said.

Grave Digger palmed the mouthpiece and whispered an address on 116th Street.

Anderson picked up the intercom and ordered the sergeant on the switchboard to alert all prowl cars and await further instructions.

'Who's in it?' Grave Digger asked.

'Ain't nobody in it at the moment,' Lady Gypsy said. 'I got a square and his girl friend up here in my seance chamber who drove up in it. They got a wild story about a lost Cadillac—'

'Hold the story,' Grave Digger said. 'And keep them there, even if you have to use ghosts. Me and Ed will be there before you can say Jack Robinson.'

'I'll send the cars on,' Anderson said.

'Give us three minutes and seal off the block,' Grave Digger said. 'Have them come in quietly with the blinkers off.'

Lady Gypsy's joint was on the second floor of a tenement on 116th Street, midway between Lexington and Third Avenues. On the ground floor was an ice and coal store.

The painted tin plaque in a box beside the entrance read:

> Lady Gypsy
> Perceptions – Divinations
> Prophesies – Revelations
> Numbers Given

The word *Findings* had been recently added. Business had been bad.

Once upon a time Lady Gypsy had lived an ultrarespectable private life in an old dark house on upper Convent Avenue with her two bosom associates: Sister Gabriel, who sold tickets to heaven and begged alms for nonexistent charities; and Big Kathy, who ran a whorehouse on East 131st Street. They were known in that uppercrust colored neighborhood as 'The Three Black Widows'. But when Sister Gabriel got his throat cut by one of the trio of con men responsible for the acid-throwing caper that permanently scarred Coffin Ed's face, the two remaining 'Widows' let the house go, relinquished respectability and holed up in their dens of vice.

Now Lady Gypsy was seldom seen outside the junk-crammed five-room apartment where she contacted the spirits and sometimes gave messages to the initiate that were out of this world.

It was a normal five-minute drive on open streets from the 126th Street precinct station, but Grave Digger made it in his allotted three. Sleet blew along the frozen streets like dry sand, making the tires sing. The car didn't skid, but it shifted from side to side of the street, as though on a sanded spot of slick ice. Grave Digger drove from memory of the streets, with the bright lights on, more to be seen than to see, because sighting through his windshield was like looking through frosted glass. His siren was silent.

A prowl car was parked in front of Lady Gypsy's but no sign of the Buick.

'Anderson jumped the gun,' Coffin Ed said.

'They might have got 'em,' Grave Digger said without much hope.

The little car skidded when he tamped the brake, and it banged into the rear bumper of the prowl car. They hit the street without giving it a thought.

Coffin Ed went first, overcoat flapping, pistol in his hand. Grave Digger slipped as he was rounding the back of the car and hit the top of the luggage compartment with the butt of his pistol. Coffin Ed wheeled about to find Grave Digger rising from the gutter.

'You're sending telegrams,' Coffin Ed accused.

'It ain't my night,' Grave Digger said.

A prowl car rounded the distant corner, siren wide open and red eye blinking.

'Makes no difference now,' Coffin Ed said disgustedly, taking the dimly lit stairs two at a time.

They found a uniformed cop standing beside the door at the head of the staircase with a drawn pistol, another in the shadows of the stairs, leading to upper floors.

'Where's the car?' Coffin Ed asked.

'There wasn't any car,' the cop said.

Grave Digger cursed. 'What are you doing here?'

'Lieutenant said to seal up this joint and wait for you.'

'What's going to stop them from going out the back?'

'Joe and Eddie got the back covered.'

Grave Digger couldn't hear him over the screaming of the siren down below.

'How's the back?' he shouted.

'Covered,' the cop shouted back.

'Well, let's see what gives,' Grave Digger said.

The siren died to a whimper, and his voice filled the narrow corridor like organ notes.

'Hold it!' a voice cried from below.

Two cops pounded up the stairs like the Russian Army.

'This beats vaudeville,' Coffin Ed said.

The cops came into sight with guns in their fists. They halted at sight of the assemblage, and both turned bright pink.

'We didn't know anybody was here,' one of them said.

'You were making sure just in case,' Coffin Ed said.

Grave Digger fingered the buzzer beside the door. From inside came the distant sound of a bell ringing.

'These doorbells always sound like they're miles away,' he said.

The cops looked at him curiously.

No one came to the door.

'Let me shoot the lock off,' a cop said.

'You can't shoot these locks off,' Grave Digger said. 'Look at them; there are more locks on this door than on Fort Knox and there're more inside.'

'There's a chance that only one is locked,' Coffin Ed said. 'If somebody left here who didn't have a key—'

'Right,' Grave Digger agreed. 'I'm too tired to think.'

A cop raised his eyebrows, but Grave Digger didn't see it.

'Stand back,' Coffin Ed said.

Everyone backed off to one side.

He backed to the opposite wall, leveled his long-barreled .38 and put four bullets about the Yale snap lock. Sound shattered the front hall windows, and doors down at the back of the hall cracked open an inch. From all directions came the sound of a sudden scurrying like rats deserting a ship.

'Let's hit it,' Coffin Ed said, coughing slightly from the cordite fumes filling the hall.

The sound of scurrying ceased.

He and Grave Digger hit the door with left shoulders, and reeled into a room.

It was a reception room. Decrepit kitchen chairs flanked opposite walls. A stained, dusty, dark-blue, threadbare carpet covered the floor. In the center, a round table-top seemed to be floating in the air. It was supported by four small steel cables, which, attached to the ceiling, were practically invisible in the dim light. On the table rested a gruesome-looking sepulcher made of dull-gray papier mâché. Out of this sepulcher was coming the ghost of Jesus Christ.

Coffin Ed caught himself, but Grave Digger reeled into the hanging table with such force that he overturned the sepulcher and the ghost of Christ went sailing across the room as though the devil had grabbed at it.

The uniformed cops followed, looking from one to the other with wide-eyed consternation.

Someone started hammering on the back door. Another bell started ringing.

'Pipe down!' Grave Digger shouted.

The noise ceased.

The walls of the room were papered with faded blue skies packed with constellations. Across from the entrance was a double doorway closed by a faded red curtain containing the gilded signs of the zodiac.

Coffin Ed stepped over the ghost of Christ and parted the zodiac.

They found themselves in the seance chamber. A crystal ball sat on a draped table. All four walls were curtained in some kind of dark satiny material covered with luminescent figures of stars, moons, suns, ghosts, griffins, animals, angels, devils and faces of African witch doctors.

The room was lit by a faint glow from the crystal ball. Their sudden entrance stirred the curtain to fluttering, and the luminescent figures flickered in and out of sight.

'Where the hell's the light?' Grave Digger roared. 'I'm getting seasick.'

A cop flashed on his torch. They didn't see another light.

'Let's find the door,' he said, tearing the curtains aside.

Behind the curtains there were doors everywhere.

He opened the first one that gave. It led to a dining room. A chandelier with four bulbs lit a square dining room table covered with a black-and-silver checked plastic cloth. Two chairs were drawn up to two dirty plates and the skeleton of a roasted opossum, lying one-sided in congealed possum grease and the remains of baked yellow yams, like the ribs of a derelict ship in shallow surf.

'Possum and taters,' Coffin Ed said, unconsciously licking his lips.

'That's what they ate, but where are they?' Grave Digger said.

'Ain't nobody here but us ghosts,' a cop said.

'Don't forget us possums,' another added.

Coffin Ed opened another door and found himself in a kitchen. He heard movement on the outside open-air stairs.

'Hey, let us in,' a voice called from without.

A cop pushed past Coffin Ed to open the back door.

Grave Digger had opened another door, which led to a bedroom.

'In here,' he called.

Coffin Ed went in, and six cops followed.

A fat, light-complexioned colored man with a flabby, sensual face and a shining, bald head lay across the bed, breathing heavily with his eyes closed. He wore a big, old-fashioned faded-yellow brassiere, holding his flopping breasts, and a pair of purple-and-golden striped boxer shorts, from which extended the fasteners of a worn garter belt attached to the tops of purple silk stockings. He was fat, but his flesh was so flabby it spread out beside his bones like melted tallow.

Another bald-headed man lay face down on the floor beside the bed. He wore a red-and-gray striped rayon bathrobe over white-dotted blue rayon pyjamas. His face was unseen, but the fringe of hair beneath his bald dome was silky white.

The white cops stared.

'What did they do with Lady Gypsy?' one asked.

'That's him on the bed,' Coffin Ed said.

'That ain't the question,' Grave Digger said. 'We got to find out who it was slugged him.'

'He isn't talking,' a white cop said.

'We'll fix that,' Grave Digger said. 'Get a bottle of vinegar from the kitchen.'

He reached over and clutched Lady Gypsy by the arm and pulled him over to the side of the bed. Then, when the cop brought the vinegar, he opened the bottle and poured the lukewarm liquid over Lady Gypsy's face.

'That the way you do it?' the cop asked.

'It works,' Grave Digger said.

'Every time,' Coffin Ed supplemented.

Lady Gypsy stirred and spluttered. 'Who is that pissing on me?' he said in a distinct, cultivated voice.

'It's me, Digger,' Grave Digger said.

Lady Gypsy sat up suddenly on the side of the bed. He opened his eyes and saw all the white cops staring at him.

'You sonofabitch,' he said.

Grave Digger slapped him with his left hand.

His head fell to one side and straightened up as though his neck were made of rubber.

'It wasn't my fault the bastard got away,' he said, fingering an egg-size lump on the back of his head. He looked down at his half-naked self. 'He took my second-best ensemble.'

'Fill us in,' Grave Digger said. 'And don't start begging for sympathy.'

Lady Gypsy flipped back the covers and wiped his face with the top end of the sheet. 'He's a rough boy,' he said. 'A square, but really rugged.' There were threads of desire and admiration in his voice. 'And he's carrying a rusty forty-five.'

'If you go patsy on me, I'll kick out your teeth,' Grave Digger said.

Again the white cops looked at him curiously.

'You don't have any compassion for anybody,' Lady Gypsy said in his cultivated voice.

'It's how you look at it,' Grave Digger said. He turned to Coffin Ed. 'Get out your stop watch, Ed. I'm going to give him ninety seconds.'

Lady Gypsy regarded him impassively through glazed, yellow-speckled brownish eyes that had the slight blue cast of age.

'You are an animal,' he said.

Grave·Digger hit him in the mouth. It made a sound like water splashing, and blood drops spurted from the corners of Lady Gypsy's mouth. But his big, flaccid body didn't move, and his flat, stoical expression went unruffled.

'I'm not scared of you, Digger,' he said. 'But I'm going to tell you what I know because I don't want to get beat up.' He wiped the blood from his bruised and swelling lips with the vinegary sheet end. 'You're forgetting it was me who tipped you.'

'Yeah, and you let him sap you and get away while you was making a pass at him,' Grave Digger accused.

'That's not so. He followed me in here and heard me phoning.' He nodded toward the telephone on the night table. 'Not that I wouldn't have if I had known what was coming,' he added.

'Forty seconds,' Coffin Ed said.

'He worked for a year as an able-bodied seaman for the South American Shipping Line.' He spoke steadily but unhurriedly. 'On the SS *Costa Brava*. Saved all his money. Bought a new Cadillac from a man called Mister Baron—'

'Baron again,' Grave Digger said, exchanging looks with Coffin Ed.

'Paid six thousand, five hundred for it,' Lady Gypsy went on unemotionally. 'Got it for a thousand dollars under the list price. A Cadillac with a golden finish—'

The white cops' mouths had come open.

'He had just paid the money and got his bill of sale, and he was taking it for a tryout when he hit an old woman—'

'Alongside the convent?'

Lady Gypsy flicked him an upward look, then dropped his gaze and stared at nothing again.

'Then you know about it?'

'You tell us.'

'I'm just telling you what he told me—'

The man on the floor stirred slightly and moaned.

'Won't you put Mister Gypsy on the bed,' Lady Gypsy said.

'Let him lay where he is,' Grave Digger said.

'So they hit this old lady and ran,' he went on tonelessly. 'They didn't get far before they were stopped by three men in cops' uniforms driving a Buick—'

'It begins to click,' Grave Digger said.

'Check,' Coffin Ed replied.

Lady Gypsy told the rest of the story in the same toneless voice. 'Then, when Mister Baron got away, they came to me,' he concluded. 'They wanted me to tell them where to find the Cadillac.'

'Did you tell them?' a white cop asked, eyes popping.

'If I could do that I wouldn't be living in this dump,' Lady Gypsy said. 'I'd be riding in a yacht on the Riviera.'

The man on the floor groaned again, and two white cops lifted him and laid him across the foot of the bed.

'How did he know about you?' Grave Digger asked.

'He didn't. His girl friend told him. Brought him, rather.'

'Who is she?'

'Sassafras Jenkins. A girl on the town.'

'Did she steer him into Baron?'

'He doesn't think so. He said he met Mister Baron at the docks in Brooklyn – where the Line has their warehouse. On his last trip in, two months ago, Mister Baron gave him a lift into Harlem; he was driving his own Cadillac convertible. Roman told him he was saving up his money to buy a car, and Mister Baron asked him how much he had saved, and he said he'd have six thousand, five hundred dollars when he came back from his next trip and Mister Baron said he'd get him a Cadillac convertible like the one he was driving for that amount—'

'He was driving a gold-finished Cadillac himself?'

'No, his was gray. But he asked Roman what color he wanted, and Roman said he wanted one that looked like solid gold.'

'What was Baron's business in Brooklyn?' Grave Digger asked.

'Sailors, Digger,' Coffin Ed said. 'Where's your thinking cap?'

Grave Digger half agreed. 'Maybe, maybe not. Maybe he was fishing frogs for snakes.'

'It's the same thing,' Coffin Ed contended. 'Sailors are everything to everybody.'

'You know Baron?' Grave Digger said to Lady Gypsy.

'It happens that I don't.'

'You know Black Beauty?'

'Yes.'

'What was his racket?'

'Pimping.'

'Pimping! That pansy!'

'You said his racket, not his pleasure. And you employed the past tense. Is he dead?'

'He was the old woman who got killed.'

'Killed? They said she wasn't hurt.'

'That's another story. But you must know Baron. He's in the clique.'

'That's what I told myself,' Lady Gypsy admitted. 'But truthfully, I don't.'

'You know the Jenkins girl, however.'

Lady Gypsy shrugged. 'I've seen her. I don't know her. She comes in here from time to time with various tricks. She's always got some little racket going.'

'With Baron?'

'You can't trick me, Digger. I've told you the truth about Mister Baron. I don't know him, and I don't think she knew him, either.'

'Okay! Okay! Where do we find her?'

'Find *her*? How would I know where to find a chippie whore?'

'You got *Findings* written on your board downstairs,' Coffin Ed put in.

'Yeah, and you'd better live up to it or you are going to find yourself where you don't want to be found,' Grave Digger added.

'You know that old courtyard between One-eleventh and One-twelfth Streets?'

'The Alley.'

'Yes. She's got a man in one of those holes in there somewhere.'

'Who's the man?'

'Just a man, Digger. I don't know who he is or what he does. You know I wouldn't be interested in a man who was interested in a chippie like that.'

'Okay, Ed, let's get going,' Grave Digger said.

'We'd better call the desk first and let Anderson know the horse got out.'

'You call him.'

Coffin Ed reached for the telephone on the night table.

Grave Digger turned to the cops and said, 'You men had

better get back to your cars; you've been off the street too
long as it is.'

Lady Gypsy said, 'I want to put in a charge against that
man for assault and battery and theft.'

'You'll have to go to the station,' Grave Digger said. 'And
you had better wear a suit.'

10

When Roman and Sassafras came running down the stairs
from Lady Gypsy's and made for the Buick parked at the
curb, it was a good thing that nobody saw them. They were
enough to catch the eyes of the blind.

Roman had stuck Lady Gypsy's fortune-telling turban, with
its big glass eye, on the side of his head – so now he had
three eyes all looking in different directions. He had draped
the rainbow-colored gown over his leather jumper and army
pants, but it was too short, and his paratrooper boots were
showing. He carried his coonskin cap in his left hand and his
big rusty .45 in his right.

'If we get caught I'm going to act crazy and start running,' he
panted hoarsely. 'They won't shoot a crazy fortune teller.'

Sassafras started giggling.

Roman gave her a dirty look as he ran around and climbed
in beneath the wheel. He put his pistol and coonskin cap on
the seat between them and took off in a hurry. But some
sixth sense told him he had a better chance of getting away
by driving slowly.

He was driving like a preacher on the way to church when
he came to Third Avenue and turned south.

The occupants of the first of the prowl cars coming fast
from the north saw the slow-moving Buick just before the
prowl car screamed around the corner into 116th Street.
They didn't give it a second thought. They hadn't seen
the driver, and they couldn't imagine anybody crawling
along at that speed in the hottest car east of the Mississippi River.

Roman drove down past 114th Street and parked in front of a mattress factory behind an open-bed truck.

'I got to give this situation some thought,' he said.

Sassafras couldn't stop giggling. Every time she looked at him it got worse.

'This ain't no laughing time,' he said hoarsely. 'You're going to make me mad.'

'I know it ain't, sugar,' she admitted, half choking. 'But ain't nobody looking at you in that get-up going to burst out crying.'

'Well, it's your fault,' he accused. 'Taking me to see that stool pigeon—'

'How was I to know he was a stool pigeon?' she flared. 'I been there lots of times before with other mens and he ain't never—' She caught herself.

'I know you has,' he said. 'You don't have to rub it in. I ain't expected you to get all rusty while I've been away. I ain't no fool.'

She put her arm about his neck and tried to pull his head down to her. 'I has been true to you, sugar,' she said. 'I swear it on a stack of Bibles.'

He pulled his head back. 'Listen, baby, this ain't no time for sweet talk. Here I is, done blowed a whole year's pay, and you is swearing to bald-face lies on stacks of Bibles.'

'It ain't no lie,' she said. 'If you'd taken the trouble to test it, instead of buying Cadillacs—'

'You wanted the car as much as me.'

'What if I did? That don't mean I think a Cadillac is the only thing God made.'

'This ain't no time to argue,' he said. 'We has got to do something – and fast. I got a notion we has been awfully lucky so far, but it ain't going to last forever. The cops is going to catch us in this hot car and then—'

She cut him off. 'We could go see a man I know who's in the automobile business. He might can help us.'

'I done seen all the men in the automobile business I needs to see,' he said. 'I has had it. What I'm thinking of doing is see if I can find some of my ship-buddies and get them to help me look for my car.'

'This man I'm talking about could do more good than

them,' she contended. 'If that big bright Cadillac is anywhere in Harlem, he is more likely to find it than anybody I know of.'

'If all these mens you know—' he began, but she wouldn't let him finish.

'What mens?'

'This bald-headed pappy passing himself off as a fortune teller—'

Her lips curled. 'You ain't jealous of him, I hope.'

'Well, he damn sure wasn't no woman.'

'This man ain't a bit like him.'

'If you think that makes me happy—'

'It ain't like that,' she said. 'I hardly know him. He's just a business acquaintance.'

'What kind of business?'

But she ignored that. 'We can ask him to look around and see what he might find,' she said. 'And also we can stay in his house whilst he's looking. You ain't got nowhere to stay.'

'I was depending on staying with you the time I wasn't staying in my car. Is you got some man staying in your room?'

'You make me sick,' she said. 'You know can't no man stay in my room, as respectable as those people is I room with.'

'Well, how is us going to pay this man for staying in his house and searching for our car?' he wanted to know. 'I gave Mister Baron my last dollar.'

'We can sell him the tires of this car,' she said. 'He's in the used-tire business.'

'I get it,' he said. 'I ain't as dumb as you think. He's a tire thief.'

'Well, what if he is,' she said. 'He's got to know where cars is at in order to steal their tires. And that's just who you need, somebody who knows something.'

'Well, all right then, let's go give him the tires off this car and get started looking. Where is he at?'

'He lives in the Alley. He's got a big place of his own.'

He started the car and drove down to 112th Street and turned back toward Lexington. Just back of the buildings facing on Third Avenue was a narrow passageway that turned at a right angle and ran between the crosstown streets.

It was a tight squeeze for a big car – there wasn't space

on either side to open the door and get out – and he had to back up three times to turn the corner.

'I'd hate to get caught in here,' he said. 'Ain't no way to go but up.'

The Alley was flanked by rows of two-story brick buildings, in varying degrees of decay, that had once been carriage-houses for the residents of 112th and 111th Streets. Now families lived on the second floors that had been servants' quarters, and the carriage stalls were filled with long-forgotten junk, in which rats bred and children played and little girls lost their maidenheads.

'It's here,' she said, indicating a rotten wooden carriage-house door spotted with patches of rusty tin. 'Let me see if he's in.'

The door was fastened by iron bars bolted to the rotten wood and a brass lock the size of a hitching block.

He stopped the car, and she got out and peered through a spyhole beside the lock.

'He ain't in,' she said. 'His motorcycle ain't here.'

'What's us going to do?' he said.

'Let me think,' she said, putting the tips of her mittened fingers to a dusty gray cheek and looking absent. 'Oh!' she said brightly. 'That reminds me. He gave me a key to the door.'

She started digging in her handbag.

'What's he doing giving you a key to his door?' he asked suspiciously.

'It's for his girl friend,' she said lightly. 'She and I is pals. And he said if she come by and he was out for me to let her in.'

To the right of the carriage-house doors was a small door that opened on to a staircase leading to the quarters above. She inserted a key in the Yale lock and said, 'There! Now we can just go inside and wait for him.'

'You know this man mighty well,' he said.

'His girl friend and me is just like that,' she said, holding up a hand with the thumb pressed tightly to the first mittened finger. 'I'll just run up and get the key to the big lock so you can put the car inside where won't nobody see it.'

'If I likes this, I likes oats in my ice-cream,' he said. 'And I ain't no mule.'

But she didn't wait to hear him. She ran up, got the key and opened the big doors, and he maneuvered the car into a dark, damp room with bare beams and a flagstoned floor smelling of tire rubber and earth mold. Hanging to toolboards on the walls were the various equipment for changing and repairing tires, but no tires were in sight.

He got out, grumbling to himself. She closed and locked the gate, switching about with a bright, excited insouciance, as though her pants were crawling with seventeen thousand queen ants.

'Now we'll just go upstairs and wait,' she said, moving as though all the ants were biting her lightly.

The upstairs was one room. There were sets of windows at both back and front, the panes covered with oiled brown paper. In the center, on one side, was a coal-burning, pot-bellied stove. The nearest corner was filled by a double bed with a chipped, white-enameled iron frame. The opposite corner was curtained off for a clothes closet. On the other side of the stove was a chest of drawers with a cracked marble top, on which sat a two-burner gas plate. A square table with dirty dishes occupied the center of the floor. Before the inside windows was a third table with a cracked white porcelain washbowl and pitcher. Water was supplied by a hose coming from a single tap at the level of the baseboards. The toilet was outside, behind the carriage house. The only covering for the bare wooden floor was a variety of men's garments.

In addition to a single drop light in the center of the room, hanging from one of the uncovered beams were several tiny wall lamps from the ten-cent stores.

Sassafras turned on the bright drop light and flung her coat across the unmade bed. She was wearing a red knitted dress to match her cap, and black lace stockings.

It was so cold in the room their breath made vapor.

'I'm going to make a fire,' she said. 'You just set down and make yourself comfortable.'

He gave her an evil and suspicious look, but she didn't notice it.

She bent over and looked into the potbellied stove, her duck-shaped bottom tightening the seat of her dress.

He put his coonskin cap on the table beside a dirty plate and placed the rusty pistol on top of it.

'There's a trap already laid,' she said, and got a box of kitchen matches from the chest of drawers.

'You don't know where he keeps his money, too, do you?' he asked.

She lit the fire and opened the draft, then turned around and looked at him. 'What're you grumbling about to yourself?'

'You're acting more at home here than a hen in a nest,' he said. 'You're sure your business with this man ain't what I'm thinking?'

She took off her cap and shook loose her short, straightened hair.

'Oh, don't be so jealous,' she said. 'You're frowning up enough to scare out the fire.'

'I ain't jealous,' he denied. 'I'm just thinking.'

She began clearing the dirty dishes from the table and stacking them beside the gas hot plate.

'You sailors is all just alike,' she said. 'If you had your way you'd handcuff a girl's legs together and take the key to sea.'

'You ain't just saying it,' he admitted, growing more and more angry as he watched her domestic activity.

The fire began roaring up the chimney, and she half-closed the damper. Then she turned and looked at him; her sloe eyes glittered like brilliants.

'Take off those Mother Hubbard clothes so I can kiss you,' she said, shaking the kinks out of her muscles.

'This place sure is making you kissified,' he complained.

'What's wrong with that?' she said. 'You can't expect a cow to chew her cud when she got a field full of grass.'

He glared at her. 'If you make eyes at this man, there's going to be asses whipped,' he said threateningly.

She moved into him and snatched off the turban with the third eye.

'That thing is galling your brains,' she said.

'It ain't my brains,' he denied.

'Don't I know it,' she said, groping at him.

'Let me get off these womanish things,' he said, and began pulling the robe up over his head. 'I feels like a rooster trying to lay an egg.'

'You is sure got chickens on your mind,' she said, tickling him in the stomach while the robe covered his face.

He jumped back, laughing like a big tickled goon, hit his calves against the edge of the bed and fell sprawling across it on his back.

She jumped on top of him and tried to smother him with the folds of colored cloth. He tore open a hole for his head to come through, and she jumped backward to her feet and bent double laughing.

He got his feet on the floor and his legs underneath him, and pushed from the bed like a young bull starting a charge. His lips were stretched, his tongue lolled from one corner; he looked as though he might be panting, but his breath was held. The frown still knotted his forehead, but his gray eyes were lit, the right one focused on her and the left one ranging off in the direction of the stove. His head peered from the folds of colored cloth hanging across his leather jacket and down his back.

He lunged for her.

She let his hands touch her, then twisted out of his grip, spinning on her toes, and went half across the room.

He put his big shoulders low, long arms outstretched like a grappling wrestler, and charged towards her. She got the table in between them. She was panting with laughter.

'Butterfingers,' she taunted, kicking off her shoes.

'I'll get you,' he panted.

He knocked over a chair trying to circle the table, but she kept just beyond his reach. Then, with a quick unexpected motion, he gripped the table by the edge, lifted it inches from the floor and threw it to one side.

Now nothing stood between them.

She shrieked and turned, but he got hold of her waist from behind and rode her face down across the bed. She was lithe, quick and strong, and she twisted from beneath him, coming face up at the foot of the bed. He jumped like a big cat and straddled her, gripping her upper arms with both hands.

She went limp for a moment and looked up at him from burning black challenging eyes. An effluvium of hot-bodied woman and dime-store perfume came up from her in a blast. It filled his mouth with tongue floating in a hot spring of saliva.

Her lips were swollen, and her throat was corded. He could feel the hardness of her nipples through his leather jacket and woolen shirt.

'Take it and you can have it,' she said.

Abruptly his mind began to work. His body went lax, his grip relaxed and his frown deepened.

'All this trouble I'm in and that's all you can think of,' he said.

'If this won't cure your troubles nothing will,' she murmured.

'We ain't got much time,' he complained.

'If you're scared, go home!' she hissed, and balled herself up to jump from the bed.

He went taut again before she got away and flattened her shoulders back.

'I'm going to cool you off,' he said.

She put her knees against his chest and pushed. He let go her arms and grabbed her stockinged legs just above the knees and began to open them. Her legs were strong enough to break a young man's back, and she put all of her strength into keeping them closed. But he hunched his overgrown muscles and began bearing down. They locked in a test of strength. Their breath came in gasps.

Slowly her legs began to open. They stared into one another's eyes. The stove had begun to smoke, and their eyes smarted.

Suddenly she gave way. Her legs went wide so quickly he fell on top of her. He clutched at flimsy cloth, and there was a tearing sound. He flung something from his hands. Buttons sailed in all directions, like corn popping.

'Now!' she screamed.

11

Three minutes after the Buick had squeezed into the Alley, a small black sedan skidded about the corner into 112th Street from Lexington Avenue.

Grave Digger was driving with the lights dimmed, and Coffin Ed was keeping a sharp lookout among the parked cars for the Buick.

The heater had suddenly begun to work, and the ice was melting on the windshield. The wind had shifted to the east, and the sleet had stopped. The tires sang softly in the shifting sleet on the asphalt street as the car straightened out; but the next moment it began going off to the right, so Grave Digger had to steer slightly left to keep it on a straight course.

'I got a feeling this is a wild-goose chase,' Coffin Ed said. 'It's hard to figure anybody being that stupid these days.'

'Who knows?' Grave Digger said. 'This boy ain't won no prizes so far.'

They were halfway down the block of dilapidated old houses and jerry-built tenements when they spied a motorcycle with a sidecar turn into the other end from Third Avenue.

They became suddenly alert. They didn't recognize the vehicle; they knew nothing of its history, its use or its owner. But they knew that anyone out on a night like that in an open vehicle bore investigation.

The rider of the motorcycle saw them at the instant they saw him. He saw a small black sedan coming crabwise down the otherwise deserted street. As much trouble as he had gone to over the years to keep out of its way, he knew it like the plague.

He wore dark-brown coveralls, a woolen-lined army fatigue jacket, and a fur-lined, dark-plaid hunter's cap.

The seat had been removed from the sidecar, and in its place were two fully-tired automobile wheels covered with black tarpaulin.

When Coffin Ed spied the tarpaulin-covered objects, he said, 'Do you see what I see?'

'I dig you,' Grave Digger said, and stepped on the gas.

If the tires had been smaller, the rider would have swallowed them the way peddlers swallowed marijuana cigarettes when the cops closed in. Instead he gunned his motorcycle straight ahead, switching on the bright light to blind the two detectives, and leaning far over to the right side out of line of fire. Motor roar filled the night like jet planes taking off.

Simultaneously Grave Digger switched on his bright lights.

Coffin Ed had his pistol out and was fumbling with the handle to the window, trying to get it down. But he didn't have time.

The two vehicles roared straight toward one another on the half-slippery street.

Grave Digger tried to outguess him. He saw the joker leaning to his right, overtop the sidecar. He knew the joker had them figured to figure he'd be leaning to the left, balancing the sidecar for any quick maneuver. He cased the joker to make a sharp last-minute turn to the right, braking slightly to make a triangle skid, and try to pass the car on the left, on the driver's side, opposite the free-swinging gun of Coffin Ed.

So he jerked the little sedan sharply to the left, tamped the brakes and went into an oblique skid, blocking off the left side of the street.

But the joker outguessed Grave Digger. He made a rollover in his seat like a Hollywood Indian on a pinto pony, and broke a ninety degree turn to his own left and gunned it to the limit for a flying skid.

His intention was to get past the sedan on the right side, and to hell with getting shot at.

Both drivers miscalculated the traction of the street. The hard, sleety coating was tricky; the tires bit in and gripped. The motorcyle sidecar hit the right-rear fender of the sedan at a tangent, and went into a full-gunned spin. The sedan wobbled on its rear wheels and threw Grave Digger off balance. The motorcycle went over the curb behind a parked car, bouncing like a rubber ball, bruised the rider's leg against a rusty iron stairpost and headed back in the direction it had come from.

Coffin Ed was stuck in the half-opened window, his gun arm pinioned and useless, shouting at the top of his voice: 'Halt or I'll shoot!'

The rider heard him over the roar of the motor as he was fighting to keep the vehicle on the sidewalk and avoid sidescraping the row of stairposts on one side and the parked cars on the other.

The sedan was across the street, pointed at an angle toward the opposite curb, but headed in the general right direction.

'I'll get him,' Grave Digger said, shifting back to first and tramping on the throttle.

But he hadn't straightened out the wheels from his sharp left turn, and, instead of the car curving back into the street, it bounded to the left and went broadside into a parked Chevy. The Chevy door caved in, and the left-front fender of the little sedan crumpled like tin foil. Glass flew from the smashed headlamp, and the rending sound of metal woke up the neighborhood.

The thing to have done was to back up, straighten out and start over.

Grave Digger was so blind mad by this turn of events he kept tramping on the throttle and scraped past the Chevy by sheer horsepower. His own crumpled left-front fender caught in the Chevy's left-rear fender, and both broke loose from their respective cars.

He left them bouncing in the street and took off after the motorcycle that had bounced back into the street and was making a two-wheeled turn north up Third Avenue.

It was pushing four-thirty in the morning, and the big transport trucks were on the streets, coming from the west, through the tunnels underneath the Hudson River, and heading north through Manhattan Island toward upstate New York – Troy, Albany, Schenectady or the Boston road.

A trailer truck was going north on Third Avenue when Grave Digger made the turn, and for a moment it looked as though he might go underneath it. Coffin Ed was leaning out the window with his pistol in his hand. He ducked back, but his gun was still in sight when they passed the driver's cabin.

The truck driver's eyes popped.

'Did you see that cannon?' he asked his helper.

'This is Harlem,' his helper said. 'It's crazy, man.'

The white driver and the colored helper grinned at one another.

The motorcycle was turning west into 114th Street when Grave Digger got the sedan steadied from its shimmy. The melting ice on the windscreen was blurring his vision, and he turned on the wipers. For a moment he couldn't see at all. But he turned anyway, hoping he was right.

He bent too sharp and bumped over the near-side corner crub. Coffin Ed's head hit the ceiling.

'Goddam, Digger, you're beating me to death,' he complained.

'All I can say is I've had better nights,' Grave Digger muttered through clenched teeth.

They kept the motorcycle in sight until it turned north on Seventh Avenue, but didn't gain on it. For a time it was out of sight. When they came into Seventh Avenue, they didn't see it.

Three trucks were lined up on the outside lane, and a fourth was passing the one ahead.

'We don't want to lose that son,' Grave Digger said.

'He's passing on the sidewalk,' Coffin Ed said, leaning out his right-side window.

'Cut one over his head.'

Coffin Ed crossed his left arm to overtop the window ledge, rested the long nickel-plated barrel atop his left wrist and blasted at the night. Flame lanced into the dark, and three blocks ahead a streetlamp went out.

The motorcycle curved from the sidewalk back into the street in front of the line of trucks. Grave Digger came up behind the truck on the inside lane and opened his siren.

At 116th Street Coffin Ed said, 'He's keeping straight ahead, Trying to make the county line.'

Grave Digger swerved to the left of the park that ran down between the traffic lanes and went up the left-hand side. The windshield wipers had cleared halfmoons in the dirty glass, and he could see an open road. He pushed the throttle to the floor, gaining on the motorcycle across the dividing park.

'Slow him down, Ed,' he said.

The park, circled by a small wire fence, was higher than the level of the street, and it shielded the motorcycle's tires. It was going too fast to risk shooting at the lamp. He threw three shots in back of it, but the rider didn't slow.

They passed two more northbound trucks, and for a time both lanes were clear. The sedan came up level with the motorcycle.

Coffin Ed said, 'Watch him close, Digger, he's going to try some trick.'

'He's as scared of these corners as we are,' Grave Digger said. 'He's going to try to crash us into a truck.'

'He's got two up ahead.'

'I'd better get behind him now.'

At 121st Street Grave Digger swerved back to the right-side lanes.

One block ahead, a refrigerator truck was flashing its yellow passing lights as it pulled to the inner lane to pass an open truck carrying sheet metal.

The motorcycle rider had time to pass on the inside, but he hung back, riding the rear of the refrigerator truck until it had pulled clear over to the left, blocking both sides of the street.

'Get a tire now,' Grave Digger said.

Coffin Ed leaned out of his window, took careful aim over his left wrist and let go his last two bullets. He missed the motorcycle tire, with both shots, but the fifth and last one in his revolver was always a tracer bullet, since one night he had been caught shooting in the dark. They followed its white phosphorescent trajectory as it went past the rear tire, hit a manhole cover in the street, ricocheted in a slight upward angle and buried itself in the outside tire of the open truck carrying sheet metal. The tire exploded with a bang. The driver felt the truck lurch and hit the brakes.

This threw the motorcycle rider off his timing. He had planned to cut quickly between the two trucks and shoot ahead before the inside truck drew level with the truck it was passing. When he got them behind him the two trucks would block off the street, and he would make his getaway.

He was pulling up fast behind the truck carrying sheet metal when the tire burst and the driver tamped his brakes. He wheeled sharply to the left, but not quickly enough.

The three thin sheets of stainless steel, six feet in width, with red flags flying from both corners, formed a blade less than a quarter of an inch thick. This blade caught the rider above his woolen-lined jacket, on the exposed part of his neck, which was stretched and taut from his physical exertion, as the motorcycle went underneath. He was hitting more than fifty-five miles an hour, and the blade severed his head from his body as though he had been guillotined.

His head rolled halfway up the sheets of metal while his body kept astride the seat and his hands gripped the handlebars. A stream of blood spurted from his severed jugular, but his body completed the maneuver which his head had ordered and went past the truck as planned.

The truck driver glanced from his window to watch the passing truck as he kept braking to a stop. But instead he saw a man without a head passing on a motorcycle with a sidecar and a stream of steaming red blood flowing back in the wind.

He gasped and passed out.

His lax feet released the pressure from the brake and clutch, and the truck kept on ahead.

The motorcycle, ridden by a man without a head, surged forward at a rapid clip.

The driver of the refrigerator truck that was passing the open truck didn't believe what he saw. He switched on his bright lights, caught the headless motorcycle rider in their beam and quickly switched them off. He blinked his eyelids. It was the first time he had ever gone to sleep while driving, he thought; and my God, what a nightmare! He switched the lights back on, and there it still was. Man or hallucination, he was getting the hell away from there. He began flashing his blinkers as though he had gone crazy; he mashed the horn and stood on the throttle and looked to the other side.

The truck carrying the sheet metal turned gradually to the right from faulty steering mechanism. It climbed over the shallow curb and started up the wide stone steps of a big fashionable Negro church.

In the lighted box out in front of the church was the announcement of the sermon for the day.

Beware! Death is closer than you think!

The head rolled off the slow-moving truck, dropped to the sidewalk and rolled out into the street. Grave Digger, closing up fast, saw something that looked like a football with a cap on it bouncing on the black asphalt. It was caught in his one bright light, but the top was turned to him when he saw it, and he didn't recognize what it was.

'What did he throw out?' he asked Coffin Ed.

Coffin Ed was staring as though petrified. He gulped. 'His head,' he said.

Grave Digger's muscles jerked spasmodically. He hit the brake automatically.

A truck had closed in from behind unnoticed, and it couldn't stop in time. It smacked the little sedan gently, but that was enough. Grave Digger sailed forward; the bottom rim of the steering wheel caught him in the solar plexus and snapped his head down; his mouth hit the top rim of the steering wheel, and he mashed his lips and chipped two front teeth.

Coffin Ed went headfirst into the safety-glass windshield and battered out a hole. But his hard head saved him from serious injury.

'Goddam,' Grave Digger lisped, straightening up and spitting out chipped enamel. 'I'd have been better off with the Asiatic flu.'

'God knows, Digger, I would have, too,' Coffin Ed said.

Gradually the taut headless body on the motorcycle spewed out its blood and the muscles went limp. The motorcycle began to waver; it went to one side and then the other, crossed 125th Street, just missing a taxi, neatly circled around the big clock atop a post at the corner and crashed into the iron-barred door of the credit jewelry store, knocking down a sign that read:

We Will Give Credit to the Dead

12

Roman got up and fastened his belt.

'When is this joker coming?' He was all for business now.

Sassafras stood up and shook down her skirts. Her face was sweaty, and her eyes looked sleepy. Her dress was stretched out of shape.

'He ought to be here any time,' she said, but she sounded as though she didn't care if he never came.

Roman began looking worried again. 'You're sure this joker can help us? I've got a notion we're up against some rough studs, and I don't want nobody messing around who's going to get rattled.'

Sassafras ran a greasy bone comb through her short, tousled hair. 'Don't worry 'bout him,' she said. 'He ain't going to lose his head.'

'This waiting around is dragging me,' he said. 'I wish we could do something.'

'You call what we been doing nothing?' she said coyly.

'I mean about my car,' he said. 'It's going to soon be daylight and ain't nobody doing nothing.'

She went over, put some coal on the fire and adjusted the damper. Her dress was pulled out of shape and hung one-sided.

'I'm going to see if he got any whiskey left,' she said, rummaging about the shoes on the floor of the curtained-off clothes corner.

He followed her and saw a green dress hanging with the men's clothes.

'This looks like your dress,' he said suspiciously.

'Don't start that stuff again,' she said. 'You think they only made one dress when they made mine. Besides which, his girl friend is about the same size as me.'

'You're sure she ain't wearing the same skin?' he said.

She ignored him. Finally she came up with a bottle of cheap blended whiskey, three-quarters full.

'Here, drink this and shut up,' she said, thrusting the bottle into his hands.

He uncorked it and let whiskey gurgle down his throat. 'It ain't bad, but it's mighty weak,' he appraised.

'How you going to know bad whiskey?' she said scornfully. 'You've been drinking white mule all your life.'

He took another drink, bringing the level down below half. 'Baby, I'm hungry enough to eat a horse off his hoof and leave the skeleton still hitched to the plow,' he said, flexing his muscles. 'Why don't you see if your girl friend's boy friend has got anything to eat in this joint?'

'If I found something, it'd just make you more suspicious,' she said.

'Anyhow, it'd fill my belly.'

She found some salt meat, a half loaf of white bread in wax-paper wrapping and a bottle of molasses in the bottom drawer. Then she opened a back window and delved into a screened cold-box attached to the sill; she found a pot half-filled with congealed hominy grits and a frozen can of sliced California peaches.

'I don't see no coffee,' she said.

'Who wants coffee?' he said, taking another swig from the bottle.

Shortly the room was filled with the delicious-smelling smoke of fried fat meat. She sliced the gelatinous hominy and browned it in the hot fat. He opened the can with his pocket knife, but the contents were frozen solid, so he put the can on top of the stove.

She couldn't find but one clean plate, so she used one slightly soiled. She polished a couple of forks with a dry cloth.

He filled his plate with fried hominy, covered it with fried meat and doused it with molasses. He stuffed his mouth full of dry bread, then packed meat, hominy and molasses on top of it.

She looked at him with disgust. 'You can get the boy out the country, but you can't get the country out the boy,' she philosophized, eating her meat daintily along with bites of bread and holding her fried hominy between the first finger and thumb, according to etiquette.

He was finished first. He got up and looked at the peaches. A core of ice still remained. He picked up the whiskey bottle and measured it with his eye.

'You want some grog mixed with peach juice?' he asked.

She gave him a supercilious look. 'I don't mind if I do,' she said in a proper voice.

He looked about for a receptacle to hold the mixture, but not seeing any, he squeezed the rim of the can into a spout and poured the peach syrup into the whisky bottle. He shook it up and took a swallow and passed it to her. She took a swallow and passed it back.

Soon they were giggling and slapping at one another. The next thing they were on the bed again.

'I wish that man would hurry up and come on,' he said, making one last effort to be sensible.

'What you want to go looking for an old Cadillac in this weather for, when here you is got me?' she said.

'Let's stop here and walk,' Coffin Ed said.

Grave Digger coasted to a stop beside the entrance to the Alley. It was a dark gray morning, and not a soul was in sight.

They alighted slowly, like decrepit old men.

'This jalopy looks as though it's been to the wars,' Grave Digger lisped.

His lips were swollen to such proportions it looked as though his face were turning wrong side out.

'You look like you've been with it,' Coffin Ed said.

'Yeah, let's hope there're no more jokers in this deck.'

He started to lock the car doors and then saw the naked front wheel, the battered rear end and the hole in the windshield, and he put the key into his pocket.

'We don't have to worry about anybody stealing it,' he lisped.

'That's for sure,' Coffin Ed agreed.

They picked their way along the uneven brick pavement, avoiding slick ice and stepping over frozen rats and cats. Garbage trucks couldn't get into the Alley, and residents piled their garbage in the street the year around. Now it presented an uneven pile of mounds along the walls of the carriage houses, composed chiefly of hog bones, cabbage leaves and tin cans. They saw one lone black cat sitting on his haunches gnawing a piece of bacon rind frozen hard as a board.

'He must have stolen that,' Coffin Ed said. 'Nobody living in here has thrown that much good meat away.'

'Let's go easy now,' Grave Digger lisped.

When they came to the door, both took out their pistols and spun the cylinders. Brass bullets showed faintly against the gleaming nickel plate. Their shadowy figures had the silence of ghosts. They were mouth-breathing now, giving off soft puffs of vapor in the frigid air.

Grave Digger switched his pistol to his left hand and fished a key from his right overcoat pocket. As he fitted the key into the lock, Coffin Ed pulled hard on the knob. The Yale lock opened without a sound. Coffin Ed pushed the door in three inches, and Grave Digger withdrew the key.

Both flattened against the outside wall and listened. From above came sounds like two people sawing wood; a man sawing dry pine board with a bucksaw and a boy sawing shingles with a toy.

Coffin Ed reached out and slowly pushed the door open with his pistol barrel. The two kept on sawing. He put his head around the doorframe and looked.

There was no door at the head of the stairs. The opening was lit by a soft pink light, revealing the naked beams of a ceiling.

Coffin Ed went up first, stepping on the outside edge of the stairs, testing each before putting down his weight.

Grave Digger let him get five steps ahead and followed in his footsteps.

At the top, Coffin Ed stepped quickly into the pink light, his gun barrel moving from left to right.

Then without turning, he beckoned to Grave Digger.

They stood side by side looking at the sleeping figures on the bed.

The man wore a plaid woolen shirt, open all the way down and the shirt-tail out, a heavy-ribbed T-shirt, army pants and stained white woolen socks. A leather jacket was piled on top of a pair of paratrooper boots on the floor beside the bed. He lay doubled up on one side, facing the woman, with an arm flung out across her stomach.

The woman wore a red knitted dress and black lace stockings. That seemed to be all. She lay half on her side, half on her back, with her legs outspread. Velvet black skin showed all the way up to her waist.

A single dim pink-shaded lamp hanging from a nail above the head of the bed made the scene look cozy.

Their gazes roved over the room, lingered on the big rusty .45 lying on the coonskin cap, went on and came back.

Coffin Ed tiptoed over and picked it up. He sniffed at the muzzle, shook his head and slipped it into his pocket.

Grave Digger tiptoed over to the bed and poked the sleeping man in the ribs with the muzzle of his own pistol.

Afterwards he admitted he shouldn't have done it.

Roman erupted from the bed like a scalded wildcat.

He came up all at once, all of him, as though released from a catapult. He struck a backhanded blow with his left hand while he was in the air, caught Grave Digger straight across his belly and knocked him on his rump.

Coffin Ed jumped over the top of Grave Digger's head and slashed at Roman with his pistol barrel.

But, while he was flat in the air, Roman doubled up and spun over, taking the blow on the fat of his hams and kicking Coffin Ed in the face with both stockinged feet.

Then the screaming began. It was high, loud, keening screaming that dynamited the brain and poured acid on the teeth. Sassafras had reared up on all fours and was kneeling in the bed with her mouth wide open.

Coffin Ed went back into the table. The legs splintered, and he crashed to the floor.

Roman landed on the flat of his shoulders and the palms of his hands while his feet were still in the air.

Grave Digger came up on his left hand, his left foot jackknifed beneath him, and tapped Roman across the top of the head with his pistol butt. But his flopping overcoat impeded the blow, and Roman gave no sign that he felt it. He doubled his feet beneath him and came up straight, like an acrobat, turning at the instant he touched floor.

Grave Digger backhanded with the same motion that tapped Roman on the head and hit his right knee cap.

Roman went down on one side, like the pier of a house giving way. Coffin Ed staggered in and kicked him solidly in the left calf.

Sassafras's hair stood out like quills of a porcupine and her eyes were glazed, but the screaming kept on.

Roman fell into Grave Digger and clutched him by the leg, and, when Coffin Ed jumped forward to kick him away, he clutched his leg.

He got to his feet, holding each big man by a leg, and banged their heads into the ceiling beams.

'Run, Sassy, run!' he shouted. 'This ain't no time for a fit.'

She stopped screaming as suddenly as she had started. She jumped to her feet and started toward the door.

Grave Digger and Coffin Ed began raining pistol blows on Roman's head.

He sank to his knees but held onto their legs.

'Run, Sassy!' he gasped.

But she stopped at the doorway to run back and snatch up her new fur coat.

Grave Digger grabbed at her but missed.

'Turn loose, tough mouth!' Coffin Ed grated as he kept pounding Roman on the head.

But Roman held on long enough for Sassafras to scamper down the stairs like a frightened alley cat. Then he relaxed his grip; he grinned foolishly and murmured, 'Solid bone . . .' He fell forward and rolled over.

Coffin Ed leaped toward the doorway, but Grave Digger called to him, lisping painfully, 'Let her go. Let her go. He earned it.'

13

It was eleven o'clock Sunday morning, and the good colored people of Harlem were on their way to church.

It was a gloomy, overcast day, miserable enough to make the most hardened sinner think twice about the hot, sun-shiny streets of heaven before turning over and going back to sleep.

Grave Digger and Coffin Ed looked them over indifferently as they drove toward Harlem hospital. A typical Sunday morning sight, come sun or come rain.

Old white-haired sisters bundled up like bales of cotton against the bitter cold; their equally white-haired men, stumbling along in oversize galoshes like the last herd of Uncle Toms, toddling the last mile toward salvation on half-frozen feet.

Middle-aged couples and their broods, products of the postwar generation, the prosperous generation, looking sanctimonious in their good warm clothes, going to praise the Lord for the white folks' blessings.

Young men who hadn't yet made it, dressed in lightweight suits and topcoats sold by color instead of quality or weight in the credit stores, with enough brown wrapping paper underneath their pastel shirts to keep them warm, laughing at the strange words of God and making like Solomon at the pretty brownskin girls.

Young women who were sure as hell going to make it or drop dead in the attempt, ashy with cold, clad in the unbelievable colors of cheap American dyes, some at that very moment catching the pneumonia which would take them before that God they were on their way to worship.

From all over town they came.

To all over town they went.

The big churches and little churches, stone churches and store-front churches, to their own built churches and to hand-me-down churches.

To Baptist churches and African Methodist Episcopal churches and African Methodist Episcopal Zionist churches; to Holy Roller churches and Father Divine churches and Daddy Grace churches, Burning Bush churches, and churches of God and Christ.

To listen to their preachers preach the word of God: fat black preachers and tall yellow preachers; straightened-haired preachers and bald-headed preachers; family preachers and playboy preachers; men preachers and lady preachers and children preachers.

To listen to any sermon their preacher cared to preach. But on this cold day it had better be hot.

Grave Digger and Coffin Ed parked their wreck in front of the Harlem Hospital and went inside to the reception desk.

They asked to speak with Casper Holmes.

The cool, young colored nurse at the desk lifted a telephone and spoke some words. She put it down and gave them a cool, remote smile.

'I am sorry, but he is still in a coma,' she said.

'Don't be sorry for us, be sorry for him,' Coffin Ed said.

Her smile froze as though the insect had talked back.

'Tell him it's Digger Jones and Ed Johnson,' Grave Digger lisped.

She stared at the movement of his swollen lips with horrified fascination.

'Tell him we're just ahead of the Confederates,' he went on. 'Maybe that will get him out of his coma.'

Her face twisted as though she had swallowed something disagreeable.

'Confederates,' she murmured.

'You know who the Confederates are,' Coffin Ed said. 'They're the people who fought to keep us slaves.'

She smiled tentatively to prove she wasn't sensitive about slavery jokes.

They stared at her, grave and unsmiling.

She waited and they waited.

Finally she picked up the telephone again and repeated their message to the floor supervisor.

They heard her say: 'No, not conferees; they said *Con-fed-erates . . . Yes . . .*'

She put down the telephone and said without expression, 'You will have to wait.'

They waited; neither moved.

'Please wait in the waiting room,' she said.

Behind them was a small nook with a table and several chairs, some occupied by others who were waiting.

'We'll wait here,' Grave Digger lisped.

She pursed her lips. The telephone rang. She listened. 'Yes,' she said.

She looked up and said, 'His room is on the third floor. Take the elevator to the right, please. The floor supervisor will direct you.'

'You see,' Grave Digger lisped. 'You don't know what those Confederates are good for.'

The room was banked with flowers.

Casper sat up in a white bed wearing a turban of white bandages. His broad black face loomed aggressively above yellow silk pajamas. He looked like an African potentate, but it wasn't a time for flattery.

French windows opened to a terrace facing the east. Two overstuffed chairs ranged along one side of the bed. On the other side, remains of a breakfast littered a wheel tray. The detectives saw at a glance that it been a substantial breakfast of fried sausage, poached eggs on toast, hominy grits with butter, fruit and cereal with cream and a silver pot of coffee. A box of Havana cigars sat beside a basket of mixed fruit on the nightstand.

The detectives took off their hats.

'Sit down, boys,' Casper said. 'What's this about Confederates?'

Grave Digger looked about for a window sill on which to rest a ham, was thwarted by the French window and compromised on the arm of a chair. Coffin Ed backed into a corner and leaned against the wall, his scarred face in the shadows.

'We were just kidding, boss,' Grave Digger lisped. 'We thought you might want to talk to us before the big brass from downtown gets up here.'

Casper frowned. He didn't like the insinuation that he preferred talking to colored precinct detectives rather than to downtown white inspectors. But since he had tacitly admitted as much by seeing them, he decided to pass it.

'A God-damned embarrassing caper,' he conceded. 'Right in my own bailiwick.'

Now he looked like a martyred potentate.

'That's what we figured,' Coffin Ed said.

Casper flicked a quick, sly look from one to the other. 'You must feel the same way,' he observed. 'Where were you at the time?'

'Eating chicken feetsy at Mammy Louise's,' Grave Digger confessed.

Casper stared at him to see whether he was joking, decided he wasn't. He opened the box of cigars and selected one, picked up a gadget from the table and carefully snipped off the end, then reached for an imported gold lighter behind the box and snapped a flame. He applied the flame like a jeweler using a miniature torch on filigree of gold, snapped shut the lighter, slowly rolled the end of the cigar about between his thick lips and blew out a thin stream of smoke. The good smell of fine tobacco dissipated the hospital odors.

As an afterthought, he extended the box toward the detectives. Both declined.

'I will tell you what I know, which isn't much,' he said. 'Then we will see what we can make out of it. You boys must have been working on it all night yourselves.'

'Still at it,' Grave Digger lisped.

'First we'll tell you what we got,' Coffin Ed said. 'A colored sailor, a country boy from Alabama, left his ship at about six o'clock last evening. He had been working for one entire year to save money to buy a car; when he got his final pay, he had six thousand, five hundred dollars in one-hundred-dollar bills in a money belt. The ship docks in Brooklyn. It was eight o'clock before he got uptown. He met his girl friend, Sassafras Jenkins. They had some drinks and then took a taxi over to an office on lower Convent Avenue, where he had an appointment to meet one Mister Baron, who was selling him the car.'

Casper smoked his cigar softly, his black face impassive.

'The appointment was for ten o'clock,' Coffin Ed went on. 'Baron was a half hour late. He rode up in the car with a white man. Roman and his girl were waiting on the sidewalk in front of the dermatological clinic near One-twenty-sixth Street. The white man got out and went upstairs to an office in the rear. Roman and his girl stayed downstairs for another half hour with Baron, inspecting the car. A small crowd of people coming from the supermarket up the street collected.

'It was a brand new Cadillac convertible with some kind of gold-like finish. Baron was selling it to Roman for six thousand, five hundred dollars.'

Casper blinked but said nothing.

'You got a Cadillac convertible. What did yours cost?' Grave Digger asked.

'With accessories over eight thousand,' Casper said.

'Roman paid six thousand, five hundred for his,' Coffin Ed said. 'The three of them went upstairs to the office where the white man was waiting, and executed the bill of sale. Sassafras witnessed it, and the white man signed as a notary public, using the name Bernard Kaufman. The white man left.

'Then the three of them took the car for a tryout at Baron's suggestion. He had Roman turn into the street south of the Convent, where there would be little if any traffic, so he could test its pickup. Roman had no sooner started accelerating than he hit an old woman crossing the street. He wanted to stop, but Baron urged him to drive on. He didn't have any insurance; the car still had dealer's plates; he couldn't apply for registration until Monday morning; and he didn't have a driver's license. His girl friend didn't think the old woman was seriously hurt, but he ran anyway. He hadn't got clear of the block when a Buick drove up and forced him to a stop. Three men in police uniforms got out and accused him of hit-and-run manslaughter and forced the three of them out of the car.'

Casper sat up straight. His face turned slightly gray.

Coffin Ed waited for him to comment, but he still said nothing.

'The phony cops forced him and his girl into the Buick, sapped Baron, took the six thousand, five hundred dollars and went away in the Cadillac.

'We've been all night running down the Buick. We got it and Roman. We got a statement from Roman. He claims that Baron confessed that the old woman got up after he had hit her. So it must have been the bandits in the Buick who hit her the second time and killed her.'

Casper looked sick. 'That's horrible,' he said.

'More than you think,' Grave Digger lisped.

'But I don't see what that has got to do with the robbery.'

'I'm coming to that,' Coffin Ed said.

Casper couldn't see Coffin Ed's face distinctly in the shadows, and it worried him. 'Come over here and sit down where I can hear you,' he said.

'I'll talk louder,' Coffin Ed said.

A flicker of anger passed over Casper's face, but he said nothing. He picked up the gold lighter, and relit his cigar and hid behind a cloud of smoke.

'So far we haven't got a line on Baron,' Coffin Ed went on. 'We checked the building superintendent where the office is located and found that it is unoccupied and for rent. The super was out last night from nine o'clock until after two.

'The Cadillac hasn't been found; there's none reported stolen. The dealers are closed on Sundays, but there's been no report that any have been broken into.

'We found the owner of the Buick – the manager of a hardware store in Yonkers. He parked his car in front of his house when he went home at seven o'clock last night and didn't miss it until this morning. But that doesn't help us any.

'We checked the listing of notary publics in Manhattan County. There was none named Bernard Kaufman; the address was bogus and the seal was counterfeit.'

'That's well and good,' Casper rasped impatiently. 'But where's the tie-in?'

'The bandits who robbed you deliberately ran down the old lady a few minutes later and killed her.'

'Just proves they're brutal mother-rapers,' Casper said, lapsing back to the Harlem vernacular of his youth. 'But that's all.'

'Not quite all,' Grave Digger lisped.

'The old lady was not an old lady,' Coffin Ed said. 'He was a sort of a pansy pimp who went by the name of Black Beauty.'

Casper strangled on cigar smoke. Grave Digger stepped beside the bed and beat him on the back. The nurse entered at that moment and looked horrified.

'It's all right,' Casper gasped. 'I just strangled.'

'I'll get you a glass of water and a sedative,' she said, looking at Grave Digger disapprovingly. 'You shouldn't talk so much, and you're not allowed to smoke either. And beating a patient on the back,' she said to Grave Digger, 'is no cure for strangulation.'

'It works,' Grave Digger lisped.

'For chrissake, don't bother me now,' Casper said roughly, wiping the tears from his cheeks with the back of his hand. 'I'm busy as all hell.'

The nurse left in a huff.

'All right, goddammit, he was a mother-raping pansy called Black Beauty,' Casper said to Coffin Ed. 'So what?'

'His straight monicker is Junior Ball,' Coffin Ed replied. 'This morning at nine-thirty o'clock your wife, Missus Holmes, appeared at the morgue and identified the body and has requested it be released to her for burial.'

Casper gave no sign of outrage or surprise or any of the

other emotions they might have expected. He began looking guttermean. He spat out shreds of wet tobacco and said in a hard, street-fighter's voice, 'So what! If his name was Junior Ball, he was her cousin.'

'What we want to know is, why would a trio of bandits who had just robbed you of fifty grand run down your wife's cousin and kill him?' Coffin Ed said.

'How in the mother-raping hell would I know?' Casper said. 'And if you think she knows then ask her.'

'We're going to ask her all right,' Grave Digger lisped.

'Then go, goddammit, and do it!' he shouted, his face turning a vivid apoplectic shade of bright purple-black. 'And don't get so mother-raping cute. I'll have you out dredging the Gowanus Canal.'

'Don't lose your temper, boss – at your age you might have a stroke,' Grave Digger lisped.

Casper harnessed his rage with an effort. His breath came out in a long, hard sigh. He threw the partly smoked cigar on the floor and picked up another one without looking. His hands trembled as he lit it.

'All right, boys, let's cut out the crap,' he said in a conciliatory voice. 'You know what I mean. I don't want my wife's name mixed up in a scandal.'

'That's what we figured,' Coffin Ed said.

'And don't forget I got you boys your jobs,' he stated.

'Yeah, you and our army records—' Grave Digger began.

'Not to mention our marks of eighty-five and eighty-seven percent in our civil service examinations,' Coffin Ed supplemented.

Casper took the cigar from his teeth and said, 'All right, all right, so you think you can't be hurt.' He spread his hands. 'I don't want to hurt you. All I want is those mother-raping bandits caught with the minimum of publicity.' He sucked smoke into his lungs and let it dribble from his wide, flat nostrils. 'And you wouldn't suffer any if these mother-rapers turned up dead.' He gave them a half-lidded conniving look.

'That's the way we got it figured, boss,' Coffin Ed said.

'What the hell do you mean by that?' Casper flared again.

'Nothing, boss. Just that dead men don't talk, is all,' Coffin Ed said.

Casper didn't move. He stared from one to the other through obsidian eyes. 'If you're insinuating what I think, I'll break you both,' he threatened in a voice that sounded very dangerous.

For a moment there was only the sound of labored breathing in the room. The sound of muted footsteps came from the corridor. Down on a nearby street some halfwit was racing a motor.

Finally Grave Digger said lispingly, 'Don't go off half-cocked, Casper. We've all known each other too long. We just figured you wouldn't want any talk from anybody with the campaign coming up you've got to organize before November.'

Casper gave in. 'All right, then. But just don't try to needle me, because I don't needle. Now I'll tell you what I know, and, if that don't satisfy you, you can ask me questions.

'First, I didn't recognize any of the mother-raping bandits, and I know goddam near everybody in Harlem, either by name or by face. There ain't nobody in this town who could pull a caper like that I wouldn't know, and that about goes for you, too.'

Grave Digger nodded.

'So I figure they're from out of town. Got to be. Now how would they know I was getting a fifty-G payoff? That's the fifty-thousand-dollar question. First of all, I haven't told nobody, none of my associates, my wife, nobody. Secondly, I didn't know exactly when I was going to get it myself. I knew I was getting it sometime, but I didn't know when until the committee secretary, Grover Leighton, came into my office last night and plunked it down on my desk.'

'Rather early for it, wasn't it? Early in the year, I mean,' Coffin Ed said.

'Yeah. I didn't expect it until April or May. That would be sooner than usual. It don't generally come through until June. But they wanted to get an early start this year. It's going to be a rough election, with all these television deals and war issues and the race problem and such crap. So how they got to know about it before I knew about it myself – I mean the exact time of the delivery – is something I can't figure.'

'Maybe the secretary let it slip,' Grave Digger suggested.

'Yeah. Maybe frogs are eating snakes this season,' Casper conceded. 'I wouldn't know. But don't you boys tackle him. Let him work it out with the other white folks—' he winked – 'The Pinkertons and the commissioners and the inspectors. Me – I don't give a goddam how they found out. You boys know me – I'm a realist. I don't want no out-of-town mother-rapers robbing me. I want 'em caught – you get the idea. And if you kill 'em that's fine. You understand. I want everybody to know – everybody on this goddam green earth – that can't no mother-rapers rob Casper Holmes in Harlem and get away with it.'

'We got you, boss,' Coffin Ed said. 'But we don't have any leads. You know everything forward and backward, we thought maybe you might have some ideas. That's why we got here ahead of the confederates.'

Casper allowed himself a grim smile. Then it vanished. 'What's wrong with your stool pigeons?' he asked. 'They got the word around in Harlem that can't nobody have the runs without your stool pigeons telling you about it.'

'We'll get to them,' Grave Digger lisped.

'Well get to them, then,' Casper said. 'Get to the whore-houses and the gambling joints and the dope pushers and the call girls. Goddam! Two hoods with fifty G's are going to splurge on some vice or other.'

'If they're still in town,' Coffin Ed said.

'If they're still in town!' Casper echoed. 'Two of 'em are niggers, and the white boy's a cracker. Where the hell they going to go? Where would you go if you pulled a caper for fifty G's? Where else would you look for kicks? Harlem's the greatest town on earth. You think they're going to leave it?'

Both detectives subdued the impulse to exchange looks.

Coffin Ed said dispassionately, 'Don't think we're not on it, Casper. We've been on it from the moment it jumped. People got hurt, and some got killed. You'll read about it in the newspapers. But that's neither here nor there. We took our lumps, but we ain't got thrown.'

Casper looked at Grave Digger's swollen mouth. 'It's a job,' he said.

14

The apartment was on the fifth and top floor of an old stone-fronted building on 110th Street, overlooking the lagoon in upper Central Park.

Colored boys and girls in ski ensembles and ballet skirts were skating the light fantastic at two o'clock when Grave Digger and Coffin Ed parked their half-wrecked car before the building.

The detectives paused for a moment to watch them.

'Reminds me of Gorki,' Grave Digger lisped.

'The writer or the pawnbroker?' Coffin Ed asked.

'The writer, Maxim. In his book called *The Bystander*. A boy breaks through the ice and disappears. Folks rush to save him but can't find him – can't find any trace of him. He's disappeared beneath the ice. So some joker asks, "Was there really a boy?"'

Coffin Ed looked solemn. 'So he thought the hole in the ice was an act of God?'

'Must have.'

'Like our friend Baron, eh?'

They went silently up the old marble steps and pushed open the old, exquisitely carved wooden doors with cutglass panels.

'The rich used to live here,' Coffin Ed remarked.

'Still do,' Grave Digger said. 'Just changed color. Colored rich folks always live in the places abandoned by white rich folks.'

They walked through a narrow, oak-paneled hallway with stained-glass wall lamps to an old rickety elevator.

A very old colored man with long, kinky gray hair and parchmentlike skin, wearing a mixed livery of some ancient, faded sort, rose slowly from a padded stool and asked courteously, 'What floor, gentlemens?'

'Top,' Coffin Ed said.

The old man drew his cotton-gloved hand back from the lever as though it had suddenly turned red hot.

'Mister Holmes ain't in,' he said.

'Missus Holmes is,' Coffin Ed said. 'We have an appointment.'

The old man shook his cotton-boll head. 'She didn't tell me about it,' he said.

'She doesn't tell you everything she does, grandfather,' Coffin Ed said.

Grave Digger drew a soft leather folder from his inside pocket and flashed his shield. 'We're the men,' he lisped.

Stubbornly the old man shook his head. 'Makes no difference to Mister Holmes. He's *The Man*.'

'All right,' Coffin Ed compromised. 'You take us up. If Missus Holmes doesn't receive us, you bring us down. Okay?'

'It's a gentleman's agreement,' the old man said.

Grave Digger belched as the ancient elevator creaked upward.

'That lets us out,' Coffin Ed said. 'Gentlemen don't belch.'

'Gentlemen don't eat pig ears and collard greens,' Grave Digger said. 'They don't know what they're missing.'

The old man gave the appearance of not hearing.

Casper had the whole top floor to himself. It had originally been built for two families with facing doors across a small elevator foyer, but one had been closed and plastered over and there was only the one red-lacquered one left, with a small, engraved brass nameplate in the middle of the upper panel, announcing: *Casper Holmes*.

'Might just as well say Jesus Christ,' Grave Digger said.

'Go light on this lady, Digger,' Coffin Ed cautioned as he pushed the bell buzzer.

'Don't I always?' Grave Digger said.

A young black man in a spotless white jacket opened the door. It opened so silently Grave Digger blinked. The young man had shining black curls that looked as though they had been milled from coal tar, a velvet-smooth forehead slightly greasy, and dark-brown eyes, with whites like muddy water, devoid of all intelligence. His flat nose lay against low, narrow cheeks slashed by a thin-lipped mouth of tremendous width. The mouth was filled with white, even teeth.

'Mister Jones and Mister Johnson?' he inquired.

'As if you didn't know,' Grave Digger said.

'Please come right this way, sirs,' he said, leading them to a front room off the front of the hall.

He came as far as the doorway and left them.

It was a big room with windows overlooking Central Park. In the distance, over treetops, the towers of Rockefeller Center and the Empire State Building loomed in the murky haze. It reminded Coffin Ed of the lounge of the City Club.

Grave Digger lifted his feet high to keep from stumbling over the thick nap of the Oriental rugs, and Coffin Ed eyed the ornate furniture warily, wondering where he should sit.

Jazz classics were stacked on a combination set, and at their entrance Louis Armstrong was doing an oldy called 'Where The Chickens don't Roost So High'.

'Me and my old lady used to dance to that tune at the Savoy – before they tore it down,' Grave Digger said, and started cutting the rug.

He still had on his hat and overcoat, and he was performing the intricate steps of an old-time jitterbug with great abandon. His swollen lips were pecking at the perfumed air, and his overcoat tails were flapping in the breeze.

Coffin Ed stood beside a Louis XIV love seat, scratching his ribs.

'Digger, you're a pappy,' he said. 'Those steps you're doing went out with zoot suits.'

'Don't I know it,' Grave Digger said, sighing.

Mrs Holmes swung into the room from an inner doorway like a stripteaser coming on stage. She stopped short in open-mouth amazement and put her hands on her hips.

'If you want to dance, go to the Theresa ballroom,' she said in a cool contralto voice. 'There's a matinee this afternoon.'

Grave Digger froze with a foot in the air, and Coffin Ed laughed: 'Haw haw.'

In unison they turned and stared at Mrs Holmes.

She had the type of beauty made fashionable in the 1930s by an all-colored musical called *Brownskin Models*. She was rather short and busty, with a pear-shaped bottom and slender legs. She had short wavy hair, a heart-shaped face, and long-lashed, expressive brown eyes; and her mouth was like a red carnation.

She wore gold lamé slacks which fitted so tight that every

quiver of a muscle showed. Her waist was drawn in by a black leather belt, four inches wide, decorated with gilt figures. Her breasts stuck out from a turtleneck blue jersey-silk pullover as though taking dead aim at any man in front of her. Black, gilt-edged Turkish slippers turned up at the toes made her feet seem too small to support her. The combination of gold fingernail polish, sparkling rings and dangling charm bracelets gave her hands the appearance of jewelry-store windows.

Both men whipped off their hats and stood there, looking gawky and sheepish.

'I was just relaxing a bit,' Grave Digger lisped. 'We've had a hard night.'

She glanced at his swollen lips and broke out a slow, insinuating smile. 'You shouldn't love so strenuously,' she murmured.

Grave Digger felt the heat spread over his face. Coffin Ed seemed to be having trouble figuring what to do with his feet.

She walked toward a pair of divans flanking an imitation fireplace on the far side of the room. Her hips rolled with the slow tantalizing motion of a natural-born teaser. Grave Digger was thinking how he could put his hands about her waist, while Coffin Ed was telling himself that she was the type of female who would set a man on fire and then direct him to a river.

Electric logs gave off a red glow. She sat down with her back to the windows and tucked a leg beneath her. She knew the red light on the colors of her skin and ensemble made her look exotic. Her eyes became luminous.

She waved them to a seat on the facing divan. Between them there was a huge circular table about knee-high, made by cutting down a dining room table. It was littered with the Sunday papers. Casper's face peered out from beneath the headlines about the robbery.

'You want to talk to me about my cousin,' she said.

'Well, it's like this,' Coffin Ed said. 'We're trying to find the connection between Black Beauty and a man named Baron.'

She frowned prettily. 'It doesn't make any sense to me. I don't know anyone named Black Beauty or Baron.'

The detectives stared at her for a moment. Grave Digger leaned forward and placed his hat atop the newspapers. Neither of them had removed their overcoats.

'Black Beauty's your cousin,' Grave Digger lisped.

'Oh,' she said. 'I've never heard him called by that name. Who told you that?'

'It's in the newspapers,' Coffin Ed said.

Her eyes widened. 'Really.' She shifted slightly so that the red light shone on her black belt with its tracery of gilded designs. 'I didn't pay any attention. I was so upset.' She shuddered and covered her face with her hands. Her breasts trembled. Looking at them, Grave Digger wondered how she did it.

'I understand,' Coffin Ed said sympathetically. 'What I don't understand is how did you know he was your cousin, Junior Ball, since all the papers referred to him as Black Beauty.'

She took her hands from her face and stared at him haughtily. 'Are you cross-examining me?' she asked in a cold, imperious voice.

'More or less,' Grave Digger lisped, his voice getting dry.

She jumped to her feet. 'Then you may leave,' she said.

Coffin Ed gave Grave Digger an accusing look, then looked up at Mrs Holmes and spread his hands entreatingly.

'Listen, Missus Holmes, we've had a long hard night. We're just trying to catch the bandits who robbed your husband. We know you want them caught as much as he does. We're not trying to antagonize you. That's the last thing we want to do. We're just following a thin lead. Won't you bear with us for a few minutes?'

She looked from him to Grave Digger. He looked back at her as though he would like to whip her.

But he said in a thick, dry lisp, 'I didn't mean it the way you took it. My nerves are kind of raw.'

'So are mine,' she said in a voice that had roughened.

She kept staring into Grave Digger's hot, rapacious gaze until her body seemed to melt; and she sat down again as though from lack of strength.

'But if you are civil I will help you all I can,' she relented.

Coffin Ed was fumbling about in his mind for a way to

phrase his questions. 'Well, the thing is,' he said. 'We'd like to know what Ball did – his occupation.'

'He was a dress designer,' she said. 'And he made articles from leather.'

She noticed Grave Digger staring at her belt and squirmed slightly.

'Did he make your belt?' he asked.

She hesitated as though she might refuse to answer, then reluctantly said, 'Yes.'

Grave Digger had made out some of the gilded designs encircling the belt. They depicted a series of Pans with nude males and females caught in grotesque postures on their horns. The thought struck him suddenly that Junior Ball got gored by one of his own Pans.

Coffin Ed picked up the idea. 'Did he ever work for Baron?' he asked. 'Design anything for him?'

'I've told you I don't know this Baron,' she said, her voice still rough. 'What has he got to do with all of this?'

'Well, I'll tell you how it goes,' he said, and related the statement they had got from Roman. 'So you see how it figures,' he concluded. 'Your cousin, Ball, and this man, Baron, were in some kind of racket.'

She frowned, but this time not prettily. 'It is possible,' she conceded. 'Although I can't see why Junior should have been mixed up in any kind of racket. He was doing well in his own field; he didn't need anything. And I still don't understand how this man, Baron, can help you find the scum who robbed Casper.'

'He got a good look at them, for one thing,' Coffin Ed said. 'He talked to them; he knows their voices.'

'And we have a hunch he knew them from before,' Grave Digger added.

She sighed theatrically. 'I've gotten used to a lot of strange things with my husband in politics,' she said. 'But all this terrible, horrible violence is too much for me.' A tremor ran over her body, making all of it shake.

Grave Digger licked his swollen lips. He was thinking about some of the lonely women about town he hadn't stopped in to see lately.

She knew what he was thinking and gave him a quick

up-from-under look, her big brown eyes stark naked for an instant; then she turned her face away and looked into the fire, and her expression became sad.

'I'd better not catch him on a dark street,' Grave Digger lisped in a voice so thick it was blurred.

She whirled about and stared at him. 'Oh!' The red light on her face seemed to be reflected from somewhere underneath the brown of her skin. 'I thought you said—' She thought he'd said, '*I'd better not catch you on a dark street.*' She was flustered for a moment. It made her furious with herself.

'I've helped you all I can,' she said abruptly. She began trembling in earnest. 'Please go. I can't stand any more of this.' Her eyes brimmed with tears. She looked even more desirable than with her brassy manner.

Coffin Ed stood up and tapped Grave Digger on the shoulder. Grave Digger came out of his trance with a start.

'Just one more thing,' Coffin Ed said. 'Do you know if Junior saw your husband last night?'

'I don't know. Don't ask me anything else,' she said tearfully. 'All I know is what I've read in the newspapers. I haven't talked to Casper. He's still in a coma. And I don't know—' She stopped as though struck by a sudden thought, then said, 'And if you're so interested in Junior's business, go down on Nineteenth Street and talk to his associate, Zog Ziegler. He ought to know.'

'Zog Ziegler,' Coffin Ed repeated in a flat voice. 'Do you know his address?'

'Somewhere on East Nineteenth Street,' she said. 'Just go down and look. You'll know the house when you see it.'

She sounded hysterically anxious for them to leave.

'Good day, Missus Holmes, and thank you,' Coffin Ed said, and Grave Digger said, 'You've helped us more than you know.'

She stiffened slightly at the subtle jibe in his words, but she didn't look up.

The wide-mouthed boy in the white jacket appeared in the doorway as though by magic. He let them out.

After an interminable delay, the creaking elevator made its appearance. The old elevator operator with the cottonboll head refused to look at them for reasons of his own. They left him to his solitude.

When they came out into the street, big fat snowflakes were drifting from a solid gray sky. The motionless air had become degrees warmer, and the snowflakes stuck where they landed, too heavy to roll over.

'She knew what I meant, the teasing bitch.'

'Didn't we all.'

'She never did answer your question.'

'She said enough.'

They stood looking at their wreck of a car for a moment before getting in.

'We'd better change buggies before going downtown,' Grave Digger said. 'We might get booked on vag.'

'We can go back to the station and get my car.'

'We might stop at Fat's for a couple of shots.'

'Whiskey ain't going to help us think any better,' Coffin Ed cautioned.

'Hell, beat as I am now it don't matter,' Grave Digger said.

15

It was four o'clock when Casper got finished with the brass and the half-brass. He had had it with the chief inspector, the inspector in charge of the Homicide squads, Lieutenant Brogan and a detective stenographer from Homicide, and two lieutenants from the Central Office Bureaus.

They had handled him gently, with all due respect for the tender sensibilities of a vote-getting politician, but he had been through the wringer nevertheless.

What they had hammered on mainly was the mystery of the leak. One or the other kept pointing out that the hoods got the tip-off from somewhere, that it didn't come from heaven, until Casper blew his top.

'I tipped them!' he had exploded. 'I leaked it. I said come on and get it. Knock out my mother-raping brains and kill a couple of people. Is that what you think?'

'It could have been somebody in your organization,' the chief inspector had said.

'All right, it was somebody in my organization. Then go out and arrest them. All of 'em! Start with my two secretaries. Haul in my associates. Don't forget my field workers. Not to mention my wife. Take 'em all downtown. Give 'em the third degree. Tickle 'em with your mother-raping loaded hose. And see what you get. You'll get nuttin', because they didn't know nuttin'. At least if they did, they didn't get it from me, because I didn't know the payoff was coming through when it did my own damn self.'

No one had batted an eye at the outburst.

'Grover Leighton said he told you several days ago that he'd bring it up Saturday night,' the chief inspector had said quietly. 'He doesn't remember the exact day.'

'He doesn't remember because he didn't do it,' Casper had raved. 'Maybe he thinks he did. But Grover has the whole fifty states to think of; and if you think he can remember every goddam little thing he has done you're giving him credit for having a mechanical brain.'

They had let it go at that.

Now Casper had a headache the likes of which would have made his professed coma preferable.

A colored trainee nurse had come in to straighten up and remove the saucers filled with cigar butts. She had opened the French windows to clear the air, and sight of the heavy fall of snow added to Casper's fury.

'Now they'll send in Canadian trackers,' he muttered.

The little girl glanced at him apprehensively; she didn't know whether she was supposed to answer or not. She began edging toward the door.

The telephone on the nightstand rang. He snatched up the receiver and shouted, 'Tell 'em I'm dead!'

The cool, controlled voice of the reception nurse asked, 'Do you care to see the press? Our lobby down here is packed with reporters and photographers.'

'Tell 'em I'm still in a coma.'

'They've seen the police leave.'

'Then tell 'em to go to hell. Tell 'em I've had a relapse. Tell 'em I've developed brain fever. No, don't tell 'em that.

Tell them I'm resting now and that I'll see them at eight o'clock.'

'Yes, sir. And there is a telephone call for you from the Pinkerton Detective Agency. Shall I put it through?'

He hesitated for an instant, waiting for his sixth sense to work; but it lay dead.

'All right, I'll take it,' he said.

A calm, soothing-type voice said, 'Mister Casper Holmes?'

'Speaking,' Casper said.

'I am Herbert Peters from the Pinkerton Detective Agency. Mister Grover Leighton has been in contact with us, and he has engaged us to arrange for an ambulance, under guard to transport you from the hospital to your home.'

'Why not a baby carriage?' Casper growled.

Peters chuckled faintly. 'If you will give us the approximate time you will be checking out, we'll make all the necessary arrangements.'

'I'll arrange for my own transportation when I leave,' Casper said. 'But I'm not thinking of leaving for two or three days.'

'Then you think you will be checking out on Tuesday?'

'That's what I think. But I don't think I need any of you. If I can't get from here to my own house, I need to go back to the nursery.'

'That's not exactly the situation, sir,' Peters said. 'It is not a matter of your ability to take care of yourself. One of our men has been killed, and, unfortunately, you are a witness to the murder. As long as you are alive, the murderers are in danger of—'

'You ain't just saying it,' Casper cut in.

'So Mister Leighton feels it is essential that we give you the protection necessary for a public figure whose life is in danger.'

'Mister Leighton has already made one mistake by going ahead on his own,' Casper said.

'That's why he doesn't want to make another,' Peters said. 'That's why we are requesting your cooperation in advance.' He paused for a moment, then added, 'We will have to cover you in any event, whether you like it or not; but it would be much better all around if we had your cooperation.'

Casper conceded. 'All right. I'll call you tomorrow and tell you when I'm checking out. Will you be there?'

'If I'm not, someone else will.'

'Okay, give me the number.'

When he had hung up, he waited for a minute, then dialed the number he'd been given.

An unfamiliar voice said, 'Pinkerton Detective Agency.'

'Let me speak to Herbert Peters.'

'Who's calling, please?'

'Casper Holmes.'

A moment later Peters' calm voice said, 'Yes, Mister Holmes?'

'I'm just checking,' Casper said. 'Being as I can't look through the telephone and see just who really is phoning me.'

'I understand, Mister Holmes. Is that all, sir?'

'That's all.'

Casper cradled the receiver and sat up in bed, thinking. The trainee had finished and closed the windows and left, but he hadn't noticed.

He lifted the receiver and told the switchboard operator not to put through any more calls.

'If someone telephones, what shall I say?'

'Say that I am sleeping and ask them to phone back after eight o'clock.'

'Yes, sir.'

'And give me an outside line.'

When he heard the central office buzz, he dialed a number. A woman's voice answered. 'Hel-looo?'

'Marie?'

'Yes. Is that you, Casper?'

'Yeah. Is Joe in?'

'Yes. I'll call him. How's your noggin?'

'Palpitating. Let me talk to Joe.'

He heard her calling, 'Jooooe! It's Casper.'

Joe Green was the biggest numbers banker in Harlem; he had a part of three lotteries.

'Casper, how's the boy?' he greeted in a husky voice.

'Ain't nothing that a little sleep won't cure.'

'Can't hurt you hitting you on the head,' Joe said. 'But

snatching all that long green off you must have given you a running fit.'

'It wasn't mine,' Casper said. 'They didn't hurt nothing but my feelings.'

'And you'll never forgive the mother-rapers for that.'

'Now that's for sure. But what I called you for is I want to borrow a couple of your boys for later in the day.'

'For bodyguards or running errands?'

'I'm going to check out here at seven-thirty in one of Clay's hearses—'

Joe chuckled. 'Just don't go by the way of the cemetery, daddy.'

Casper laughed. 'By way of Clay, neither. Naw, I'm going home. I want to dodge the newsboys; I got a pop call to make on the way. I just want them to trail me.'

'It's done,' Joe said. 'How 'bout Big Six and George Drake in the Cadillac? They ought to handle any situation that might jump up. Or do you want another one?'

'Naw, they'll do. I want them to pick up the hearse at Clay's and stay with it, but not too close. I don't want it looking like no procession.'

'I got you, daddy. What time?'

'I'm leaving here at seven-thirty. They'd better get to Clay's by seven.'

Joe hesitated. 'Can't you make it earlier, daddy? If this snow keeps coming down like it is now, ain't much going to be moving by seven-thirty.'

'I'm going to be moving,' Casper said.

'Okay, daddy, I got you covered,' Joe said. 'Don't do nothing I wouldn't do.'

'It's made then,' Casper said. 'I'll see you in church.'

When the connection was broken, he began dialing another number without putting down the receiver.

A proper male voice said, 'H. Exodus Clay's Funeral Parlor. Good afternoon. May we be of service to you?'

'I don't want to be buried, if that's what you mean,' Casper said. 'Just let me speak to Clay.'

'Mr Clay is resting; he's having his customary afternoon nap. Perhaps I can help you.'

'Wake him up,' Casper said. 'This is Casper Holmes.'

'Oh, Mister Holmes. Yes sir, right away, sir.'

A few moments later Clay's thin, querulous voice came over the wire. 'Casper. I was hoping to do some business with you.'

'You are, Hank, but not the kind you want.' Only a few people in Harlem knew that the H in Clay's name stood for Henry; most people thought it stood for either Heaven or Hell. 'I want to hire a hearse.'

'For yourself, or for a friend?'

'For myself.'

'The reason I asked, I have three hearses now. I use the old one for poor folks, the middle one for rich and the new one for celebrities. I'll give you the new one.'

'Naw, give me the middle-newest. I don't want to attract any attention to myself. I want to slip away from this hospital without anybody seeing me. And let Jackson drive it; nobody going to look at him twice.'

'Jackson!' Clay echoed. 'Listen, Casper, I don't want any shenanigans with my hearse. I never will forget the time Jackson was running all over town dodging the police with my hearse full of dead bodies.'

'What are you beefing about?' Casper said. 'He made you a lot of business.'

'I'd rather get my business in the normal way; I'm not expecting a depression.'

'All right, Hank, have it your way. I just want to get this hearse over here at the back door at seven-thirty sharp.'

'The streets will be snowed under by that time,' Clay complained. 'Can't you make it earlier, or wait another day?'

'Naw. Just put some chains on it. And there's going to be some boys of Joe Green's following it. So don't let that worry you.'

'Boys of Joe Green's!' Clay exclaimed apprehensively. 'Listen Casper, if anything happens to my hearse, I'm going to bill the national party for it.'

'Okay, you do that. And tell Jackson to drive me first to my office on One-twenty-fifth Street.'

'Tell him yourself,' Clay said, losing interest and already drifting back to sleep.

Casper cradled the receiver and picked up his wrist watch

from the nightstand. It was thirteen minutes past five o'clock. He peered between the drawn curtains at the drifting snow. Everything that met his eye was white, except the gray sky. He selected a cigar, clipped it carefully, stuck one end between his lips and rolled it about. Then he put it down on the edge of the nightstand, picked up the receiver again and began dialing.

'Do you want an outside line?' the operator asked.

'What the hell do you think I'm dialing for?' he said.

He waited for the dial tone and began over. He heard the phone ringing at the other end.

A cool, contralto voice said, 'Yes.'

'Leila. Casper,' he said.

'How are you, sugar,' she said in the same tone that she had said yes.

'Listen, I'll be home around eight o'clock,' he said. His voice was as impersonal as hers. 'I want you to stay there until after I get there – or say until nine o'clock. Then you can go wherever in the hell you want to. Understand?'

'I'm not deaf.'

'Naw, but you're dumb sometimes.'

'That blow on your head hasn't changed your disposition,' she observed.

'If anybody phones me, tell them I'm still in the hospital and won't be home until Tuesday. Tell them I've had a relapse and am in a coma again. Get that?'

'Yes, sugar, I got it.' Under her breath she added, 'And I'm going to keep it, too.'

'What's that?'

'I didn't say anything. Somebody must be talking on your end.'

'All right. And for once keep your lip buttoned up.'

'Is that all?'

He put down the receiver and reached for his cigar. Before he could pick it up, the phone rang. He picked up the receiver again.

'What is it?'

'Washington, D.C. calling,' the operator said. 'A Mister Grover Leighton. Shall I put him through?'

'Yes.'

Grover's sunshiny, glad-handing Pennsylvania voice came on. 'Casper. How are you?'

'Fine. Just resting. It's all I can do at the moment.'

'That's the thing to do. Just keep it up. We've all been worried about you.'

'Nothing to worry about. You can't hurt an old dog like me.' Casper's voice had taken on a subtle obsequious quality.

'That's what I told them,' Grover said cheerfully. 'And don't you worry, either. We'll come through again soon with the same score.'

'Oh, I'm not worrying about that,' Casper said. 'But some of the city brass here have been making it a little rough.'

'For you?' Grover sounded slightly shocked. 'Why so?'

'They're trying to figure out how the hoods got the tip-off,' Casper said. 'And the chief inspector claims that you told him that you had told me sometime early last week that you were stopping by last night with the payroll.'

There was a pause as though Grover was trying to remember. 'Well, I guess I did tell him something like that,' he said finally. 'But I thought I told you about it Wednesday, or was it Thursday, when we talked on the phone about the precinct units.'

'Listen, Grover, I want you to think, try to remember. Because I'm sure you didn't tell me then. You might forget a thing like that, but I wouldn't. All I've got to think of is my little group in Harlem, while you've got the whole country on your mind. And I'm sure I wouldn't have forgotten your telling me that, because that's what starts the cart to rolling.'

'Maybe you're right,' Grover conceded. 'It was in my mind to tell you, but it must have slipped. But that's not important, is it?'

'Not to you and me; but the brass here are insinuating that the leak came from me.'

'My God!' Grover sounded really shocked. 'They must be crazy. They're not trying to push you around, are they?'

'Naw, it's not that. But I don't like all the innuendo, especially at the beginning of a campaign.'

'You're right. I'll telephone the chief inspector and put an end to that. And when they're arrested we'll find out where they got their information. But I telephoned you about another matter. I have asked the Pinkerton Agency in New York to keep an eye on you; we don't want a duplication of this business, and we certainly don't want anything to happen to you. And they are involved now also, since they lost one of their men.'

'You know I'll cooperate, Grover. Be glad to. It's as much to my interest as to anyone's.'

'That's what I told them. I asked them to arrange for an ambulance with a guard to take you home when you leave there – unless, of course, you have arranged something else.'

'Naw, I haven't made any arrangements,' Casper said. 'That suits me fine. One of the men phoned from the agency, said you had spoken to them. I told him I'd let him know in advance when I planned to leave.'

'Well, then, it's all settled.' Grover sounded relieved. 'Take care of yourself, Casper. We don't want anything to happen to you. The Harlem vote is going to be mighty important in this coming election. It might mean the balance that will swing the whole state of New York in our favor.'

'I'm going to take damn good care of myself from now on,' Casper said.

Grover laughed. 'Good fellow! Let us know if there is anything we can do for you.'

'Nothing at the moment, Grover. Thanks for everything.'

'Don't mention it. We'll be thanking you before it's done with.'

When they had hung up, Casper lit his cigar and sat smoking it slowly, looking thoughtful.

'It's in the fire now,' he said to no one, and picked up the receiver again.

'Give me a line, honey,' he said.

He dialed a downtown number.

'Now who can this be?' a voice of indeterminate gender asked with an affected lisp.

'Let me speak to Johnny.'

'Oh, and not with me?'

Casper didn't answer.

'And who shall I tell him is calling, dear?'

'None of your God-damned business.'

'Oh! You're rude!'

He heard the receiver dropped on a table-top. After what seemed to him much longer than was necessary, a pleasant male tenor voice said, 'Hello, Casper, it couldn't be anybody but you who'd be so unkind to Zog.'

'I'm going home around eight o'clock,' Casper said, 'I want you to come up later.'

'I knew they couldn't hurt you,' Johnny said, and then, 'How much later?'

'Around ten o'clock. Use your own key and come on in.'

'Will do,' Johnny said.

When Johnny had hung up, Casper jiggled the hook and asked the operator to have the supervising nurse come up to his room.

16

It was past four o'clock when Grave Digger and Coffin Ed got away from Fats's Down Home Restaurant – just about the time Casper had got finished with the brass.

They hadn't intended to stay that long. But the place was filled with gamblers and whorehouse madams, all curious about the Casper caper, and they had been fishing themselves, to see what they could pick up about any new jokers in town on a kick binge.

The gamblers hadn't run across any fresh money; if they had, they wouldn't admit it. The madams hadn't come across any new customers, not with big money, anyway.

'If I had,' one madam confessed, 'I'd have handcuffed each of 'em to two girls, and foot-chained 'em to the bed, bad as I need money.'

Pee Wee, the gaint black bartender, had fixed them some hot bourbon teas to stave off grippe and pneumonia. Before they had a chance to test what those potent drinks might stave off, they were clutched in the throes of tremendous appetites.

Then Fats had appeared, looking like the scalded and scraped carcass of a hippopotamus, and said he was taking a Smithfield ham out of the oven. That did it.

They ate baked ham and sweet potatoes while Grave Digger held everybody entranced giving a detailed account of the joker getting his head cut off.

By the time they got back outside, they were both willing to believe the gremlins had done it.

The snow was drifting down like endless fields of cotton, and the street was covered an inch thick. The wreck of a car, sitting at the curb, looked like an abandoned derelict. They hadn't got to the precinct station as yet.

Grave Digger took hold of Coffin Ed's sleeve and detained him for a discussion on criminology.

'Take a detective,' he said. 'Like you and me. A man gets robbed in the street. The robber taps his victim on the head, knocks him unconscious and runs. Ain't nobody seen him; the victim don't know him. Then we come up. We don't know a damn thing. Don't even know the man's been robbed. All we got is his word for it. But everybody expects us to run off and nab the criminals as if we got a robber's preserve.'

'Maybe they expect us to crawl along and sniff them out, like human bloodhounds,' Coffin Ed said. 'Maybe they think we got the nose for it.'

'That Casper,' Grave Digger said. 'He got more twists in him than a barrel full of snakes.'

They got into the car. Normally at that hour it would have been dark, but the blanket of snow seemed to illuminate the streets. The few cars out were crawling along like snails, leaving black lines on the white blanket.

'Two bull alligators like you and me ain't going to catch anything in that goldfish bowl downtown,' Coffin Ed stated. 'We're just going to scare the living hell out of everybody and get the deep freeze for our effort.'

'We'll bait the hook,' Grave Digger suggested.

'I was thinking the same thing.'

Captain Rice was on duty in the precinct station. They asked his permission to take the prisoner along to identify Baron in case they unearthed him.

The captain said a Homicide detective had taken Roman Hill down to the Bureau of Criminal Identification at Headquarters, but he gave them an order to pick him up. He was still a precinct prisoner until he appeared before the magistrate's court the next morning.

They changed over to Coffin Ed's new Plymouth and went down the East Side Drive. Coffin Ed took the wheel; he didn't mind riding with Grave Digger in a city-owned car, but he had paid his own money for the Plymouth.

The small tractor-type snowplows were already at work on the main arteries, scurrying about like orange bugs, piling the snow along the curbs for the trucks to pick up and dump into the river.

The tires sang in the coating of snow, and the windshield wipers clicked back and forth.

They talked about the blizzard of 1949, when city traffic had been paralyzed by thirty-nine inches of snow.

Off to their left, unseen tugboats with green and red lights, barely discernible through the white curtain, raised a cacophony of foghorns. The lights of the petroleum companies across the East River were blanked out.

A ferryboat was docked at the 79th Street pier when they passed, unloading day workers from Welfare Island.

'Damn, this day is moving,' Grave Digger remarked.

They began feeling the pressure of time. A slow build-up of apprehension sobered them.

Coffin Ed stepped on the gas.

They found Roman in the Gallery on the first floor of Headquarters on Centre Street.

Headquarters, and the Annex across the street, were the only lighted buildings in the area. Skyscrapers in the adjacent Wall Street district loomed dark and ghostly against the bottomless gray sky.

They gave the Homicide detective Captain Rice's order and took the prisoner. He looked scarcely the worse for the head-whipping he had taken; just a mass of unnoticeable clotted wounds in his thick curly hair.

'Do you want the other one, too?' the detective asked. 'The bartender from the Paris Bar?'

'You still got him?'

'Got him and going to keep him until he looks at every picture on record – unless you want him.'

'You keep him,' Grave Digger said. 'Nothing we can do with him.'

They handcuffed Roman and took him out to the Plymouth. Coffin Ed had left the motor running and the windshield wipers working. But he had to brush the snow from all the windows before he could move on.

They went a couple of blocks beyond Headquarters and stopped.

'You got a sailor suit?' Coffin Ed asked.

'Yeah, but I don't wear it,' Roman said.

'Where is it?'

'It's aboard ship.'

'All right, we're going over to Brooklyn to get it, and you're going to put it on,' Coffin Ed said, easing the car off slowly through the snow.

When the telephone rang again, Leila Holmes thought it was Casper calling back.

'Yes.' She sounded cold enough to make icicles.

'Leave me talk with Casper,' a man's voice said.

The hand holding the receiver began to tremble. She thought she recognized the voice, but she wasn't certain.

'He's still in the hospital,' she said, a sudden indeterminable fear making her voice sound parrotlike. 'He's had a relapse; he's in a coma.'

'Can the bull,' the voice said. 'That li'l lick on a booger's head ain't putting him in no coma.'

She felt certain of it now. It was a Southern voice with a Mississippi accent. It was a white man's voice.

She began trembling all over, her breasts moving in the jersey-silk pullover like molded Jell-O.

'Telephone the hospital if you don't believe me,' she said, furious with herself for sounding defensive, but she couldn't help it. She was scared witless. There was something sadistic and inhuman about the voice. 'He is in a coma,' she contended.

'If he wants any of his fifty G's back, he better come out of it,' the voice said. 'And nigger-quick.'

The use of the epithet steadied her fear and scalded her with rage.

'Who are you, you mother-raping peckerwood,' she flared.

An evil chuckle came over the wire. 'I'm the man who can help him get his money back – for a split,' the voice said.

She tried to think, but she didn't know where to start. 'You'd better call Casper at the hospital,' she said.

'You call him, sugar pie. I've called six times and can't get through to him. So you do it, honey chile.'

'What shall I tell him?' she asked, then added viciously, 'Redneck.'

'I'll make your li'l neck red if I get hold of you,' the voice said, then added, 'just tell him what I told you, and if he wants to do business, he better take my call.'

She remembered what Casper had told her about keeping her lip buttoned up. If she did the wrong thing, he'd be furious. She didn't know what to do.

'It can keep, can't it?' she said.

'Keep until when?'

'Until he gets out the hospital.'

'When will that be?'

'When?' She felt trapped. 'I don't know when. Ask at the hospital.'

'You ain't doing him no good, baby doll,' the voice taunted. 'He ain't going to like it when he finds out what he's missed.'

'All right, sonofabitch!' she flared. 'I'll call him and you call me back.'

'What good is that going to do? I got to do business with him. And it ain't going to keep. If Casper wants to lie in the hospital with his head underneath the pillow, that's just going to be his bad luck. And I'll figure out some other way to get my split.'

Her mind exploded with vulgarity, as it always did when she felt cornered.

'For chrissakes, call back after eight o'clock,' she said exasperatedly. 'I don't know what the hell—'

She didn't get a chance to finish it. A soft click sounded from the other end, and the line went dead. She sat staring at the receiver. She began trembling again. Scare went through her like acid.

'Now what the hell did I say?' she wondered.

It was twenty minutes past six when the telephone rang.

A proper male voice answered. 'H. Exodus Clay's Funeral Parlor. Good evening. May we be of service to you?'

'This is the Pinkerton Detective Agency,' the voice said at the other end. 'Leave me speak to the boss.'

It was a Southern voice with a Mississippi accent. It was a white man's voice.

The attendant said, 'Yes, sir. Right away, sir.'

A moment later Clay's querulous voice came on the line, 'What is it now?'

'This is the Pinkerton Detective Agency,' the voice repeated.

'You said that before,' Clay snapped. 'This is my funeral parlor. Now let's get on.'

'We are sending three men up to your place to guard the ambulance you're sending for Mister Holmes,' the voice informed him.

During the past hour, the voice had repeated the same words to sixteen other ambulance services and funeral homes in Harlem without the desired result. But this time the voice struck pay dirt.

'It's not an ambulance I'm sending,' Clay said tartly. 'It's a hearse.'

A chuckle came over the wire. 'That's just the right thing,' the voice said. 'What time are you sending it?'

'Casper has arranged for his own guards,' Clay replied with a note of racial pride in his thin, peevish voice. 'We're all local people up here. We don't need any big-time race-track detectives with machine guns just to go a few blocks down the street. Inform your employers that it's already covered.'

'That's mighty fine,' the voice said. 'But we've been employed by the national party. We'll cover the coverers.'

'Well, you'd better hurry then. It'll leave here in half an hour.'

'That'll work out fine,' the voice said. 'We won't interfere with any of the arrangements; we'll keep in the background. You don't even have to mention us.'

'You needn't worry about that,' Clay said sarcastically. 'I don't get paid to advertise the Pinkertons.'

With that rejoinder he clapped down the receiver.

There was a traffic jam on the Brooklyn Bridge.

A trailer truck had skidded on a spot of slick ice caused by the overheated radiator of a passenger car that had passed a short time previously, and sideswiped a passenger bus.

There were no casualties, but the truck bumper had gored a hole in the side of the bus and it took time to get them apart.

Grave Digger and Coffin Ed sat in the stalled line of cars and fumed. They had the feeling that time was rushing past like a maniac with a knife and they were caught barefooted with their hands tied. They couldn't back out, couldn't squeeze through; they couldn't abandon the car on the bridge and walk.

Roman sat in the back in his sailor's suit, white cap stuck on the back of his head and his manacled hands in his lap.

Grave Digger looked at his watch. It was twenty minutes past six. The snow was coming down.

'I'd rather be bit in the rear by a boa constrictor than sitting here waiting for something to happen, and I can't even guess what,' he complained bitterly.

'All I'm waiting to happen is for them to get those wrecks apart,' Coffin Ed grated.

It was three minutes past seven when they turned into East 19th Street from Third Avenue and began looking for the house.

They had no trouble finding it. It had a four-story yellow brick-veneer front, with candy-striped awnings at all the upper windows sagging with snow. The first-floor lounge had a wide picture window overlooking a three-foot strip of lawn. The window curtains were a translucent pale-blue silk, behind which the silhouettes of people moved in a frantic saraband. Black steps led up to a door covered with a plate of blackened bronze set in a white frame. In the upper panel was a knocker that looked vaguely obscene; overhead was a carriage lamp.

Coffin Ed drove past and parked three houses beyond. In unison they turned about and looked at Roman.

'We want you to go in that house back there and ask for Junior Ball,' Grave Digger lisped.

'I didn't understand you,' Roman said.

'Let me talk,' Coffin Ed said to Grave Digger.

Grave Digger waved him ahead.

Coffin Ed repeated the order.

'Yes, sir,' Roman said, then asked, 'What do I say to him if he's there?'

'He ain't there,' Coffin Ed said. 'He's dead. They know he's dead, but you're not supposed to know. You just got off ship-board and you came looking for him at this address that he gave you last time your ship was in.'

'I'm supposed to be one of those?'

'That's right.'

'What do I do when they tell me he's dead?'

'They're not going to tell you. They're going to invite you in and ask you to wait; they'll tell you they expect Junior to arrive any minute.'

'What do I do while I'm waiting?'

'Hell, boy, where have you been all your life? It's a pansy crib. They'll find things for you to do.'

'I don't go for that stuff,' Roman muttered.

'What kind of square are you? This ain't the docks. These are high-brows. Who do you think you're going to find in a hundred-thousand-dollar house a block away from Gramercy Square? They're going to try to make you, but they're going to test you first. You just sit there and drink your cocktails and look embarrassed—'

'That ain't going to be hard.'

'Act like you're waiting for Junior. Then, after about five minutes, start looking impatient. Let your eyes rove around. Then ask whoever you're talking to what time will Baron be in.'

'Baron!' Roman sat up straight. 'Mister Baron? The man who sold me my car? Is he going to be in there?'

'We don't know. He might; he might not. If you see him when you go in, you just grab him and yell for help.'

'I won't need no help,' Roman declared.

'Yes, you will,' Coffin Ed said. 'Because we don't want him hurt. You just grab him and hold on to him and start yelling.'

'What if he tries to draw a pistol on me?' Roman wanted to know.

'If you hold him tight enough he'll forget it.'

'I's ready if you is,' Roman said.

'Okay,' Coffin Ed said. 'We're going to back up and park next door. When you hear me blowing on the horn one time long and twice short, you come on out.'

'Yes, sir, but I sure hope to see Mister Baron before that.'

'So do we, so do we,' Coffin Ed said.

Grave Digger leaned over the back of the seat, unlocked the handcuffs about Roman's wrists and removed them.

'Okay, go ahead,' he said. 'Just remember one thing. You might run, but you can't hide.'

'I ain't going to run,' Roman said.

They watched him walking in his rolling sailor's gait back to the bronze door and stand looking at the knocker as though he didn't know what to do with it. They saw him knock on the door with his knuckles.

'He must have never left his ship,' Coffin Ed observed.

Grave Digger grunted.

They saw the door open; a moment later they saw him go inside; they saw the door close. Coffin Ed started the motor and backed up the car.

17

A black Cadillac limousine with scarcely any metal trimmings was parked on 134th Street, a few doors down from Clay's Funeral Parlor, on the opposite side of the street. It might have been a funeral car judging from its somber appearance.

The motor was idling, but it couldn't be heard. The defroster was on, the lights were off. The windshield wipers clicked back and forth.

George Drake sat behind the wheel, cleaning his fingernails

with a tiny, gold-handled penknife. He was an ordinary-looking colored man of indeterminate age. Even the expensive dark clothes he wore looked ordinary on him. His only distinguishing features were his slightly popping eyes. He didn't look bored; he didn't look impatient; he didn't look patient. He looked as though waiting for someone was his job.

Big Six sat beside him, picking his teeth with a worn whale-bone toothpick. He looked enormous in a bright-tan belted polo coat and wide-brimmed black velour hat pulled low over his eyes. His pock-marked face looked oversized; he had big gaps between big stained teeth.

A white drunk staggered past in the ankle-deep snow. A dark felt hat, mashed out of shape as though he had stepped on it in the snow, was stuck precariously on the back of his head. Thick, coarse, straight black hair was plastered back from a forehead as low as that of the Missing Link. The blue-white face with its beetle-brows, high cheekbones, coarse features and wide, thin-lipped mouth looked part Indian. A dark blue overcoat smeared with snow on one side flagged open, showing a wrinkled, double-breasted, unstylish blue serge suit.

The drunk stopped suddenly, opened his trousers and began urinating on the right front fender of the Cadillac, teetering back and forth.

Big Six opened the window and said, 'Push off, mother-raper. Quit pissing on this car.'

The drunk turned and peered at him through bloodshot black eyes. 'I'll piss on you, black boy,' he muttered in a Southern voice.

'I'm gonna see you do it,' Big Six said, stuck the toothpick in his change pocket and opened the door.

'Let him go on,' George Drake said. 'Here comes Jackson down the stairs.'

'I'm gonna flatten him is all,' Big Six said. 'Ain't gonna take a second.'

In the right side mirror, George noticed two colored men coming from beside the house in front of which he was parked. They were carrying battered Gladstone bags like Pullman porters on their way to work. They started across the street. The back window of the Cadillac was coated with snow, and he lost them in the rear-view mirror.

'Hurry up, man!' he called just as Big Six reached out a hand to clutch the drunk by the shoulder.

The drunk swung a long arc with his right hand, which he had held out of sight, and plunged the blade of a hunting knife through Big Six's head. It went in above the left temple, and two inches of the point came out on a direct line above the right temple. Big Six went deaf, dumb and blind, but not unconscious. He teetered slightly and groped about aimlessly like an old blind man.

'Gooooodammmmm!' George Drake said, pushing open the door with his left hand, while reaching inside of his coat for his pistol with his right.

He had his left foot down on the street, buried in the snow, and his left hand gripping the edge of the door for leverage, when a noose was dropped over his head and he was jerked backward. A knee caught him in the back, and he felt as though his spine was broken. His hat fell off. The sap landed right above his left ear, and lights exploded in his head as he lost consciousness.

'Put him in the back,' the white man said from the other side of the car. 'And put the kiesters in the trunk.'

He turned his head, gave a last look at Big Six and forgot him.

Big Six was walking slowly down the sidewalk, dragging his feet in the snow. The wound bled scarcely any; a thin trickle ran down his cheek from where the point of the knife protruded. His eyes were open; his hat was on his head. But for the bone knife-handle sticking from one temple and two inches of blade from the other, he looked like the usual drunk. He was calling silently for George to help him.

The white man got into the back of the car and took hold of the end of the noose. One of the colored men got behind the wheel; the other was at the back, putting away the Gladstone bags.

A shining black hearse backed carefully from the garage beside the funeral parlor. It straightened up and pulled to the curb. A fat black man in a dark chauffeur's uniform got out and closed the garage door. He looked across the street toward the Cadillac.

'Blink your lights once,' the white man said from the rear.

The driver hit the bright lights for an instant.

Jackson waved his right hand and got into the hearse.

The snowplows hadn't got into the small side streets, and the hearse made slow progress until it came to Seventh Avenue. The Cadillac followed half a block behind with the lights dimmed.

The white man turned George Drake over on the floor, placed one foot on his back between the shoulder blades, the other on the back of his head, and drew the noose as tight as it would go. He kept it like that while the Cadillac followed down the cleaned traffic lane in Seventh Avenue and turned into 125th Street.

Scores of colored laborers, willing to pick up a few extra bucks on their off day, were shoveling the piles of snow into city dump trucks.

Cars were out again in the cleaned streets, and gay, laughing drunks were bar-hopping. Jokers were chucking light, loose snowballs at their girl friends, who ran screaming in delight. A mail truck passed, emptying the boxes.

Big Six kept shuffling slowly toward Seventh Avenue with the knife stuck through his head. He passed a young couple. The woman gasped and turned ashy.

'It's a joke,' the man said knowingly. 'You can buy those things in the toy stores. Magical stuff. You stick 'em on each side of your head.'

The woman shuddered. 'It ain't funny,' she said. 'A big grown man like him playing with kid stuff.'

He passed a woman with two children, on their way to the movies to see a horror film. The children shrieked. The woman was indignant.

'You ought to be ashamed of yourself, frightening little children,' she accused.

Big Six kept on slowly, lost to the world. 'George!' he was calling silently in the rational part of his mind. 'George. The mother-raper stuck me.'

He started across Seventh Avenue. Snow was banked against

the curb, and his feet plowed into the snow bank. He slipped but somehow managed not to fall. He got into the traffic lane. He stepped in front of a fast-moving car. Brakes shrieked.

'Drunken idiot!' the driver cried. Then he saw the knife sticking from Big Six's head.

He jumped from his car, ran forward and took Big Six gently by the arm.

'My God in heaven,' he said.

He was a young colored doctor doing his internship in Brooklyn hospital. They had had a case similar to that a year ago; the other victim had been a colored man, also. The only way to save him was to leave the knife in the wound.

A woman started to get out of the car.

'Dick, can I help?' She had only seen the handle of the knife. She hadn't seen the blade coming out the other side.

'No-no, don't come near,' he cautioned. 'Drive to the first bar and telephone for an ambulance – better cross over to Small's; make a U-turn.'

As she drove off, another car with two men stopped. 'Need any help?' the driver called.

'Yeah, help me lay this man on the sidewalk. He's got a knife stuck through his head.'

'Jumping Jesus!' the second occupant exclaimed, opening the far door to get out. 'They think of new ways every day.'

Cars were double-parked on Lexington Avenue in front of the hospital, and a large crowd of people milled about on the slushy sidewalks. Photographers and newsmen guarded the front door and the ambulance driveway, looking sharply at everyone who left. Somehow word had got out that Casper Holmes was leaving the hospital, and they were determined he wouldn't get past.

Two prowl cars were parked across the street; uniformed cops stood about, beating their gloved hands together.

The heavy snow drifted down, leaving a mantle of white on hats and overcoats and umbrellas.

When the hearse drew up the cops cleared the entrance to the driveway.

A reporter opened the door of the driver's compartment and flashed a light into Jackson's face.

'It's just the chauffeur,' he called over his shoulder to his colleagues; then he asked, 'Who are you taking, Jack?'

'The late Mister Clefus Harper, a pneumonia victim,' Jackson replied with a straight face.

'Anybody know a Clefus Harper?' the reporter asked.

No one knew him.

'Don't let me hold you up, Jack,' he said.

The hearse purred slowly down the driveway toward the back exit.

'Keep on going,' the white man in the rear of the Cadillac limousine said. 'They're going to take a little time to get him out, and we got to get rid of this stiff.'

The driver stepped it up, went past the double-parked cars and crossed 121st Street.

'Is he dead?' his companion asked.

'He ain't alive,' the white man said as he bent over and began removing the noose from George Drake's neck.

When he had finished he began emptying all of Drake's pockets.

'Where we going to dump him?' the driver asked, as they approached 119th Street.

The white man looked about. He was not very familiar with Harlem.

'Turn down this street,' he said. 'It looks all right.' The big car floundered in inches of snow.

'Can you get through to Third Avenue?' the white man asked.

'Sure,' the driver said confidently. 'A little snow like this won't stop a Cadillac.'

The white man looked up and down the street. There was no one in sight. He opened the curb-side door.

'Pull in a little,' he said.

The driver brushed the curb.

The white man rolled the body of George Drake out into the deep snow on the sidewalk. He closed the door and looked back once. The body looked like that of a fallen drunk, only there were no footsteps.

'Step it up,' he said.

* * *

Jackson pulled up before the back door of the hospital from which the dead were removed. He was no stranger there.

He got out, went around, opened the back of the hearse and began dragging out a long wicker basket.

Two grinning colored attendants came from within the hospital and took the wicker basket inside with them.

Jackson got back into the driver's seat and waited. He listened to an argument going on inside.

'You can't come back here and poke your nose into these dead baskets,' an indignant voice was saying.

'Why not,' a laconic voice replied. 'It's a city hospital, ain't it?'

'I'll get the supervisor,' the first voice threatened.

'All right, I'll go,' the laconic voice acceded. 'I wasn't looking for anyone; I was just curious as to how many people die in this joint during an average day.'

'More than you think,' the first voice said.

Eight minutes passed before the attendants reappeared, staggering beneath the weight of the loaded wicker basket. The lid was sealed with a metal clamp, to which was attached a namecard in a metal frame:

> *CLEFUS HARPER – male Negro*
> *FOR: H. Exodus Clay Funeral Parlor*
> *134th Street*

They slid the basket into the coffin compartment and started to shut the doors.

'Let me do it,' Jackson said.

The attendants grinned and re-entered the hospital.

'Where you want to go, Mister Holmes?' Jackson asked in a stage whisper.

'We're alone?' Casper asked in a low voice from within the basket.

'Yes, sir.'

'Joe Green's boys are following in the Cadillac?'

'Yes, sir, they's waiting outside in the street.'

'No one knows they're tailing us?'

'No, sir, not as far as I know of. They's keeping about a half a block behind.'

'Okay. Then drive me to my office on 125th Street. You know where that is?'

'Yes, sir, up over the Paris Bar.'

'Double-park somewhere close,' Casper instructed. 'Then get out and come back and open the basket. Then stand there as if you're doing something and watch the street. When it's safe for me to get out without being seen, give me the word. You got that?'

'Yessir.'

'All right, let's go.'

Jackson closed the back door and climbed back into the driver's seat. The hearse purred slowly up the driveway.

Before reaching the street it was stopped again by newspaper reporters. They looked at the name tag on the basket. One of them made a note of it. The others didn't bother.

The hearse turned toward 125th Street. Half a block distant it passed Joe Green's black Cadillac limousine. Jackson glanced at the Cadillac. It looked unoccupied. He began to worry. He drove slowly, watching it in his right-side fender mirror. When he had gone another half block, the Cadillac's bright lights blinked once and went off. He was relieved. He blinked his own lights in reply and kept driving slowly until he had made the turn into 125th Street and saw the black Cadillac make the turn half a block behind him.

He crossed Park, Madison, Lenox, keeping to the right, letting the fast traffic pass him.

At Seventh Avenue he waited for a snowplow to pass, pulled around a dump truck, parked in front of the clock, that was being loaded by a gang of well-liquored men. They stopped and watched the hearse cross the avenue.

'Somebody going by way of H. Clay,' one of them remarked.

'Don't ask who it is,' another replied. 'It might be your mammy.'

'Don't I know it,' the first one replied.

A Cadillac limousine pulled around the truck in the wake of the hearse and carefully crossed the avenue.

'That's Joe Green's big Cat,' a third laborer stated.

'Warn't his men in it,' another replied.

'How you know? You running Joe's business?'

'Most generally he got George Drake driving and Big Six sitting in the front.'

'Warn't Joe in the back, neither.'

'Come on, you sports, and bend your backs,' the truck driver said. 'You ain't getting paid to second-guess Joe Green.'

The hearse double-parked beside a Ford station wagon in front of the drugstore adjacent to the Paris Bar. The drugstore was open for business, and a few customers were moving about inside. The Paris Bar seemed crowded as usual. Its plate-glass windows were steamed over, and from within came the muted sound of a jump tune issuing from the juke box.

The Cadillac double-parked at the corner in front of the United Cigar Store.

Jackson got out on the driver's side, came around the front of the hearse and looked up and down the street. A couple of men issued from the Paris Bar, glanced at the hearse and went the other way.

Jackson went to the back, opened the doors and cut the metal seal on the wicker basket with his pocket-knife.

Casper lay in the basket, fully dressed except for a hat. He wore the same dark clothes he had worn into the hospital. A soft black hat with the crown crushed in lay atop his stomach.

'Want me to help you up?' Jackson asked in a whisper.

'I can get up,' Casper said roughly. 'Close the doors and watch the street.'

Jackson left the doors slightly ajar and looked one way and the other and then across the street. Cars passed in the street, a bus went by; people came and went along the sidewalks, trampling the deep snow into slush.

'Where's Joe's car parked?' Casper asked from the crack between the doors.

Jackson jumped. He wasn't used to people talking to him from the back of the hearse. He looked down the street and said, 'In front of the Cigar Store.'

'When you leave, give 'em a blink,' Casper instructed. 'How is it now?'

For a moment there was no one nearby; no one seemed to be looking in that direction.

'All right, if you come fast,' Jackson said.

Casper came fast. He was down on the street in one jump, the black hat pulled low over his silver white hair. He cleared the back end of the station wagon in two strides, leaped over the snow banked along the curb, slipped in the slush but caught himself, and the next instant was close to the doorway of the stairs leading to his offices above. His back was to the street as he inserted the key in the lock; no one had noticed him jump from the hearse; no one had recognized him; no one was paying him the least bit of attention. He got the door open and went inside, turned once and glanced at Jackson through the upper glass panel, signaled him to go on.

Jackson got back into the driver's seat, blinked his bright lights and looked into the rear-view mirror.

The Cadillac's bright lights blinked in reply.

The hearse drove slowly away.

The Cadillac pulled up and double parked in the same position beside the station wagon.

'What you going to do with this heap?' the driver asked.

'Leave it right here, with the motor running,' the white man said. 'If Joe Green's a big shot, which he's gotta be, ain't nobody going to bother with it.'

He took his short-barreled police special from his right overcoat pocket, held it in his lap and spun the chamber, then put it back into his pocket.

'I'll go first,' he said.

He got out and crossed the sidewalk, side-stepped two men and a woman and tried the handle to the door.

The two colored men closed in behind him.

The handle turned; the door opened.

'He made it easy for us,' the white man said, and started up the stairs, keeping close to the edges and walking on the balls of his feet.

The colored men followed.

'Lock the door behind you,' the white man whispered over his shoulder.

18

Grave Digger and Coffin Ed sat in the car with the lights off on 19th Street, and waited. The motor was idling and the wind-shield wipers working.

Snow drifted down. The superintendents of the swank high-rent apartment houses flanking the private residences had their helpers out cleaning the sidewalks. Snowplows had already passed. The streets in this neighborhood were kept clean.

'I got a feeling we're missing something,' Grave Digger lisped.

'Me, too,' Coffin Ed agreed. 'But we got to have somewhere to start.'

'Maybe the sailor boy will hit it.'

Coffin Ed looked at his watch.

'It's a quarter past seven. He's had ten minutes. If he hasn't hit it by now, he ain't never going to hit it.'

'Blow for him then.'

Coffin Ed touched the horn, giving the prearranged signal. They watched in the rear-view mirrors.

Roman came out. Someone stood out of sight in the open door, watching him. He put his hat on the back of his head and started along the street.

When he came level, Grave Digger reached back, opened the door and said, 'Get in.'

A head came out of the open door, peered briefly and then withdrew. The door closed.

'What did you make of it?' Coffin Ed asked.

'Whew!' Roman blew. A film of sweat shone on his smoothtan skin. 'Nobody knew Mister Baron,' he said. 'Least-wise they all said they didn't.' He blew again. 'Jesus God-amighty!' he exclaimed. 'Them people! And they's rich. And educated, too!'

'They knocked you out, eh?' Coffin Ed said absently.

He and Grave Digger stared at one another.

'We'd better stop by the hospital again,' Coffin Ed suggested. He sounded dispirited and perplexed.

'We're losing time,' Grave Digger said. 'We had better phone.'

Coffin Ed drove around Gramercy Square and stopped in front of a quiet, discreet-looking bar on Lexington. He got out and went inside.

Well-dressed white people were drinking apéritifs in a dimlighted atmosphere of gold-lined wickedness. Coffin Ed fitted like Father Divine in the Vatican. He didn't let it bother him.

The bartender informed him with a blank face that they didn't have a phone. Bar customers on high stools looked at him covertly.

Coffin Ed flashed his shield. 'Do that once more and you're out of business,' he said.

Without a change of expression the bartender said, 'In the rear to the right.'

Coffin Ed restrained the impulse to yank him over the bar and hurried back to the telephone booth. A man was coming out; one was waiting to enter. Coffin Ed flashed his shield again and claimed priority.

He got the reception desk at the hospital.

'Mister Holmes is resting and cannot be disturbed,' the cool voice said with a positive accent.

'This is Precinct Detective Edward Johnson on a matter of police business of an urgent nature,' Coffin Ed said.

'I'll switch you to the supervisor,' the reception nurse said.

The supervising nurse was patient and polite. She said that Mr Holmes was not feeling well and could not for any reason be disturbed at that time; he had postponed his scheduled press conference until ten o'clock, and the doctor had given him a sedative.

'I can't say that I believe it, but what can I do?' Coffin Ed said angrily.

'Precisely,' the supervisor said and hung up.

He phoned Casper's house. Mrs Holmes answered. He identified himself. She waited.

'Have you been in contact with Casper?' he asked.

'Yes.'

'When?'

'He telephoned this afternoon.'

'Not during the past hour?'

'No.'

'Might I ask when he is expected home?'

'He said that he will come home Tuesday evening – if there are no complications.'

He thanked her, hung up and went back to the car.

'I don't like this,' Grave Digger said.

Coffin Ed drove up Lexington Avenue, going fast, and turned over to Park Avenue at 35th Street, where the traffic moved faster. He skirted Grand Central Station on the upper ramp, skidding on the sharp corners and causing taxi drivers to shout at him.

'If I know Casper he'd get the hell out of that hospital as soon as he could,' he half muttered as he accelerated up the slope toward 50th Street.

'Unless he's hiding,' Grave Digger offered.

From the back seat Roman said, 'If you-all are talking about Mister Holmes, he done already left the hospital.'

The car slewed about and just missed a Lincoln limousine high-balling in the middle lane. Coffin Ed pulled over to the curb, easing between two fast-moving cars, and parked at the corner of 51st Street. He joined Grave Digger in staring at Roman.

'Leastwise, that's what them people were saying in that house back there,' Roman added defensively. 'He'd phoned one of 'em from the hospital and said he'd be home by eight o'clock – one named Johnny.'

'It's thirteen minutes to eight now,' Coffin Ed said, looking at his watch. 'I'd like to have that supervisor—'

'He fixed her; you know Casper,' Grave Digger said absently.

They were both thinking hard.

'If you were Casper and you wanted to slip out, how would you do it?' Grave Digger asked.

'I ain't Casper, but I'd hire an ambulance.'

'That's too obvious. The joint is crawling with newsmen, and, if anybody was laying for him, they'd spot it too.'

'A hearse,' Coffin Ed suggested. 'As many people as die in that hospital—'

'Clay!' Grave Digger said, cutting him off.

He looked about; the street was flanked with new sky-scraper office buildings and a few remaining impregnable apartment houses.

'We got to get to a phone,' he said, then added on sudden thought, 'Drive over to the Seventeenth.'

The 17th Precinct was on 51st Street, between Lexington and Third Avenues. They were there in two minutes.

Coffin Ed telephoned Clay with Grave Digger standing by. They had left Roman handcuffed in the car.

'Clay's burial home,' came the old man's querulous voice.

'Clay. Ed Johnson and Digger Jones this end. Did you send a hearse to take Casper home?'

'I'm getting sick and tired of everybody wanting to guard the hearse I sent for Casper,' the old man said tartly. 'He already had Joe Green's boys – as if he couldn't take care of himself, mean as he is. And besides which he wanted it kept quiet. Then the Pinkertons sent men up—'

'What? The Pinkerton Agency?'

'That's what they told me. That they were sending three men on orders from—'

'Jesus Christ!' Coffin Ed said, breaking the connection. 'Get the Pinkerton Detective Agency,' he asked the switchboard operator.

When he had finished talking, he and Grave Digger looked at one another with as much fear in their eyes as either had ever seen.

'They no doubt got him by now – but why?' Coffin Ed said.

'That ain't the question now,' Grave Digger lisped. 'It's where?'

'There's got to be a tie-in,' Coffin Ed said. 'We've just missed it is all.'

'We got one more card that we can play; we can make like we're a joker called Bernard Kaufman.'

'We'd need to know his straight moniker.'

'Makes no difference; we can play that one, since it's all we got to play,' Grave Digger argued. 'It might flush Baron into the open.'

Coffin Ed began getting the idea. 'You know, it might work

at that,' he conceded. 'But we're going to need Roman's girl friend.'

'Let's go get her, and let's hurry. We've just about run out of time.'

They went outside to their car and braced Roman.

'We're going to set a trap for Baron, son, and we're going to need your African queen to identify him,' Coffin Ed said.

'I can't do that,' Roman said. 'You-all don't need her.'

'We want you both, and there isn't any time to argue about it. A man's life might depend on this, a big man's life, an important man to us colored people any way you look at it – the way things are set up. If you help us now, we'll help you later. But if you don't we'll crucify you. Have you ever been cold?'

'Yes, sir, lots of times.'

'But not as cold as we'll make you. We'll take you over to the river, handcuff your feet together, and let you hang in the water with all that snow they're dumping from the bridges.'

Roman began to shiver just thinking about it.

Afterwards Coffin Ed admitted it might only have worked on an Alabama boy.

'If I tell you where she's at, you won't arrest her, will you?' Roman begged. 'She ain't done nothing.'

'If she helps us catch Baron, we'll decorate her,' Coffin Ed promised.

They stood in the deserted office of the boathouse beside the lagoon, across from the apartment house in which Casper Holmes lived, using the telephone.

It was cold and damp; an inch-thick coating of ice covered the floor.

Coffin Ed was on the telephone, talking through the fine-tooth end of a gutta-percha comb held tight against the mouthpiece.

'This Bernie,' he said. 'Just listen, don't talk. There's a police tap on your line. Have Baron get in touch with me immediately.'

'I don't know what you're talking about,' a voice said coldly at the other end of the wire.

He hung up.

Grave Digger looked a question.

He shrugged.

Roman and Sassafras, standing to one side and handcuffed together, stared at him as though he had taken leave of his senses.

'If you is trying to imitate the Mister Bernard Kaufman, who stamped that bill of sale Mister Baron gave to Roman, you don't sound nothing like him,' Sassafras said scornfully.

But the detectives had considered this.

'Well, let's go see if it works,' Grave Digger lisped.

They took the handcuffed couple outside and crossed the sidewalk to Coffin Ed's Plymouth.

It was parked between two snow-covered cars of indistinguishable make, directly across 110th Street from the entrance to Casper's apartment house. Nothing about it indicated a police car.

Coffin Ed unlocked it, got in and started the motor and the windshield wipers. Grave Digger got into the front beside him; Roman and Sassafras piled into the back.

Roman was still wearing his sailor suit; Sassafras wore the same ensemble she had the day before, with the exception of the red knitted cap, which she had exchanged for a green one.

Passing pedestrians, half-blinded by the snow, paid them no attention.

Sassafras leaned close to Roman and whispered conspiratorially, 'I ain't heard yet from my friend.'

She had been in hiding all day and hadn't learned that her friend with the experience had finally lost his head.

'But as soon as I do—'

'Hush your mouth!' Roman said tensely. 'You ain't going to.'

'Well, I like that!' she exclaimed indignantly and withdrew to the other side.

The Plymouth was pointed toward Fifth Avenue, which bounds Central Park on the east. All Fifth Avenue buses going north turned the corner into 100th Street and branched out toward their various destinations further on. The line's control office, where the schedules were checked and the personnel changed, was directly around the corner on the north side of

110th Street. Adjacent was a bar, facing the circular square. It contained the nearest public telephone.

Coffin Ed turned about on his seat and said, 'Listen, we want you to watch the door across the street. If you see anyone come out that you know – anyone at all – tell us who it is.'

'Yes, sir,' they replied in unison and stared across the street.

A short, fat man came from the apartment. He was wearing a blue chesterfield overcoat, white scarf and a black Homburg. Grave Digger looked from Roman to Sassafras. Neither showed any sign of recognition.

A middle-aged couple came out; a woman with a little girl went in; a tall man in a polo coat rushed out.

Leila Holmes came out. She was wearing dark slacks, black fur-lined boots and a flowing ranch-mink coat. A wheat-colored cashmere scarf was wrapped about her head.

She began walking hurriedly toward the corner of Fifth Avenue.

Coffin Ed pushed the button for *drive* and eased the Plymouth out into the traffic lane. He drove ahead of the hurrying woman on the other side of the street and slowed down.

A street lamp spilled a circle of white light on the white snow.

When Leila came into the circle of light, Sassafras exclaimed, 'There's Mister Baron!'

Roman stiffened, leaned forward peering; his eyes popped. 'Where?'

'Across the street!' Sassafras cried in her high keening voice. 'In that fur coat! That's him!'

'That's a woman!' Roman shouted. 'Has you gone crazy?'

''Course he's a woman.' Sassafras shrieked in an outraged voice. 'I'd know that bitch anywhere.'

Coffin Ed had already pulled ahead and was making a U-turn to head Leila off.

'Goddammit, girl, why didn't you tell me!' Roman raved in a popeyed fury.

'You think I was going to tell you he was a woman?' Sassafras said triumphantly.

The Plymouth had drawn abreast of Leila. Grave Digger got out, stepped over the snowbank and passed between two parked cars. Leila didn't see him until he took her by the arm.

Her face jerked up, tight with panic; her big brown eyes were pools of fear. Her smooth brown skin had turned powdery gray.

Then she recognized him. 'Get your dirty hands off me, you stinking cop!' she screamed in a sudden rage and tried to jerk her arm free from his grip.

'Let's get into the car, *Mister* Baron,' Grave Digger lisped in a cottony voice. 'Or I'll slap you down right here in the street.'

Blood surging to her face had given it the bright painted look of an Indian's. Her eyes had slitted like a cat's and glittered with animal fury. But she ceased to fight. She merely said in a strangled voice, 'Play tough, buster; I'll have Casper break you for this.'

'Casper ain't going to live that long, unless we find him quick,' he lisped.

'Oh God!' she said with a moan and went limp.

He had practically to carry her to the waiting car. Coffin Ed opened the front door, and they installed her between them on the front seat.

'How did you make me?' she asked.

'It figures,' Coffin Ed explained. 'You had to be a woman or you'd be in the clique. And no one in the clique knew you.'

'They only knew Casper,' she said bitterly.

Grave Digger looked at his watch. 'It's nineteen minutes past eight,' he lisped. 'Our only chance rides on how tough Casper is; and how much you're going to tell us; and how fast you're going to tell it.'

She began to bridle. 'I wasn't in with it, if that's what you think—'

'Save it,' Coffin Ed grated.

'I just guessed it,' she said. 'I recognized the white man when they stopped us, after they'd run down Junior. I don't know why—'

'That can wait.'

'I'd seen him talking to Casper Friday morning. I knew

he was a stranger. Then I remembered Casper putting in a long-distance phone call to Indianapolis on Thursday night, right after he'd got the phone call from Grover Leighton. I wondered at the time what he was up to—'

Grave Digger exploded. 'For chrissakes, get to the point!'

'Then when I found out they were the same ones who had robbed Casper, I knew he had hired them to do it.' She took a deep breath, and her face twitched strangely. 'Nobody could rob Casper unless he let them do it.'

'It figures,' Coffin Ed admitted.

'But why the snatch? What do they want with him now?' She sighed. 'He probably swung out on them.'

'Double-crossed them?' Coffin Ed sounded slightly startled. 'He'd double-cross these dangerous hoods?'

'Why not?' Leila said. 'Casper would double-cross his own mother; and he's not scared of anybody who walks on two feet. He'd double-cross them and then job them. He probably had his brief case stuffed with newspapers when they pulled off that phony heist.'

'They're going to kill him,' Coffin Ed said.

'Not before they get the money,' Grave Digger amended. 'Where would he plant it?' he asked Leila.

'Somewhere in his office building,' she said dully. 'He didn't get to go anywhere else.'

Grave Digger looked at his watch again. It was twenty-four minutes past eight.

The Plymouth was already rolling.

'Hold out, son,' Grave Digger lisped in his cottony voice as he pulled his long-barreled, nickel-plated revolver from its shoulder sling and began checking the cartridges in the cylinder. 'We're coming.'

19

'Here goes nothing,' Leila Baron Holmes said to herself.

She took a large ring of keys from her mink-coat pocket and began searching for the one that fitted the lock.

One side of her head and shoulders were highlighted in the upper glass panel by the red light of the neon sign from the Paris Bar next door.

In the pitch darkness at the head of the stairs, a man crouched, watching her. He shifted the .38 Colt automatic to his left hand, wiped his sweating right palm against his overcoat and renewed his grip on the butt. He sucked his bottom lip and waited.

Leila found the right key and got the door open. She returned the keys to her pocket and groped for the light switch on the wall to the right. Her gloved fingers touched it; she pushed the button, but no lights came on.

'Oh, damn!' she said in a tremulous voice that she had tried vainly to make sound annoyed.

She turned, locked the door behind her and began ascending the stairs. Her body was trembling from head to foot, and she had to force her reluctant feet to make each step.

A strong, nerve-tingling, aphrodisiacal scent of a French perfume preceded her.

The man at the top of the stairs drew back out of sight and waited.

When her foot touched the runner in the corridor, the man put his right forearm about her throat and his left elbow between her shoulder blades and lifted her from the floor, cutting off her wind.

She kicked and beat him futilely with her hands as he carried her down the corridor.

'Cut it out or I'll break your neck,' he whispered thickly, blowing her perfumed hair out of his face.

She stopped fighting and began to squirm.

He stopped before the last door toward the front and kicked softly on the bottom panel.

The upper panel was frosted glass with the words:

Casper Holmes and Associates
Public Relations

spelled out in gold letters. But there was no light behind or in front, and the letters were a vague glittering.

The door opened inward abruptly. Nothing but the whites

of the eyes of the man inside could be seen. The sound of Leila's strangled breathing was loud in the pregnant silence.

'What you got?' a whisper asked.

'A woman – can't you smell her?' the lookout whispered in reply, and stepped into Casper's reception room, still holding her suspended by the neck.

'What is it?' a Mississippi voice asked from the other room.

'A woman,' the lookout repeated, unconsciously accenting the word.

Leila was rubbing herself seductively against him for all she was worth. Before arriving she had drenched herself in the aphrodisiacal perfume, and its scent, along with his own tongue swelling with lust, was choking him. Her trembling was setting him on fire. He lowered her to her feet and slackened his grip so she could breathe.

Suddenly a light came on in the private office, and the rectangle of a door appeared in the corner.

'Bring her in,' the voice ordered.

The lookout pushed Leila through the doorway; the other man followed.

Her eyes widened in abject terror, and she moaned.

The office was a shambles. Drawers hung open, papers littered the floor, the leather upholstery was slashed, spare clothes from the closet were torn into shreds, the safe in one corner stood open.

A heavy green shade covered the window opening onto the inside airwell, and Venetian blinds were closed tightly over the two front windows.

Street sounds came faintly, muffled by the snow. There was the soft sound of snow falling into the airwell and water running in the drainpipes. No other sounds came from inside. They had the building to themselves.

Casper lay on his back on the dark maroon rug; his legs were spread-eagled, with his ankles lashed to the legs of the desk with halves of an extension cord. He was stripped to his underwear. His arms were twisted behind him so that his hands extended above his shoulder blades and were manacled with a set of handcuffs looped across his throat. He was gagged with his own black silk scarf, tightly twisted and passing through his mouth to a knot behind his head. Blood trickled from his eyelids, seeped steadily from his huge, flaring nostrils, ran from the corners of his mouth and flowed down his cheeks alongside the scarf that gagged him.

The desk lamp had been placed on the floor and focused into his face. It supplied the only light.

His eyes were closed, and he looked near death. But Leila knew intuitively that he was conscious and alert. The knowledge kept her from fainting, but it didn't help her terror.

The white man knelt beside him with a bloodstained knife pressed tightly against his throat. He had used the knife to slit Casper's eyelids and jab inside his nostrils and slash his tongue, and he had threatened to use it next to relieve him of his manhood.

His coarse black hair was still plastered to his head, but his nostrils had whitened at the corners. He stared at Leila from black eyes that had the bright enameled look of a snake's.

'Who's she?' he asked as though without interest.

'I don't know, she came up here with her own key.'

'I'm Leila Holmes,' she said in a voice that sounded as though her tongue had stuck to her teeth.

'Casper's whore,' the white man said, getting to his feet. 'Hold her, I'll stab her.'

Leila whimpered and pushed closer to the lookout for protection. 'You're not going to let that cracker hurt me,' she begged in a tiny terror-stricken voice.

Suddenly, there was a horse of another color.

The black lookout shoved her to one side and drew his .38 automatic. He didn't aim it at the white man, but he showed it to him.

'I ain't going for that,' he muttered.

The white man looked at him without expression.

'Go back and keep watch,' he ordered.

'Door's locked,' the lookout said.

'Go back anyway.'

The lookout didn't move. 'What you going to do with her?'

'Kill her, goddammit, what you think?' the white man said flatly. 'You think I'm going to let her live and send me to the chair?'

'We can use her to make him talk,' the lookout argued.

'You think he's going to talk to save this whore?'

Leila had inched over to the partition separating the two rooms and now began edging slowly toward the inside window.

'Don't let him kill me,' she begged in her little-girl's voice to keep their attention distracted.

Her mouth was open; the tip of her tongue slid across her dry lips to make the red paint glisten. She stuck out her breasts and made her body sway as though her pelvic girdle was equipped with roller bearings. She was playing her sex along with her race for all it was worth; but her big brown eyes were dark pools of terror.

The white man turned his back on the lookout and moved toward her with the knife held in a stabbing position.

The second colored man said, 'Wait a minute; he's going to shoot you.'

The white man halted but kept staring at Leila without turning around. 'What's the matter with you niggers?' he said. 'The bitch has got to be silenced; and we ain't got all night to fool around.'

The word *nigger* estranged him. Where before they were divided by a woman, now they were separated by race. Neither of the colored men moved or spoke.

Down below in the Paris Bar someone had put a coin in the juke box, and the slow hypnotic beat of an oldtime platter called 'Bottom Blues' came faintly through the floor.

The second colored man decided to act as peacemaker. 'Ain't no need of you two falling out about a woman,' he said. 'Let's consider it.'

'Consider what?' the white man said. His big, sloping shoulders beneath the loose blue coat seemed suspended in motion.

Moving inch by inch, Leila played the lookout with eyes that promised a thousand nights of frenzied love. All of her life she had played sex for kicks; now she was playing it for her life and it didn't work the same; she felt as sexless as a leg of veal. But everything depended on it, and she forced words through her numb trembling lips.

'Don't let him kill me, please, I beg of you. I'll give you

money – all the money you want. I'll be every kind of woman you can think of; just don't let him—'

'Shut up, whore,' the white man said.

'Let's talk it over,' the lookout mouthed. Lust was shaking him like electric shocks, half choking him, draining his stomach down into his groin.

'We've talked too much already,' the white man said, moving into Leila and raising the knife.

Leila's hand flew to her mouth but she didn't dare scream.

The lookout moved forward and stuck the gun muzzle against the small of the white man's back, then pulled it back a few inches so it could breathe; it was an automatic, and if he had to shoot it needed air.

The white man got the message. He froze with his hand raised. 'You ain't going to shoot me,' he said. His voice sounded as dangerous as a rattlesnake's warning.

'Just don't hurt her is all,' the lookout said in a voice that sounded equally as dangerous.

The second colored man drew his own .38 police special, holding it down beside him in his left hand.

'This is getting too tight for me,' he said. 'I got fifteen grand wrapped up in this deal myself, and if it gets blown away we're all going to go.'

'Chicken feed,' Leila whispered, holding the lookout with her eyes.

Sweat had filmed on her temples and upper lip; a vein in the left side of her throat was throbbing. She breathed as though she couldn't get enough air; her breasts in the jersey-silk pullover were rising and falling like bellows. She was playing a sex pot if there ever was one; but all she wanted in this world was to get to the window, and it seemed like ten thousand miles away.

Unseen by the lookout, the white man turned the knife in his hand and gripped the point.

'This bitch is going to scream any minute,' he said.

The lookout made an offer. 'I'll give you my share for her.'

Leila edged closer to the window. 'You won't lose,' she promised.

Nobody spoke. In the silence the slow, hypnotic beat coming

from below repeated itself endlessly, changing instruments for eight-bar solos.

'It's a deal,' the white man said. 'Now get back on the door.'

'I'll stay here – let Lefty take the door.'

Leila turned her back to the window and groped behind her for the shade. Her fingers found the drawstring.

'Kill him!' she screamed and jerked the string.

Everything happened at once.

The shade flew up and spun at the top in sudden chopping sound like a runaway ratchet wheel.

Leila dropped toward the floor as the white man threw the knife. It caught her in the stomach and went in up to the hilt.

The lookout swung his automatic, searching for a target.

Glass shattered, and the room exploded with the big, hard, head-splitting roar of a high-powered .38 as Grave Digger, standing on the snow-covered fire escape, shot through the iron window grill and put two slugs less than an inch apart in the gunman's heart.

Simultaneously, two shots sounded from the corridor; metal broke and wood crashed, and cold air rushed into the room.

The left-handed gunman spun toward the connecting door-way and went through with his pistol down at his left hip in the Hollywood gunslinger's fashion. He ran into a brace of slugs and came reeling back with two sudden eyes in his forehead, his coat flapping in the hard percussion of sound.

With no expression whatsoever in his beetle-browed, brutal face, the white man drew from the shoulder. He was light-ning fast.

But Grave Digger had already taken a bead on him with the long nickel-plated barrel resting on an iron crossbar. He put the first one in the white man's right arm, just above the elbow, and the second one in his left kneecap.

The pistol dropped from the white man's hand as he pitched to the rug on his face. The pain in his knee was excruciating, but he didn't make a sound. He was like a wounded tiger, silent, crippled, but still as dangerous a killer as the jungle ever saw. Without looking up, knowing that he didn't have a chance, he turned over and lunged for his fallen pistol with his left hand.

Coffin Ed came in from the reception room and kicked it out of his reach, then crossed the room and shot the padlock off the window grill.

Grave Digger kicked it in, knocked out the broken window glass with the side of his shoe and came into the room. Snow followed him.

Leila was curled up against the baseboard with her hands gripping the handle of the knife, crying softly and moaning.

Grave Digger knelt down, pulled her hands away gently and handcuffed them behind her back.

'You can't pull it out,' he said. 'That would only kill you.'

Coffin Ed was occupied handcuffing the white man's good left hand to his good right leg. The white man looked at him without expression.

Finally Casper opened his eyes. The scene was stained red by the blood on his eyeballs.

Coffin Ed undid the gag.

'Get me loose quick,' Casper said thickly, talking through a mouthful of blood.

Grave Digger unlocked the manacles and Coffin Ed freed his legs.

Casper got to his hands and knees and looked about. He saw the manacled white man. Their gazes met. Casper saw the white man's revolver on the floor beside the desk. He crawled to it bear fashion and picked it up. Everyone was watching him, but no one except the white man expected it. He pumped three slugs into the white man's head.

Coffin Ed went crazy with rage. He kicked the pistol from Casper's hand and aimed his own revolver at Casper's heart.

'God-damned sonofabitch, I'll kill you!' he raved. 'He was ours; he wasn't yours. You God-damned sonofabitch, we worked all night and all day and took every God-damned rapefiend risk to get this hoodlum, and you kill him.'

'It was self-defense,' Casper said thickly, blood spattering from his slashed tongue. 'You saw the mother-raper trying to shoot me – didn't you!'

Coffin Ed drew back his pistol as though to club him across

the head. 'I ought to knock out your God-damned brains and call it an accident,' he raved.

'Easy, Ed, easy man,' Grave Digger cautioned. 'You ain't God either.'

Leila was laughing hysterically. 'You knew what kind of man he is when you were risking me and everybody else to save him.'

Grave Digger watched Casper pull to his feet and stagger toward the closet for some clothes to put on.

'Man, does money mean that much to you?' he asked.

'What money?' Casper said.

Down below on 125th Street was a crowd scene. Traffic was stopped. Joe Green's big black Cadillac limousine sat in a line of cars a block long, the motor running and nobody in it. The sidewalks on both sides of the street were jammed. The Paris Bar and the Palm Café and the Apollo Bar had erupted their clients. The three movie houses had been deserted for the bigger attraction.

'Gawwwaheddamnnnn. A shooting every night,' a joker crowed triumphantly. 'It's crazy, man, crazy.'

Prowl cars converged from all directions, weaving in and out of the stopped cars, on the right side and on the wrong side of the street, jumping the curb when necessary to get by. Their sirens were screaming like the souls of the damned; their red lights were blinking like eyes from hell.

Cops jumped out, big feet splattering in the ankle-deep slush, went up the stairs like the introduction to the television series called *Gang Busters*.

Their eyes popped at the sight that greeted them.

Coffin Ed was telephoning for an ambulance.

Grave Digger looked up from the floor, where he was kneeling beside Leila Baron, stroking her forehead and consoling her.

'It's all over but the lying,' he lisped.

20

Casper Holmes was back in the hospital.

His eyes and mouth were bandaged; he could not see nor talk. There were tubes up his nostrils, and he had been given enough morphine to knock out a junkie.

But he was still conscious and alert. There was nothing wrong with his ears, and he could write blind.

He was still playing God.

At eleven o'clock that night he held the press conference which he had last scheduled for ten o'clock, against the considered advice of the staff doctors and his own private physician.

His room was packed with reporters and photographers. His chin jutted aggressively. His hands were expressive. He was in his métier.

He had scribbled a statement to the effect that the robbers had evidently been tipped off that he had received another payroll and had attempted a second robbery before getting out of town.

He had equipped himself with a small scratch pad and stylo with which to answer questions.

The questions came hard and fast.

He scribbled the answers, ripped off the pages and flung them toward the foot of the bed.

Question: Were you given a second payoff?
Answer: Hell no.
Question: Where did they get the information?
Answer: Ask a Ouija board.
Question: How did they find out about the first payoff?
Answer: Can't say.
Question: Why did you slip out of the hospital in a hearse?
Answer: Safety first.
Question: Why did you stop by your office?
Answer: Private reasons.
Question: How did it happen your wife was there?

Answer: I asked her to meet me.

Question: How did detectives Jones and Johnson locate you?

Answer: Ask them.

Question: How do you feel about it all?

Answer: Lucky.

So it went. He didn't give away a thing.

Afterwards he held a private session with his colored attorney, Frederick Douglas Henderson. He scribbled some instructions:

Get charges against sailor Roman Hill nol-prossed, give him your check for his $6,500 and get him out the country on first ship leaving. Then file claim in his name for the $6,500 found on the white robber's body. Then I want you to phone Clay and tell him to keep effects of body for me personally. Got all that?

Attorney Henderson read the instructions thoughtfully.

'Whose body?' he asked.

Casper wrote: He'll know.

When he left, Casper scribbled across a page: Keep your lip buttoned up.

He rang for the nurse and wrote: Get me an envelope.

She returned with the envelope. He folded the note, put it into the envelope and sealed it. He wrote across the face: Mrs Casper Holmes. He handed it to the nurse.

Leila was in the adjoining room, but the nurse did not deliver the note.

She had been in an oxygen tent, taking plasma transfusions, ever since the operation. It was touch-and-go.

Big Six was in another smaller, cheaper private room, which was being paid for by Joe Green.

He had lapsed into a coma. The knife was still in his head. Orders were to leave it there until an encystment had formed about it in the brain, permitting its removal to be attempted. There was no record of such an operation being successful, and brain specialists all over the country had been alerted to the case.

* * *

George Drake's body was found shortly after midnight by a waiter on his way home from work.

He was the eighth victim taken to the morgue from Harlem that weekend resulting from what later became known as the Casper caper.

Grave Digger and Coffin Ed worked all night in the precinct station, writing their report. They stuck to the bare unadorned facts, omitting all references to Casper's private affairs and domestic life. Nevertheless, it filled fourteen sheets of foolscap paper.

It snowed all night, and Monday morning there was no letup in sight. The big suction-type snow removers had been put into use at midnight, and the city's snow crews had worked unceasingly in a slowly losing race against the snow.

At eleven o'clock that morning Roman Hill shipped out on a cargo vessel bound for Rio de Janeiro. He put $6,500 in cash in the captain's keeping before going to work.

Sassafras saw him off. As she was leaving the docks she met a man who reminded her of him very much. The man had a room in Brooklyn and invited her to a bar nearby to have a drink. She saw no reason why she should go all the way back to Harlem in that snow when you could find the same things in Brooklyn while the snow lasted.

At five minutes before noon two detectives from the Automobile Squad made a strike. They located the golden Cadillac in the showroom of a Cadillac dealer on midtown Broadway. It had been sitting outside the entrance to the service department, covered with snow, when the mechanics had shown up for work that morning.

No one admitted knowing how it had got there. It had been inside with the other demonstrator models when everybody left, and the place was locked eight o'clock Saturday evening.

One of the company's oldest salesmen, Herman Rose, closely resembled the description that Roman Hill had given of the man posing as Bernard Kaufman, who had notarized the phony bill of sale Mister Baron had given him.

But there were no charges against him and no one to identify him, so nothing could be done.

Grave Digger and Coffin Ed were summoned to the Chief Inspector's office in the Headquarters building on Centre Street shortly after lunch.

The office was filled with Brass, including an assistant D.A. and a special investigator from the Commissioner's office.

They had been asked why they had attempted to apprehend the robbers single-handed, using Mrs Holmes as a front, instead of contacting their precinct station and getting instructions from the officer in charge.

'We were trying to save his life,' Coffin Ed replied. 'If the block had been surrounded by police, those hoods would have killed him for sure.'

The Chief Inspector nodded. It was a straw-man question anyway.

What the Brass really wanted was their opinion as to Casper's guilt.

'Who knows?' Grave Digger lisped.

'It hasn't been proven,' Coffin Ed said. 'All we know is what his wife said she guessed.'

'What was her racket?' the Chief Inspector asked.

'We haven't figured it out,' Coffin Ed admitted. 'We got wound up in this other business and we haven't worked on it.'

The Chief Inspector admitted that a crew of detectives from the Safe, Loft and Truck Squad and two experts from the Pinkerton Detective Agency had searched Casper's office and the entire office building, and had questioned all of the other tenants and the building superintendent. But they had not turned up with the $50,000.

'You men know Harlem, and you know Holmes,' the Chief said. 'Where would he hide it?'

'If he's got it,' Grave Digger lisped.

'That's the fifty-thousand dollar question,' Coffin Ed said.

'All that I have to say about this business,' the assistant D.A. said, 'is that it stinks.'

Now it was Monday night.

The snow crews had lost the race. The city was snowed in.

The customary metropolitan roar was muffled to an eerie silence by sixteen inches of snow.

Grave Digger and Coffin Ed were in the captain's office in the Harlem Precinct station, talking over the case with their friend and superior officer, Lieutenant Anderson.

Grave Digger sat with one ham perched on the edge of the captain's desk, while Coffin Ed leaned against a corner radiator in the shadow.

'We know he did it,' Grave Digger lisped. 'But what can you do?'

Veins throbbed in Anderson's temples, and his pale-blue eyes looked remote.

'How did you figure the tie-in between Baron's racket and Casper's caper?' Anderson asked.

Grave Digger chuckled.

'It was easy,' Coffin Ed said. 'There wasn't any.'

'We were just lucky,' Grave Digger admitted. 'It was just like she said; she guessed it.'

'But you uncovered her,' Anderson said.

'That's where we were lucky,' Coffin Ed replied.

'What was her racket?'

'Maybe we'll never know for sure, but we figure it like this,' Coffin Ed explained. 'Leila Baron knew this salesman, Herman Rose. Casper bought his Cadillac from there. When she met Roman and found out he had saved up sixty-five hundred dollars to buy a car, she got Rose to come in with her and Junior Ball – or Black Beauty if you want to call him that – on a deal to trim him. Rose provided the car; he probably has a key to the place; he's been there long enough, and he's trusted. And he also acted as notary public. Then his part was finished. Baron was going to take Roman down the deserted street where Black Beauty, masquerading as an old woman, was going to fake being hit. They had no doubt worked out some way to get the car back from Roman and keep the money, too; we'll never know exactly unless she tells us. Probably she planned to scare him into leaving the country.

'Anyway, these hoods masquerading as cops turned into the street as they were making their own getaway in time to see the whole play. They saw the Cadillac knock the old woman down; they saw the old woman getting up. They knew immediately it was a racket, and they decided on the spur of the moment to use it for their own purposes. They could get another car, which wouldn't be reported as stolen, and pick up some additional money too. So they hit the phony victim deliberately to kill.'

'They wouldn't have had to do that,' Anderson said. 'They could have got the Cadillac and the money anyway.'

'They were playing it safe. With the phony victim really killed, no one could go to the police. They could use the Cadillac as long as they wanted without fear of being picked up.'

'Vicious sons of bitches,' Anderson muttered.

'That was how we got the idea that the cases were connected,' Grave Digger said. 'There was an extraordinary viciousness about both capers.'

'But why did they take the car back to the dealer's?' Anderson wondered.

'It was the safest thing to do when they finished with it,' Coffin Ed contended. 'The dealer's name and address were on a sticker in the rear window. Roman and his girl just didn't notice it.'

Anderson sat for a time, musing.

'And you don't think his wife was connected in any way with his caper?' he asked.

'It doesn't figure,' Grave Digger said. 'She hates him.'

'She'd have tipped the police if she had known about it in advance,' Coffin Ed added.

'She tried to give us a lead, but we didn't pick it up,' Grave Digger admitted. 'When she sent us down to Zog Ziegler's crib. She figured that somebody down there would probably know about it, and we could find it out without her telling us.'

'But we figured she was tipping us on Baron, and we missed it,' Coffin Ed said.

'But she helped you to save him in the end,' Anderson said. 'How do you figure that?'

'She didn't want him taken by those hoodlums who had knocked her out and robbed her,' Grave Digger said.

'Besides, she might still think Casper is a great man,' Coffin Ed said.

'He is a great man,' Grave Digger said. 'According to our standards.'

Anderson took his pipe from his side coat pocket and cleaned it with a small penknife over a report sheet. He filled it from an oilskin pouch and struck a kitchen match on the underside of the desk. When he had the pipe going, he said:

'I can understand Casper pulling off a caper like that. He probably wouldn't even think he was hurting anybody if he got away with it. The only people who'd get hurt would be some out-of-town hoods. But why would his wife get mixed up in a cheap chiseling racket like that? She's a lovely woman, a socialite. She had a hundred activities to keep her occupied.'

'Hell, the reason is obvious,' Coffin Ed said. 'If you were a woman and you had a husband who played about with the little boys, what would you do?'

Anderson turned bright red.

Several minutes passed. No one said anything.

'You can hear your own thoughts moving around in this silence,' Coffin Ed said.

'It's like an armistice, when the guns stop shooting,' Anderson said.

'Let's hope we don't have to go through that again,' Grave Digger said.

'What I have been thinking about is why Casper went by his office when it's obvious by now that he doesn't have the money hidden there,' Anderson said.

'That's the big question,' Coffin Ed admitted.

They brooded over it in the eerie silence.

'Maybe to throw off the Pinkertons who were onto him by then, or maybe to set a trap for the hoods if they were still in town. It was a red herring, anyway.'

'Yeah,' Grave Digger said. 'We're missing something.'

'Just like we missed that tip-off on Ziegler.'

Grave Digger screwed about and looked at Coffin Ed.

'Yeah, maybe we're missing the same thing.'

'You know what it is?' Coffin Ed said.

'Yeah, it just now came to me.'

'Me, too. It was thinking about the clique that did it.'

'Yeah, it's as obvious as the nose on your face.'

'That's the trouble. It's too God-damned obvious.'

'What are you talking about?' Anderson asked.

'We'll tell you about it later,' Coffin Ed said.

There was no way to drive down 134th Street.

Grave Digger and Coffin Ed left the Plymouth on Seventh Avenue, which had been kept open for the interstate trucks, and waded through snow that came up to their knees.

Mr Clay was lying on his side on an old couch covered with faded gray velvet in the first-floor front room that he used for an office. His face was toward the wall and his back was toward the street of falling snow, but he was not asleep.

The dark-shaded floor lamp in the window that he kept lit permanently threw the room in dim relief.

He was a small, dried-up old man with parchmentlike skin, washed-out brown eyes and long, bushy gray hair. As was customary, he was dressed in a frock coat, black-and-gray striped morning pants and old-fashioned black patent-leather shoes with high-button, gray-suede leather tops. He wore a wing collar and a black silk ascot tie held in place by a gray pearl stickpin. Pince-nez glasses, attached to a long black ribbon pinned to the lapel of his coat, were tucked into a pocket of his gray double-breasted vest.

When Grave Digger and Coffin Ed walked into the office, he said without moving, 'Is that you, Marcus?'

'It's Ed Johnson and Digger Jones,' Coffin Ed said.

Mr Clay turned over, swung his feet to the floor and sat up. He clipped the pince-nez onto his nose and looked at them.

'Don't shake the snow on my floor,' he said in his thin, querulous voice. 'Why didn't you clean yourselves outside?'

'A little water won't hurt this place,' Grave Digger lisped. 'It'll help settle all this dust in here.'

Mr Clay looked at his swollen mouth. 'Hah, somebody gave it to you this time,' he said.

'I can't always be lucky,' Grave Digger replied.

'Hot as you got it in here, you must be making mummies,' Coffin Ed observed.

'You didn't come here to complain about the heat,' Mr Clay snapped.

'No, we came to examine the effects of a body you got in here.'

'Whose body?'

'Lucius Lambert.'

Mr Clay refused flatly. 'You can't see them.'

'Why not?'

'Casper doesn't want them disturbed.'

'Did Casper claim his body from the morgue?'

'A relative claimed him, but Casper is paying for the funeral.'

'That don't give him any legal rights,' Coffin Ed said. 'We'll get an order from the relative. Who is he?'

'I don't have to tell you,' Mr Clay said peevishly.

'Naw, but you're going to have to do one or the other,' Grave Digger lisped. 'You can't hold bodies here without the proper authority.'

'What did you want with his effects?'

'We just want to look at them. You can come with us if you want.'

'I don't want to look at them; I've seen them. I'll send Marcus with you.' He raised his voice and called, 'Marcus!'

A tall, light-skinned, loose-lipped man affecting the latest English fashion came into the room. He was the embalmer.

'Show these dicks Lambert's effects,' Mr Clay directed. 'And see that they don't take anything.'

'Yes, sir,' Marcus said.

He took them to a basement storeroom, adjacent to the embalming room, where the clothes and effects of the bodies were kept in small wicker baskets until claimed by relatives.

Marcus took one of the baskets from a shelf and placed it on the table.

'Help yourself,' he said, and started from the room. At the door he turned and winked. 'There's nothing in it worth taking, except a box of stockings, and the old man has already spotted them,' he said.

'I'll bet you know,' Coffin Ed said.

It didn't take but a few moments. Grave Digger pushed the clothes aside until he found the box of stockings.

It was a black box with a gold stripe across it, intended for twelve pairs of stockings. It was sealed with a tiny bit of Scotch tape.

Grave Digger peeled back the tape and removed two pairs of sheer silk stockings wrapped separately in gold cellophane paper. Underneath was another package wrapped in similar paper. He placed the package on the table and opened it.

It contained fifty brand-new thousand-dollar bills.

'It had to be,' he said. 'Snake Hips was the only one he could have passed it to. And we missed it all this time.'

'It was right there in front of our eyes,' Coffin Ed admitted. 'This boy would never have been dancing in the street half dressed on a night as cold as Saturday just to bitch off that square bartender. We ought to have known that.'

'And he was in the clique, too. That's how we should have known. Casper passed him the package as he went by.'

'Why do you think he left it here, Digger?'

'Safer here than anywhere else, and probably didn't figure us to dig Snake Hips' straight moniker as Lucius Lambert.'

'What are we going to do with it?'

'Let's just seal up this package and put it back and don't say anything about it,' Grave Digger said.

'And keep the money?'

'Damn right keep the money.'

'Casper's going to know we got it.'

'Damn right he's going to know we got it. And there ain't going to be a damn thing he can do about it. That's what's going to hurt him. He's going to want to job us, but you can't job two detectives with twenty-five thousand bucks in their kicks. And as much as we know about him now, he knows he'd better not try.'

'I'd like to see his face when he comes for it,' Coffin Ed said.

'Yeah, there's going to be some arteries bursting for sure.'

Two days later, the *New York Herald Tribune* Fresh Air Fund, which sends New York City boys of all races and creeds on vacations in the country during the summer, received an anonymous cash donation of $50,000. The executives of the fund didn't bat an eye; they were used to this kind of money.

On the same day, as he was about to leave the hospital, Casper received an anonymous telegram.

It read: *Crime doesn't pay.*

The Heat's On

1

'You're my friend, ain't you?' the giant asked.

He had a voice that whined like a round saw cutting through a pine knot.

'What do you need with a friend, as big as you are?' the dwarf kidded.

'I is asking you,' the giant insisted.

He was a milk-white albino with pink eyes, battered lips, cauliflowered ears and thick, kinky, cream-colored hair. He wore a white T-shirt, greasy black pants held up with a length of hemp rope, and blue canvas rubber-soled sneakers.

The dwarf put on an expression of hypocritical solicitude. He flicked back his sleeve and glanced at the luminous dial on his watch. It was 1.22 a.m. He relaxed. There was no need to hurry.

He was a hunchback with a dirty yellow complexion, shades darker than that of the albino. Beady black eyes that could not focus on anything looked out from a ratlike face. But he was dressed in an expensive blue linen, handstitched suit, silk-topped shoes and a black panama hat with a dull orange band.

His shifty gaze flicked for a moment on the rope knot at the giant's belly, which was on a level with his own eyes. The giant could make four of him, but he was not scared. The giant was just another sucker as far as he was concerned.

'You know I'm your friend, daddy-o. I'm old Jake. I'm your real cool friend.' He spoke in a wheezing voice that was accustomed to whispering.

The giant's battered white face knotted into a frown. He looked up and down the dimly lit block on Riverside Drive.

On one side was a wall of big dark buildings. Not one lighted window was visible. On the other side was a park. He could make out the shapes of trees and benches, but he could only smell the flowers and the recently watered grass. A block away was the squat dark shape of Grant's Tomb.

None of that interested him.

The park sloped sharply to the West Side Highway. He saw the scattered lights of late motorists going north toward Westchester County. Beyond the highway was the Hudson River, flickering vaguely in the dark. Across a mile of water was the New Jersey shore. It might have been the Roman walls for all he cared.

He put his ham-size hand on the dwarf's small bony shoulder. The dwarf's back seemed to bend.

'Don't give me that stuff,' he said. 'I don't mean no real cool friend. You is everybody's real cool friend. I mean is you my sure enough, really and truly friend?'

The dwarf wriggled irritably beneath the weight of the giant's hand. His shifty gaze traveled up the huge white arm and lit on the giant's thick white neck. Suddenly he realized that he was alone with a giant halfwit on a dark deserted street.

'Look here, Pinky, ain't Jake always been your friend?' he said, pumping earnestness into his wheezing whisper.

The giant blinked like a dull mind reacting to a sudden apparition. Knobs of scar tissue shading his pink eyes moved like agitated lugworms. His cauliflowered ears twitched. His thick scarred lips drew back in a grimace. Rows of gold-crowned teeth flashed like a beacon in the semidark.

'I don't mean no always-been-your-friend friend,' he whined angrily, his grip tightening involuntarily on the dwarf's shoulder.

The dwarf winced with pain. His gaze flicked up toward the giant's agitated face; but it bounced right off. It lighted for a moment on the twenty-two-story tower of the Riverside Church, rising in the dark behind the giant's back. He became increasingly apprehensive.

'I mean is you my friend through thick and thin?' the giant insisted. 'Is you my friend through smoke and fire?'

The sound of a fire engine sounded faintly from the distance.

The dwarf heard it ... *smoke and fire* ... He began to get the connection. He struggled to break from the giant's grip.

'Turn me loose, fool!' he cried. 'I got to split.'

But the giant held on to him. 'Can't split now. You got to stay and back me up. You got to tell 'em for me, friend.'

'Tell who what, you fool?'

'The firemen, thass who. You got to tell 'em how my pa is gonna get robbed and murdered.'

'Shit!' the dwarf said, trying to push the giant's hand from his shoulder. 'Ain't nothing going to happen to Gus, you mother-raping idiot!'

But the giant only tightened his grip; his first finger and thumb closed about the dwarf's neck.

The dwarf squirmed like a pig in a sack, becoming panic-stricken; his beady black eyes bulged from their sockets. He hammered at the giant's thick torso with his puny fists.

'Turn me loose, you big mother-raper!' he screamed. 'Can't you hear those sirens? Are you stone-deaf? We can't be seen together on this plushy street. We'll get nabbed for sure. I'm a three-time loser. I'll get life in prison.'

The giant leaned forward and pushed his face before the face of the dwarf. The scar tissue on his blurred white face seemed to be jumping with a life of its own, like snakes in a hot fire. His body trembled and his nostrils flared and his eyes gleamed like pink coals as he stared into the beady black eyes of the dwarf.

'Thass why I been asking is you my friend through thick and thin,' he whined in a desperately urgent whisper.

The quiet environs of Riverside Drive were shattered with ear-splitting noise as fire engines and police cruisers poured into the street.

The dwarf stopped beating futilely at the giant's torso and began frantically to fish little square paper packets from his own pockets and eat them up. He stuffed them into his mouth, one after another, chewed desperately and swallowed. His face turned purple as he began to choke.

At the same instant, firemen jumped from the still-moving engines and rushed toward the church, brandishing axes. Some burst through the front doors and rushed about in the black dark 215-foot nave, stumbling over pews and banging into pillars, looking for burning timbers to chop away. Others rushed around the sides of the building, searching for other accesses.

The fire captain was already in the street, shouting orders through his megaphone.

A church sexton came from a dark recess beside the huge front doors where he had been hiding.

He leveled an accusing finger at the giant albino and cried, 'There's the man who put in the false alarm!'

The captain saw him but could not hear him. 'Get that civilian out of the danger zone!' he shouted.

Two prowl car cops on the alert for trouble rushed forward and seized the sexton.

'All right, buddy, get back,' one of them ordered.

'I am trying to tell you,' the sexton said through gritted teeth. 'That big man there put in the fire alarm.'

The cops released the sexton and turned toward the giant.

'What's going on here? Why are you choking that shrimp?' the vocal one asked in a hard voice.

'He's my friend,' the giant whined.

The cop reddened with anger.

The dwarf gurgled as though choking and his eyes popped.

The cop looked from one to the other, trying to decide which one to slug. They both looked guilty, he had no choice.

'Which one of you guys put in the alarm?' he asked.

'He did,' the sexton said, pointing at the giant.

The cop looked at the giant and decided to call the fire captain. 'We got the man who put in the alarm, sir.'

The fire captain called back, 'Ask him where the fire is.'

'Fire?' the giant said as though he didn't know what it was.

'Fire!' the sexton echoed in outrage. 'There isn't any fire! That's what I been trying to tell you.'

The two cops looked at one another. All these fire engines and no fire, they thought. Suddenly one was reminded of that song by Louis Armstrong, 'All that meat and no potatoes . . .'

But the fire captain purpled with rage. He moved toward the giant with balled fists.

'Did you put in the alarm?' he asked dangerously, his chin jutting forward.

The giant released his grip on the dwarf and said, 'You tell him, Jake.'

The dwarf tried to run but one of the cops caught him by the neck of his coat collar.

'I saw him when he did it,' the sexton said.

The captain wheeled on him. 'Why didn't you stop him? Do you know what it costs the city to put all these engines into operation?'

'Hell, look at him,' the sexton replied. 'Would you have stopped him?'

They all looked at him. They understood what the sexton meant. One of the cops flashed his light into the giant's face to see him better. He saw the white face with the Negroid features and white hair. He had never seen an albino Negro. He was astonished.

'What the hell are you?' he asked.

'I'm his friend,' the giant said, pointing at the dwarf struggling in the other cop's grip.

The captain's eyes stretched. 'By God, he's a nigger!' he exclaimed.

'Well, kiss my foot!' the first cop said. 'I thought there was something damn funny about him to be a white man.'

The dwarf took advantage of the distraction and broke from the other cop's grip. He ran around the rear of the fire captain's car and started across the street.

Brakes squealed and a fast-moving car slewed sidewise to keep from running him down.

Two big loose-jointed colored men wearing dark battered felt hats and wrinkled black alpaca suits emerged in unison from opposite sides of the front seat and hit the pavement in identical flat-footed lopes.

They came around the front of their little black sedan and converged on the running dwarf. Coffin Ed reached out a hand and caught hold of a thin, bony arm. It felt as though it might break off in his hand. He spun the hunchback around.

'It's Jake,' Grave Digger said.

'Look at his face,' Coffin Ed said.

'He's been eating it,' Grave Digger observed.

'But he ain't digested it yet,' Coffin Ed concluded, gripping the dwarf from behind by both arms.

Grave Digger hit the dwarf in the stomach.

The dwarf doubled over and began to vomit.

Grave Digger took out a handkerchief and spread it on the ground so that the dwarf vomited into it.

Half-chewed packets of paper came out with bits of boiled tongue and dill pickle.

Suddenly the dwarf fainted. Coffin Ed carried him over to the edge of the street and laid him on the grass border.

Grave Digger carefully folded the vomit-filled handkerchief and inserted it into a heavy manila envelope which he stuck into his leather-lined side coat pocket.

They left the dwarf lying on the ground and moved over to see what the commotion was about.

The giant was saying to the fire captain, 'Jake can tell you, boss. He's my friend.'

'Jake ain't talking,' Grave Digger said.

The giant looked stunned.

'He's halfwit,' one of the white cops said.

By now the giant was encircled by several cops and a number of firemen.

'Halfwit or not, he's going to answer my question,' the captain said, pinning his bloodshot gaze onto the giant's pink eyes. 'Why did you ring the fire alarm, boy?'

Sweat flowed down the giant's cheeks like tears.

'Boss, I didn't go to start all this,' he whined. 'All I wanted was for somebody to come and stop 'em from robbing and murdering my pa.'

Grave Digger and Coffin Ed tensed.

'Where at?' Grave Digger asked.

'He works for the janitor of the apartment house three doors up the street,' the sexton volunteered.

'He's my pa,' the giant said.

'Shut up, all of you, and let me ask the questions,' the fire captain grated. He leaned toward the giant. He was over six feet tall but he only came up to the level of the giant's flat nose. 'I want to know why you came here and rang the special fire alarm for Riverside Church?' he insisted. 'You're not such an idiot that you don't know there is a special fire alarm just for this famous church.'

'He told you,' Coffin Ed said.

The fire captain ignored him. His teeth clenched so fiercely the muscles knotted in his purple-tinted jaws. 'Why didn't you phone the police? Why didn't you put in a police alarm? Why didn't you ring some other fire alarm? Why didn't you just yell for help?'

The giant looked bewildered. His flat white face began twitching. He licked a pink tongue across colorless lips.

'It was the closest,' he said.

'Closest to what?' the fire captain rasped.

'Closest to where he lives, obviously,' Grave Digger said.

'This is my business!' the fire captain shouted. 'You keep out.'

'If it's murder or robbery it's our business,' Grave Digger replied.

'Do you believe this idiot?' a white cop asked scornfully.

'It won't take long to find out,' Coffin Ed said.

'I'm going to find out first why he rang this alarm and got all these engines out here,' the fire captain said.

He reached forward with his left hand to clutch the giant in a vise, but he didn't find any place to take hold. The giant's T-shirt was too flimsy and his sweaty white skin was too slippery. So the fire captain just held out his hand with the palm forward as though to push the giant in the chest.

'Who's trying to rob your pa?' Grave Digger asked quickly.

'There's an African and my stepma; they is teaming up on him,' the giant whined.

The fire captain rapped him on the chest. 'But you knew there wasn't any fire.'

The giant looked about for help. There wasn't any.

'Nawsuh, boss, I didn't exactly know there wasn't any fire,' he denied. He glanced at the captain's face and admitted, 'But I didn't seen any.'

The fire captain blew his top. He hit the giant in the stomach with all his might. His fist bounced back as though he had hit the tire of a truck.

The giant looked surprised.

'There ain't no need of that,' Coffin Ed said. 'He's willing to talk.'

The fire captain ignored him. 'Let's take him, boys,' he said.

A fireman took hold of the giant's right arm while the fire captain looped a left into his hard rubber stomach.

The giant grunted. He reached out his left hand and took the captain by the throat.

'Easy does it!' Grave Digger shouted. 'Don't make graves.'

'Keep out of this,' a white cop warned him, drawing his police revolver.

The captain's eyes bulged and his purpling tongue popped out.

A fireman hit the giant in the back with the flat of his ax. A sound came from the giant's mouth like a wet cough.

Another fireman raised his ax.

Grave Digger caught it by the handle in midstroke and drew his long-barreled, nickel-plated, .38-caliber revolver. He swung the barrel against the back of the giant's hand. The pain went through the giant's hand into the captain's Adam's apple and the captain's head filled with a shower of blue-pointed stars.

The giant's grip went slack and the captain fell.

At sight of the captain on the ground, tempers flared.

The fireman snatched his ax from Grave Digger's grasp and made as though to chop at him.

From the other side, Coffin Ed's revolver flashed in the dim light as he warned, 'Don't do it. Don't lose your head. Your ass goes with it.'

The fireman whirled his ax and hit the giant a glancing blow across the back of the neck.

The giant cried like an enraged stallion and began to fight. He elbowed the fireman on his right in the jaw, knocking him unconscious. He couldn't close his left hand, but he flailed out with his left arm and flattened two firemen with axes.

Firemen reversed their axes and began whaling at him with the hickory handles. Some were getting through and making deep purple welts on the giant's sensitive white skin. Firemen were going down from the giant's pumping right fist and bodies were piling up as though a massacre were taking place. Still others closed in. The giant showed no signs of weakening, but he was slowly turning black and blue.

The sexton was standing to one side, wringing his hands

and beseeching the irate firemen, 'Be calm, gentlemen, it's divine to forgive.'

Grave Digger and Coffin Ed were doing their best to stop the fracas.

'Easy does it,' Grave Digger was repeating.

Coffin Ed was imploring, 'Let the police have him.'

But their pleas had no effect.

A fireman hit the giant across the shins. He went down. Firemen swarmed over him, trying to pin his arms behind him. But the muscles beneath his greasy purpling skin were rock hard. Fingers couldn't get a grip. It was like trying to hold a greased pig at a state fair.

The giant got to his hands and knees and pushed to his feet, shaking off firemen like a dog shedding water. He put his head down and started to run, plowing through a rain of blows.

'The sonofabitch ain't human,' a fireman complained.

He got across the sidewalk and stepped onto the grass. His foot sunk into the belly of the unconscious dwarf. Globules of vomit spewed from Jake's mouth. No one noticed.

He vaulted over the hood of a fire engine and got a lead on his pursuers.

'Stop him, he's getting away,' a white cop shouted.

Grave Digger and Coffin Ed had moved out into the street, anticipating the breakaway. They had the giant blocked.

The giant drew up as though skidding on his heels. For an instant he stood like a cornered animal, his back to the fire engine, looking for a way out. He had the bruised, bleeding, bewildered look of a bull when the picadors have finished.

'Shall we take him?' Coffin Ed asked.

'Hell, let him go if he can make it,' Grave Digger said.

They drew apart and let the giant through.

Cops and firemen were closing in from both ends of the fire engine. The detectives' car stood obliquely in the street and two prowl cars flanked the other side.

The giant leaped onto the hood of the little black sedan. His rubber-soled sneakers gripped. His next leap took him to the top of a white-and-black prowl car. For a brief instant he was caught in the glare of a fire engine spotlight, a grotesque figure in the strained, shocking, ugly position of panic-stricken flight.

Automatically, as though the target were irresistible, a cop drew a bead with his service revolver. At the same instant, as though part of the same motion sprung from another source, Coffin Ed knocked his arm up with the long nickel-plated barrel of his own revolver. The cop's pistol went off. The giant seemed to fly from the roof of the prowl car and crashed into the foliage of the park.

For a moment everyone was sobered by the sound of the shot and the sight of the giant crashing to earth. All were gripped by the single thought – the cop had shot him. Reactions varied; but all were held in a momentary silence.

Then Coffin Ed said to the cop who had fired the shot, 'You can't kill a man for putting in a false fire alarm.'

The cop had only intended to wing him, but Coffin Ed's rebuke infuriated him.

'Hell, you killed a man for farting at you,' he charged.

Coffin Ed's scarred face twitched in a blind rage. It was the one thing in his career which touched him to the quick.

'That's a goddamned lie!' he shouted, his pistol barrel flashing in a vicious arc toward the white cop's head.

There was just time for Grave Digger to catch the blow in his hand and spin Coffin Ed around.

'Goddammit, Ed, control it, man!' he said. 'It's a joke.'

The white cop was being forcibly held by two of his uniformed mates. 'These two black bastards are crazy,' he mouthed.

Coffin Ed allowed himself to be drawn off by Grave Digger, but he said, 'It ain't no joke to me.'

Grave Digger knew that it was useless to explain that Coffin Ed had shot a different boy, one who was trying to throw perfume into his face. He had thought the boy was throwing acid; and he already bore the scars of one acid bath in his face. Everyone in the department knew the straight story, but some of the white cops distorted it to needle Coffin Ed.

The fracas didn't last more than a minute, but it gave the giant a chance to get away. The park dropped steeply from the manicured fringe bordering Riverside Drive through a rocky jungle of brush down to a wire fence enclosing the tracks of the New York Central Railroad's freight lines and the elevated platform of the six-lane West Side Highway.

A cop heard the giant threshing through the brush and shouted, 'He's making for the river!'

The pursuit commenced again. No one had believed the giant's story of robbery and murder taking place.

'Let 'em go,' Grave Digger said bitterly.

'I ain't stopping 'em,' Coffin Ed said. 'With the start he's got now they won't catch him anyway.'

Grave Digger took off his heavy felt hat and rubbed his palm across his sweat-wet short kinky hair.

They looked at one another with the unspoken communication they had developed during the years they had served as partners.

'You think there's anything in it?' Grave Digger asked.

'We'd better try to find out. It'd be a hell of a note if somebody was being murdered during all this comedy we're having.'

'That would be the story.'

Coffin Ed walked over and looked down at the unconscious dwarf. He bent over and felt his pulse.

'What about our friend Jake?'

'He'll keep,' Grave Digger said. 'Let's go. This halfwit Pinky may be right.'

2

By that time Riverside Drive was wide-awake. Vaguely human shapes hung from the dark open windows of the front apartments like an amphitheater of ghosts; and the windows of the back apartments were ablaze with lights as though the next war had begun.

The apartment house they sought was a nine-story brick building with plate-glass doors opening into a dimly lit foyer. The night latch was on. There was a bell to one side above a shiny chrome plate announcing: SUPERINTENDENT. Coffin Ed reached toward it, but Grave Digger shook his head.

Even though the street was packed with fire engines, prowl cars, uniformed cops and firemen, the residents peering from the upper windows watched the two black men suspiciously.

Coffin Ed noticed them and remarked, 'They think we're burglars.'

'Hell, what else they going to think about two spooks like us prowling about in a white neighborhood in the middle of the night?' Grave Digger said cynically. 'If I was to see two white men in Harlem at this time of night I'd figure they were looking for whores.'

'You would be right.'

'No more than them.'

At the side of the building was a narrow cement walk closed off by a barred iron gate. The gate was locked.

Grave Digger grabbed the top bar with one hand, put a foot on the middle crossbar, and went up and over. Coffin Ed followed.

From somewhere above came the sound of an outraged gasp. They ignored it.

Halfway down the side of the building was a barred window on a level with the sidewalk. Purple light poured out onto the opposite wall in a rectangular bar. They approached it quietly and knelt, one on each side.

The window opened into a room that appeared to have been furnished by the castoffs of decades of tenants. Nothing had escaped. Lowboys and highboys were stacked against the walls, interspersed with marble statuettes, grandfather clocks, iron jockey hitching posts, empty birdcages, a broken glass aquarium, two moth-eaten stuffed squirrels and a molted stuffed owl. On one side was a round-topped dining table, surrounded by a variety of dilapidated chairs, and covered by a faded red silk curtain. Between two doors opening to the kitchen and bedroom respectively stood an old-fashioned organ, atop which was a menagerie of china animals. Opposite were two out-of-date television sets, one atop the other, crowned by a radio from the pre-television age. An overstuffed davenport, flanked by two overstuffed armchairs, were drawn up before the television sets close enough to reach through the screens and manhandle the performers. The linoleum floor was piled with threadbare scatter rugs.

A lamp with a blue bulb burned on a lowboy, vying with a red-bulbed lamp on the dining table. A small fan atop an oakstained highboy was stirring up the hot air.

The television screen was dark but the radio was playing. It was tuned to a late record program. The voice of Jimmy Rushing issued from the metallic sounding speaker, singing: '*I got that old-fashioned love in my heart . . .*'

A young black man wearing a soiled white turban and a flowing robe of bright-colored rags sat in the center of the davenport, eating a pork chop sandwich and looking over his shoulder with an animated leer.

Behind him a high-yellow woman was doing a chickentail shuffle around the dining table with a dark Jamaica rum highball in one hand. She was wearing a garment that looked like a bleached flour sack with holes cut out for the arms and head. She was a tall, skinny woman with the high sharp hips of a cotton chopper and the big loaded breasts of a wet nurse. As she shuffled barefooted on the pile of rugs, her bony knees poked out the sack in front while her sharp shaking buttocks poked it out in the back like the tail feathers of a laying hen. Up above, her breasts poked out the top of the sack like the snouts of two hungry shoats.

She had a long bony face with a flat nose and jutting chin. Masses of crinkly black hair, dripping with oil, hung down to the middle of her back. Her slanting yellow eyes were doing tricks in the African's direction.

Grave Digger rapped on the window.

The woman gave a start. Liquid sloshed from the glass over the table cover.

The African saw them first. His eyes got white-rimmed.

Then the woman turned and saw them. Her big, wide, cushion-lipped mouth swelled with fury.

'You niggers better get away from that window or I'll call the police,' she shouted in a flat unmusical voice.

Grave Digger fished a felt-lined leather folder from his side coat pocket and showed his buzzer.

The woman went sullen. 'Nigger cops,' she said scornfully. 'What you whore-chasers want?'

'In,' Grave Digger said.

She looked at the drink in her hand as though she didn't

know what to do with it. Then she said, 'You cain't come in here. My husband ain't at home.'

'That's all right, you'll do.'

She looked around at the African. He was getting to his feet as though preparing to leave.

'You stay, we want to talk to you too,' Grave Digger said.

The woman jerked her gaze back toward the window. Her eyes were slits of suspicion. 'What you want to talk to him for?'

'Where's the door, woman?' Coffin Ed said sharply. 'Let us ask the questions.'

'It's in the back; where you think it's at?' she said.

They stood up and went around to the back of the building.

'It's been a long time since I've seen a real cat-eyed woman,' Coffin Ed remarked.

'I wouldn't have one for my own for all the tea in China,' Grave Digger declared.

'You just ain't saying it.'

Steps led down to the green-painted basement door. The woman had it open and was waiting for them, arms akimbo.

'Gus ain't in no trouble, is he?' she asked. She didn't look worried; she looked downright evil.

'Who is Gus?' Grave Digger asked, stopping on the bottom.

'He's my husband, the super.'

'What kind of trouble?'

'How would I know? Trouble is your sugar. What would you be doing messing around here at this time of night unless—' She broke off; her slitted yellow eyes became malevolent. 'I just hope ain't none of these grudging-assed white folks has accused us of stealing something, just 'cause we is going to Ghana,' she said in her flat outraged voice. 'It'd be just like 'em.'

'Ghana!' Grave Digger exclaimed. 'Ghana in Africa? You're going to Ghana?'

Her expression became suddenly triumphant. 'You heard me.'

'Who's *we*?' Coffin Ed asked over Grave Digger's shoulder.

'Me and Gus, that's who.'

'Let's go inside and get this straightened out,' Grave Digger said.

'If you think we has stole something, you're beating up the wrong bush,' she said. 'We ain't took nothing from nobody.'

'We'll see.'

She wheeled and went down the brightly lighted, whitewashed corridor, her square bony shoulders held high and stiff while her hard sharp buttocks wiggled like a tadpole.

A dark green steamer trunk stood against the wall beside the elevator doors. It bore luggage stickers reading: SS QUEEN MARY – CUNARD LINE – *Hold*.' Both handles were tagged.

The detectives' interest went up another notch.

The door to the janitor's suite opened directly into the over-stuffed parlor. When they entered, the African was sitting on the edge of a straight-backed chair with the rum highball shaking in his hand.

The radio was silent.

As she turned to close the door, an animal appeared silently in the kitchen doorway.

The detectives felt their scalps twitch.

At first sight it appeared to be a female lion. It was tawny-colored with a massive head, upright ears and lambent eyes. Then a low growl issued from its throat and they knew it was a dog.

Coffin Ed slipped his revolver from its holster.

'She won't hurt you,' the woman said scornfully. 'She's chained to the stove.'

'Are you taking this animal with you?' Grave Digger asked in amazement.

'It don't belong to us; it belongs to an albino nigger called Pinky who Gus had around here to help him,' she said.

'Pinky. He's your son, ain't he?' Grave Digger needled.

'My son!' she exploded. 'Do I look like that nigger's ma? He's already older than I is.'

'He calls your husband his father.'

'He ain't no such thing, even if he is old enough. Gus just found him somewhere and took pity on him.'

Coffin Ed nudged Grave Digger to show him four tan

plastic suitcases which had been hidden from their view by the dining table.

'So where is Gus?' Grave Digger asked.

She got sullen again. 'I don't know where he's at. Out watching the fire up the street, I suppose.'

'He didn't go out to get a fix, did he?' Grave Digger took a shot in the dark, remembering their prisoner, Jake.

'Gus!' She appeared indignant. 'He ain't got the habit – no kind of habit, unless it's the churchgoing habit.' She thought for a moment and added, 'I guess he must have went to take the trunk from the storage room; I see somebody put it in the hall.'

'Who's got the habit?' Coffin Ed insisted.

'Pinky's got the habit. He's on H.'

'How can he afford it?'

'Don't ask me.'

Grave Digger let his gaze rest on the nervous African.

'What's this man doing here?' he asked her suddenly.

'He's an African chief,' she said proudly.

'I believe you; but that don't answer my question.'

'If you just must know, he sold the farm to Gus.'

'What farm?'

'The cocoa plantation in Ghana where we is going.'

'Your husband bought a cocoa plantation in Ghana from this African?' Coffin Ed said incredulously. 'What kind of racket is this?'

'Show him your passport,' she told the African.

The African fished a passport from the folds of his robe and held it out toward Grave Digger.

Grave Digger ignored it, but Coffin Ed took it and examined it curiously before handing it back.

'I don't dig this,' Grave Digger confessed, removing his hat to scratch his head. 'Where's all this money coming from? Your husband can afford to buy a cocoa plantation in Ghana on a superintendent's salary, and his helper can afford a heroin habit.'

'Don't ask me where Pinky gets his money from,' she said. 'Gus got his on the legit. His wife died and left him a tobacco farm in North Carolina and he sold it.'

Grave Digger and Coffin Ed looked at one another with raised brows.

'I thought you were his wife,' Grave Digger said to the woman.

'I is now,' she said triumphantly.

'Then he's a bigamist.'

She tittered. 'He ain't no more.'

Grave Digger shook his head. 'Some folks have all the luck.'

From outside came the sound of fire engines starting and beginning to move away.

'Where was the fire?' she asked.

'There wasn't any fire,' Grave Digger said. 'It was Pinky who turned in the fire alarm. He wanted to call the police.'

Her slanting yellow eyes stretched into the shape of almonds. 'He did! What did he want to do that for?'

'He said that you and this African were murdering and robbing his father.'

She turned a dirty muddy color. The African jumped to his feet as though he had been stung in the rear by a wasp; he started sputtering denials in a guttural-sounding, strangely accented English. She cut him off harshly, 'Shut up! Gus will take care of him. The dirty mother-raping white nigger! After all we has done for him, trying to make trouble for us on our last day.'

'Why would he do that?'

'He don't like Africans is all. He's just envious 'cause he ain't got no color in his own fishbelly skin.'

Grave Digger and Coffin Ed shook their heads in unison.

'Now I've heard everything,' Grave Digger said. 'Here's a white colored man who puts in a false fire alarm that Riverside Church is on fire, getting half the fire equipment in New York City on the roll and all the police in the neighborhood up here – and why? I ask you why?'

'Because he don't like black colored people,' Coffin Ed said.

'You can't blame that on the heat,' Grave Digger said.

The front doorbell began to ring. It rang long and insistently, as though someone was trying to jab the button through the wall.

'Now who in the hell is that at this hour of the night?' the woman said.

'Maybe it's Gus,' Coffin Ed said. 'Maybe he's lost his key.'

'If Pinky done put in another false fire alarm, he better watch out,' the woman threatened.

She opened the door to the corridor and went to answer the bell. The detectives followed her up the stairs into the front foyer.

Through the glass-paneled doors, uniformed cops were seen swarming about the entrance.

The woman flung open the doors.

'Now what you all want?' she demanded.

The white cops looked suspiciously at the two colored detectives.

'We got several reports that two colored prowlers have been seen around this house,' one of them said in a hard challenging voice. 'You know anything about it?'

'That's us,' Grave Digger said as he and Coffin Ed flashed their buzzers. 'We've been prowling around.'

The white cop reddened.

'Well, don't blame us,' he said. 'We got to check on these reports.'

'Hell, we ain't blaming you,' Grave Digger said. 'It's the heat.'

They left with the other cops and went up the street to look for Jake the dwarf, but he was gone. A prowl car cop still lingering in the vicinity said he had been taken to the hospital.

The fire engines had gone but several deserted prowl cars were still parked haphazardly in the street. Some cops were still searching for Pinky, the giant albino, but they had not found him.

Coffin Ed glanced at his watch.

'It's twelve after two,' he said. 'This joke has lasted for more than an hour.'

'The bars have closed,' Grave Digger said. 'We'd better take a look in the valley before checking in.'

'What about Jake?'

'He'll keep. But first let's look see what's cooking in all this heat.'

They got into their little black sedan and drove off, looking like two farmers who had just arrived in town.

3

It was 3:30 a.m. before they finally got back to the precinct station to write out their report.

The heat had detained them.

Even at past two in the morning, 'The Valley,' that flat lowland of Harlem east of Seventh Avenue, was like the frying pan of hell. Heat was coming out of the pavement, bubbling from the asphalt; and the atmospheric pressure was pushing it back to earth like the lid on a pan.

Colored people were cooking in their overcrowded, over priced tenements; cooking in the streets, in the after-hours joints, in the brothels; seasoned with vice, disease and crime.

An effluvium of hot stinks arose from the frying pan and hung in the hot motionless air, no higher than the rooftops – the smell of sizzling barbecue, fried hair, exhaust fumes, rotting garbage, cheap perfumes, unwashed bodies, decayed buildings, dog-rat-and-cat offal, whiskey and vomit, and all the old dried-up odors of poverty.

Half-nude people sat in open windows, crowded on the fire escapes, shuffled up and down the sidewalks, prowled up and down the streets in dilapidated cars.

It was too hot to sleep. Everyone was too evil to love. And it was too noisy to relax and dream of cool swimming holes and the shade of chinaberry trees. The night was filled with the blare of countless radios, the frenetic blasting of spasm cats playing in the streets, hysterical laughter, automobile horns, strident curses, loudmouthed arguments, the screams of knife fights.

The bars were closed so they were drinking out of bottles. That was all there was left to do, drink strong bad whiskey and get hotter; and after that steal and fight.

Grave Digger and Coffin Ed had been held up by an outburst of petty crime.

Thieves had broken into a supermarket and had stolen 50 pounds of stew beef, 20 pounds of smoked sausage, 20 pounds of chicken livers, 29 pounds of oleomargarine, 32 pounds of cooking lard, and one TV set.

A drunk had staggered into a funeral parlor and had refused to leave until he got 'first-class service.'

A man had stabbed a woman because she 'wouldn't give him none.'

A woman had stabbed a man whom she claimed had stepped on the corn on her left little toe.

Then on their way in they got held up again by a free-for-all on Eighth Avenue and 126th Street. It had been started by a man attacking another man with a knife in a dice game in a room back of a greasy spoon restaurant. The attacked man had run out into the street and grabbed a piece of iron pipe from a garbage can where he had cached it for just such an emergency before joining the dice game. When the man with the knife saw his erstwhile victim coming back with the iron pipe, he did an about-face and took off in the opposite direction. Then a friend of the man with the knife charged from a dark doorway wielding a baseball bat and began to duel the man with the pipe. The man with the knife turned back to help his friend with the baseball bat. Upon seeing what was happening, the cook came from the greasy spoon, wielding a meat cleaver, and demanded fair play. Whereupon the man with the knife engaged the cook with the cleaver in a separate duel.

When Grave Digger and Coffin Ed arrived at the scene, the hot dusty air was being churned up by the slinging and slashing of weapons.

Without engaging in preliminaries, Coffin Ed began pistol-whipping the man with the knife. The man was staggering about on the sidewalk, holding on to his knife which he was too scared to use; his legs were wobbling and his knees were buckling and he was saying, 'You can't hurt me hitting me on the head.'

With his left hand, Grave Digger began slapping the face of the man with the baseball bat, and with his right hand fanning the air with his pistol to keep back the crowd; at the same time shouting, 'Straighten up!'

Coffin Ed was echoing, 'Count off, red-eye! Fly right!'

Both of them looked just as red-eyed, greasy-faced, sweaty and evil as all the other colored people gathered about, combatants and spectators alike. They were of a similar size and build to other 'working stiffs' – big, broad-shouldered, loose-jointed and flatfooted. Their faces bore marks and scars similar to any colored street fighter. Grave Digger's was full of lumps where felons had hit him from time to time with various weapons; while Coffin Ed's was a patchwork of scars where skin had been grafted over the burns left by acid thrown into his face.

The difference was they had the pistols, and everyone in Harlem knew them as the 'Mens'.

The cook took advantage of this situation to slip back into his kitchen and hide his meat cleaver behind the stove. While the man with the pipe quickly cached his weapon inside his pants leg and went limping rapidly away like a wooden-legged man in a race of one-legged men.

After a little, peace was restored. Without a word or backward glance, Grave Digger and Coffin Ed walked to their car, climbed in and drove off.

They checked into the precinct station and wrote their report.

When Lieutenant Anderson finished reading the statement of the janitor's wife as to the reason Pinky put in the false fire alarm, he asked incredulously, 'Do you believe that?'

'Yeah,' Grave Digger replied. 'I'll believe it until some better reason comes along.'

Lieutenant Anderson shook his head. 'The motives these people have for crimes.'

'When you think about them, they make sense,' Coffin Ed said argumentatively.

Lieutenant Anderson wiped the sweat from his face with a limp dirty handkerchief.

'That's all right for the psychiatrists, but we're cops,' he said.

Grave Digger winked at Coffin Ed.

'*If you're white, all right*,' he recited in the voice of a school-boy.

Coffin Ed took it up. '*If you're brown, stick around . . .*'

Grave Digger capped it, '*If you're black, stand back.*'

Lieutenant Anderson reddened. He was accustomed to his two ace detectives needling him, but it always made him feel a little uneasy.

'That might all be true,' he said. 'But these crimes cost the taxpayers money.'

'You ain't kidding,' Grave Digger confirmed.

Coffin Ed changed the subject. 'Have you heard whether they caught him?'

Lieutenant Anderson shook his head. 'They caught everyone but him – bums, perverts, whores, tricks, and one hermit.'

'He won't be too hard to find,' Grave Digger said. 'There ain't too many places for a giant albino Negro turning black-and-blue to hide.'

'All right, let's stop the clowning,' Anderson said. 'What about this charge against a drug pusher?'

'He's one of the big sources of supply for colored addicts up here, but he's smart enough to keep out of Harlem,' Grave Digger said.

'When we saw him choking, we knew he'd been eating the decks he had on him, so before he could digest them we got enough out of him to convict him of possession anyway.'

'It's in that envelope,' Grave Digger said, nodding toward the desk. 'When it's analyzed, they'll find five or six half-chewed decks of heroin.'

Anderson opened the end of the brown manila envelope lying atop the desk which the detectives had turned in as evidence. He shook out the folded handkerchief and opened it.

'Phew!' he exclaimed, drawing back. 'It stinks.'

'It doesn't stink any more than a dirty pusher,' Grave Digger said. 'I hate this type of criminal worse than God hates sin.'

'What's the other stuff with it?' Anderson asked, pushing the mess about with the tip of his pencil.

Coffin Ed chuckled. 'Whatever he last ate before he started eating evidence.'

Anderson looked sober. 'I know your intentions are good, but you can't go around slugging people in the belly to collect evidence, even if they are felons. You know that this man has been taken to the hospital.'

'Don't worry, he won't protest,' Grave Digger said.

'Not if he knows what's good for him,' Coffin Ed echoed.

'Every precinct's not like Harlem,' Anderson cautioned. 'You get away with tricks here that'll kick back in any other precinct.'

'If this kicks back, I'll eat the foot that did it,' Grave Digger said.

'Talking about eating reminds me that we ain't ate yet,' Coffin Ed said.

Mamie Louise was sick and the other all-night greasy spoons and barbecue joints had no appeal. They decided to eat in the Great Man nightclub on 125th Street.

'I like a joint where you can smell the girls' sweat,' Coffin Ed said.

It had a bar fronting on the street with a cabaret in back where a two-dollar membership fee was charged to get in.

When the detectives flashed their buzzers they were made members for free.

Noise, heat and orgiastic odors hit them as they entered through the curtained doorway. The room was so small and packed that the celebrants rubbed buttocks with others at adjoining tables. Faces bubbled in the dim light like a huge pot of cannibal stew, showing mostly eyes and teeth. Smoke-blackened nudes frolicked in the murals about the fringes of the ceiling. Beneath were pencil sketches of numerous Harlem celebrities, interspersed with autographed photos of jazz greats. A ventilator fan was laboring in the back wall without any noticeable effect.

'You want stink, you got it,' Grave Digger said.

'And everything that goes with it,' Coffin Ed amended.

Some joker was shouting in a loud belligerent voice, 'I ain't gonna pay for but two whiskeys; dat's all I drunk. Somebody musta stole the other three 'cause I ain't seen 'em.'

Behind a dance floor scarcely big enough to hold two pairs of feet, a shining black man wearing a white silk shirt kept banging the same ten keys on a midget piano; while a lank black woman without joints wearing a backless fire-red evening gown did a snake dance about the tables, shouting *Money-money-money-honey,* and holding up her skirt. She was bare beneath. Whenever someone held out a bill, she changed the lyric to, 'Ohhhweee, daddy, money makes me feel so funny,' and gave a graphic demonstration by accepting it.

The proprietor cleared a table in the back corner for the two detectives and showed them most of the amalgam fillings in his teeth.

'I believe in live and let live,' he said right off. 'What you gentlemen wish to eat?'

There was a choice of fried chicken, barbecued pork ribs and New Orleans gumbo.

They chose the gumbo, which was the specialty of the house. It was made of fresh pork, chicken gizzards, hog testicles and giant shrimp, with a base of okra and sweet potatoes, and twenty-seven varieties of seasonings, spices and herbs.

'It's guaranteed to cool you off,' the proprietor boasted.

'I don't want to get so cooled off I can't warm up no more,' Grave Digger said.

The proprietor showed him some more teeth in a reassuring smile.

They followed the gumbo with huge quarters of ice-cold water-melon which had black seeds.

While they were eating it, a chorus of four hefty, sepia-colored girls took the floor and began doing a bump dance with their backs to the audience, throwing their big strong smooth-skinned hams about as though juggling hundred-pound sacks of brown sugar.

'Throw it to the wind!' someone shouted.

'Those hams won't stay up on wind,' Coffin Ed muttered.

The tight close air was churned into a steaming bedlam.

The temptation was too great for Coffin Ed. He filled his mouth full of watermelon seeds and began spitting them at the live targets. It was a fifteen-foot shot and before he got the range he had hit a couple of jokers at ringside tables in the back of their necks and almost set off a rumpus. The jokers were puffing up to fight when finally Coffin Ed's shots began landing on the targets. First one girl and then another began leaping and slapping their bottoms as though stung by bees. The audience thought it was part of the act. It was going over big.

One joker was inspired to give an impromptu rendition of 'Ants in Your Pants.'

Then one of the black seeds stuck to the cream-colored bottom of one of the girls and she captured it. She held it up and looked at it. She stopped dancing and turned an irate face toward the audience.

'Some mother-raper is shooting at me with watermelon seeds,' she declared. 'And I'm gonna find out who it is.'

The other three dancers examined the seed. Then all four of them, looking evil as housemaids scrubbing floors, began pushing between the tables, roughing up the customers, shaking down the joint for someone eating watermelon.

Grave Digger had the presence of mind to whip the plates containing the rinds and seeds from atop the table and hide them on the floor underneath their chairs. No one else was eating watermelon, but Coffin Ed went undiscovered.

When finally the dancing was resumed, Grave Digger let out his breath. 'That was a close shave,' he said.

'Let's get out of here before we get caught,' Coffin Ed said, wiping his mouth with the palm of his hand.

'*We!* What we?' Grave Digger exploded.

The proprietor escorted them to the door. He wouldn't let them pay for the dinners. He gave them a big fat wink, letting them know he was on their side.

'Live and let live, that's my motto,' he said.

'Yeah. Just don't think it buys you anything,' Grave Digger said harshly.

It was pressing 5 a.m. when they came out into the street, almost an hour past their quitting time.

'Let's take a last look for Gus,' Grave Digger suggested.

'What for?' Coffin Ed asked.

'For reference.'

'You don't never give up, do you?' Coffin Ed complained.

It was 5:05 when Grave Digger drove past the apartment over on Riverside Drive. He kept on down to Grant's Tomb, turned around and parked on the opposite side of the street, three houses down. Gray dawn was slipping beneath an overcast sky and the sprinklers were already watering the browned grass in the park surrounding the monument.

They were about to alight when they saw the African come from the apartment, leading the mammoth dog by a heavy iron chain. The dog wore an iron-studded muzzle that resembled the visor of a sixteenth-century helmet.

'Sit still,' Grave Digger cautioned.

The African looked up and down the street, then crossed over and walked in the opposite direction. His white turban and many-colored robe looked outlandish against the dull green background of foliage.

'Good thing I'm in New York,' Grave Digger said. 'I'd take him for a Zulu chief out hunting with his pet lion.'

'Better follow him, eh?' Coffin Ed said.

'To watch the dog piss?'

'It was your idea.'

The African turned down steps descending into the park and passed out of sight.

They sat watching the apartment entrance. Minutes passed. Finally Coffin Ed suggested, 'Maybe we'd better buzz her; see what's cooking.'

'Hell, if Gus ain't there, all we'll find is dirty sheets,' Grave Digger said. 'And if he's home he's going to want to know what we're doing busting into his house when we're off duty.'

'Then what the hell did we come for?' Coffin Ed flared.

'It was just a hunch,' Grave Digger admitted.

They lapsed into silence.

The African ascended the stairs from the park.

Coffin Ed looked at his watch. It read 5:27.

The African was alone.

They watched him curiously as he crossed the street and pressed the bell to the apartment. They saw him turn the knob and go inside. They looked at one another.

'Now what the hell does that mean?' Coffin Ed said.

'Means he got rid of the dog.'

'What for?'

'The question is, how?' Grave Digger amended.

'Well, don't ask me. I'm no Ouija board.'

'Hell with this, let's go home,' Grave Digger decided suddenly.

'Don't growl at me, man, you're the one who suggested this nonsense.'

4

Pinky peered through the plate-glass window of a laundrymat at the corner of 225th Street and White Plains Road in the Bronx. There was an electric clock on the back wall. The time read 3:33.

The sky was overcast with heavy black clouds. The hot sultry air was oppressive, as before a thunderstorm. The elevated trestle of the IRT subway line loomed overhead, eerie and silent, snaking down the curve of White Plains Road. As far as he could see, the streets were empty of life. The silence was unreal.

He reckoned it had taken him more than an hour to get there from the Riverside Park in Manhattan. He had covered part of the distance by hopping a New York Central switch engine, but afterwards he had slunk along endless blocks of silent, sleeping residential streets, ducking to cover when anyone hove into view.

Now he began to feel safe. But his body was still trembling as though he had the ague.

He turned east in the direction of the Italian section.

Apartment buildings gave way to pastel-colored villas of southern Italian architecture, garnished with flower gardens and plaster saints. After a while the houses became scattered, interspersed by market gardens and vacant lots overgrown with weeds in which hoboes slept and goats were tethered.

Finally he reached his destination, a weather-stained, one-storied, pink stucco villa at the end of an unfinished street without sidewalks. It was a small house flanked by vacant lots used for rubbish dumps. Oddly enough, it had a large gabled attic. It sat far back of a wire fence enclosing a front yard of burnt grass, dried-up flowers and wildly thriving weeds. In a niche over the front door was a white marble crucifixion of a singularly lean and tortured Christ, encrusted with bird droppings. In other niches at intervals beneath the eaves were all the varicolored plaster saints good to the souls of Italian peasants.

All of the front windows were closed and shuttered. Save for the faint sounds of a heavy boogie beat on a piano, the house seemed abandoned.

Pinky vaulted the fence and followed a path through tall weeds around the side of the house, taking care to avoid a concrete birdbath, an iron statue of Garibaldi and a large zinc vase of artificial roses.

There was a deep backyard enclosed by a high plank fence. The back door opened onto a grape arbor with thick clusters of purple grapes hanging between the dusty leaves. To one side was a rotting tool-and-wood shed adjoining a chicken coop and rabbit hutch. From the door of the tool shed a tethered nanny goat gazed at Pinky from sad wise eyes. Beyond was a dusty vegetable garden dying from thirst and neglect. But along the back fence a patch of well-watered, carefully tended marijuana weeds grew adjacent to a garage of corrugated steel.

Pinky halted in the dark beside the arbor and listened. He breathed in a choking manner and tears streamed down his cheeks.

Now the sound of music was loud and defiant. Vying with the hard banging of piano notes was the ratchetlike rhythm of someone strumming an accompaniment on a double-sided wooden washboard. It sounded like a cross between bone-beating and rim-rapping.

The two attic windows were wide open. Through the left-side one, from where he stood, Pinky saw the back of an upright piano, atop which sat a kerosene lamp and a half-filled bottle of gin. As he watched, a black, pudgy-fingered hand rose from the far side of the piano and grasped the gin bottle. The tempo of the piano changed. Instead of two-handed playing with the steady bass beat marching alongside the light fantastic tripping on the treble keys, there followed a wild left-hand riffing the whole length of the board.

The hand holding the bottle reappeared. The hand withdrew. The bottle remained. The level of the gin had lowered noticeably. Suddenly the bass came in again like John Henry driving steel and the treble notes ran through the night like the patter of rain.

Then another black hand appeared from the other side of the piano and took down the bottle. The sound of rim-rapping ceased and only the sound of beating bones continued. One side of the washboard had conked out. The hand and the bottle reappeared. After which the rapping went wild.

Through the right-side window could be seen vague figures of shirt-sleeved men and black-shouldered women swaying back and forth, locked in tight embrace; the locked liquid motions steady and unchanging despite the eccentricity of the music, sometimes keeping on the beats, sometimes in between. The Bear Hug and the Georgia Grind were being performed with a slow steady motion. Black skin gleamed like oily shadows in the dim yellow rays of the single flickering light of the kerosene lamp.

'Missa Pinky,' came a soft small voice from the dark.

Pinky jumped and wheeled about.

Big white circles shone from a small black face almost invisible in the dark. The skinny barefooted figure was clad in a patched mansize overall jumper.

'Boy, what you want at this time of night?' Pinky said roughly.

'Will you please, sir, go up and ask Sister Heavenly for two pods of Heavenly Dust for Uncle Bud?'

'Why don't you go up and get it yourself?'

'She won't sell it to me. I is too young.'

'Why don't Uncle Bud come get it hisself?'

'He's feeling po'ly. That's why he sent me. He ain't got the faith no more.'

'All right, give me the money.'

The boy stuck out a hand holding two crumpled dollar bills.

Pinky went beneath the arbor and knocked on the back door.

'Who dat?' a disembodied voice asked from within.

'Me, Pinky.'

Two white crescents flickered briefly in a glass pane of the upper-door panel. There was the click of a simple mortise lock and the door swung open.

With his eyes accustomed to the dark, Pinky made out the vague figure of a stone-old, gray-haired man clad in a blue cotton nightgown which seemed to float about the pitch-dark kitchen. Faint bluish gleams came from a double-barreled shotgun which the old man held cradled in his right arm.

'How is you, Uncle Saint?' Pinky greeted politely.

'Middling,' the old man replied. His voice seemed to come from another part of the room.

'I's going up to see Sister Heavenly.'

'You got feet, ain't you?' Now his voice seemed to come out of the floorboards between Pinky's feet.

Pinky grinned dutifully and went through the kitchen toward the stairs in the back hall.

He found Sister Heavenly sitting on a high throne chair in the corner of the attic farthest from the light. In the dark shadows she was an indistinguishable shape wrapped in dull black cloth.

A sick man lay on a stretcher on the floor at her feet.

Sister Heavenly was a faith healer. Pinky didn't dare approach her while she was 'ministering'.

'You is going to be happy,' she crooned in an old, cracked voice which still retained remnants of a bygone music. 'You is going to be happy – if you got the faith.'

Her body swayed from side to side in time with the slow steady beat of the bass.

The man on the stretcher said in a weak voice, 'I is got the faith.'

She crept down from the throne and knelt by his side.

Her thin, clawlike, transparent hand extended a silver spoon containing white powder toward his face.

'Inhale,' she said. 'Inhale deeply. Breathe the Heavenly Dust into your heart.'

The man sniffed rapidly four times in succession, each stronger than the previous.

She climbed back into her throne.

'Now you is going to be healed,' she crooned.

Pinky waited patiently until she deigned to see him. She forbade interruptions.

Sister Heavenly prided herself on being an old-fashioned faith healer with old-fashioned tried-and-true methods. That was why she used old-fashioned gin-drinking musicians and directed her clients to dance old-fashioned belly-rubbing dances. It was the first stage of the cure. She called it 'de-incarnation'.

She had kept Black Key Shorty on the piano for fifteen years. Washboard Wharton had come later. Both were relics of a bygone time. Washboard sat beside the piano holding a double-sided washboard which he strummed with rabbit-leg bones between his legs. Black Key had learned to play the piano in flats. Both were gin drinkers. They were the only ones she permitted to drink gin in her 'Heavenly Clinic.' There was nothing wrong with them. But she had to heal the sick people who came to her with Heavenly Dust.

'What you want, Pinky?' she asked suddenly.

He gave a start; he didn't think she had seen him.

'You got to help me, Sister Heavenly, I is in trouble,' he blurted out.

She looked at him. 'You've been beat up.'

'How can you tell that, in all this dark?'

'You don't have no milk shine like you generally does.' On second thought she added sharply, 'If it's the police who done it, you git away from here. I don't want no truck with the police.'

'It weren't the police,' he said evasively.

'Well then you tell me about it later. I ain't got no time to listen to it now.'

'It ain't only that,' he said. 'There's a little tadpole down in the backyard wants two pods of Heavenly Dust for Uncle Bud.'

'I ain't selling no pods to little punks,' she snapped.

'It ain't for him, it's for Uncle Bud; and you don't have to give it to him, I'll do that,' he said.

'Well, give me the money,' she said impatiently.

He handed her the two crumpled dollar bills.

She examined the money with disgust. 'I ain't selling no pods for a dollar no more. Leastways not at this time of night.' She took one small paper packet from somewhere beneath her layers of garments and handed it to him. 'You give him this and tell him the price is two dollars,' she directed, grumbling to herself. 'How do them cheapskates expect to get healed for a dollar, with prices of everything as high as they is?'

'Another thing,' he said hesitantly. 'I need a fix bad.'

'Go see your friend,' she said shortly. 'He'll stake you to a fix.'

'He ain't my friend no more. He's in jail.'

She wheeled about on her throne. 'Don't tell me you were in the rumble with him, 'cause if you've come here with yourself all hot, I'll turn you in myself.'

'I weren't with Jake when they caught him,' he denied evasively.

She was staring at him sharply as though she could see in the dark.

'Well, go down and open the buck rabbit and take a pill out,' she relented. 'And don't take but one, it's all you'll need, it's a speedball. And be sure to close him up good. The spike's in my bureau drawer.'

As he started to turn away, she added, 'And don't think you're putting nothing over on me 'cause I ain't through with you yet. You just wait until I get time to talk to you.'

'I got to talk to you too,' he said.

The man on the stretcher was twitching in time to the music. 'It's cool, Sister Heavenly,' he said in the voice of a convert giving a testimonial. 'I got the real cool faith.'

Black Key Shorty was driving piles on the bass with his steady left hand while his right hand was frolicking over hot dry grass in a nudist's colony. Washboard Wharton was giving out with grunting sounds like a boar hog in a pen full of sows.

The strong orgiastic smell of sweat and red-hot glands was pouring from the windows into the hot sultry air.

It didn't mean a thing to Pinky. He felt so much like crying he was thinking only of a fix. He went down the stairs to the hallway and passed through the kitchen.

Uncle Saint floated from the shadows with his double-barreled shotgun.

'I'll be right back,' Pinky said. 'Sister Heavenly sent me to tap the rabbit.'

'Don't tell me your troubles, I ain't your pappy,' Uncle Saint said, unlocking the door. His voice sounded as though it had come from the bottom of a well.

The little boy in the overall jumper was waiting for Pinky in the grape arbor. He had discovered the grapes but was scared to take any.

'Did you get 'em, Missa Pinky?' he asked timidly.

Pinky fished the packet from his pocket. 'Here, you give this to Uncle Bud and tell 'im the price has gone up. Tell him Sister Heavenly say don't expect to get healed for nothing.'

Reluctantly the little boy accepted the single pod. He knew he'd get a beating for bringing back only one. But there wasn't anything to do about it.

'Yessa,' he said and went slowly into the shadows.

Pinky went to the rabbit hutch, reached through the hatch and caught the buck by the ears. With a deft motion of his free hand, he removed a small square of adhesive tape covering the rabbit's rectum, then withdrew a long rubber plug with a tiny metal handle like a sink stopper. The rabbit remained motionless, staring at him from enormous fear-frozen eyes. He squeezed the rabbit's stomach and a small aluminum capsule popped out. He put the capsule into his pants pocket and restoppered the rabbit.

He wondered what other hiding places Sister Heavenly had. He was her nephew and her only living relative, but she had never told him anything. He reckoned she was getting ready to eat the rabbit if she let him know that much.

At the kitchen door he again went through the amenities with Uncle Saint.

'I'm going to Sister Heavenly's room for a bang.'

'You must think I'm the recording angel,' Uncle Saint grumbled. His voice sounded as though it came out of the oven. 'Go to the devil, for all I care.'

Pinky knew this wasn't true, but he didn't challenge it. He knew that Uncle Saint would curse up a fit if he went somewhere in the house without telling him in advance.

The top bureau drawer looked like the last stand of a

hypochondriac. He found the hypodermic needle lying in the midst of syringes, thermometers, hatpins and hairpins, tweezers, shoe buttoners, and old-fashioned glass-topped bottles containing enough varicolored poisons to decimate an entire narcotic squad. The alcohol lamp sat openly on a marble-topped table in the corner, alongside a battered teapot and a set of stained test tubes. The sugar spoon was in a sugar bowl on the night table beside the bed.

He lit the lamp and sterilized the needle over the flame. Then he emptied the white powdered cocaine and heroin from the aluminum capsule into the sugar spoon and melted it over the flame. He drew the liquid through the needle into the syringe and, holding the spike in his right hand, banged himself in the vein of his left arm while the C & H was still warm.

'Ahhh,' he said softly as the drug went in.

Afterwards he put out the lamp and returned the spike to the medicine drawer.

The speedball had immediate effect. He went back to the kitchen stepping on air.

He knew Sister Heavenly wouldn't be ready for him yet, so he passed the time with the ancient gunman.

'How long is you been a ventriloquist, Uncle Saint?'

'Boy, I been throwing my voice so long, I don't know where it's at anymore myself,' Uncle Saint said. His voice seemed to come from the bedroom Pinky had just quit. Abruptly he laughed at his own joke, 'Ha-ha-ha.' The laughter seemed to come from outside the back door.

'You're going to keep on throwing it around until it gets away some day,' Pinky said.

'What business is it of yours? Is you my keeper?' Uncle Saint crabbed. He sounded like a ghost lurking underneath the floor.

Upstairs, Black Key Shorty was riffing with his left hand again. Pinky knew that the gin bottle was pressed to his lips. Washboard Wharton was making like a skeleton with the galloping itch, waiting his turn.

Pinky listened to the steady clumping of feet on the wooden floor. Everything was crystal clear to him again. He knew just what he had to do. But it was getting late.

5

The pilgrims had finally gone.

Sister Heavenly was sitting up in bed, wearing a pink crocheted bed jacket trimmed in frilly lace. Long, curly, midnight-blue hair of a wig hung down over her shoulders.

She was so old her face had the shrunken, dried-up leathery look of a monkey's. The corneas of her eyes were a strange shade of glazed blue resembling an enameled surface, while the pupils were a faded ocher with white spots. She wore perfect fitting plates of brilliant, matched, incredibly white teeth.

As a young woman her skin had been black; but daily applications of bleach creams for more than half a century had lightened her complexion to the color of pigskin. Her toothpick arms, extending from the pink jacket, were purple-hued at the top, graduating to parchment-colored hands so thin and fragile-looking as to appear transparent.

In one hand she held a scalding hot cup of sassafras tea, with her little finger extended according to the dictates of etiquette; in the other a small, dainty, meerschaum pipe with a long curved stem and a carved bowl. She was smoking the finely ground stems of marijuana leaves, her only vice.

Pinky sat beside the bed on a green leather ottoman, wringing his ham-size, milk-white hands.

The only light in the room came from a pink-shaded light on the other side of the bed. The soft pink light gave Pinky's bruised white skin the exotic coloring of some unknown tropical sea monster.

'How come you think they's going to croak him?' Sister Heavenly asked in her deep, slightly cracked, musical voice.

'To rob him, that's why,' Pinky said in his whining voice. 'To get his farm in Ghana.'

'A farm in Ghana!' she said scornfully. 'If Gus got a farm in Ghana I got a palace in heaven.'

'He got a farm, all right. I has seen the papers.'

'Taking he got a farm – which he ain't – how they going to get it by croaking him?'

'She's his wife. He done willed it to her.'

'His wife! She ain't no more his wife than you is his son. If they croak him, it'll go to his relatives – if he got any relatives.'

'She his wife all right. I has seen the license.'

'You has seen everything. Suppose they croak him. They can't go live on his farm. That's the first place the police will look.'

He realized she wasn't convinced about the farm. He took another tack.

'Then it's his money. They'll get that and run away.'

'His money! I is too old and time is too short for this bullshit. Gus ain't never had two white quarters to rub together in his life.'

'He got money. A whole lot of money.' He looked away evasively and his voice changed. 'His other wife in Fayetteville, North Carolina, died and left him a big tobacco farm and he sold it for a heap of money.'

She took a long puff from her pipe and held it down by sipping tea. Her old faded eyes regarded him with cynical amusement over the rim of her cup. Finally, when she let the smoke dribble from her lungs, she said, 'What you trying to con me out of?'

'I ain't trying to con you.'

'Then what's all this 'bout his other wife and his other farm, an' all his money? You must be seeing double.'

'It's the God's truth,' he said, avoiding her eyes. 'I swear it.'

'You swear it. Long as I knowed Gus he ain't never let no woman get no legal hold on him. And if you think any woman what knows that is fool enough to die and leave him something, you don't know the female race.'

'He got something,' he maintained urgently. 'He made me promise not to tell, but I knows it's what they's after.'

She smiled evilly. 'Then why don't you get it yourself, if it's worth anything – poor as you is?' Her voice dripped sarcasm.

'I couldn't rob Gus. He the only one who ever been good to me.'

'You get it and let them rob and murder you, if you is so set on protecting him.'

His face took on a desperate expression. Sweat trickled from the borders of his hair. Tears welled up in his eyes.

'You sitting there, making fun, and he might be dead,' he accused in his whining voice.

Slowly she put down her cup on the night table. She rested the pipe across her stomach and studied him deliberately. She saw that something was troubling him. She realized with faint surprise that he was deadly earnest.

'Ain't I been good to you, too, treating you like my own son – if I had a son?' she cajoled.

'Yassum,' he replied obediently. 'But he took me in and called me his son.'

'Ain't I told you time and again that you is my heir?' she insisted. 'Ain't I told you that you is going to inherit all that I got when I die?'

'Yassum, but you ain't helping me now.'

'You ain't got no right to hold out on me like this. God won't like it,' she said.

'I ain't holding out,' he whined, looking trapped. 'It's just that I promised not to tell.'

She leaned forward and held his eyes in a hypnotic stare. 'Is it in a trunk?'

Her eyes were like two balls of colored fire bearing down on him.

'Not when I seen it.'

'Is it in a sack?'

He felt his power to defy her slipping away.

'Twarn't in no sack when I seen it.'

'Were it hidden in the house?'

He shook his head.

'In the closet? ... Beneath the floor? ... Behind the wall?'

He felt himself growing dizzy in a holocaust of lights.

'That ain't how it were hidden,' he admitted.

'He got it on him,' she said triumphantly.

He was too worn out by her eyes to resist further.

'Yassum. In a money belt.'

Intense thought wrinkled her face like a prune.

'It's jewelry,' she concluded. 'He's stolen some jewelry. Is it diamonds?'

His willpower gave way. He slumped forward and sighed. 'It's a treasure map,' he confessed. 'It tells how to find a whole mess of buried treasure in Africa.'

Her eyes popped open as though the lids had broken.

'Treasure map!' she screamed. 'Lost treasure! You still believe in lost treasure, as old as you is?'

'I know how it sound, but that's what it is all right,' he maintained stubbornly.

She stared at him speculatively until he felt himself withering.

'Did you see it?' she asked finally.

'Yassum. It shows a river and the sea and just where the treasure is buried on the bank.'

'A river!' Her eyes glittered as her brain worked lightning fast. 'Where did he get it?'

'He's had it.'

Her eyes narrowed. 'When he show it to you?'

He hesitated before answering. 'Last night.'

'Don't nobody but you know he got it?'

'His wife and the African know. He's going to give it to the expressmen who come for his trunk this morning. They're going to send it on to his farm in Ghana so can't nobody rob him of it before he gets there. But I knows that woman and the African plan to kill him and take it before the expressmen get there – if they ain't already done it.'

'Why didn't you stay with him and protect him?'

'He wouldn't let me; he said he had something to do. He went off and I didn't know where he was at. That's why I rung the fire alarm.'

'What time are the expressmen due?'

'Six o'clock.'

She drew from inside her gown an old-fashioned locket-watch attached to a thin gold chain. It read 5:27.

She jumped out of bed and began to dress. First she snatched off the black wig and substituted a gray one.

'You'll find some green stuff in a bottle in the drawer,' she said. 'Give yourself a shot. It'll calm you. You're too jumpy with all that C.'

While he was loading the spike and banging himself, she dressed rapidly. She paid him no attention.

She put on a flowing black gown over numerous petticoats, low-heeled black shoes and black silk gloves, elbow length. She pinned a small black straw hat to her gray wig with a long steel hatpin.

'Go start the car,' she said.

She listened until he had gone out of the back door. Then she picked up a large black-beaded handbag, got a black-and-white striped parasol from the closet, and went into the kitchen.

Uncle Saint had already dressed. He now wore a black chauffeur's uniform and cap, several sizes too large for him, and of a fashion popular during the 1920s.

'Did you get it?' she asked tersely.

'I heered him,' he replied straight from his mouth. 'If Gus's cut is big enough to buy a farm, it can't be chicken feed – whatever it is.'

'I have an idea what it is,' she said. 'If we ain't too late.'

'Let's go then.'

She went outside. He picked up his shotgun from beside the doorway and followed her, closing and locking the door behind him. He was high as a kite.

Although objects were already visible in the gray dawn light, they did not see Pinky. But they heard him. He was on his knees on the hard-packed dirt floor of the garage, gripping the doorposts with his hands, trying to get to his feet, breathing in loud hard gasps. The muscles of his neck, arms and torso were corded; his blood vessels stood out like ropes.

'He's got the constitution of an ox,' Uncle Saint said.

'*Shhh,*' Sister Heavenly cautioned. 'He can still hear.'

His sense of hearing was unbearably heightened, and he heard every word they said as distinctly as though they had shouted. His mind was lucid. She gave me a knockout drop, he was thinking. But he could feel consciousness leaving him like a wrecked ship sinking slowly into the sea. Finally his muscles collapsed and he went down onto his face between the doorposts. He didn't hear Sister Heavenly and Uncle Saint when they approached.

Uncle Saint reached inside the garage and turned on

the light. A 1937 black Lincoln Continental sprang into view.

They stepped over Pinky without comment and left him lying there. Sister Heavenly got into the back. Uncle Saint placed the shotgun within easy reach on the floor of the front seat, then went forward to open the double doors.

He followed a dirt road across an abandoned field, pushing up to fifty, bouncing over rocks and ruts, leaving a cloud of dust. A gardener in his undershirt, wearing a straw hat, was milking a goat tethered to a tree. He paid no attention to the black limousine; it was a common sight. But when Uncle Saint got onto the macadam streets and pushed up to seventy and seventy-five, early-morning workers, milkmen and garbage collectors, turned to stare.

6

Uncle Saint sat in the Lincoln and watched the entrance to the apartment. It was parked in the same place Grave Digger and Coffin Ed had vacated less than an hour earlier.

Sister Heavenly had gone inside to look for Gus. But Uncle Saint didn't take any stock in Pinky's story about a map. The way he figured, Gus was a connection for racketeers smuggling diamonds or maybe gold. He was picking it up somewhere and passing it on.

Sister Heavenly reckoned that Gus was carrying the boodle on him. But Uncle Saint didn't figure it that way. Whatever it was would be in the trunk, he decided. You had to figure that racketeers who would use an old square like Gus for a connection knew what they were doing. And a trunk was still the best means of smuggling anything hot – because it was so obvious. All the smart federal men and slick city dicks would figure racketeers too smart to use an old worn-out gimmick like a trunk. And that was where the racketeers could outsmart them. Just plain human nature. Like the best mark is the one who has been clipped before; he figures then that he knows everything.

As he sat there and turned it over in his mind, Uncle Saint resolved to get that trunk for himself.

For more than twenty-five years he had flunkied for Sister Heavenly, serving her as guard, cook, nurse and toady – doing her dirty work. Before that he had been her lover. But when she had thrown him over, he had hung around like a homeless dog through a long succession of subsequent lovers. Now all he had for her was hate, but he couldn't leave her because he didn't have anywhere else to go, and she knew it.

So he decided to cross her, get the boodle and cut out. Leave her taking the rap. See how she'd handle a mob of racketeers.

He saw a green panel truck pull up before the apartment house entrance. It looked similar to a Railway Express Company truck except for the name in white letters on its sides: Acme Express Co.

Two white men in hickory-striped uniforms and blue-visored caps got out. One was tall and thin, the other medium height and heavyset. Both were clean-shaven and neither wore glasses. That was all Uncle Saint noticed.

Both men glanced toward the Lincoln. It was the only parked car with an occupant. But sight of the old liveried colored pappy behind the wheel allayed their suspicions.

Uncle Saint had a sour grin as they turned their backs and walked toward the door. They had him cased as a square like old Gus, he figured. On the one hand it rankled; but on the other it worked in his favor.

He waited until they had gone inside, then started the motor and kept it idling. He figured he was going to have to hijack the trunk. But not here in front of the apartment house. It was too open and there was no telling what Nosy Parker might be watching him from behind some curtained window, wondering what a strange limousine was doing in the neighborhood at this hour of morning. He just hoped Sister Heavenly wouldn't do anything to rank his play.

Sister Heavenly was sitting in the janitor's parlor, covering the janitor's wife and the African with a blunt-nosed .38-caliber revolver, when the doorbell rang.

'I got to go and open the front door,' the janitor's wife said. 'It's most likely Gus.'

She was standing beside the African, who was seated before the table, where she had backed when Sister Heavenly got the drop on her.

'Can the bullshit and press the buzzer,' Sister Heavenly said, motioning with the barrel of the pistol from where she sat on the arm of the davenport. 'When they get here we'll see who it is.'

The janitor's wife shuffled sullenly over toward the door and pressed a button releasing the latch on the entrance door. She was barefooted and still wore the same cotton shift as before, but now it looked as though she had been rolling in it. Her face was greasy and her slanting yellow eyes glittered evilly.

'You ain't going to get nothing by this, whatever it is you is after,' she muttered in her gravelly voice.

'Just get back over there and shut up,' Sister Heavenly said with an arrogant wave of the gun barrel.

The janitor's wife shuffled back to the side of the African.

The African sat with drooping body, like a melted statue, his white-rimmed eyes staring at the pistol as though hypnotized.

They waited. Only their heavy breathing was audible in the surrounding silence.

The two expressmen saw the trunk in the basement corridor beside the elevator and took it away without seeing anyone.

Uncle Saint was watching when they returned to the street, carrying a large green steamer trunk, stickered and tagged for shipping. They put the trunk into the body of the truck, closed the doors, and looked once again toward the parked Lincoln.

Without appearing to notice them, Uncle Saint leaned out the car window and looked up toward the front windows of the third-story apartment as though listening to someone speaking to him.

The expressmen looked in the same direction, but they didn't see anything.

'Yassum,' Uncle Saint called in a flunkey's voice. 'Right away, mum.'

He put the Lincoln in gear and drove past the express truck without giving it a look and kept on down Riverside Drive, keeping within the twenty-five-mile speed limit.

The expressmen got into the compartment of the truck. The driver started the motor and the truck took off behind the limousine at a more rapid speed.

Uncle Saint accelerated, watching the following truck in his rearview mirror. He kept well ahead, lengthening and shortening the gap between as though driving naturally.

He knew he was playing a dangerous game, especially alone. But he was too old and had lived too long on the edge of violence to be scared of death. What scared him was the idea of what he planned to do. What was in his favor was the fact nobody knew him. No one but Pinky and Sister Heavenly knew his straight monicker; in recent years but few people had seen him in the light. If he could get it and get away, only those two would know who had done it, and even they wouldn't know where to look for him.

He accelerated gradually as he realized the truck was headed downtown, and pulled far ahead. He was two blocks ahead on the almost empty drive when he came to the entrance to the Yacht Club at 79th Street. He swerved into the curving driveway and slowed down, hidden by the dense foliage of the crescent-shaped park. He got a glimpse of the truck passing on Riverside Drive. He came back into the drive a block behind it and kept a bakery truck in between down as far as 72nd Street.

The truck turned east on 72nd Street to Tenth Avenue, and went south. It was a southbound avenue, feeding the Lincoln and Holland tunnels underneath the Hudson River, and was fairly covered with commercial traffic at this hour. That made it easy. The express truck had only one rearview mirror on the left front fender. Uncle Saint kept far to the right, and always kept some vehicle in between.

At 56th Street when the truck turned toward the Hudson River, the Lincoln was exposed for a moment or two; but when the truck turned south again alongside the overhead trestle of the New York Central Railroad line, he was covered again. On the west side of the wide brick-paved avenue, the whole length of North River was closed in by the docks of the great oceangoing lines. Underneath the trestle, as far as the eye could see, trucks and truck-trailers were parked side by side. The southbound lane was heavy with traffic feeding the docks.

Already the funnels of the *Queen Mary* at dock could be seen overtopping the wharf of the French Line adjoining the Cunard pier. The express truck swerved toward the curb and braked to a sudden stop behind a black Buick sedan parked less than fifty yards from the entrance to the French Line dock.

The maneuver was executed so quickly Uncle Saint didn't have a chance to stop behind the truck and had to pull ahead of the Buick to park.

It was a no-parking zone and two cops in a prowl car looked meaningfully at the three parked vehicles as they drove slowly by. Being as one was a chauffeur-driven limousine and another an express truck, the cops let them slide for a moment.

Two dark-suited, straw-hatted, somber-looking men sat in the front seat of the Buick and watched the prowl car pass the Cunard dock and drop out of sight in the traffic. The man on the curb side opened the door and stepped out onto the sidewalk. He was a heavyset, black-haired man with a thick-featured, olive-skinned face and a bulging belly. His black single-breasted coat was buttoned at the bottom. He came down the street, looking anxiously toward the exit of the French Line wharf.

Uncle Saint watched in the rearview mirror, concentrating on the men in the express truck.

The driver of the Buick sat with his right hand on the wheel, his left hanging loosely through the open window.

When the heavyset man came level with the curb-side window of the Lincoln, he turned with a quick, catlike motion, unexpected in a man of his build, and came toward the car. He clapped his left hand on the car top, flipped open his coat and drew from a left shoulder sling. When he bent over to peer through the window, as though speaking to the gray-haired old chauffeur, his flapping coat shielded the pistol from view. It was a single-shot derringer with a six-inch perforated silencer attached. Without speaking a word, he took careful aim at the softest spot in Uncle Saint's head. His dull dark eyes were impassive.

Abruptly from behind him a hard voice shouted, 'Get 'em up or I'll shoot!'

He didn't see the faint motion of Uncle Saint's lips. He wheeled about convulsively, the back of his head striking the top of the doorframe, knocking off his hat onto the seat of the car.

Uncle Saint lunged for his shotgun lying on the floor.

The gunman wheeled back, his eyes bugging out, as Uncle Saint was bringing up the muzzle of the double-barreled shotgun.

Both fired simultaneously.

The small coughing sound of the silenced derringer was lost in the heavy booming blast of the shotgun.

In his panic, Uncle Saint had squeezed the triggers of both barrels.

The gunman's face disappeared and his thick heavy body was knocked over backward from the impact of the 12-gauge shells.

The rear light of a truck parked beneath the trestle in the middle of the avenue disintegrated for no apparent reason.

The air stunk with the smell of cordite and burnt flesh as the driver of the Buick leaned out the window and emptied an automatic pistol held in his left hand.

Holes popped into the back of the Lincoln's tonneau and the left-side rearview mirror was shattered.

Uncle Saint hadn't been touched, but his nappy hair was standing up like iron filings beneath a magnet.

Abruptly a woman began to scream in high, piercing, repetitious shrieks.

Uncle Saint felt as though the top of his head was coming off.

Then men began to shout; horns blew; a police whistle shrilled, and there was a sudden shower of running feet.

Both cars took off at once.

A trailer truck was passing on the left side and a taxi coming from the French Line dock blocked the traffic lane ahead. Porters and stevedores were running up the sidewalk and a uniformed cop with a pistol in his hand was trying to break through.

Uncle Saint was looking through a blind haze of panic. His brain had stopped working. He was driving instinctively, like a fox encircled by hounds.

The truck was to his left, the taxi was in front; he pulled to the right, up over the curb, heading behind the taxi. The running men scattered, diving for safety, as the two cars roared down the broad sidewalk, the Buick following the Lincoln bumper to bumper.

At the entrance to the dock a porter was loading luggage from a taxi onto a four-wheeled cart. He didn't see the Lincoln until it hit the cart. He sailed into the air, clinging to the suitcase as though running to catch a train waiting somewhere in the sky, while other luggage flew past like startled birds. The cart raced down the pier and dove into the sea. The porter came down feetfirst on top of the following Buick, did a perfect somersault and landed sitting on the suitcase, his astounded black face an ellipsoid of white eye-balls and white teeth.

In front of the Cunard Line dock Uncle Saint found an opening back to the street. He turned into it but couldn't straighten out fast enough and crossed in front of the same trailer truck he had already passed on the sidewalk. It was so close the truck bumper passed overtop and left rear fender of the Lincoln as he barely missed the concrete pier of the railroad trestle on the other side.

Rubber screamed on the dry brick pavement as the truck driver applied air brakes. The truck horn bleated desperately. But it didn't save the Buick following in the wake of the Lincoln. The truck hit it broadside. The sound of metal rending metal shattered the din. A senseless pandemonium broke out up and down the street.

The truck had overturned the Buick and the front wheels had run overtop it. Hundreds of people were running in all directions, without rhyme or reason.

Uncle Saint got away.

He didn't see the accident or hear the sound. He was on the inside traffic lane and it was clear for nine straight blocks. Instinctively he looked into the rearview mirror. Behind him the avenue was empty.

Traffic had been stopped at the scene of the accident. The first two prowl cars to arrive had blocked off the street. For the moment the black Lincoln had been forgotten. By the time the cops got around to gathering evidence, Uncle Saint had passed 42nd Street. None of the witnesses had recognized the make of the car; no one had thought to take the license number; all descriptions of the driver were conflicting.

Suddenly Uncle Saint found himself caught in one of the clover-leaf approaches to the Lincoln Tunnel. The three traffic lanes were jammed with vehicles, bumper to bumper. There was no turning back.

As he crawled along in back of a refrigerator truck, his panic cooled to a sardonic, inverted scare. The killing didn't bother him whatever. 'Thought the old darky was tame,' he muttered to himself.

A subtle change came over him. He reverted to the legendary Uncle Tom, the old halfwit darky, the white man's jester, the obsequious old white-haired coon without a private thought.

During one of the stops as the long lines of traffic were halted at the toll gates, he hid the shotgun underneath the back seat and tossed the gunman's straw hat on top of the seat.

The toll gates looked like the entrance to a wartime military post housing nuclear weapons. Booted and helmeted cops sat astride high-powered motorcycles beside the toll booths; beyond were the white-and-black police cars that patrolled the tunnel.

The guard took the fifty cents toll and waved Uncle Saint on, but a motorcycle cop strolled over and stopped him.

'What are these holes in the back of this car, boy?'

Uncle Saint grinned, showing stained decayed teeth, and his old bluish-red eyes looked sly.

'Bullet holes, sah,' he said proudly.

'What!' The cop was taken aback; he had expected Uncle Saint to deny it. 'Bullet holes?'

'Yas sah, gen-you-wine bullet holes.'

The cop pinned a beetle-brow stare onto Uncle Saint.

'You make 'em?'

'Naw sah, Ah was goin' the other way.'

The toll guard could not repress a smile, but the cop scowled.

'Who made 'em?'

'My boss, sah. Mistah Jeffers. He made 'em.'

'Who was he shooting at?'

'Shooting at me, sah. He always shoots at me when he's

had a liddle too much. But he ain't never hit me though –
he-hee.'

The toll guard laughed out loud, but the cop didn't like
it.

'Pull over there and wait,' he ordered, indicating the parking
space for the patrol cars.

Uncle Saint drove over and stopped. The cops in the cars
looked at him curiously.

The motorcycle cop went into the glass-enclosed toll booth
and studied the list of wanted cars. The Lincoln was not on
the list. He fiddled about for fifteen minutes, looking more
and more annoyed. Finally he asked the toll guard, 'Think I
ought to hold him?'

'Hold him for what?' the guard said. 'What's an old darky
like him ever done but steal his boss's whiskey?'

The cop came out of the booth and waved him on.

It was only a quarter past seven when Uncle Saint came
out of the tunnel into Jersey City.

He left the parkway at the first turn-off and went north along
the rutted, brick-paved streets that bordered the wharves. He
drove slowly and carefully and obeyed all the traffic signs. It took
him an hour to reach the first New Jersey approach to the George
Washington Bridge. He crossed over into Manhattan and fifteen
minutes later crossed the Harlem River back into the Bronx.

Before arriving at Sister Heavenly's he threw out the dead
gunman's hat, then retrieved the shotgun, reloaded it, and
placed it on the floor of the front seat within reach.

'Now let's see which way the cat's gonna jump,' he said
to himself.

It was about 8:30 o'clock. The clock in the car didn't work
and Uncle Saint didn't have a watch. But time meant nothing
to him one way or another.

7

Grave Digger was sound asleep.

His wife shook him.

'Telephone. It's Captain Brice.'

Grave Digger knuckled the sleep from his eyes. On duty all of his senses were constantly on the alert. Coffin Ed had once summed it up by saying, 'Blink once and you're dead.' To which Grave Digger had rejoined, 'Blink twice and you're buried.'

But at home, Grave Digger relaxed completely. His wife somtimes called him 'Slowpoke'.

He was still sleep-groggy when he took the phone and said grumpily, 'Now what gives?'

Captain Brice was a disciplinarian. He never fraternized with the men under him and played no favorites. The Harlem precinct was his command. Grave Digger and Coffin Ed were under his supervision, although their hours at night rarely permitted them to see him.

'Jake Kubansky is dead,' he said in a voice without inflection. 'I have orders to present you to the commissioner's office at nine o'clock.'

Grave Digger became abruptly alert. 'Has Ed been notified?'

'Yes. I wish we'd had time for you to drop by here and go over this business, but the order just came in. So you had better go straight down to Centre Street.'

Grave Digger looked at his watch. It read 8:10.

'Right, sir,' he said and hung up.

His wife looked at him anxiously. 'Are you in trouble?'

'Not as far as I know.'

That didn't answer her question, but she had learned not to press him.

Grave Digger and Coffin Ed lived only two blocks apart in Astoria, Long Island. Coffin Ed was waiting in his new Plymouth sedan. 'It's going to be another scorcher,' he greeted.

'Let it burn up,' Grave Digger said.

Everyone was in shirtsleeves.

The commissioner, deputy commissioner, inspector in charge of detectives, an assistant D.A., an assistant medical examiner, Captain Brice and Lieutenant Anderson from the Harlem precinct, three firemen and two patrol car cops from the horde who had answered the false fire alarm the previous night.

The hearing was being held in a big barren room in the headquarters annex across the street from the headquarters building. It had begun at 9:55; now it was 11:13.

Hard yellow sunlight slanted in from the three windows looking out on Centre Street and the room was sweltering hot.

The charge of 'unwarranted brutality' resulting from the death of Jake had been lodged against Coffin Ed and Grave Digger.

First the assistant M.E. had testified that the autopsy had shown that Jake had died from a ruptured spleen caused by severe external blows in the region of the stomach. In the opinion of the Examiner's Office he had either been kicked in the stomach or pummeled by a heavy blunt instrument.

'I didn't hit him that hard,' Grave Digger had contradicted from where he sat with one ham perched on the window ledge.

Coffin Ed, backed against the wall on the shady side of the room, said nothing.

The commissioner had raised a hand for silence.

Lieutenant Anderson gave a verbal account of the detectives' report and produced photostats of the pages of the precinct blotter where the entry had been made.

Captain Brice explained the special detail to which he had assigned the two detectives, sending them to all trouble spots over Harlem during all hours of the night.

The three firemen and the two patrol car cops testified reluctantly that they had witnessed Grave Digger hit the victim in the stomach while Coffin Ed held his arms pinned behind him.

Then Grave Digger and Coffin Ed had taken the stand in their own defense.

'What we did is routine procedure,' Grave Digger said. 'You take these pushers, when they're peddling dope they work in the street. They carry their decks in a pocket where they are convenient to dispose of. The officer has to apprehend them while they still have the junk on their person, or he has to swear he has seen them dispose of it. So when you close in on a pusher and he sees he can't get rid of his load, he stuffs it into his mouth and eats it. They all carry some kind of physic which they take a short time afterwards – and there goes your evidence—'

The commissioner smiled.

'You know they've been selling dope; you've seen 'em; but you can't prove it,' Grave Digger continued. 'So Ed and me use this method to make them vomit up the evidence before they take the physic and dissipate it.'

Again the commissioner smiled at the use of the word *dissipate*.

'However, if that were permitted, what is there to prohibit an officer from punching a person in the stomach suspected of drunken driving?' the assistant D.A. remarked.

'Nothing,' Grave Digger replied in a thick, dry voice. 'If he's run over somebody and killed 'em.'

'You're forgetting that you are primarily a peace officer' the assistant D.A. reminded him. 'Your duty is to maintain the peace and the courts will punish the offenders.'

'Peace at what price?' Coffin Ed put in, and Grave Digger echoed thickly:

'You think you can have a peaceful city letting criminals run loose?'

The assistant D.A. reddened. 'That's not the point,' he said sharply. 'You've killed a man suspected of a minor crime, and not in self-defense.'

Suddenly the room was filled with tension.

'You call dope peddling a minor crime?' Grave Digger said, pushing to his feet.

At the sound of his thick, dry voice, every eye in the room turned in his direction. The arteries in his neck became swollen from rage and veins throbbed in his temples.

'All the crimes committed by addicts – robberies, murders, rapes . . . All the fucked-up lives . . . All the nice kids sent down the drain on a habit . . . Twenty-one days on heroin and you're hooked for life . . . Jesus Christ, mister, that one lousy drug has murdered more people than Hitler. And you call it *minor!*' His voice sounded like it was filtered through absorbent cotton.

The assistant D.A. reddened. 'He was merely a peddler,' he stated.

'And who gets it into the victim's blood?' Grave Digger raved. 'The peddler! He sells the dirty crap. He makes the personal contact. He puts them on the habit. He's the mother-raper who gets them hooked. He looks into their faces and puts the poison in their hands. He watches them go down from sugar to shit, sees them waste away. He puts them out to stealing, killing, starts young girls to hustling – to get the money to buy the kicks. I'll take a simple violent murderer any day.'

'Let's put it this way,' Coffin Ed said, trying to mollify both parties. 'Everybody here knows how the big-time operators work. They buy junk abroad – mostly heroin nowadays. They get a lot of it from France – Marseille – for about five thousand dollars a kilo – two pounds and three ounces. The French don't seem to able to stop the traffic. It comes to New York and the wholesalers pay from fifteen thousand dollars to twenty thousand dollars a kilo for it. The U.S. federal agents don't seem to be able to catch them either. So the wholesalers dilute the stuff, which is about eighty per cent pure to begin with – they add enough sugar of milk or quinine to get it down to two per cent pure. Just plain shit. And this is the stuff the peddler sells. It grosses a half million dollars a kilo. All of you know that. But who's stopping it? All Digger and me can do is try to catch the peddlers in our precinct. So one gets hurt—'

'Killed,' the assistant M.E. corrected.

'By accident,' Coffin Ed amended. 'If that is what killed him. In all that excitement up there last night he might have been trampled to death for all we know.'

The commissioner looked up. 'What excitement?'

'The firemen were trying to detain a firebug who got away.'

'Oh, that.' His glance flicked from Lieutenant Anderson to the red-faced firemen.

'We are going to have these detectives indicted,' the assistant D.A. stated. 'There has been too much police brutality in Harlem. The public is indignant.'

The commissioner pressed the tips of his fingers together and leaned back in his chair.

'Give us time to make a more thorough investigation,' he said.

The assistant D.A. was reluctant. 'What more investigation is needed? They have admitted beating the deceased.'

The commissioner passed over him. 'In the meantime, detectives Jones and Johnson, you are suspended from the force until further notice. Captain Brice,' he added, turning his head slightly, 'have them turn in their shields and strike their names from the roll.'

Grave Digger's swollen face turned gray around the mouth and the grafted skin on Coffin Ed's face twitched like a tic.

'And that's that,' Grave Digger said to their friend, Lieutenant Anderson, as they stood outside in the glaring hot sunshine. 'For a mother-raping pusher.'

'It's just the newspaper pressure. We're suffering from the customary summer slack in news. It'll blow over,' Lieutenant Anderson consoled. 'The papers are on one of their periodic humanitarian kicks. Don't worry. Nothing's coming out of it.'

'Yeah, humanitarian,' Grave Digger said bitterly. 'It's all right to kill a few colored people for trying to get their children an education, but don't hurt a mother-raping white punk for selling dope.'

Lieutenant Anderson winced. As accustomed as he was to these two colored detectives' racial connotations, that one hurt.

8

Uncle Saint hung about the garage for a long time before he got up enough nerve to enter the house.

Three of the bullets had made holes which he plugged with putty and sprayed with quick-drying black enamel. But there were two big dents and one long seam atop the left rear fender which couldn't be concealed. He had no mirror to replace the broken one, so he removed them from both front fenders and sprayed the marks they had left. That didn't help much either; the bolt holes still remained. The license plates presented no problem. He had several changes of plates, none of which had the legitimate registration number. He put on some Connecticut plates.

Still he kept fiddling about. Once he thought of painting the whole car another color; or at least the upper half. But finally his jag began thinning out and he got jumpy. He knew he'd have trouble sure as hell with Sister Heavenly if he got too jumpy, so he decided to go inside and have it out.

She would just have to look after him, he told himself. She had kept him helpless and homeless for twenty-five years and he wasn't going to jump up and run off by his lonesome just because he was in a little trouble. If he went down he was going to take her with him. It had been her idea anyway, he justified himself. He had just been trying to do her business.

He slunk up the path toward the house, holding the shotgun cradled in his arm as though stalking an enemy.

Only the screen door was closed. He became wary. When he poked his head into the kitchen, his eyes popped. Sister Heavenly was sitting at the kitchen table drinking sassafras tea and smoking a pipe of marijuana and looking content with the world. For a brief moment he thought she had gotten it and his head exploded with rage. But the next instant he realized she couldn't have. He stepped inside and closed the door.

The kitchen had windows on the side and back but their shutters were closed tight to keep out the heat and the only light came in through the screened back door. The kitchen table, covered with blue-and-white checked oilcloth, sat before the side window. The stove stood against the inside wall and Uncle Saint's bunk, covered with army blankets, lay beneath the back window.

Sister Heavenly was dressed as before. She sat sidewise to the table, one leg crossed over the other exposing the ruffles of her petticoats, and her little finger was extended properly as she held the steaming teacup to her lips. Her black beaded bag lay atop the table and her black-and-white striped parasol was propped against the wall beside her.

A small electric fan atop the refrigerator stirred the reeking scent of marijuana and the fragrant aroma of sassafras tea.

She regarded Uncle Saint curiously over the rim of the cup.

'Well, you're finally back,' she said.

Uncle Saint coughed. 'You see me,' he grunted.

Pinky sat across the table from Sister Heavenly, his torso looming so high above her he looked like a barrel-chested midget standing in the chair. He looked from one to the other.

'Did you see Gus?' he asked Uncle Saint in his whining voice.

'I said I would tell you in a minute,' Sister Heavenly snapped at him.

Uncle Saint couldn't make out her game, so he decided to keep his mouth shut. He sat on his bunk, placed the loaded shotgun close beside him, and reached underneath and dragged out a rusty iron lockbox in which he kept everything he owned. From his side pants pocket he took a single key attached to a long brass chain hanging from his belt and unlocked the tremendous Yale padlock which secured his box.

Two pairs of eyes followed his every movement, but he studiedly ignored them. He had his own alcohol lamp, teaspoon and spike, and he would use no other.

Silently they watched him mix a deck of heroin and a deck of cocaine, light the lamp and cook it in a spoon, load the spike. He banged himself in a vein just above his left wrist. His brown decayed teeth bared like an animal's when the spike went in, but his mouth went loose and sloppy in a soft sighing sound as he drew out the spike.

Sister Heavenly finished her cup of tea and waited a few minutes for his speedball to work, slowly swallowing the sweet marijuana smoke.

'What happened to the trunk?' she asked finally.

Uncle Saint looked around as though expecting to find it in the kitchen. He hadn't made up any kind of a story and all his furtive looks at her didn't tell him anything. Outwardly she looked indifferent and serene, but he knew from past experience that didn't mean a thing. Finally he decided to lie to the bitter end. He had lost the mother-raping trunk and had blown some mother-raper's brains out to boot, and wasn't nothing going to change that. He was too mother-raping old to worry about every little thing that came along.

He licked his dry lips and muttered, 'We been barking up

the wrong tree. There wasn't nothing in that trunk. Them expressmen come and got it and took it straight to the docks and left it there. I followed them, but when I seen there wasn't nothing in it I figured there had been a switch, so I turned around and highballed it back uptown looking for you, but you has gone. So I figures you has already got it – if there was anything to get.'

'That's what I thought,' she said enigmatically. 'We been on a wild-goose chase.'

Pinky's battered face contorted in a fit of rage. 'You was after Gus's treasure map,' he accused. 'That's why you give me that knockout shot. You was trying to steal Gus's treasure map and you done let him get kilt.'

'He ain't no more dead than you is,' Sister Heavenly said calmly. 'I saw him talking to the expressmen when—'

'You saw Gus alive!' Pinky exclaimed. His eyes bugged out in an expression of horror.

Sister Heavenly went on as though she hadn't noticed. 'Not only saw him but I felt him. He talked to the expressmen when they came for the trunk and gave them the treasure map to mail.'

Pinky stared at her in disbelief. 'You saw Gus give the expressmen the treasure map?' he echoed stupidly.

'What are you so het up about?' she asked sharply. 'Ain't you the one who said he was going to give them the treasure map to mail to him in Ghana?'

'But I thought he was already kilt by now,' Pinky stammered in confusion.

Uncle Saint was staring from one to another with a fixed expression of imbecility. He wondered if he was hearing right.

'He might be killed by now but he was alive when I was there,' she said. 'And Ginny and the African was getting the bags ready to leave. Ginny was straightening up for the new couple what comes in today.'

Pinky looked flabbergasted. He opened his mouth to say something but was stopped by the sound of an automobile horn from the street in front.

'That's Angelo,' she said casually, and looked sharply from one to the other to see their reactions.

Both looked suddenly guilty and trapped.

She smiled cynically. 'Sit still,' she said. 'I'll go out and see what he wants this early in the morning.'

'But it ain't his day,' Pinky whined.

Uncle Saint threw him a black look.

But Sister Heavenly merely said, 'It sure ain't,' as she got to her feet.

The front door was never opened, so she went out the back door and circled the house by the path. Her long skirt caught in the high dry weeds and burs clung to the hem but she paid it no attention.

A thickset, swarthy, black-haired man wearing a navy blue straw hat with a fluted gray silk band, Polaroid sunglasses in a heavy black frame, a charcoal-gray suit of shantung silk, white silk shirt and knitted maroon tie, sat behind the wheel of a shiny black MGA sports car with white-wall tires. He was a precinct detective sergeant.

Rows of even white teeth showed in his heavily tanned face at sight of her.

'How's tricks, Sister H?' he greeted in a jovial voice.

She rested her black-gloved hands on the door of the car and looked at him questioningly. 'Same as usual.' In the bright sunshine, her black straw hat atop the gray wig glittered like a cockroach.

'Are you sure?' His voice was insinuating.

'Now what do you mean by that?'

'I just came from the station,' he said. 'As soon as I got the reader I came straight to see you. It's the least I could do for an old friend.'

She looked at the dark green lens of his sunglasses, trying to see his eyes, but she only saw her own reflection. She felt trouble coming on and looked across the street to see if they were being watched.

The villa opposite was the only other house in the block. It was occupied by a large Italian family, but they were so accustomed to seeing the sergeant's flashy car parked in front of Sister Heavenly's, and to all the other strange goings-on in that house, they paid it no attention. At the moment none of the brood was in sight.

'Let's finish with the bullshit,' Sister Heavenly said.

'Finished,' he agreed. 'There was a shotgun killing took place down near the French Line dock at about half past six this morning,' he went on, watching her expression sharply from behind his trick glasses, but her expression didn't change.

'It seems that a man standing on the sidewalk was shotgunned to death by a man sitting in a parked car. They found a derringer with a silencer attached on the sidewalk near the victim. It had recently been fired. Homicide figures the man with the derringer tried to gun the man in the car and got himself shotgunned instead.

This sort of rod is a professional's tool. Anyway, the killer got away,' he added offhandedly, waiting for her reaction.

She didn't show any reaction. All she said was, 'What's that mean to me?'

He shrugged. 'Nobody can get any sense out of it. You see, there're a lot of conflicting descriptions of both the car and the killer. All they could get for certain about the car is that it was a black low-slung limousine, but no one knew the make. But there was one guy who described the killer as a little dried-up darky with gray kinky hair who was wearing a chauffeur's uniform; and he can't be shaken.'

'Well, now ain't that lovely!' Sister Heavenly exclaimed in disgust.

'You ain't just saying it,' Angelo agreed. 'Don't make any sense at all. But one thing is for sure. The car is marked. It seems the victim had a friend in a car parked behind the killer's. When this friend saw his buddy shot down he opened up with an automatic and put some holes in the back of the killer's car. That's the lead homicide is following.'

She chewed over that for a time. 'How about this second gunman?' she asked. 'Did he get away too?'

'Nope. That's where the killer got lucky. While this second party was following the killer's car he drove in front of a truck and was run over and killed too.'

A veil dropped over Sister Heavenly's old blue-rimmed ocher eyes as her mind worked furiously. 'Did anybody make them?' she asked.

'Not yet,' he said. 'But they had all the marks of professionals, and they ain't going to be hard to identify.'

'All right,' she conceded finally. 'I got the message. What's it worth?'

He took a small black cheroot from a black leather case which he carried in his breast pocket and slowly applied a flame from a solid gold Flaminaire lighter imported from France. It looked as though he were doing a takeoff on a private eye.

Finally he said, 'Well, Sister H, seeing as how your nephew Pinky is wanted too for putting in that false fire alarm last night, I figure for the two of them together, fifteen C's ain't too much. And while you're at it, you better give me next month's sugar at the same time. With all this shooting going on, who knows where we'll be by then.'

'Two G's!' she exploded. 'Hell, you can have 'em both right now. They ain't worth that much to me.'

He blew out a cloud of smoke and grinned at her. 'You didn't get the message. Homicide is going to wonder what it's all about. They ain't going to bite on the idea that one old darky chauffeur dreamed it up – and nobody else, if you get what I mean.'

She didn't argue. There was no use.

'Let's see if I've got that much,' she said and turned back toward the house.

'Look good and look fast,' he called after her.

She halted and her body stiffened.

'You know this is a lamster's hangout up here in these sticks,' he said. 'And I'm the authority on it. People are going to be asking me questions pretty damn soon, and I got to know how to answer.'

She resumed walking, her long skirts catching in the weeds again as she went around the side of the house. The tethered nanny goat was bleating for water and she stopped for a moment to untie it. Then she kept on through the blistered garden, trampling over the withered vegetables indiscriminately, and looked into the garage. One glance at the Lincoln was enough.

'Who did he think he was fooling,' she murmured to herself, then added half aloud, 'Anyway, I was damn right.'

She returned to the house and entered her bedroom.

Uncle Saint and Pinky had disappeared.

She knelt before the chest of drawers, took out her bunch of keys and selected one and unlocked the bottom drawer. The front of the drawer swung down on hinges, revealing a built-in safe. She spun the dial and opened a small, rectangular door. Then she selected another key and opened an inner compartment which was stuffed with packets of banknotes. She took two packets from the top, closed and locked all three doors and left the room.

A tall, emaciated colored man flashily dressed in a Palm Beach suit and a hard straw hat with a red band stood beside the door. She quickly slipped the money inside of her dress.

'I ain't got no Heavenly Dust now, Slim,' she said. 'Come back later.'

'I need it,' he insisted.

'Well, I ain't got it,' she snapped impatiently, brushing past him toward the sidewalk.

He followed reluctantly. 'When you gonna have it?'

'At one o'clock,' she said over her shoulder.

He looked at his watch. 'It ain't but nine-thirty now. That's three hours and a half,' he whined, following her into the street.

'Beat it,' she snarled.

He looked from her to the detective sitting in the car. Angelo turned his head slightly and made a motion with his thumb. Slim hastened down the street. Angelo watched him in the rearview mirror until he turned into a path across a vacant lot.

'It's clear now,' he said.

Sister Heavenly took the packets of banknotes from inside her dress and placed them in his hand. He counted them carefully without looking up or taking any precaution at concealment. Each packet contained ten one-hundred-dollar notes. Negligently he slipped them into his inside coat pocket.

'Pretty soon you'll be turning in this heap for a Jaguar,' Sister Heavenly said sarcastically.

'You ain't just kidding,' he replied.

The high-powered motor roared into life. She watched him back the car at high speed into the first cross street, turn and speed away.

Pinky had the key, she thought. But the question was how to get it out of him.

Instead of returning to the kitchen she went on to the rabbit hutch to see if Pinky had taken another speedball in her absence. The buck rabbit was huddled in a corner of his cage, watching her with terrified eyes. She dragged him out by the ears and removed the stopper from his rectum. The three capsules of C & H that should have been there were gone.

No wonder he was talking so strange, she thought. He must be leaping and flying.

She put the buck back into his cage and walked slowly toward the kitchen, carrying the stopper in her hand.

I'll just play it dumb, she decided, and see what those speedballs tell him to do next.

9

The house didn't have a basement. It had been built by Italian immigrants unused to the cold winters of the Bronx and who didn't have sufficient money for such a luxury.

Sister Heavenly's bedroom and the kitchen composed one half of the house. The other half was composed of a large front parlor that was kept shuttered and closed and a small back bedroom which Sister Heavenly had converted into a bathroom.

The stairway to the attic led up from the kitchen and took up part of the short front hall, which, like the parlor, was never used. The bottom of the stairway which extended into the kitchen was detachable.

When Sister Heavenly returned to the kitchen she spoke apparently to no one: 'You can come out now, he's gone.'

The bottom of the stairs moved slowly out into the kitchen, revealing an access to a dugout beneath the house.

Pinky's head appeared first. His kinky white hair was covered with cobwebs. On his battered face, ranging in colors from violent purple to bilious yellow, was a look of indescribable stupidity. His shoulders were too large for the opening and he had to put one arm through first and perform a series of contortions. He looked like some unknown monster coming out of hibernation.

The next thing that appeared was Uncle Saint's shotgun, which seemed to drag Uncle Saint behind it.

Pinky shoved the staircase back into place and then stood close to Uncle Saint as though for spiritual comfort.

Neither of them met Sister Heavenly's scornful gaze.

She couldn't restrain from taunting: 'You two innocents are acting mighty strange for people with clear consciences.'

'Ain't no need of going looking for trouble,' Uncle Saint said sheepishly.

Sister Heavenly consulted her old-fashioned locket-watch. 'It's quarter to ten. How about all us going down to the dock and seeing Gus and Ginny off?'

If she had exploded a bomb filled with ghosts, she couldn't have gotten stranger reactions.

Uncle Saint had a sudden heart attack. His eyes rolled back in his head and three inches of tongue fell suddenly from the corner of his dirty-looking mouth. He clutched his heart with his left hand and reeled toward his bunk, taking good care to hold on to the shotgun with his right hand.

Simultaneously Pinky had an epileptic fit. He fell to the floor and had convulsions, contortions and convolutions. His muscles jumped and jerked and quivered as he thrashed about on the floor. Foam sprayed from his mouth.

Sister Heavenly backed quickly from the danger zone of flying legs and arms and took up a position behind the stove.

Pinky's eyes were set in a fixed stare; his spine stiffened, his legs jerked spasmodically, his arms flailed the air like runaway wind-mills.

Sister Heavenly stared at him in admiration. 'If I had known you could throw wingdings like that I could have been using you all along as a sideline to faith healing,' she said.

Seeing that Pinky was stealing the show, Uncle Saint sat up. His eyes were popping and his jaw was working in awe.

'I'd have never thunk it,' he muttered to himself.

Sister Heavenly looked at him. 'How's your heart attack?'

He avoided her gaze. 'It was just a twinge,' he said sheepishly. 'It's already let up.'

He thought it was a good time to get out and let Pinky carry on. 'I'll go start the car,' he said. 'We might have to take him to the doctor.'

'Go ahead,' Sister Heavenly said. 'I'll nurse him.'

Uncle Saint hastened off toward the garage, still carrying his loaded shotgun. He raised the hood and detached the distributor head, then began to work the starter.

Sister Heavenly could hear the starter above the gritting sounds of Pinky's teeth and realized immediately that Uncle Saint had disabled the car.

She waited patiently.

Pinky's convulsions eased and his body turned slowly rigid. Sister Heavenly stepped over and looked into his staring eyes. The pupils were so distended his eyes looked like red-hot metal balls.

Uncle Saint came in and said the car wouldn't start.

'You stay here and look after Pinky, I'll take a taxi to the docks,' Sister Heavenly decided.

'I'll put some ice on his head,' Uncle Saint said and began fiddling about in the refrigerator.

Sister Heavenly didn't answer. She picked up her black beaded bag and black-and-white striped parasol and went out of the back door.

She didn't have a telephone. She paid for police protection and protected herself from other hazards and her business was strictly cash and carry. So she had to walk to the nearest taxi stand.

Outside she opened the parasol, went around the house by the path through the weeds, and set out walking down the middle of the hot dusty road.

Crouching like an ancient Iroquois, still carrying the loaded shotgun in his right hand, Uncle Saint skulked from corner to corner of the house, watching her. She kept straight on down the street in the direction of White Plains Road without looking back.

Satisfied that she was not coming back, he returned to the kitchen and said to the rigid epileptic on the floor, 'She's gone.'

Pinky jumped to his feet. 'I got to get out of here,' he whined.

'Go ahead. What's stopping you?'

'Looking like I am. The first cop sees me gonna stop me, and I is wanted anyway.'

'Git your clothes off,' Uncle Saint said. 'I'll fix that.'

He seemed possessed with an urgency to be alone.

Sister Heavenly kept to the road until she knew she couldn't be seen from the house, then she turned over to the next street and doubled back.

The house nearest to hers on the same side of the street was in the next block. It was owned by an old Italian couple who lived alone. They were good friends of Sister Heavenly. The man ran a provision house and was away from home during the day.

When Sister Heavenly called, his wife was in the kitchen, straining and bottling wine.

Sister Heavenly asked permission to sit in the attic. She often did this. There was a side window in the attic which offered a clear view of her own house, and whenever she found it necessary to check up on Uncle Saint she sat there watching for an hour or two. The old couple had even provided her with a rocking-chair.

Sister Heavenly climbed the stairs to the attic and, after opening the shutters, settled into her chair.

It was hot enough in the attic to roast a goose, but that didn't bother Sister Heavenly. She liked heat and she never perspired. She sat rocking gently back and forth, watching the front and back of her own house at the end of the adjoining block.

An hour later Uncle Saint said to Pinky, 'You is dry enough, put on some clothes and git.'

Pinky didn't have a change of clothes in the house and he was more than twice the size of Uncle Saint. The black pants and T-shirt he had taken off were bloodstained and filthy.

'Where am I gonna git some clothes?' he asked.

'Look in the souvenir trunk,' Uncle Saint said.

The souvenir trunk sat beneath a small dormer window in the attic.

'Take a chisel, it's locked,' Uncle Saint added as Pinky started ascending the stairs.

There wasn't any chisel in the kitchen and Uncle Saint wouldn't go to the garage to get one. Pinky couldn't go because he was buck naked, so he took the poker for the stove.

It was an old-fashioned steamer trunk with a domed lid and was bound with wooden hoops. Sunshine slanted on the dustcovered top and when Pinky began prying at the old rusty lock, dust motes filled the air like glittering confetti. All of the windows had been closed after the night's performance to keep out the heat and now the sweaty odor of the dancers lingered in the blazing heat. Pinky began to sweat. Sweat drops splattered in the dust like drops of ink.

'Hey, this stuff is coming off,' he called down to Uncle Saint in a panic.

'That's just the excess,' Uncle Saint reassured him. 'The main part ain't coming off.'

With sudden haste, Pinky levered the poker and the lock flew apart. He raised the lid and looked into the trunk.

The souvenir trunk was where Sister Heavenly kept various garments left by her former lovers when they had lammed. Pinky rummaged about, holding up pants and shirts and cotton drawers with back flaps. Everything was too small. Evidently Sister Heavenly hadn't counted any giants amongst her lovers. But finally Pinky came across a pair of peg-top Palm Beach pants which must have belonged to a very tall man at least. He squeezed into a pair of knee-length cotton drawers and pulled the peg-top trousers over them. They fitted like women's jodhpurs. He looked about until he found a red jersey silk shirt worn by some sharp cat in the early 1930s. It stretched enough for him to get it on. None of the shoes were possible, so he closed the trunk and went down to the kitchen and put on his same old blue canvas sneakers.

'Why didn't yer git a hat?' Uncle Saint said.

Pink turned around and went back up the stairs and rummaged in the trunk for a hat. The only hat which fitted was a white straw hat with a wide floppy brim and a peaked crown like the hats worn by Mexican peons. It had a black chin strap to keep it on.

'Look around and see if there's some sunglasses,' Uncle Saint called.

There was a shoe box of nothing but sunglasses but the only pair that fitted Pinky had white celluloid frames and plain blue glass lenses. He put them on.

Uncle Saint surveyed his handiwork when Pinky stood before him.

'Not even you own mother would recognize you,' he said proudly, but he called a warning as Pinky started off. 'Keep out the sun or that stuff'll turn purple.'

Sister Heavenly's eyes popped. She stopped rocking and leaned forward.

From out of her own front yard came the blackest man she had ever seen, and Sister Heavenly had specialized in black men. This man was so black he had blue-and-purple tints to his skin like wet bituminous coal glinting in the sunshine. Not only was he the blackest, but he was the sportiest man she had ever seen. She hadn't seen anyone dressed that sporty since minstrel shows went out.

He was walking fast and there was something about him, especially down around the legs, which reminded her of one of her short-time lovers called Blackberry Slim, but his legs were thicker than Slim's. And that red jersey silk shirt rising from those peg-top legs was identical with one that Dusty Canes used to wear. But that hat – that big white flopping hat with a chin strap, and those blue-tinted sunglasses with a white frame; she had never seen anyone wear a hat like that but Go-Go Gooseman.

'My God!' she exclaimed aloud as she suddenly recognized the man. 'That's Pinky and he's been in my souvenir trunk!'

Her mind started working lightning fast ... Pinky in disguise. She had expected him to make a move but she hadn't expected to get such a lucky break. Naturally he was headed for the cache.

She jumped up so quickly she overturned the rocking chair. The old Italian woman tried to stop her in the kitchen to share a bottle of wine but she hurried past and went around the house. She stood behind a green lattice gate and watched Pinky loping past. He didn't look in her direction.

She folded up her parasol to make herself as inconspicuous as possible, and kept well in back of him.

He went directly to the subway stop on White Plains Road and climbed the stairs to the waiting platform. Sister Heavenly was blowing and puffing by the time she reached the turnstile. She acted as though she hadn't recognized Pinky and went down to the other end of the platform.

Looking around he saw her and gave a start. There was no place for him to hide. His only chance was to brazen it out. Everyone was staring at him. Once her gaze wandered in his direction. He stared back at her from behind his blue sunglasses. She looked at him for a moment curiously, then turned as though she had not recognized him and watched the train approach.

Two cars separated them. Both of them remained standing so they could peek around the doors when the train stopped and see if the other was getting off. But neither saw the other peeping.

They rode like this down to Times Square. Pinky jumped off just as the doors were closing. Before Sister Heavenly saw him, the doors were closed. She saw him stop and turn and look directly at her as her coach passed.

She got off at 34th Street and taxied back to Times Square, but he had disappeared. Suddenly she realized that he was trying to outsmart her. He had ridden down to Times Square and had given her the slip on the chance that she might have recognized him. He figured he was throwing her off his tracks. But there was only one place he could have anything cached, and that was the apartment on Riverside Drive.

She hailed a taxi and told the driver to step on it.

The driver leaned over a little to peer at her through the rearview mirror. My God, she's still trying, he thought. But all the time she's already had, if she ain't made it yet she'll never make it now.

Sister Heavenly had him stop in front of Riverside Church. She got out and paid him. He paused for a moment to watch her, making as though he was writing in his record sheet. He was curious. She had rushed him up here as though it were a matter of life and death, and all she wanted was to go to church.

Some of these old ladies think all God has got to do is wait on them, he thought sourly and shifted into gear.

Sister Heavenly waited until he had driven out of sight. Then she walked across the street into the park and selected a bench where she could watch the entrance to the apartment unobserved unless Pinky deliberately looked about for her.

Whistles began to blow as she took her seat. She pulled out her locket-watch to see if it was correct. It read twelve noon on the dot.

10

It was twelve noon sharp when Coffin Ed turned his Plymouth sedan into the northbound stream of traffic on lower Broadway.

'What do two cops do who've been kicked off the force?' he asked.

'Try to get back on,' Grave Digger said in his thick, cotton-dry voice.

He didn't say another word all the way uptown; he sat burning in a dry, speechless rage.

It was twelve-thirty when they checked into the Harlem precinct station to turn in their shields to Captain Brice.

They stood for a moment on the steps of the precinct station, watching the colored people pass up and down the street, all citizens of Harlem who stepped out of the way to let the white cops by who had business in the station.

The vertical rays of the sun beat down.

'First thing to do is find Pinky,' Grave Digger said. 'All we had on Jake is possession. If we get evidence he was peddling H too, that might give us a start.'

'He's got to talk,' Coffin Ed pointed out.

'Talk! TALK! You think he ain't going to talk! Much as you and me need a few kind words. Ain't no mother-raper who ever knew Jake going to refuse to do a little talking.'

Fifteen minues later they pulled up before the apartment on Riverside Drive.

'Do you see what I see?' Coffin Ed remarked as they alighted.

'There couldn't be but one of 'em,' Grave Digger said.

The dog was lying in front of the iron gate to the rear entrance. It lay on its side with its back to the gate and all four feet extended. It seemed to be asleep. The vertical rays of the midday sun beat down on its tawny hide.

'It must be cooking in this heat,' Coffin Ed said.

'Maybe she's dead.'

It still wore the heavy muzzle reinforced with iron and the brass-studded collar with the chain attached.

They walked toward it by common accord.

Its lambent eyes half opened as they approached and a low growl, like distant thunder, issued from its throat. But it didn't move.

Green flies were feeding from a dirty open wound in its head from which black blood oozed.

'The African did a poor job,' Grave Digger observed.

'Maybe he was in a hurry to get back.'

Grave Digger reached down and took hold of the chain close to the collar. The rest was underneath the dog. He pulled gently and the dog climbed slowly to her feet in sections, like a camel getting up. She stood groggily, looking disinterested.

'She's about done in,' Coffin Ed said.

'You'd be done in too if you were knocked in the head and thrown in the river.'

The dog followed docilely as they went back to the front entrance and rang the superintendent's bell. There was no answer. Coffin Ed stepped over to the mailboxes and pushed buttons indiscriminately.

The latch clicked with a ratchetlike sound that went on and on.

'Everyone's expecting.'

'Looks like it.'

As they were descending the stairs to the basement, Coffin Ed said curiously, 'What do we do if we run into trouble?'

They were still in their shirtsleeves and they had left their revolvers at home that morning.

'Pray,' Grave Digger said thickly, the rage building up in

him again. 'Don't forget we're subject to the charge of impersonating officers if we claim to be cops.'

'How can I forget it,' Coffin Ed said bitterly.

The first thing they noticed was that the trunk was gone.

'Looks like we're too late.'

Grave Digger said nothing.

There was no reply to the janitor's bell. Grave Digger looked at the Yale lock above the old-fashioned mortise lock. He passed the dog's chain to Coffin Ed to hold and took a Boy Scout's knife from his pants pocket.

'Let's just hope the night lock ain't on,' he said, opening the screwdriver blade.

'Let's just hope we don't get caught, you mean,' Coffin Ed amended, turning to watch all the entrances.

Grave Digger forced the blade between the doorjamb and the lock, slowly forced back the bolt and pushed open the door.

Both of them grunted from shock.

The body of the African was lying in a grotesque position in the center of the bare linoleum floor with its throat cut from ear to ear. The wound had stopped bleeding and the surrounding blood had coagulated, giving the impression of a purple-lipped monster's mouth.

Blood was everywhere, over the furniture, the floor, the African's white turban and crumpled robe.

For a moment there was only the sound of their labored breathing and the buzzing of an electric fan somewhere out of sight.

Then Coffin Ed reached behind him, knocking the dog aside, and closed the door. The sound of the clicking of the lock released them from their trance of shock.

'Whoever did that wasn't joking,' Grave Digger said soberly, the anger drained from him.

'As many as I've seen, I always get a shock,' Coffin Ed confessed.

'Me too. This mother-raping senseless violence!'

'Yeah, but what you gonna do?' Coffin Ed said, thinking about themselves.

'Hell, meet it is all.'

The dog inched forward unnoticed and suddenly Coffin

Ed looked down and saw it sniff at the cut throat and lick the blood.

'Get back, Goddammit!' he shouted, snatching up the chain.

The dog backed up and cringed.

Finally they got around to noticing that the room was in a shambles. Rugs were scattered; drawers were emptied, the contents strewn about the floor; the stuffed birds and animals had been gutted, the statuettes smashed, the overstuffed furniture slashed and the packing ripped apart; the broken-down TV sets and the radio had been pried open, the housing of the organ bashed in.

Without commenting, Coffin Ed looped the handle of the dog chain over the doorknob. Then he and Grave Digger poked into the other rooms, taking care not to step into the blood. Doors led from the parlor into the kitchen and one bedroom, beyond which was a bathroom. There was the same disorder in all. They went back and stared at the body of the African.

The macabre hideousness of the bloody corpse was accentuated by the buzzing of the fan. Grave Digger bent over and sent his gaze along the floor, underneath the blood stained shattered furniture, searching for it. The fan lay overturned beneath the dining table, half hidden by a broken television screen. He located the wall socket and jerked out the plug.

Silence came down. It was the dinner hour and the basement was deserted.

They could almost hear their thoughts moving around.

'If what the janitor's wife said about Pinky is true, he might have cut the African's throat.' Coffin Ed spoke his thoughts aloud.

'I don't figure him for this,' Grave Digger said. 'What would he be looking for?'

'Search me. What about her? Cat-eyed women are known for cutting throats.'

'And search her own house?' Grave Digger said.

'Who knows? All this heat is affecting people's minds. Maybe she thought her husband had something hidden here.'

'Why would she kill the African? It looked to me like

they were cooking with the same gas. It was obvious he was laying her.'

'I don't dig this at all,' Coffin Ed confessed. 'Somebody wanted something bad, but they didn't find it.'

'That's obvious. If they had found it, there would be at least one small place that wasn't torn up, some indication where the search had stopped.'

'But what the hell could they be looking for important enough to murder? What could one old colored janitor have that valuable?'

Grave Digger began considering the sex angle. 'You think he's that old? Old enough to kill the African out of jealousy? Or you think he found out they were crossing him in some way?'

'I ain't figuring him for doing it. But it figures he was old. And old men don't generally take chances.'

'Who told you that?'

'Anyway, there're a hell of a lot of questions here need answering,' Coffin Ed said.

With unspoken accord, they approached the body, picking their way through the blood. Coffin Ed grimaced and his face began to twitch.

Grave Digger lifted one of the African's arms, holding the wrist between his thumb and first finger, then let it drop. The body was still limp even though the blood had coagulated.

'How do you account for that?' Coffin Ed asked.

'Maybe it's the heat. In weather this hot it might take some time for rigor mortis to set in.'

'It might be that he ain't been dead long too.'

They looked at one another with the same sudden thought. A chill seemed to come into the room.

'You think he came in and interrupted the search? And that's why he got killed?'

'It figures,' Coffin Ed said.

'Then the chances are the murderer might not have finished when we arrived.'

'Or *they*. It don't have to be just one person.'

'In that case they might still be hiding somewhere in this basement.'

Coffin Ed didn't reply immediately. The grafted patches of skin on his face contorted and the tic set in.

For a time they stood without moving, holding their breath to listen. Vague sounds drifted in from the street – passing automobiles, the distant horn of a ship, the muted, unidentifiable thousand sounds of the city forming an unnoticeable undertone. The rat-tat-tat of a woman's heels hurrying down the hallway overhead was followed by the rumbling of the elevator starting. But no sound came from the vicinity of the basement. It was a quiet residential street and during this hour most of the tenants, grownups and children alike, were at lunch.

At the same time both were trying to reconstruct the layout of the basement from what little they had seen of it. On their previous visit they had noticed that the laundry was to the right of the back entrance facing a corridor which ran parallel to the back wall. Next to the laundry were the elevator, staircase to the front hall, a toolroom and the door to the janitor's suite; all of which faced the blank whitewashed wall of the storeroom entered from the other side. Another hall running parallel with the front of the house turned off at right angles at the janitor's door and no doubt continued around the other side of the house, encircling the basement. They had both noticed that the door to the boiler room opened off the front hall.

'I'd feel a hell of a lot better if I was heeled,' Grave Digger confessed.

'I got a notion we're making rattlesnakes out of tadpoles,' Coffin Ed said.

'Let's play it safe,' Grave Digger said. 'Whoever cut this boy's throat wasn't kidding.'

Coffin Ed unhooked the dog's chain from the doorknob, cracked the door and peered cautiously down the corridor.

'This situation is funny,' he said. 'Here we are, supposed to be tough cops, and are scared to poke our heads out of this door in the basement of one of the safest houses in the city.'

'You call this safe?' Grave Digger said, indicating the gory stiff. 'And it wouldn't be so funny if you got your head blown off.'

'Well, we can't stay holed up like two rats,' Coffin Ed said and threw open the door.

Grave Digger leaped to one side and flatted himself against the wall flanking the door, but Coffin Ed stood out in the open.

'You remind me of a Spanish captain I read about in a book by Hemingway,' Grave Digger said disgustedly. 'This captain figured the enemies were all dead so he charged the dugout single-handed, beating his chest and yelling at them to come out and shoot him, showing how brave he was. And you know what – one of 'em rose up and shot him through the heart.'

'Does that look like any enemy is out there?' Coffin Ed demanded.

In both directions, the brightly lit, whitewashed corridors were deserted and serene. The door to the laundry was open but the doors to the toolroom and boiler room were closed. But they had wire mesh in the place of upper panels and not a sound came from either room. It looked as peaceful as a grave. The idea of killers lurking in ambush seemed suddenly absurd.

'Hell, I'm going to look around,' Coffin Ed said.

But Grave Digger was still for playing it safe. 'Not without a gun, man,' he cautioned again. Suddenly he was struck by an idea. 'Let's send out the dog to sniff around.'

Coffin Ed glanced at her scornfully. 'She couldn't hurt a mouse with that muzzle on.'

'I'll fix that,' Grave Digger said and stepped over to the bitch and removed the muzzle and unhooked the chain.

He pushed her out into the corridor but she merely looked over her shoulder at him as though she wanted to come back in. He looked about for something to throw but everything movable was bloody, so he took off his hat and sailed it down the corridor in the direction of the boiler room door.

'There, boy, there, boy, go get it,' he urged.

But the bitch suddenly turned around with her tail between her legs and ran into the kitchen. They could hear her lapping up water.

'I'm going to call homicide,' Grave Digger said. 'Have you seen a phone?'

'In the kitchen.'

'That's a house phone.'

Coffin Ed stepped outside and looked up and down the corridors. 'Here's a pay phone beside the door. You got a dime?'

Grave Digger fished some change from his pocket. 'Yeah.'

It was an old-fashioned telephone box attached to the wall with the mouthpiece on a level with the average man's mouth. Grave Digger stepped around the corner, lifted the receiver and put in a dime. He held the receiver to his ear, waiting for the dial tone.

'I'm going to get a couple of wrenches or something we can use for saps, just in case,' Coffin Ed said, stepping over toward the toolroom.

'Why don't you let it alone and let's just wait for some cops with pistols,' Grave Digger called over his shoulder.

But Coffin Ed thought better. He pushed open the toolroom door and leaned inside, reaching for the light switch.

He never knew what hit him. Lights exploded in his head as though his brain had been dynamited right behind the eyes.

Grave Digger had just gotten the dial tone and had stuck his right index finger on the figure 7 when he heard the flat whacking sound made by the impact of a blunt instrument against a human skull. There could be no mistaking the sound; he had heard it often enough. He was moving, his head wheeling and ducking, before the sound of the following grunt reached his ears.

He never got around but his head had moved enough so that the bullet intended for his temple struck the gutta percha receiver in his left hand, shattered it but was deflected so that it merely burned a blister across the back of his neck.

The gunman was a marksman with a pistol. He was using a derringer with a sawed-off barrel and a silencer attached, similar to the one used by the gunman whom Uncle Saint had killed. At the sound of Coffin Ed opening the toolroom door, he had stepped from the boiler room into the corridor and had taken a bead on Grave Digger's head, resting the meat side of his trigger hand in the crook of his raised left arm. But even the best of marksmen could miss with a one-shot gun, so he also held a .38-caliber police positive in his left fist as insurance.

Grave Digger's left hand and the whole left side of his head went numb and he felt as though he had been kicked in the head by a mule. But he was not stunned. He erupted into motion like the snapping of a clock spring. He went down into a rolling plunge toward the open door of the janitor's suite.

He wasn't looking toward the gunman; his eyes, his mind, his straining muscles, and all his five senses were concentrating on escape. But somehow his mind retained the impression of a face – a dead-white, death's head face with colorless lips pulled back from small yellow teeth and huge deep-set eyes like targets on a pistol range: black balls rimmed with a thin line of white about which were large irregular patches of black – a hophead's face.

The gunman straightened out his left arm and fired the police positive.

The bullet caught Grave Digger in his spin as he was turning on a long slant, almost horizontal to the floor. It went in underneath the left shoulder blade and came out three inches above the heart.

Grave Digger grunted once like a stuck hog and was knocked flat on his face. But he didn't lose consciousness. He felt his face skidding across the slick cool surface of linoleum and he knew he had got inside the room. With a quick convulsive movement which consumed the last of his strength, he rolled over on his back like a cat turning in midair and kicked with his left foot toward the door, trying to close it. He missed it and his foot was in the air. His stabbing, desperate gaze went across it, and he found himself looking straight down the barrel of the police positive.

He thought fleetingly, without fear or regret, Digger, your number's up.

That's the last he knew.

Hopped to the gills, the gunman stalked forward on the balls of his feet to place another slug in the absolutely motionless body, but the second gunman, standing by the toolroom door, shouted, 'For chrissakes, cummon, Goddammit! Did you have to use that sonofabitching cannon?'

The hopped-up gunman paid him no attention. He was intent on pumping another slug into his victim.

But suddenly a woman let out a scream. It was a scream of

unbelievable volume and immeasurable terror. You could tell it was a colored woman screaming by the heart she put into it. It was the loudest screaming the hopped-up gunman had ever heard and it shattered his control like glass breaking.

He started to run blindly and without direction. He ran head-long into the second gunman, who grappled with him and they struggled furiously for a brief moment.

The colored maid was standing as she had stepped from the elevator. The basket of soiled clothes lay overturned on the floor where it had fallen from her hands. Her body was rigid. Her mouth formed an ellipsoid big enough to swallow an ostrich egg, showing the chewing edges of her molars, a white-coated tongue flatted between the bottom teeth and humped in the back against the tip of a palate which hung down like a blood-red stalagmite. Her neck muscles were corded. Her popeyed stare was fixed. Screams kept pouring from her mouth with an unvarying, nerve-shattering resonance.

The second gunman got his left arm free and slapped the hopped-up gunman twice across the face.

Sanity returned to the dilated pupils, along with terror.

He holstered the police positive in a right-shoulder sling, dropped the derringer into his right coat pocket, and went up the stairs as though the furies were after him.

'Not so fast, you hophead bastard!' the second gunman called from behind him. '*Walk* out into the street.'

11

The *Queen Mary* sailed at twelve noon sharp.

Wharf attendants said they had never witnessed so much confusion at the sailing of a Cunard Line ship.

Two of the tugboats on hand to ease the big ship from its mooring ran together. An able-bodied seaman was knocked into the drink and one of the tugboat captains choked on his false teeth.

Two stout businessmen celebrating the departure of their

wives, along with a fat lady seeing off her daughter, fell off the dock and the *Queen* had to backwater until they were fished out.

The dock police trying to keep the people behind the guard lines were mobbed. Fights broke out; several people were trampled.

Fifteen hundred passengers were on board and five thousand people on the dock to see them off. With the blowing of the tugboat whistles, the shouting of orders, the screaming of goodbyes from six thousand five hundred throats, there was enough noise to arouse the inhabitants of a cemetery.

Authorities said it was due to the excessive heat. The threat of a thunderstorm had passed over and the sun beat down from a cloudless sky.

In the general confusion, no one gave Pinky a second glance. An international atmosphere prevailed; thoughts dwelled on faraway places and people. Those who saw him put him down as either an African politician, a Cuban revolutionary, a Brazilian snake charmer, or just a plain ordinary Harlem shoeshine boy.

Pinky was looking for the trunk.

While everyone's attention was directed to the confusion on the dock, he looked through the pile of freight inside the shed at the end of the wharf.

One of the guards came back and caught him there.

'What you doing in here, boy? You know you ain't got any business here.'

'I'm looking for Joe,' Pinky said, ducking and dodging like a halfwit to divert the guard's suspicions.

Like all colored people, Pinky knew if he acted stupid enough the average white man would pass him off as a harmless idiot.

The guard looked at Pinky and suppressed a smile.

Pinky was sweating and where the dye had run he had big purple splotches across the back of his red jersey silk shirt, down the front, underneath the arms and on the seat of his Palm Beach pants. Sweat was running down his face, collecting on the knot of his chin strap to his hat and dripping to the floor.

'Joe who?' the guard asked.

'Joe the porter. You know Joe.'

'Look upstairs where they keep the passenger luggage; porters don't work here,' the guard said.

'Yassah,' Pinky said and shuffled off.

A moment later the guard told a co-worker who had come over to join him, 'See that darky there?' He pointed. 'The one in the white hat and red shirt going upstairs.'

The second guard looked dutifully.

'He's sweating ink,' the first guard said.

The second guard smiled indulgently.

'I mean it,' the first guard said. 'Look there on the floor. That's where he sweated.'

The second guard looked at the purple blots on the gray concrete floor and grinned unbelievingly.

The first guard grew indignant. 'You don't believe it? Go look at him for yourself.'

The second guard conceded with a nod.

The first guard relaxed. 'I've heard of darkies sweating ink,' he said. 'But this is the first time I've ever seen it.'

Pinky saw the trunk the moment he approached the section for the luggage that went aboard ship. All the luggage that had surrounded it had been loaded and it stood by itself.

He didn't go near it. He seemed satisfied just by the sight of it.

The next thing was to find the African.

He took up a station behind a concrete pier underneath the railroad trestle and watched the people as they left the wharf. He didn't anticipate any difficulty in locating him among the throng. He gonna look like a fly in a glass of buttermilk, he thought.

But after an hour he gave it up. If the African had been there to see Gus and Ginny off, he would have left by then.

He decided to go uptown and check with the African's landlady. If he lost the African he was going to be caught holding the bag.

The African had a room at 145th Street and Eighth Avenue. The hell of it was how to get there without getting nabbed by the cops. It had occurred to him that he was beginning to look conspicuous with the dye running all over his clothes. Besides which he didn't have but fifteen cents, and he couldn't take a taxi if he had found a driver willing to take him.

While he was giving this some thought an old sandwichman shuffled along the sidewalk opposite the wharves, looking wistfully into all the bars he passed. Pinky's mind was cool and sharp from the four speedballs he had loaded his veins with that morning.

He read the advertisement on the signboards hanging fore and aft the old man's shoulders:

BLINSKY'S BURLESQUE
in
Jersey City

50 *Beautiful Girls* 50
10 *Glamorous Striptease Artistes* 10
6 *Zippy Comedians* 6
GREATEST DISPLAY ON EARTH

Underneath some wit had written in red drawing crayon:

Beats Picasso

Pinky studied the old man, took in the battered straw hat, the bulbous red nose, the white stubble of two days' whiskers, the ragged cuffs of baggy pants and the beat-up shoes with one sole flapping loose showing beneath the signboards. He tabbed him as a bum from Hoboken.

He cut across the traffic lane and approached the old bum.

'Is it true what they say?' he asked, shuffling from one foot to another and acting like a natural son of Uncle Tom. 'Ah just come from Mississippi and Ah wants to know is it true.'

The old bum looked up at him from rheumy eyes.

'Is what true, Sam?' he said in a whiskey voice.

Pinky licked his purple lips with his big pink tongue. 'Is it true all them white women shows theyself mother naked?'

The old bum grinned, exposing a couple of dung-colored snaggleteeth.

'Mother naked!' he croaked. 'They ain't even that. They done shaved off the feathers.'

'Ah sho do wish Ah could see 'em,' Pinky said.

That gave the bum an idea. He had been down there all morning hustling up trade among the truck drivers and longshoremen, and the barmen wouldn't even let him enter the bars wearing his sign.

'You hold this sign while I go inside and see a friend and I'll see what I can do for you,' he promised.

'Ah sho will,' Pinky said, helping the old bum pull the boards up over his head.

The old bum beat it for the nearest bar and disappeared inside. Pinky took off in the opposite direction and turned out of sight at the first corner. Then he stopped and hooked the boards over his head. It was a tight fit and the boards stuck out back and front like some newfangled water wings, but he felt covered. He walked toward Columbus Circle to catch the Broadway subway without any qualms.

He got off at 145th Street and Lenox Avenue. As soon as he came up from the subway kiosk, he took off the sandwich boards. He was in Harlem now and he didn't need them anymore.

He walked to Eighth Avenue and started to enter a doorway to one side of the Silver Moon Bar.

'*Pst, pst,*' someone called from the adjoining doorway.

He looked around and saw an old colored woman beckoning to him. He went over to see what she wanted.

'Don't go in there,' she warned him. 'They's two white 'licemen in there.'

She didn't know him from Adam's tomcat, but it was the rigid code of colored people in Harlem to stick together against white cops; they were quick to warn one another when white cops were around, there was no telling who might be wanted.

He looked around for the prowl car, tensed and ready to take off.

'They's plainclothes dicks,' she elaborated. 'And they snuck up here in that ordinary-looking Ford.'

He gave one look at the parked Ford sedan and took off down Eighth Avenue without waiting to thank her. His real cool brain was thinking up a breeze. He figured the only reason two white dicks could be in that tenement at that particular time was they were looking for the African. That was just what he wanted. The only thing wrong was they were looking for the African too soon. That meant they had got something on the African he didn't know about.

After covering two blocks he figured it was safe enough to turn into a bar. Then he remembered he didn't have any money, so he had to keep on down to 137th Street where he had a friend who ran a tobacco shop as a front for a numbers drop and a connection where the pushers dropped by and sold teenage school kids sticks of marijuana and doctored up decks of heroin.

His friend was an old man called Daddy Haddy who had white leprous-looking splotches on his leathery tan skin. It was choking hot in the small, dark, musty shop but Daddy Haddy wore a heavy brown sweater and a black beaver hat pulled down low enough to touch the rims of his black smoked glasses. He looked at Pinky without a sign of recognition.

'What you want, Mac?' he asked suspiciously in a high falsetto voice.

'What's the matter with you?' Pinky said angrily. 'You going blind? Can't you see I is Pinky?'

Daddy Haddy looked at him through his smoked glasses. 'You is ugly as Pinky,' he admitted. 'And you got the size for it. But what is you doing in that skin? You fall in some blackberry juice?'

'I dyed myself. The cops is looking for me.'

'Git out of here, then,' Daddy Haddy said in alarm. 'You want to get me knocked off?'

'Ain't nobody seen me come in here, and you seen for yourself that don't nobody know me,' Pinky argued.

'Well, say what you want and then beat it,' Daddy Haddy conceded grudgingly. 'The way that dye is running you ain't going to be blue for long.'

'All I want you to do is send Wop up to the corner of 145th Street to look out for a African and warn him not to go back home 'cause the police is looking for him.'

'Umph!' Daddy Haddy grunted. 'How he going to know a African from anybody else?'

'This African don't look like nobody else. He wear a white head rag and a Mother Hubbard dress in four different colors over his pants.'

'What's he done?'

'He ain't done nothing. That's how he dress all the time.'

'I mean done for the police to be looking for him.'

'How I know what he's done,' Pinky whined irritably. 'I just don't want him to get caught yet.'

'Besides which, Wop is high,' Daddy Haddy said. 'He's so high everything looks like four colors to him and he's liable to stop some old woman, thinking she's the African.'

'I thought you was my friend,' Pinky whined.

The old man looked at his purple-dyed face knotting up and gave the matter a second thought.

'Wop!' he shouted.

A coal-black boy, wafer thin, with a long egg-shaped head and slanting eyes, came in from the back room. He wore the white T-shirt, blue jeans and canvas sneakers of any other black boy his age in Harlem. The difference was he had long, straight black hair and there were no whites to his obsidian eyes.

'What you want?' he asked in a gruff, unpleasant voice.

'You tell him,' Daddy Haddy said.

Pinky gave him the picture.

'What if the 'licemens already got him?' Wop asked.

'Then you hightail it away from there.'

'All right,' Wop said. 'Press the skin.'

'I'll see you tonight at Sister Heavenly's,' Pinky promised. 'If I ain't there I'll leave a sawbuck with Uncle Saint.'

'All right, daddy-o,' Wop said. 'Don't make me have to look for you.'

He took a pair of smoked glasses from his blue jeans, fitted them to his head, put both hands into his hip pockets and opened the door with his foot and stepped out into the light.

'Don't bet too much on him,' Daddy Haddy warned.

'I ain't,' Pinky said and followed Wop outside.

They went off in opposite directions.

12

'I know she got it,' Uncle Saint muttered to himself as he dug up the half-pint bottle of nitroglycerin he had buried in the garage. 'Trying to look so innocent that butter wouldn't melt in her mouth. Think she can con old Uncle Saint. Long as I has knowed that double-crossing bitch.'

He muttered to himself as he worked. He was in a driving hurry, but he had to be careful with the stuff. Only five minutes had elapsed since Pinky left the house, but there was no telling when Sister Heavenly would return and he had to have it and be gone by then.

'Don't believe any more she's going down to see Gus off than I believe in Santa Claus,' he muttered. 'The truth ain't in that lying bitch. She's just as soon gone down to sell me to the police for some more protection as she is to have gone to fence the stuff, whatever it is.'

The nitroglycerin was in a green glass bottle filled to the tip and closed securely with a rubber stopper to make it airtight. He had buried it there fifteen years before when she had started thinking about getting rid of him because one of her lovers had objected to having him around.

'She going to get rid of me all right,' he muttered. 'But she going to pay for twenty-five years of service.'

He had wrapped the bottle in a section of rubber inner tube, binding it with a roll of adhesive tape. The ground had hardened during fifteen years and the bottle seemed to have gone in deeper. He dug at first with a spade, measuring the excavation with a wooden folding ruler. He had buried it two feet deep. When he got down to twenty inches he discarded the spade and began digging with a kitchen spatula. But he had to go another ten inches before he scraped the top of the package and it had been slow work with the spatula. Time was passing. Sweat poured from him like showers of rain. He still wore the ancient chauffeur's uniform and cap and he felt like he was inside a coke oven.

But now he worked very carefully, scraping the dirt from around the rotten package with a kitchen spoon.

Both the tape and the rubber had disintegrated and came away from the bottle like rotten cork. He went to extreme pains not to touch the bottle with the spoon.

'Wouldn't that bitch be happy?' he muttered. 'Come home and find me gone. Wouldn't even have to bury me. Just have to fan away the dust.'

Finally the green bottle was uncovered. When he lifted it carefully, inch by inch from its resting place, the top of the rubber stopper fell away, but a thin layer remained covering the nitroglycerin. He held his breath until he straightened it right side up, then he gave a deep sigh.

The loaded shotgun lay on the ground beside him. Holding the bottle of nitroglycerin in his right hand, he reached out with his left hand and picked up the shotgun, then got to his feet like a weight lifter arising with two tons of steel.

He didn't want the nitroglycerin to get in the sunshine so he held it over his heart beneath his coat. Sweat trickled from the band of his chauffeur's cap and stung his eyes as he picked his way across the uneven surface of the dried-up garden like a tightrope walker crossing Niagara Falls.

When he came to the kitchen door, he propped the shotgun against the wall and opened the door with his right hand, making a complete turn to step into the kitchen to be certain of not bumping the edge of the door with the bottle. Inside he eased the door shut and looked about for a place to set the bottle. The kitchen table looked as safe as anywhere. He placed it on the center of the top of the oilcloth cover.

Now he had to go back to the garage for another package containing an electric drill with a 3/8-inch diamond-pointed bit, a 12-inch length of fuse, and two feet of 1/4-inch rubber tube.

The package was wrapped in a plastic doily and hidden inside of an old tire hanging from the rafters. He had gotten hold of these things eleven years after he had buried the nitroglycerin, during his second serious crisis with Sister Heavenly. That one had resulted from Sister Heavenly's conclusion that his hanging around was the chief reason she was so unsuccessful in getting a reliable new lover.

He had only left the kitchen for a few minutes, but during his absence the nanny goat had opened the screen door and entered and was in the act of eating the oilcloth table cover. She had eaten a hole several inches deep, pulling the cover toward the edge as she ate. The bottle of nitroglycerin had been moved more than six inches and was perilously nearing the edge, but it still remained upright.

She was just about to take another bite when he cried, 'Hah!' She paused and looked at him through her cold yellow eyes, then turned back to continue eating.

He jerked up the muzzle of the shotgun and aimed it at her head. 'Git away from there or I'll blow your mother-raping head off,' he said in a dry, dangerous voice.

Sweat broke out in the palms of his hands, but he didn't dare shoot.

Slowly the goat turned her head about and looked at him. The goat didn't know he was scared to shoot. He looked to her like he was going to shoot and she believed him.

Maintaining her dignity, she turned and walked daintily from the kitchen, pushing the door open with her head. And he didn't dare kick her in the rear.

He moved the bottle of nitroglycerin back to the center of the table and placed the other package beside it. Then he sat on his bunk and pulled out his lockbox, unlocked the big padlock, took out his lamp and spoon, and cooked a shot of straight heroin to calm his nerves. His hands were trembling violently and his mouth was working but no sound was issuing forth.

'Ahhhh!' he moaned as he banged himself straight into the vein at the wrist.

He put away his paraphernalia, locked the box and pushed it beneath the bunk, and sat waiting for the drug to take effect.

'How she got it? What I care?' he started muttering again to himself. 'That tricky bitch could steal the cross from under Christ without him ever missing it.' He let out a dry cackling laugh. 'But old Uncle Saint going to out-trick her.'

By then his hands had steadied and his head was filled with a sense of omniscience. He felt as though he could make a *four* by two deuces with the first roll of the dice.

He stood up and opened the package, fitted the bit into the electric drill. Holding it in his right hand, he stepped over to the bunk and retrieved his shotgun with his left hand, and went into Sister Heavenly's bedroom.

He placed the shotgun on the floor in front of the chest of drawers, then unplugged the cord to the bed lamp to plug in the cord to his drill.

The outside lock didn't give him any trouble. He bored a series of holes around it until the flap fell forward. Then he began drilling a hole into the safe about an inch to the right of the dial. The hard safe-steel didn't give like butter; it had almost worn the diamond point from the bit before it broke through.

Now came the ticklish part. He inserted the 1/4-inch tube into the 3/8-inch hole until it struck bottom inside of the door. More than a foot hung out. He cut it off so that only an inch protruded. Then he made a funnel out of a sheet of white writing paper and fitted the small end into the rubber tube.

He went back to the kitchen and picked up the bottle of nitroglycerin and took it into the bedroom. With the end of a safety pin he fished out the thin layer of rubber in the neck of the bottle. With infinite precaution, holding his breath all the while, he emptied the bottle into the funnel, pouring in a thin steady stream. When it was finished he stood the empty bottle on the floor and let out his breath in a long heartfelt sigh.

Now he began feeling elated. He had it made now. He removed the funnel and fitted the fuse into the end of the rubber tube. He started to gather up the drill and bit and the empty bottle, but then he thought, 'What the hell for?'

He picked up his loaded shotgun and started to strike a match. He heard someone at the kitchen door. He swung the shotgun around and cocked both barrels and stepped into the kitchen. But it was only the nanny goat trying to get back inside. In a sudden squall of rage, he reversed the gun and started to club her across the head. But he was struck by a sudden idea.

'You want to come in, come on in,' he muttered and opened the door wide for her to enter.

She stared at him appraisingly, then came inside slowly

and looked around as though she had never been there before.

He chuckled evilly as he returned to the bedroom and struck the match. The goat followed him out of curiosity and was bending her neck to peer around his leg when he lit the fuse. He hadn't seen the goat follow him into the bedroom. The instant the fuse began to burn he wheeled about and started to run. The goat thought he was after her and wheeled about to run also. But she wheeled the wrong way, and he didn't see her until it was too late. He tripped over her and fell face forward toward the floor.

'Goat, beware!' he cried as he was falling.

He had forgotten to uncock the shotgun, which he still held with the butt forward as when he had intended clubbing her in the head.

The butt struck the floor and both barrels went off. The heavy charge of buckshot struck the front of the safe, behind which was one-half pint of nitroglycerin.

Strangely enough, the house disintegrated in only three directions – forward, backward and upward. The front went out across the street, and such items as the bed, tables, chest of drawers and a handpainted enamel chamber pot crashed into the front of the neighbor's house. Sister Heavenly's clothes, some of which dated back to the 1920s, were strewn over the street like a weird coverlet of many colors. The back of the house, along with the kitchen stove, refrigerator, table and chairs, Uncle Saint's bunk and lockbox, crockery and kitchen utensils, went over the back fence into the vacant lot. Afterwards the hoboes who camped out in that section prepared their Mulligan stews in unheard-of luxury for months to come. The corrugated iron garage was moved in one piece a hundred feet away, leaving the Lincoln Continental standing naked in the sunshine. While the top of the house, attic included, along with the old upright piano, Sister Heavenly's throne and souvenir trunk, sailed straight up into the air, and long after the sound of the blast had died away the piano could be heard playing up there all alone.

The outer door of the safe was blown off and went out the back way along with the kitchen stove. The steel inner door was punctured like a blown-up paper sack hit by a hard fist, and the safe proper went out the front. Scraps of hundred-dollar bills floated in the air like green leaves in a hurricane. Later in the day, people were picking them up as far as ten blocks away and some of the neighbors spent all winter trying to fit the pieces together.

But the floor of the house remained intact. It had been swept clean of every loose scrap, every pin and needle, every particle of dust, but the smooth surface of the wood and linoleum went undamaged.

It was hard to determine afterwards which way Uncle Saint and the nanny goat went, but whichever way they went, they went together, because the two assistants from the Medical Examiner's Office of Bronx County couldn't distinguish the bits of goat meat from the bits of Uncle Saint's meat, which was all there was left for them to work on.

The trouble was, Uncle Saint had never blown a safe before. One-fifth of the nitro would have blown the safe without taking him and the house along with it.

13

Sister Heavenly figured there was more than one way to skin a cat. If Pinky didn't show up soon, she was going to trick Uncle Saint into making like he had found the stuff, and force Pinky to show his hand.

Then she heard the shots. Nothing sounds like pistol shots but pistol shots. She had heard too many of them to be mistaken.

She sat up on the park bench across from Riverside Church and screwed her head around.

Next she heard the screaming.

In the back of her old jaded mind she thought cynically that the sequence was logical – when men shot off pistols, women screamed.

But the front of her mind was alive with conjectures. If anyone else got killed the stuff was going to get so hot it couldn't be touched, she thought.

Then she saw two men come quickly from the apartment house. It was quite a distance to see faces distinctly and both wore their hats pulled low over their eyes, but she knew she'd never forget them.

One was a fat man, definitely fat, with a round greasy face but fair-skinned. His shoulders were broad and he looked as though he might be strong. He wore a dark blue Dacron single-breasted suit. He had the other man by the arm and seemed to be pushing him along.

The other man was thin with a too-white, haggard face and dark circles about his eyes. Even from that distance she made him as a junkie. He wore a light gray summer suit and was shaking as though he had a chill.

They turned and walked quickly in the opposite direction. She saw them get into a Buick Special sedan of ordinary battleship-gray. There was nothing about the car to distinguish it from any car of the same make. From that distance she couldn't read the license number, but the plates were Empire State issue.

She figured she might have something valuable; something she could sell. She didn't know how valuable, but she would wait and see.

She didn't have to wait long. The first of the prowl cars showed up in a little over two minutes. Within five minutes the street was filled with police cars and two ambulances.

By then people were hanging out the windows and the customary crowd had collected. The police had formed lines, keeping the front of the house clear.

She figured it was safe to get closer. She saw a figure on a stretcher brought out and shoved quickly into an ambulance. A third attendant had walked alongside it, holding a bottle of plasma. The siren sounded and the ambulance roared off.

She had recognized the face.

'Grave Digger,' she whispered to herself.

A cold tremor ran down her spine.

Coffin Ed came out walking, assisted by two ambulance attendants whom he was trying to shake off. They managed to get him into the second ambulance and it drove off.

Sister Heavenly was backing off to leave when she heard

someone say, 'There's another one, an African with his throat cut.'

She backed away fast. As she was leaving she saw two heavy black sedans filled with plainclothesmen from homicide pull up. She figured what she had was too damn valuable to sell. It was valuable enough to get her own throat cut.

She walked quickly up the hill to Broadway, looking for a taxicab. She was so disconcerted she forgot to raise her parasol to protect her complexion from the sunshine.

After she had hailed a taxi, got inside and felt it moving, she began to feel secure again. But she knew she had to get rid of Uncle Saint and the red-hot Lincoln, or she was going to find herself up a creek.

When she arrived on the street where she had left her house, she found it filled with fire trucks, police cars, ambulances, and thinly dressed people, for the most part Italians with a sprinkling of Negroes, cooking in the noonday heat, risking sunstroke to satisfy their morbid curiosity.

The whole city was running amok, she thought, from the sugar side to the shabby side.

As the taxi drew nearer, she craned her neck, looking for her house. She didn't see it. From the window of the taxi, looking over the heads of the crowd, she couldn't see the floor that remained. It looked to her as though the entire house had disappeared. The only thing she could see was the Lincoln, standing out like a red thumb in the bright sunshine.

She stopped the taxi before it got too close to the police lines and hailed a passerby.

'What happened down the street?'

'Explosion!' the bareheaded Italian-looking worker gasped, breathing hard as though he couldn't get enough of the hot dusty air into his lungs. 'Blew the house up. Killed the old couple who lived there. Saint Heavenly they were called. No trace of 'em. Musta had a still.'

He didn't pause to see her reaction. He was scrabbling around, like scores of others, picking up scraps of paper.

Well now, ain't that just too beautiful for words? she thought. Then she asked the taxi driver, 'See what that is they're picking up.'

He got out and asked a youth to see a sample. It was the

corner of a hundred-dollar bill. He brought it back to show to Sister Heavenly. The youth followed him suspiciously.

'Piece of a C-note,' he said. 'They must have been making counterfeit.'

'That tears it,' Sister Heavenly said.

The two of them stood staring at her.

'Give it back to him and let him go,' she said.

She knew immediately that Uncle Saint had tried to blow her safe. It didn't surprise her. He must have used an atom bomb, she thought. She wished he had picked a better time for the caper.

The taxi driver climbed back into his seat and looked at her with growing suspicion. 'Ain't that the house where you wanted to go?'

'Don't talk foolish, man,' she snapped. 'You see I can't go there 'cause the house ain't there no more.'

'Don't you wanna talk to the cops?' he persisted.

'I just want you to turn around and drive me back to White Plains Road and put me out by the playground.'

At that hour the treeless playground was deserted. The sandpits baked in the sunshine and heat radiated from the iron slides. The slatted bench on which Sister Heavenly sat burned stripes up and down her backsides. But she didn't notice it.

She took out her pipe and filled it with the finely ground stems of marijuana from an oilskin pouch and lit it with an old gold-initialed pipe lighter. Then she opened her black-and-white striped parasol and holding it over her head with her left hand, she held the pipe in her right hand and sucked the sweet pungent marijuana smoke deep into her lungs.

Sister Heavenly was a fatalist. If she had ever read *The Rubáiyát of Omar Khayyám*, she might have been thinking of the lines:

> The moving finger writes,
> And having writ moves on;
> Nor all your piety nor wit
> Nor all your tears
> Shall cancel half a line of it . . .

But instead she was thinking, Well, I'm back on my bare ass where I started, but I ain't yet flat on my back.

It was life that had taught Sister Heavenly not to cry. A crying whore was a liability; and she had started as a whore. At fifteen she had run away from the sharecropper's shack her family had called home, with a pimp to be a whore because she was too cute and too lazy to hoe the corn and chop the cotton. He had told her that what she had to sell would find buyers when cotton and corn were a drug on the market. The memory brought a smile. He was a half-ass pimp but he was sweet, she thought. But in the end he had kicked her out like the others had afterwards with nothing but the clothes she had on her back.

Then her thoughts turned cynical: Even cotton got rotten with age and corn got too wormy to shuck.

Anyway, after she'd got onto the faith healing pitch, she had lived high on the hog, which meant she could eat pork chops and pork roasts instead of pig's feet and chitterlings. It had been the other way around after that; she had been the ruler of the roost and had kicked her lovers out when she got tired of them.

She knocked out her pipe and put it away. The ocher-colored pupils of her eyes had become distended with a marbleized effect and pink splotches had formed beneath her leathery skin.

As she walked up White Plains Road the drab-colored buildings took on blinding bright hues in the sunshine. She hadn't been that high in more than twenty years. Her feet seemed to glide through the air, but she was still in full command of her mind.

She began to suspect she had cased the whole caper wrong from the very beginning. She had figured it as a shipment of H, but maybe it wasn't that at all.

It couldn't be a mother-raping treasure map, she thought with exasperation. That old con game went out when airplanes came in.

Or could it? another part of her mind asked. Could it be that some gang had come up with some treasure somewhere and had made a map of its whereabouts? But what the hell kind of treasure? And how the hell would the map get into the hands of a square like Gus, a simple-minded apartment house janitor?

The weed jag made her thoughts dance like jitterbugs. She turned into a supermarket drugstore and ordered black coffee.

She didn't notice the man next to her until he spoke. 'Are you a model, may I ask?'

She flicked him an absent-minded glance. He looked like a salesman, a house-to-house canvasser type.

'No, I'm one of the devil's mistresses,' she said nastily.

The man reddened. 'Excuse me, I thought maybe you were a model for some advertising agency.' He retired behind a newspaper.

It was the afternoon *Journal American* and she saw the streamer on the page turned toward her:

Two Harlem Detectives Suspended for Brutality

A column was devoted to the story. To one side the pictures of Grave Digger and Coffin Ed looked like pictures of a couple of Harlem muggers taken from the rogues' gallery.

She read as much of the story as she could before the man folded the paper.

So they killed Jake, she thought. In front of Riverside Church.

That must have been when Pinky put in the false fire alarm.

Her thoughts churned furiously. She tried to remember everything Pinky had said, how he had looked and acted. A pattern was beginning to take shape, but the answer eluded her.

Suddenly she jumped to her feet. Her table mate drew back in alarm. But she merely paid her bill and rushed outside and started walking rapidly to the nearest taxi stand.

She looked at her locket-watch when she had paid off the taxi driver in front of Riverside Church. It read 3:37.

She looked up and down the street. The prowl cars had gone and there was no sign left of the police unless it was the black sedan parked down the street from the entrance to the apartment.

She had a sinking sensation in her stomach as the thought occurred to her that it might already be too late.

She opened her parasol and holding it in her left hand and her heavy black beaded bag on her right arm, took hold of her skirt on the right side and lifting it slightly, sailed down the street and turned into the apartment house.

A big stolid-looking white cop was on guard at the door. He did a double take.

'Hey, whoa there, ma'am,' he said, stopping her. 'You can't go in here.'

On second thought he added, 'Unless you live here.'

'Why not?' she countered. 'Is it quarantined?'

'What do you want in here, if you don't live here?' he reiterated.

'I'm taking up subscriptions for the colored peoples' Old Folks Home,' she said blandly.

But he was a conscientious cop. 'Do you have a license?' he demanded. 'Or at least any identification or something to show who you are?'

She arched her eyebrows. 'Do I need any? After all, I'm a sponsor.'

'Well, you'll have to come back later, I'm afraid. You see, the police are conducting a search in there right now and they don't want any strangers in the house.'

'A search!' she exclaimed, giving the impression of horrified shock. 'For a body buried in the basement?'

The cop grinned. She reminded him of a character out of a stage play he had seen once.

'Well, not exactly a body, but a buried treasure,' he said.

'My land!' she said. 'What's the world coming to?'

His grin widened. 'Ain't it awful?'

She started to turn away. 'Well, if they find it, don't forget the old colored people,' she said.

He laughed out loud. 'Never!' he said.

She went into the next-door apartment house and took up a station in the foyer from which she could watch the entrance next door. Passing tenants looked at her curiously, but she paid them no attention.

One thing was for sure, she was thinking; if it was there,

the police would find it. But on the other hand, why hadn't the two gunmen found it, since they would know exactly what they were looking for?

Her head swam with doubts.

I wish to Jesus Christ I knew what the hell I was looking for, she thought.

She saw a small panel truck pull up before the house next door. It had the letters S.P.C.A. painted on the sides.

Now what the hell is this? she thought.

She saw two men wearing heavy leather gloves and long white dusters alight from the compartment and enter the house.

A few minutes later they returned, leading Pinky's dog Sheba by a heavy chain leash.

And all of a sudden it exploded in her head. All this goddamn time wasted! she thought disgustedly. And there it was all the time.

It fitted like white on rice.

She watched the attendants put the dog into the body of the S.P.C.A. truck and drive away. She had to fight back the impulse to rush out and call the bitch by name and claim her. But she knew she'd wind up in the pokey and they'd still have the dog. It was like watching a friend go down in the middle of the sea, she thought. You could feel for him but you couldn't reach him.

She started racking her memory trying to figure out what S.P.C.A. stood for. It couldn't be *Special Police for Collaring Animals*. That didn't make any sense. What would they have special police to collar animals for when any policeman could do it?

Then suddenly she remembered: *Society for the Prevention of Cruelty to Animals*. Where she had heard about it she didn't know, but there it was.

She left her station and walked over to Broadway and entered the first bar. It took a little time to find the telephone number of the Manhattan branch of S.P.C.A.

A woman's pleasant, impersonal voice answered her call.

'I've heard you sell stray dogs,' Sister Heavenly said. 'I'd like to buy a dog.'

'We don't actually sell the stray dogs that are brought in

to us,' the woman explained. 'We try to find congenial homes for them where they will fit in with the families, and we ask for a donation of two dollars to help carry on the work of the foundation.'

'Well, that's all right,' Sister Heavenly said. 'I can spare two dollars. Have you got any dogs on hand?'

'Well, yes, but is there any particular kind of dog you would like?'

'I want a big dog. A dog as big as a lion,' Sister Heavenly said.

'We seldom have dogs that size,' the woman said doubtfully. 'And we are very particular about whom we let take them. Could you give me an idea of your reasons for wanting a dog that size?'

'It's like this,' Sister Heavenly said. 'I have a roadhouse in New Jersey. It's not far from Hoboken. And to be frank with you, it's not the most law-abiding place you can find. But there's a big fenced-in yard for the dog to run. And of course there're always plenty of bones, not to mention meat, for him to eat.'

'I see. You need it for a watchdog?'

'Yes. And he can't be too big. Our last watchdog was fairly big. He was a German dog. But prowlers killed him.'

'I see. You say *him*. Does it make any difference if the dog is female?'

'That's all the better. As long as she's big.'

'It so happens that you have called at an opportune time,' the pleasant-voiced woman said. 'There might be a large female dog available within a few days. Would you mind giving me your name and address?'

'A few days!' Sister Heavenly exclaimed, filling her voice with dismay. 'I thought I could get one today. I'm leaving tomorrow on two weeks' vacation and I want to leave the dog there with the caretaker while I'm gone.'

'Oh, that's not possible, you see we have to check ... But ... Won't you hold on for a moment, perhaps ...'

Sister Heavenly held on.

After a time the pleasant voice said, 'Hello, are you there?'

'Yes, I'm still here.'

'Well, it's quite likely that you may get your big dog today just as you wish. It's highly irregular of course, but one has just come in and – if you will call me back an hour from now we will give you a definite answer. Okay?'

'Okay,' Sister Heavenly said and hung up.

She looked at her watch. It read 4:03.

She telephoned back at exactly 5 o'clock.

The pleasant-voiced woman said she was so sorry, but a detective had come and had taken the dog away.

Sister Heavenly knew just how people felt when they said 'Doggone!'

14

Coffin Ed was in a crying rage, caught up in an impotent self-tormenting fury that gave to his slightly disfigured face a look of ineffable danger.

'These miserable mother-raping crumbs,' he grated through clenched teeth. 'These sonofabitching rathole snakeshit hopped-up sons of syphilitic whores with their doctored rods trying to play tough by shooting an unarmed man in the back. But they ain't seen nothing yet.'

He was talking to himself.

There was an electric clock on the wall at the end of the dazzling white hospital corridor. It read 2:26.

He thought bitterly, Yeah, they suspended us for punching a mother-raping pusher in the guts and ain't three hours passed before some drugged-up killer has got Digger.

Tears were seeping from his eyes and catching in the fine scar ridges between the patches of grafted skin on his face as though his very skin was crying.

Nurses and interns passing down the corridor gave him a wide berth.

What made it all the worse, he felt a sense of guilt. If I hadn't been so mother-raping cute and had listened to Digger and just let it alone until the guys from homicide came he might not have got it, he thought.

Grave Digger lay on the operating table beyond the closed white door. Death wasn't two feet off. He needed blood and they had used the one lone pint of his type blood they had in store. It wasn't enough. The only other place they had it was in the Red Cross blood bank in Brooklyn. A police car led by two motorcycle cops opening up the city traffic was bringing it as fast as anything could possibly move in the big congested town. But time was rapidly running ut.

Coffin Ed had just been told he didn't have the type of blood Grave Digger needed.

Now I can't even do this for him, he thought. But one thing is for sure, if he goes down, he ain't going alone.

He had a lump on the side of his head, back of the left ear, as big as a goose egg, and his head seemed split in all directions by a blinding headache that began behind the eyes. The doctors had said he had concussion and had tried to put him to bed. But he had fought them off with a raving scarcely controlled violence and they had gotten the hell away from him.

It was a high-class, well-equipped hospital, the nearest to the scene of the shooting; and he knew if Grave Digger could be saved, they would save him there. But that did nothing to assuage his self-condemning rage.

Down at the end of the corridor he saw his and Grave Digger's wife ascending the head of the stairs. He turned and fled through the first doorway. He found himself in a room for minor surgery. The lights were off and it was temporarily out of use.

He couldn't bear to face Grave Digger's wife and he didn't want to see his own. His daughter was in a summer camp in the Catskills. There was no one to hinder him. Mentally, he thanked someone for this small favor.

The wives were not permitted in the operating room. They stood outside the door in the corridor, their brown faces set like graven images. From time to time Grave Digger's wife touched a handkerchief to her eyes. Neither of them spoke.

Coffin Ed looked for a way to get out. There was a connecting door at the end of the room but it was locked. He raised the bottom half of the frosted-glass window. It opened onto a fire escape. He went outside. A group of medical students in an adjoining building stopped to watch him. He didn't notice them. He went down one story and the swing ladder dropped to the paved driveway that led to the emergency entrance at the rear.

He went out to the street and walked bareheaded in the blinding midday sunshine to where his car was parked on Riverside Drive. Heat shimmered before his vision, distorting his perspective. His head ached like rheumatic fever of the brain.

Half an hour later he pulled into the driveway of his house in Astoria, Long Island. How he managed to get there he never knew.

He had been given a sedative at the hospital to take home. The label on the bottle read: *One teaspoonful every hour.* He tossed it into the trash can outside the kitchen door and let himself into the kitchen.

He put the Silex coffee maker on the gas stove, with enough coffee in it to make mud. While waiting for it to boil he stripped off his clothes and piled them on the chair beside the bed. In the bathroom medicine cabinet he found a bottle of Benzedrine tablets. He took two and drank water from the washbowl faucet in his cupped hand. He heard the coffee maker boiling and went into the kitchen and turned off the fire.

After that he took a shower, turning it from lukewarm to as cold as he could bear. He held his breath and his teeth chattered as the cold needles bit into his skin. His head felt as though sheets of lightning were going off in his brain, but the lethargy left his limbs.

He toweled and went into the bedroom and put on jockey shorts, nylon socks, lightweight black shoes with rubber soles, the pants to his brand-new dark gray summer suit, and a blue oxford cloth shirt with a button-down collar. He omitted the tie. He didn't want anything to be in his way when he reached for the handle of his revolver.

His shoulder holster hung from a hook inside the door of the clothes closet. The special-made, long-barreled, nickel-plated .38-caliber revolver, that had shot its way to fame in Harlem, was in the holster. He took it out, spun the chamber, rapidly ejecting the five brass-jacketed cartridges, and quickly cleaned and oiled it. Then he reloaded it, putting a U.S. army tracer bullet into the last loaded chamber and leaving the one under the trigger empty so there wouldn't be an accident in case he had to club some joker across the head with the butt.

He placed the revolver on the bed and took down the holster. From the shelf in the closet he took a can of seal fat and smeared a thick coating on the inside of the holster. He wiped the excess off with a clean handkerchief, tossed the handkerchief into the soiled-clothes hamper, and strapped on the shoulder sling. When he had cradled the revolver, he strapped a stopwatch to his left wrist.

He chose a knockout sap from the collection in his dresser drawer. It was made of plaited cowhide covering a banana-shaped hunk of soft solder, with a whalebone handle. He stuck this into a hip pocket made especially for that purpose.

He slipped a Boy Scout knife into his left pants pocket. As an afterthought he stuck a thin flat hunting knife with a grooved hard-rubber handle, sheathed in soft pigskin, inside the back of his pants alongside his spinal column, and snapped the sheath to his belt. Not that he thought he would need it, but he didn't want to overlook anything that might keep him living until his job was done.

I'd drink some *everlasting* water if I knew where some was at, he thought grimly.

Then he put on his coat. He had chosen that suit because the coat was bigger than any of his others and it had been tailor-made to accommodate his shoulder sling.

He dropped a new box of cartridges into the leather-lined pocket on the left side, then put a handful of cartridges with tracer bullets into the leather-lined pocket on his right side.

He went into the kitchen and drank two cups of scalding hot, mud-thick coffee. It recoiled in his empty stomach like cold water on a hot stove, but stayed down. The Benzedrine had killed his appetite and left a dry brackish taste in his mouth. He scarcely noticed it.

Just as he was about to leave the house the telephone rang. For a moment he debated whether to ignore it, then went back into the bedroom and picked up the receiver.

'Johnson,' he said.

'This is Captain Brice,' the voice said from the other end. 'Homicide wants you to get in touch – Lieutenant Walsh. And keep out of this. Stay home. Let the men with the shields have it. If you get in any deeper I'm not going to be able to help you.' After a pause he added, 'Nobody is.'

'Yes sir,' Coffin Ed said. 'Lieutenant Walsh.'

'They got the blood from Brooklyn, in case you haven't heard,' the captain added.

Coffin Ed held on to the receiver, but he didn't have the nerve to ask.

'He's still hanging on,' Captain Brice said, as though reading his thought.

'Yes sir,' Coffin Ed said.

The phone began to ring again as soon as he cradled the receiver. He picked it up again.

'Johnson.'

'Ed, this is Lieutenant Anderson.'

'How goes it, Lieutenant?'

'I called to ask you.'

'He's still in there fighting,' Coffin Ed said.

'I'm going over there now,' Anderson said.

'I ain't any use. He don't know anybody yet.'

'Right. I'll wait 'til it's time.' A pause, then, 'Keep out of this, Ed. I know how you feel, but keep out of this. You don't have any authority now and anything you do is going to make it worse.'

'Yes sir.'

'What?' Anderson was startled. Coffin Ed had never said *yes sir* to him before.

But Coffin Ed had hung up.

He telephoned the West Side homicide bureau and asked for Lieutenant Walsh.

'Who's calling?'

'Just tell him Ed Johnson.'

After a while a deliberate, scholarly-sounding voice came on.

'Johnson, I'd like to know what you think about this.'

'Up until we found the African's corpse, I didn't think anything about it. We couldn't figure that from any angle. Then when they got Digger, that changed the story. There must have been two—'

'We know that,' Lieutenant Walsh cut him off. 'Two

professional gunmen. We know they were after something. The whole place is being gone over by a crew from the safe and loft squad. But they haven't found anything, or even anything to indicate what they're looking for. What do you think it might be? If we knew that, we might know where to start.'

'I think it might be H; a shipment of H that's taken off.'

'We thought of that. The narcotics squad is working on it. But a shipment of heroin, even as pure as it comes, large enough to induce murder is not easy to hide. A really valuable shipment, considering all the wrappings it would need, would run to about the size of a football. By this time anything that size would have been found by the crew at work on it.'

'It doesn't have to be a shipment. It can be a key.'

'A key. I hadn't thought of that; I don't know about the searchers. Just a key to a plant somewhere. Maybe you're right. I'll pass the suggestion on. Anyway, they're going to keep after it until they're satisfied there's nothing there.'

'If it isn't that I don't know what it is.'

'Right. By the way, what do you think has happened to the janitor and his wife? Gus and Ginny Harris, they are called. And they had a helper, an ex-pug called Pinky.'

'Gus and Ginny were supposed to sail on the *Queen Mary* today and Pinky's on the lam.'

'They had booked passage but they didn't sail. All three of them have just dropped out of sight.'

'They can't stay hidden forever.'

'They can if they're at the bottom of the river.'

Coffin Ed waited. He had said all he had to say.

'That's all for the time, Johnson. Stick around. We might want to get in touch with you again. And Johnson—'

'Yes sir.'

'Keep out of this. Let us handle it. Okay?'

'Yes, sir.'

Coffin Ed went into the kitchen and drank a glass of water from the refrigerator bottle. His throat felt bone dry.

Then he went into the garage and put a suit of paint-smeared coveralls into a large canvas bag left behind by the painters who had worked on his house. He put the bag into the back of his car and got in and drove down the street to Grave Digger's house.

He knew the doors would be locked so he walked around to the back and jimmied the kitchen window. His body had a light weightlessness that put an edge on his reflexes, making them a shade too quick. He'd have to be careful, he cautioned himself. He'd kill someone before he knew it.

Two of the neighborhood children, a little boy and girl, stopped playing in the yard next door and looked at him, accusingly.

'You're breaking into Mister Jones's house,' the little boy piped up, then shouted at the top of his voice, 'Mama, there's a burglar breaking into Mister Jones's house.'

A woman came quickly from the back door of the next-door house just as Coffin Ed got one leg over the window ledge.

He nodded toward her and she smiled. They were all colored people on that street and the grown-ups knew one another; but the children seldom got sight of the detectives, who were sleeping most of the day.

'That's just Mister Jones's partner,' she told the children. 'Mister Jones has been hurt.' She figured that explained it.

Coffin Ed closed and locked the window and went into the bedroom and opened the clothes closet. A long-barreled nickelplated .38-caliber revolver identical with his own was cradled in a holster hanging from an identical hook inside the door. He slipped it from the holster, spun the cylinder to make certain it was loaded, then stuck the barrel down inside the waistband of his trousers with the handle angled toward the left side.

'Almost ready,' he said out loud, and inside of his splitting head he felt the tension mount.

He went into the living room, searched about in the writing desk, and scribbled on a sheet of stationery: STELLA, *I've taken Digger's gun.* ED.

He brought it back and propped it on top of the dressing table.

He was turning away to leave when a sudden thought struck him. He stepped over to the night table and picked up the phone and dialed homicide again.

When he got Lieutenant Walsh, he asked, 'What happened to the janitor's dog?'

'Ah yes, she was turned over to the S.P.C.A. Why?'

'I just remembered that it was hurt and I wondered if anybody was taking care of it.'

'That's what I forgot to ask,' Lieutenant Walsh said. 'Do you happen to know how she got that wound in the head?'

'We saw the African take her down toward the river early this morning and then come back without her. That was early this morning – a little after five. We didn't have any reason to be suspicious, so we didn't question him. When we got back to the place around one o'clock she was lying in front of the side gate with that hole in her head.'

'That clears up that,' Walsh said. 'How's Jones coming on?'

'He's still breathing – the last I heard.'

'Right,' Walsh said.

They both hung up at the same instant.

Coffin Ed telephoned the hospital. He identified himself.

'I'm calling to find out how is Detective Jones.'

'His condition is grave,' the impersonal woman's voice replied.

Pain flashed in Coffin Ed's head.

'I know that,' he said through clenched teeth, trying to control his unreasonable rage. 'Is it any graver?'

The impersonal voice thawed slightly. 'He has been placed in an oxygen tent and has passed into a coma. We are doing all we can for him.'

'I know that,' Coffin Ed said. 'Thank you.'

He hung up and went outside through the front door, locking it on the snap latch, and got into his Plymouth sedan.

He stopped in the neighborhood pharmacy to get four and a half pounds of sugar of milk. The pharmacist had only half the amount in supply, so Coffin Ed told him to fill it out with quinine.

The pharmacist stared at him goggle-eyed, torn between suspicion and amazement.

'It's for a gag,' Coffin Ed said. 'I'm playing a joke on a friend.'

'Oh,' the pharmacist said, relaxing, then added with a grin, 'As a matter of fact, this mixture is good for a cold.'

Coffin Ed had him wrap it securely and seal all the seams with Scotch tape.

From there he drove into Brooklyn and stopped in a sporting goods store. He bought a square yard of rubberized silk, in which he carefully wrapped the package from the pharmacy. The clerk assisted. They sealed the seams with rubber cement.

'That'll keep it dry on the bottom of the sea,' the clerk said proudly.

'That's what I want,' Coffin Ed said.

He bought a small blue canvas utility bag and put the package inside of it. Then he bought a pair of dark green goggles and a soft woolen Scotch beret large enough so that it wouldn't press too hard on the knot on his head.

On first glance he looked like a beatnik escaped from Greenwich Village. But that impression was quickly dispelled by the bulge beneath his breast pocket and the frightening tic in his dangerous-looking face.

'Good luck, sir,' the clerk said doubtfully.

'I'll need it,' Coffin Ed said.

15

It was one of those big, old-fashioned, four-story houses on 139th Street between Seventh and Eighth avenues. It had a limestone façade flanked by Ionic columns and a hand-carved mahogany door with crystal glass panels which had been enameled black. There was a carriage entrance on one side. The carriage house had been converted into a garage.

Years back, when the street had been inhabited by the nouveau riche, it had claimed pretensions. Then during the 1920s a smart colored real estate promoter filled the old mansions with socially ambitious Negro professionals, and it became known throughout the length and breadth of Harlem as 'Strivers' Row'.

But during the depression of the 1930s, hard times came upon the strivers like a storm of locusts and the street went rapidly down from sugar to shucks. The houses were first partitioned into flats, then the flats were divided into rooms. Then the madams took over and filled the rooms with prostitutes.

Coffin Ed parked his Plymouth in front of the house, got out and opened the back door. He reached inside and grasped the handle to a chain and pulled out the oversize dog. She was muzzled again but the wound on her head had been neatly bandaged and she looked more respectable.

He led her around the side of the house, past the carriage entrance, and rang the back door bell.

The kitchen door was wide open. Only the heavy screen outer door was locked. Coffin Ed watched a fat kimono-clad woman waddle in his direction.

She peered through the screen and said, 'My God, it's Coffin Ed.'

She unlocked the door and opened it for him to enter, then drew back quickly at sight of the dog. 'What's that thing?'

'It's a dog.'

Her eyebrows went up. She had hennaed hair almost the same shade as her eyes, and wrinkled skin which was heavily coated with Max Factor pancake makeup and copper-red suntan powder. She was called Red Marie.

'It won't bite, will it?' she asked. Her voice sounded as though she had something down her throat, and her thickly painted, greasy red lips curled and popped, exposing gold teeth smeared with lipstick.

'It can't bite,' he said, pushing into the kitchen.

It was a modern electrical kitchen. Everything was spotlessly clean and dazzling white. A young whore, still active and competing, dreams of diamonds and furs. But an old whore, no longer active and competing, whether she's gone down to a toothless hag or up to a rich landprop, dreams of a kitchen like this. It contained every kind of electrical gadget imaginable, including a big white enamel electric clock over the stove.

Coffin Ed looked at the clock. It read 4:23. Time was getting short.

On a small white enamel table to one side a white enamel radio stood on top of a blond oak television set. A television program was showing but the sound was turned off.

A big slouchy man with short kinky red hair growing in burs about a bald spot sat in a tubular stainless-steel chair with his elbows propped on top of a large white enamel kitchen table.

'We was just listening to the radio,' he said. 'It said Digger has been shot up and you both is off the force.'

He sounded happy about it; but not happy enough to get his teeth knocked out.

Coffin Ed stood in the center of the floor, holding the dog loosely by the chain.

'Listen,' he said. 'You can make it light on yourselves. I ain't got much time. Where can I find Pinky?' His voice sounded forced, as though he had a stricture in his throat, and the tic was running away.

The man glanced at him, then looked back at the bottle of whiskey before him on the table and reaching out, touched it with the fingertips of both hands.

He had a broad flat face, rough reddish skin and little reddish eyes from which tears leaked continuously. He was called Red Johnny. He might have been related to Pinky.

He wore a white silk shirt open at the throat, green-and-red checked suspenders, tan gabardine pants, white-and-tan wing-tipped shoes, and the usual heavy gold jewelry denoting a successful pimp: gold ring with a huge milky stone of unknown origin, gold ring with three-quarter-carat yellow diamond, and a gold lodge ring with the outline of an owl with two ruby eyes.

He crossed glances with Red Marie, standing to the left and behind Coffin Ed, then he spread his thick-fingered hands and looked at the gun bulge on Coffin Ed's shoulder.

'We're clean,' he muttered. 'We keeps squared off with the captain and you ain't rightly got no authority no more.'

'We don't even know nobody called Pinky,' Red Marie spoke up.

'All you're doing is asking for trouble,' Coffin Ed said. His jaw muscles rippled beneath the tic as he tried to control his rage. 'You ain't got one mother-raping reason on earth to cover for Pinky. It's just that I'm the law and you resent me. Now you can show it. But you're making a mistake.'

'What mistake?' Red Johnny asked. He could barely keep the insolence from his voice.

'You're over fifty,' Coffin Ed said. 'You spent thirteen years in stir on a second-degree murder rap. Now you're doing all right. You got this house through a lucky hit on the numbers and you set this ex-hustler up as a madam. I know you both. She did her bit too in stir for stabbing a teen-age whore not quite to death. Then when she got back on the bricks she streetwalked for a chickenshit pimp called Dandy who got his throat cut by a square for playing around with the deck in a five-and-ten-cent blackjack game. Now you're both going great. Times are good. Tricks are walking. The streets are full of lains. Squares everywhere. The money's rolling in. You're paying off the man. You're sitting pretty. But you're making one mistake.'

'You said that before. What mistake?'

Coffin Ed let the handle to the dog chain drop to the floor. 'I ain't playing,' he said.

Red Johnny folded his arms and leaned back in his chair. His gaze dropped slightly to the impression of the gun stick in Coffin Ed's belt.

'Course you ain't rightly got no authority to come in here and ast me no questions 'bout nobody,' he began, and from across the table Red Marie warned, 'Don't push him, Johnny.'

'I ain't pushing him and I ain't going to let him push me neither. I done already told him I don't know no Pinky and he can—'

He never got to say what Coffin Ed could do. One whole side of Coffin Ed's face convulsed in a muscular spasm as his right hand flashed toward his hip. Red Johnny moved out of animal reflex; his head jerked about, eyes following the movement of Coffin Ed's hand; his left foot braced against the floor; his left arm flew up instinctively to ward off the blow. He didn't see the motion of Coffin Ed's left hand at all as it came from the front with Grave Digger's pistol and smashed the barrel in a backhanded swing straight across his loose-lipped mouth.

The whole front line of Red Johnny's teeth caved into his mouth, two of the bottom teeth flew out sidewise like corn popping, and Red Johnny spun over backward in the tubular chair. The back of his head hit the linoleum floor with a dull thud while at the same instant his feet flew upward and kicked the bottom of the enamel table. The whiskey bottle rose six inches in the air and shattered the drinking glass when it came down.

The abrupt ear-shattering din panicked the dog. She leapt over Red Johnny's face, making for the inner door. Red Johnny thought she was leaping for his throat and tried to scream. Nothing came out but a spray of blood and he choked on his teeth.

Coffin Ed didn't see it. He had swung back to take a left-handed bead on Red Marie's stomach, and had frozen her in midstride, her right hand waving out in front, left hand floating out behind, her big sloppy fat body poised on the ball of her right foot like a rip-roarious burlesque of a ballerina executing a movement in *Swan Lake*.

But no one thought it was funny. Her face was distorted with terror and Coffin Ed looked like a homicidal maniac.

The chair scraped as Red Johnny rolled over, clawing at his throat, making choking sounds.

The inside of Coffin Ed's head was one great flaming-red blast of pain, through which sound trickled like curses. From somewhere came the thought that Red Johnny was trying to draw a gun. He wheeled back and kicked Red Johnny on the base of the jaw.

'Ugh!' Red Johnny grunted and fainted.

The dog pushed open the inner door and ran down the hall, her chain clanking behind her.

Red Marie grabbed at the table edge for support; her fingers slipped off and she fell to the floor with a crash.

From the front of the house came the sound of women screaming.

Coffin Ed stood in the center of the floor with the long-barreled nickel-plated pistol in one hand and the sap in the other, looking as dazed as though he had just emerged from a shock treatment for insanity.

On the television screen three shrunken lunatics, arms about one another's shoulders, were dancing frantically back and forth, eyes rolling and lips flapping but no sound coming out.

Coffin Ed's head suddenly cleared; only a shrill, almost imperceptible whistling in both ears still remained.

He pocketed the sap, stuck the pistol back into his belt, and reached down and rolled Red Johnny over onto his stomach.

'Lawd, don't kill him,' Red Marie wailed. 'I'll talk.'

'Give me a tablespoon and shut up,' Coffin Ed grated. 'He'll do his own mother-raping talking.'

She crawled on all fours around the table and got a spoon from the drawer.

'Bring it here,' Coffin Ed said, kneeling beside Red Johnny and lifting his head.

Red Johnny had swallowed his tongue. Coffin Ed stuck the spoon down Red Johnny's throat and kept levering until he got enough tongue out so he could reach in with his other hand and grab hold of the tip. The tongue was so slippery with blood it took half a dozen tries before he got hold of the tip and yanked it back into position. Blood gushed over his hands onto the floor and four broken teeth fell out.

'Here, you hold his tongue down until he gets his breath,' he ordered Red Marie and made her take the handle of the spoon.

He got up and went to the sink and washed the blood from his hands with cold water from the tap, dried them on a kitchen towel. There was a small bloodstain on the cuff of his blue shirt, but he didn't bother it.

He came back and stood over the two people on the floor. 'I'm going to ask some questions—'

'I'll answer 'em,' Marie said.

'Let him answer them. When the answer is yes, nod your head. You hear me?'

Red Johnny's head nodded carefully.

'When the answer is no, shake your head. And don't make any more mistakes.'

Again Red Johnny nodded.

'It hurts him,' Red Marie said.

'I want it to hurt him,' Coffin Ed said. 'You run a shooting gallery in here?'

Red Johnny nodded.

'It ain't really no regular shooting gallery,' Red Marie said defensively. 'It's just we have some jags here sometimes, just folks with a chicken habit—'

'And pushers,' Coffin Ed cut in.

Red Johnny shook his head.

'If I catch you lying—'

'I hope God may kill me,' Red Marie blurted. 'We don't let no pushers come in here. It's just parties we has and folks bring their own stuff. We gets a few skinpoppers but the H they has ain't even strong enough to be habit-forming. Ain't none of 'em real addicts. Most of 'em just blows weed. Just to get a kick. That ain't our racket. We just sells poontang here.'

'Pinky is an addict.'

'Yes, but—'

'Let him answer.'

Red Johnny nodded.

Coffin Ed stepped back from the pool of blood that was reaching toward his feet.

'Lawd be my secret judge, he don't come here for it,' Red Marie said. 'He don't come for the jags neither. He just buys pussy.'

'Has he got any particular choice?'

'He too ugly to score a home here; he's like Jesus, he loves 'em all.'

'Was he here today?'

Red Johnny shook his head.

'Last night?'

Again Red Johnny shook his head.

'Know where he lives?'

The answer was the same.

'You've been doing so much talking; talk some now,' Coffin Ed said to Marie.

'We don't know nothing 'bout Pinky, I swear 'fore God; he just come here to see the girls and I wish to heaven he had picked on somebody else for that; I don't need his money and I can't stand his looks.'

'Where does he hang out?'

'Hang out?' She started to parry, but one glance at Coffin Ed's face loosened her tongue so that she began to stammer. 'Kid Blackie's gym is all I know. I heered him say once he'd just come from there. You know somewheres else, Johnny?'

Red Johnny shook his head.

'All right,' Coffin Ed said. 'That's Pinky's dog I got. I'm gonna take it through this house and let it sniff around. If I find out you're lying—'

'As God be my benefactor and protector and my haven—' Marie began, but Coffin Ed cut her off.

'You're making me puke. How is it that all you worn-out whores get so chummy with God?'

'It ain't really Him,' Marie said solemnly. 'It's Jesus.'

He couldn't tell whether she was in earnest or not. He pushed open the door and went toward the front hall and called the dog.

'She's here!' a woman's voice replied.

He went up the front stairs to the second floor and traced the voice to an open bedroom at the rear. A brownskin whore in a negligee was stuffing cream chocolates into the side of the dog's mouth through the muzzle. The bitch loved it.

Coffin Ed took the chain leash and led the dog. He didn't know exactly what he was looking for, but he was playing out a hunch. Nothing came of it but some curses from some whores working at their trade.

'Gawddammmm!' one of the girls said disgustedly when her white customer became suddenly deflated at sight of the big colored man and monstrous dog poking into the room. 'As long as it took to get this slow-John started—'

Upon seeing a pay telephone in the front hall, Coffin Ed stopped and telephoned the hospital.

The answer was the same.

Red Johnny and Red Marie were nowhere in sight when he passed through the kitchen.

He led the dog around on the other side of the table from the pool of blood, through the back door and around the house. He didn't encounter anyone. The whole block looked deserted.

He put the dog in the back of the Plymouth and got into

the front seat behind the wheel. He looked at his watch. It read 4:51.

He had a sudden crazy, desperate feeling that he was looking for a needle in a haystack, wasting time; and that time was the most precious thing on earth.

16

Kid Blackie was a short black man with a face like a monkey's and a shining bald head. His torso was naked in the dim-lit stinking heat of the small dirty gym. Big flopping breasts shaped like gourds with rusty-looking teats as big as a woman's hung down to his navel. His flabby muscles seemed about to drop from the bones and his bay window was big enough to give birth to quintuplets.

He had his thumbs hooked in frayed suspenders holding up baggy-seated pants that looked loaded, and was chewing the stub of a cigar in the corner of his mouth, as he watched two young chocolate-skinned middleweights work out on the greasy square of canvas.

'Wait a minute, Ed,' he said and blew on a whistle that hung from a string about his neck.

The boys stopped punching and stared at him.

He climbed into the ring and squared off with one of the boys.

'Like this,' he said, the cigar butt wobbling in the corner of his mouth, and jabbed a left at the boy's face.

When the boy's guard flew up automatically, he crossed a right to the boy's stomach, bringing it down. The boy's right shoulder dropped as he started a looping right hook. Kid Blackie hooked a left to the boy's jaw so fast the boy never saw it. The boy sat down, looking dazed.

Kid Blackie turned to the other boy. 'You seen how I done it?'

The boy nodded mutely.

'You try it.'

The boy jabbed with his left. Kid Blackie went under it

and left-hooked him in the stomach. The boy bent in slightly, dropping his left arm, and tried to cross with his right. But he wasn't fast enough. Kid Blackie threw an overhand right to his jaw and knocked him unconscious.

He spat frayed tobacco to the canvas and climbed down out of the ring. His old glassy brown eyes looked sad.

'These boys that turn up nowadays,' he bemoaned. 'If they was chicks they'd never get hatched.'

Kid Blackie had been lightweight champion of the world at one time. Rumor had it that he had squandered over a million dollars on white women and Cadillacs. He didn't look as though he regretted it.

'All old people say the same thing,' Coffin Ed dissented. 'There're always some good and some bad. You don't expect everybody to be like you.'

'Maybe you're right.' He watched the two boys helping one another up. 'What's on your ass?'

'I'm looking for Pinky.'

Kid Blackie scratched his bald head. 'That's funny. Some bitch was just in here looking for him too. Cat-eyed woman. Ain't been more'n ten minutes ago.'

Coffin Ed tensed and his tic started jumping.

'By herself?'

Kid Blackie wasn't looking directly at him, but he didn't miss the sudden change.

'Yeah,' he said. 'She come up by herself but I got curious. Only reason for a bitch like her be looking for Pinky would be to shoot him, so when she left I looked out the window. She got in a car with two white jokers – looked like mobsters.' He let it go at that.

Coffin Ed felt his heart constrict and his breath turned rockhard in his lungs. I'm on your tail now, you mother-rapers, he thought. Pain flooded his head like a sudden hemorrhage and his tic went spasmodic. He tried to control his voice.

'Get a look at 'em?'

'Not much. Come on, let's take a gander. Maybe they're still hanging around.'

They walked to the grimy flyspecked window and looked down on 116th Street.

'Had a gray Buick – little one,' Kid Blackie added.

Their gazes searched the parked cars lining the curbs.

The sun was on the south side and the street lay in shadow. Colored people dressed for the heat milled about on the wide sidewalks, shiny black faces peering from beneath a variety of headgear, black arms protruding from light cotton fabrics.

A two-wheel pushcart loaded with slices of watermelon packed in ice and covered with wet gunnysacks was parked behind an empty ice truck. A hand-lettered sign on one side read: SUGAR TOOF GORGIA MELON, with the S turned around. Water dripped from the bottom.

Farther down an old man with a smaller pushcart was selling glasses of flavored ice. The varicolored bottles stood in a rack about a block of ice covered with wet newspaper. Fronting on the sidewalk behind it was an open hot-dog counter with big glass bottles of orange-flavored ice water and a grill covered with franks like soldiers on parade.

Venetian blinds covered the windows of the bars. Signboards in the lobby of a movie theater depicted gangsters never seen on land or sea shooting it out with blasting rods. On the street in front of it, skinny black children wearing loincloths romped in a stream of water gushing from a fire hydrant.

Coffin Ed had left the dog in his Plymouth and she had her head out of the window, panting. A crowd had collected to stare at her. They kept a respectful distance despite her muzzle.

One little boy was holding up his mongrel in his arms to see the big dog. The mongrel didn't like that business.

There was no sign of a gray Buick.

Kid Blackie shook his head. 'They musta gone.'

The distant blaring of a jukebox came from a bar somewhere below. A bottle fly buzzed against the grimy windowpane.

'You didn't get a look at 'em?' Coffin Ed asked finally, trying to keep the disappointment from his voice.

'I didn't see 'em too good,' Kid Blackie confessed. 'The mugs looked like mugs look anywhere. One looked sort of bony, whitefaced, like he was sick, a hopheaded-looking character. Other was a fatty, too light to be a greaser, maybe a Swede.

Both of 'em was wearing straw hats and smoked glasses. That mean anything to you?'

'They sound like the ones who sapped me and got Digger.'

Kid Blackie clicked his tongue. 'Too bad about Digger. Think he'll make it?'

There wasn't much sympathy in his voice, but Coffin Ed understood it. Kid Blackie liked Digger, but he was so old he was glad it was somebody else dying and not himself.

'Can't tell 'til the deal's down,' he said.

'Wish I could help you. The woman was dressed sharp, had on a light green suit—'

'I know her.'

'Well, that's all I seen.'

'Every little bit helps. You ain't seen Pinky?'

'Not since three days ago. What you think these mobsters want with him?'

'Same as me.'

Kid Blackie looked at Coffin Ed's face through the corners of his eyes and dropped it.

'Too bad about that big ape,' he said. 'He might have made the grade if it wasn't for his skin.'

'What's the matter with his skin?' Coffin Ed asked absently. He was thinking of the janitor's wife, trying to figure this new angle.

'Bruises too easily,' Kid Blackie said. 'Touch him with a feather and he'll turn black-and-blue. In the ring it always looks like he's getting beat to death when he ain't even hurt. I remember once the ref stopped the fight and Pinky wasn't even—'

'I ain't got much time, Kid,' Coffin Ed cut him off. 'You got any idea where I can find him?'

Kid Blackie scratched his shiny bald head. 'Well, he's got a pad somewhere on the Riverside Drive.'

'I know that, but he's on the lam.'

'Yeah? In that case I couldn't say.' Kid Blackie screwed up his eyes and gave Coffin Ed a tentative look. 'A man can't ask you no questions, can he?'

'It ain't that,' Coffin Ed said. 'I just ain't got time to answer.'

'Well, I heered he got an aunt up in the Bronx somewheres,' Kid Blackie volunteered. 'Called Sister Heavenly. You ever heered of her?'

Coffin Ed was thinking. 'Yeah, once or twice. But I've never seen her.'

'From the stone age they say. She got a faith healing pitch. Cover-up they say.'

'For what?'

'Pushing H they say.'

Inside of his blinding headache Coffin Ed's thoughts were jumping like ants frying on a red-hot stove. Whichever way it went, it came back to H, he was thinking.

'Has she got a temple?' he asked.

'I couldn't say.' Kid Blackie shook his head. 'Pinky says she's got a pisspot full of money but she wouldn't give him the sweat off her ass. She must got some kind of joint.'

'Know whereabouts it's at?'

'I couldn't say. Somewheres in the sticks.'

'That don't help much. There're sticks all over the Bronx.'

Kid Blackie decided finally to give up on the cigar butt. He spit it to the floor and carefully picked the shreds from his snaggle-tooth mouth.

'Who might know is Daddy Haddy,' he said. 'You know where he's at?'

'Yeah,' Coffin Ed said, turning about to leave. 'See you.'

'Don't tell him I told you.'

'I won't.'

All the time he was there Kid Blackie had been looking him over covertly. His wise old eyes hadn't missed a thing. He had made the two guns and the sap and he figured they weren't all.

He let Coffin Ed reach the head of the staircase, then called, 'Wait a minute. You got some blood on your shirt cuff.'

He was curious to know whose blood it was but it was too risky to ask outright.

Coffin Ed didn't even look at his cuff; he didn't stop walking; he didn't look around. 'Yeah,' he said. 'And there's going to be some more.'

17

Unlike the opium derivatives and cocaine, marijuana gives one an esoteric appetite.

Sister Heavenly had just come from seeing Daddy Haddy. After listening to Daddy Haddy's recital of Pinky's latest brainstorm, she had a sudden wild craving for something she'd never eaten before. She couldn't even think until she ate; she couldn't figure out what it meant.

Twenty-five minutes later she left her hired car and the driver on 116th Street and staggered up an alley to a small, dirty 'Home-Cooking' restaurant where she knew the cook. It stood in back of a store that advertised: *Seafood – Eggs – Chicken-on-the-Feet – Southern Specialties*. That gave her an idea.

She ordered a half dozen shelled raw oysters, a bottle of sorghum molasses, three raw eggs and a glass of buttermilk.

The big fat black woman who ran the joint had to send next door to fill the order, and she stood over Sister Heavenly and watched her pour sorghum molasses over the oysters and eat them and mix the raw eggs with the buttermilk and drink it.

'Honey, if I didn't know you I'd swear you was knocked up,' she said.

'I ain't knocked up,' Sister Heavenly said. 'But I'm barefooted.' To herself she added, 'And that ain't no lie.'

Suddenly she jumped up and rushed outside in the alley and was sick. Even the hungry dogs wouldn't touch the mess. She came back and ordered fried chicken.

'Thass more like it,' the big fat cook said.

When Sister Heavenly had finished with the chicken she pushed back her chair and opened her beaded bag below the level of the table to check its contents. Aside from cosmetics it contained a billfold with five one-hundred-dollar bills, three tens and two ones, a handful of loose change rattling around in the bottom, her pipe and pouch of marijuana, a key ring with 13 keys, a .38 Owl's Head revolver with the barrel sawed off to an inch in length and loaded with dumdum bullets, a spring-blade knife with a bone handle, a box of calling cards reading *Sister Heavenly – Healing by Faith*, three lavender initialed linen handkerchiefs, three French teasers that looked like miniature beartooth neck-laces, a picture of a slick-haired black man with buck teeth inscribed, *To Choochy from Hoochy*, and an imitation deputy sheriff's badge.

'That don't spell *whore*,' she said bitterly to herself. 'It don't spell nothing.'

She didn't think about Uncle Saint, her blown-up cache or her lost house. She was too old to regret.

It was time that was worrying her now. She knew her time was short. If the devil don't get me, the cops will, she thought. If the cops hadn't already made the hot Lincoln, they would soon. She gave herself until morning. If she hadn't scored by then it would be too late. She couldn't let the sun catch her again in these parts.

After talking to the pleasant-voiced woman at the S.P.C.A. she had figured that the dick who took Pinky's dog was looking for Pinky. She had started looking for Pinky in the hopes of finding the dog.

Her next stop was Kid Blackie's gym.

She had hired an old Mercury sedan driven by a rape-fiend-looking colored man who worked it as a taxi without buying a license. He was a lean, rusty-black, nervous-looking joker with bright red buck-wild eyes. He was a weedhead and she figured she could trust him.

He was drowsing behind the wheel, sucking on a stick of weed, when she came out and got into the back.

'Turn around and go back toward Lenox,' she said.

He shifted into gear and executed the U-turn with flourishes like a maestro.

'I know you can drive; you don't have to prove it,' she said cynically.

He grinned at her in the rearview mirror, narrowly missing a woman with a baby buggy crossing the street.

They had got past Eighth Avenue and were headed east when she casually noticed a Plymouth sedan passing on the other side of the street, headed west. At just that moment the dog stuck its head out of the window on her side.

'Sheba!' she screamed. 'Turn around!'

The driver was teaed to the gills and on a livewire edge and her sudden scream scared the living hell out of him. He knew his name wasn't *Sheba* and he didn't know who *Sheba* was. But he figured if *Sheba* was enough to scare the old witch he was chauffeuring about, that was enough for him. He didn't stop to see.

He put his shoulders to the wheel and turned.

Tires squealed. People screamed. Two cars behind him telescoped. A crosstown bus coming from the opposite direction braked so hard it scrambled the passengers into the aisle.

The Mercury lurched and went up over the opposite curb. A sad-looking cripple leaped like a kangaroo through the door of a bar. An old lady was run over by a black-clad preacher shouting, 'Praise God and run for your lives!'

The front bumper knocked over a wooden stand displaying religious booklets and twenty-four marijuana cigarettes were scattered about the sidewalk.

The driver didn't see a thing. He was standing on the gas and trusting to fate.

'Follow that car!' she screamed.

'What car?' The street was full of cars.

'It turned up Eighth!'

He was already on top of Eighth Avenue, on the inside lane, pushing past 50 miles an hour. But he made another do-or-die turn, going in between a yellow taxi and a cabin truck with not more than a few inches give-or-take each way; tires screaming, drivers cursing. He came into the avenue so fast he almost climbed up in the back seat of a beat-up convertible carrying ten passengers.

The women in the back seat screamed.

Somewhere behind, a police whistle was blowing frantically.

'Don't stop!' Sister Heavenly cried.

'Is I stopping?' he threw over his shoulder as he wrenched the car around the back of the convertible and gave it the gas.

The bug-eyed driver of the convertible looked out from

his galaxy of chicks and shouted threateningly, 'Don't you run into my car, nigger!'

But the Mercury was past and closing rapidly in behind Coffin Ed's Plymouth.

'It's the car!' Sister Heavenly hollered. 'Don't get too close.'

'Hell, I gonna pass it,' he said.

Coffin Ed noticed the beat-up Mercury when it passed. At another time he might have taken on the duties of a traffic cop and run it down. But he didn't have the time.

It was just another automobile racer, a black Stirling Moss trying out his car for a 'Grand Prix' somewhere. Harlem was full of 'em. They got teaed on weed and imagined they could drive those old V-8 gas gluttons straight up in the sky, he thought. He noticed that the back seat was empty. He figured some cop up the line would get him if he didn't get himself killed. He put it from his mind.

The Mercury was out of sight when he pulled up before Daddy Haddy's joint.

The little hole-in-the-wall had a red painted front like the big chain of United Tobacco Stores. But Daddy Haddy had named his *Re-United Tobacco Store*; there wasn't anything anybody could do about that.

The shades were drawn.

Coffin Ed glanced at his watch. It read 6:07.

The tenement across the street threw a shadow on the store. But it was too early for it to be closed. Coffin Ed felt his stomach knot.

He got out of his car, walked across the sidewalk and tried the door. It was locked. A sixth sense told him to wipe his prints from the doorknob, get back into his car and drive – he wouldn't get anything here. He was a civilian on a manhunt; he had no authority to investigate what he suspected might reveal a crime; he was outside of the law himself. 'Phone the station, report your suspicions, and let it go at that,' an inner voice told him.

But he couldn't let it go. He was in it; he was committed; he was like the airplane over the middle of the ocean that had passed the point of no return. He thought fleetingly of Grave

Digger, but that wouldn't bear thinking about. The pain in his head and the brackish taste in his mouth had become normal, as though he had always had them.

He took a deep breath and looked up and down the street to see if there were any police in sight. He took out his Boy Scout knife, opened the round, needle-point pry, and began fiddling with the Yale lock.

The door had been closed on the latch. Whoever had last left had just pulled it shut. In a moment it was open. He closed and locked it behind him, groped about until he found the light switch, and turned on the light.

There were no surprises.

He found the body of Daddy Haddy behind the glass-enclosed counter. There was a hole in the center of his forehead filled with a glob of blackish blood. It was encircled by powder burns more than an inch in diameter. He put his toe beneath the shoulder and turned the body just enough to see the back of the head. There was a small hard lump at the base of the hairline where the bullet had come out of the skull without force to penetrate the skin and had coursed downward and stopped.

A clean job! he thought without any emotion whatever. No blood. No noise. Someone had held a pistol with a silencer a few inches in front of Daddy Haddy's head and had pulled the trigger. Daddy Haddy had not expected it. So much for that. Daddy Haddy had had it.

The joint had been searched hurriedly but thoroughly. Shelves, drawers, cases, boxes had been turned out, the contents dumped helter-skelter over the floor. Among the unopened packages of cigarettes, scattered cigars, matches, lighters, flints, fluids, pipes and cigarette and cigar holders was a sprinkling of neatly folded decks of heroin and carefully rolled marijuana cigarettes of bomber size. There was still the faint odor of cordite fumes in the hot, close, stinky air.

He waded through the debris and opened the door at the rear. It showed a tiny storeroom containing two padded straight-backed chairs. The air was redolent with marijuana smoke. The treatment was the same.

It was obvious the searchers hadn't found what they were looking for.

Two people already dead. And Digger—? The thought broke off, then came on again: Small-time dog-ass little Harlem hustlers on the fringe of the narcotics racket. Pee-wee colored scrabblers for a dirty buck. How do they get mixed up in this business? This is mob stuff from downtown. Hired gunmen from a syndicate ...

He hadn't discovered any lead to Uncle Saint, so he didn't know there were already three others dead from the caper.

He wondered if he oughtn't back out before it got to be more than he could handle. Drop it back into the lap of homicide and the narcotics squad. Let 'em call in the feds.

Then he thought if he reported the crime he'd be detained, held up for hours, questioned. His superiors were going to want to know what he was doing in this business when he had been warned by all of them to keep out.

'They ain't going to like it, Ed.' He didn't realize he had spoken aloud.

But on the other hand, they were going to dig him anyway. He hadn't made any effort at concealment; his prints were everywhere. They'd find witnesses to testify he had been there. On one side was the devil, on the other the deep blue sea.

He thought of Grave Digger again. He thought of having to break in a new partner – that is, if he ever got back on the force. He knew the Harlem hoodlums would make life rough with Grave Digger gone. He thought of how Grave Digger had tracked down the hoodlum who had thrown acid in his face; how he had shot him through both eyes. He thought of the effect on the Harlem gunslingers. He knew if he backed down now, he'd never live it down.

There was nothing in there that he found of any use. Nothing he didn't know before he came inside.

I can't find them, so the only thing for me to do now is let 'em find me, he thought and went outside and pulled the door shut behind him.

A little girl about eleven or twelve years old had the back door of his car open and was trying to entice the dog onto the sidewalk. But she was too scared of the dog to reach inside and get the leash. She stood back a distance on the sidewalk and said, 'Here, Sheba. Here, Sheba. Come on, Sheba.'

It struck Coffin Ed as odd that she knew the dog's name but didn't know the dog.

But before his mind had a chance to work on this, he caught a picture from the corners of his eyes that reacted instinctively on his brain. A youth was standing on the other side of Eighth Avenue at the corner of 137th Street looking up at the sky. Coffin Ed knew automatically there wasn't anything in the sky at that moment to attract the attention of a Harlem youth.

'Let her alone,' he told the little girl and closed the car door.

The little girl ran up the street. He didn't give her another thought.

He walked around the car as though he were going to get in behind the wheel. He had the door open. Then he seemed to think of something and closed the door and turned and started to cross Eighth Avenue.

Two cars were coming along the other side and he had to stop and let them pass.

The youth turned and began sauntering slowly up 137th Street toward St Nicholas Avenue as though he didn't have a thing on his mind.

There was a small chain grocery store on the corner. Coffin Ed headed for it. He knew that in his Scotch beret, green goggles and suit with a coat, he didn't look like a Harlem character out shopping for dinner. But it couldn't be helped; it had to appear he was headed for some definite place until he had closed the gap.

The youth walked faster. He was a coal-black boy, wafer thin, with a long egg-shaped head from which fell locks of long straight black hair. He wore a white T-shirt, blue jeans, canvas sneakers and smoked glasses. The only thing to set him apart from other Harlem youths was his watching Coffin Ed. Harlem youths kept the hell away from Coffin Ed.

Going toward St Nicholas Avenue, 137th Street became residential. It was nearing the dinner hour and the smell of cooking seeped into the street and mingled with the smell of heat and motorcar exhaust. Half-clad people lounged in the doorways, sat on the stoops; naked black torsos gleamed in the sunshine on the upper windows; women's long fried hair glistened and grease trickled down their necks.

Anything was welcome that broke the monotony.

When Coffin Ed yelled to the youth, 'Halt!' everyone perked up.

The youth began to run. He kept to the sidewalk, dodging the people in his path.

Coffin Ed drew Grave Digger's pistol from his belt because it hampered his running. But he didn't dare fire the customary warning shot into the air. He couldn't afford to draw the cops. It was the first time he found himself trying to avoid the cops. But it wasn't funny.

He ran in a long-gaited, flat-footed, knee-straining lope, as though his feet were sinking into the concrete. The light rubber-soled shoes helped, but the heavy artillery weighed him down, and each step set off explosions in his head.

The thin agile youth ran in a high-stepping, light-footed, ground-eating sprint, ducking and dodging between the people pouring into the street.

Sides were taken by the enthusiastic spectators.

'Run, buster, run!' some shouted.

'Catch 'im, daddy!' others echoed.

'Look at them niggers picking 'em up and putting 'em down,' a big fat lady crowed jubilantly.

'Dig the canon, Jack!' a weedhead exclaimed as Coffin Ed ran past.

Two jokers jumped from a parked car at the corner of St Nicholas Avenue and split in an effort to catch the fleeing youth. They didn't have anything against him; they just wanted to join in the excitement.

The youth ducked to the right and one of the jokers lunged at him like a baseball catcher trying to stop a wild pitch. The youth bent low and went underneath the out-stretched hand, but the other joker stuck out his foot and tripped him.

The youth skidded forward on his hands and elbows, scraping off the skin, and Coffin Ed closed in.

Now the two jokers decided to take the youth's part.

They turned toward Coffin Ed grinning confidently and one said in a jocular voice, 'What's the trouble, daddy-o?'

Their eyes popped simultaneously. One saw the nickel-plated revolver and the other saw Coffin Ed's face.

'Great Godamighty, it's Coffin Ed!' the first one whispered.

How the people up and down that noisy street heard him is one of those mysteries. But suddenly everybody started drawing in. The two jokers took off, running in opposite directions.

By the time Coffin Ed had reached down and grabbed the youth by the back of his neck and yanked him to his feet, the street was deserted save for heads peeking furtively around corners.

Coffin Ed took the youth by the arm and turned him around. He found himself looking into a pair of solid black eyes. He had to fight down the impulse to take Grave Digger's pistol and start beating the punk across the head.

'Listen to me, snake-eyes,' he grated in a constricted voice. 'Walk back to the car ahead of me. And if you run this time I'm going to shoot you in the spine.'

The boy walked back in that high-stepping, cloud-treading gait that marijuana gives. Blood was dripping from his skinned elbows. Silence greeted them along the way.

They crossed Eighth Avenue and stopped beside the car. The dog was gone.

'Who got it?' Coffin Ed asked in a voice that seemed to come from a dried-up throat.

The youth glanced at the tic in Coffin Ed's face and said, 'Sister Heavenly.'

'You're sure it wasn't Pinky?'

'Nossuh, 'twere Sister Heavenly.'

'All right, fine, you know the family. Go around and get inside on the front seat and we're going away where we won't be disturbed and talk.'

The youth started to obey but Coffin Ed reached out again and took him by the arm. 'You want to talk, don't you, sonny?'

The youth glanced again at the tic in Coffin Ed's face and choked, 'Yessuh.'

18

'It's here,' Sister Heavenly told her red-eyed chauffeur.

He pulled the Mercury to the curb beside a red-painted fireplug in front of the Harlem Hospital, cut the motor and reached behind his car for the marijuana butt. There were spaces to park in front and behind.

'Pull away from this fireplug, you lunatic,' Sister Heavenly said. 'You want the cops to nab you?'

'Fireplug?' He turned his head and stared. 'I didn't seen it.'

Nonchalantly he shifted into gear and pulled up a space.

'Watch my dog and don't let nobody steal it,' Sister Heavenly said and got out.

She didn't hear him mutter, 'Who'd want it?' She went across the street to a glass-fronted, white-trimmed surgical supply store.

They were getting ready to close but she told the white clerk it was urgent.

She ordered a large package of absorbent cotton, an eight-ounce bottle of chloroform, a scalpel, elbow-length rubber gloves, a full-length rubber apron, a rubber sheet, and a large enamel basin.

'You forgot the forceps,' the clerk said.

'I don't need any forceps,' she said.

The clerk looked her up and down. She was still carrying her parasol along with her beaded bag, but it was closed. He wanted to be sure to remember her in case of an investigation.

'You ought to leave these things to the hospitals,' he said seriously. 'There're hospitals in the city where they'll do it if it's necessary.'

He thought she was planning to perform an abortion. She dug him.

'It's *my* daughter,' she said. 'I'll do it myself.'

He shrugged and wrapped up the bundle. She paid him and left.

When she returned to the Mercury, the dog was whining, either from thirst or hunger. She got in and put the bundle on the floor and stroked the bitch's head. 'It won't be long now,' she said gently.

She had her chauffeur drive her to a fleabag hotel on 125th Street, a block distant from the 125th Street railroad station, and wait for her while she went inside.

A glass-paneled door hanging askew permitted a hazardous entry into a long, narrow hall with a worn-out linoleum floor and peeling wallpaper, smelling of male urine, whore stink, stale vomit and the cheapest of perfume. What was left on the wallpaper was decorated with graffiti that would have embarrassed the peddlers of obscene pictures in Montmartre.

At the back, underneath the staircase, was a scarred wooden counter barricading a padded desk chair behind which hung a letter box holding identical dime store skeleton keys. A hotel bell stood on the counter; above it on the wall was a pushbutton with the legend NIGHT BELL.

No one was in sight.

Sister Heavenly slapped her gloved palm on the hotel bell. No sound came forth. She picked it up and looked underneath. The clapper was missing. She leaned her thumb on the night bell. Nothing happened. She took the handle of her parasol and banged the side of the hotel bell. It sounded like a fire truck.

A long time later a man emerged from a half-door in the dark recess behind the desk chair. He was a middle-aged brownskin man with a face full of boils, a head full of tetter, and glazed brown eyes. He had a thick, fat, powerful-looking torso; his collarless shirt was open showing a chest covered with thick nappy hair.

He limped forward, his heavy body moving sluggishly, and put his hands on the counter.

'What can I do for you, madame?' he said in the voice of a baritone singer. His diction was good and his enunciation distinct.

Sister Heavenly was past being surprised by anything.

'I want a quiet room with a safe lock,' she said.

'All of our rooms are quiet,' he said. 'And you are as safe here as in the lap of Jesus.'

'You have a vacancy?'

'Yes, madame, we have vacancies all the time.'

'I'll bet you do,' she said. 'Just a minute while I go get my luggage.'

She went out and paid off her chauffeur and took the dog by the leash and her bundle by the string. When she returned, the proprietor was waiting at the foot of the stairs.

He had an atrophied leg, evidently from polio, and he looked like a spider climbing the stairs. Sister Heavenly followed patiently behind him.

From behind a door on the second floor came loud voices raised in argument: 'Who you talking to, you blue-gum nigger!'

'You better shut up, you piss-colored whore . . .'

From behind another came the sound of pots and pans banging around and the smell of boiling ham hocks and cabbage.

From a third the sound of bodies crashing against furniture, objects falling to the floor, feet scuffling, panting grunts and a woman's voice shrilling, 'Just wait 'til I get loose—'

The proprietor limped slowly ahead without giving the slightest notice as though he were stone-deaf.

They ascended slowly to the third floor and he opened a door with one of the ten-cent skeleton keys and said, 'Here you are, madame, the quietest room in the house.'

A window looked down on 125th Street. It was the rush hour. The roar of the traffic poured in. Directly below was a White Rose bar. A jukebox was blasting and the loud strident voice of Screaming Jay Hawkins was raised in song. From the room next door came the blaring of a radio tuned up so loud the sound was frayed.

The room contained a single bed, straight-backed chair, chest of drawers, six eight-penny nails driven into a board on the inner wall to serve as a clothes closet, a chamber pot, and a washbasin with two taps.

Sister Heavenly went across the room and tried the taps. The cold water ran but the hot water tap was dry.

'Who wants hot water in this weather?' the proprietor said, carefully touching his face with a dirty handkerchief.

'I'll take it,' Sister Heavenly said, tossing her bundle onto the bed.

'That will be three dollars, please,' the proprietor said.

She gave him three dollars in small change.

He thanked her and snapped the inside bolt back and forth suggestively and limped off.

She closed the door, locked it on the inside, and snapped the bolt. Then she laid her bag and parasol on the bed beside the bundle, removed her hat and wig, sat on the side of the bed and took off her shoes and stockings. When she stood up she was baldheaded and barefooted.

The dog began to whine again.

'In just a moment, honey,' she said.

She took out her pipe, loaded it with the finely ground stems of marijuana and lit it with her gold-plated lighter. The dog laid its head in her lap and she stroked it gently as she sucked the smoke deep into her lungs.

Someone knocked on the door and a slick, ingratiating voice said, 'Hey Jack, I hears you, man. Leave me blow a little with you. This is old Playboy.'

Sister Heavenly ignored him. After a while the disgruntled voice said, 'I hopes the man catches you, stingy mother-raper.'

Sister Heavenly finished her pipe and put it away. Then she rolled up her skirt, exposing her thin bird's legs, and pinned it above her knees. She peeled off her silk gloves and put on the rubber ones; and hooked the long rubber apron over her head and fastened it securely behind.

She took the package of cotton, the bottle of chloroform and the chair and sat in front of the open window.

'Here, Sheba,' she called.

The dog came and nuzzled her bare feet. She hooked the handle of the leash onto the lower half of the sash lock, tore off a swab of cotton, saturated it with chloroform and held it to the dog's nose. The dog reared back and broke off the lock. She chased it across the room and stuck the saturated cotton inside the nose of the muzzle. The dog gave a long pitiful howl and broke for the window. She grabbed the end of the chain leash and swung the dog around just before it jumped, then quickly she grabbed the open bottle of chloroform and poured

it over the dog's nose. The howling stopped. The dog gasped
for breath and settled slowly to the floor, legs extended stiffly
front and back. Its lips drew back, exposing clenched teeth,
its eyes became fixed; it shuddered violently and lay still.

Quickly she spread the rubber sheet in the center of the
floor and placed the enamel basin on it. She dragged the
dog and laid its head in the basin and cut its throat with the
scalpel. Then she lifted it by the rear legs and let it bleed.

She dumped the blood into the washbasin, turned on the
water and left it running. She brought the enamel basin back
and began to disembowel the carcass.

It was bloody, dirty, filthy work. She opened the stomach
and split the intestines. She was nauseated beyond description.
Twice she vomited into the filth. But she kept on.

Down below, the jukebox blasted; next door the radio
blared. Strident voices sounded from the street; horns blared
in the jammed traffic. Colored people swarmed up and down
the sidewalks; the bars were packed; people stood in line in
front of the cafeteria across the street.

The hot poisonous air inside of the room, stinking of blood,
chloroform and dog-gut, was enough to suffocate the average
person. But Sister Heavenly stood it. There wasn't anything
she wouldn't do for money.

When finally she had convinced herself there wasn't anything inside of the dog but blood and filth, she threw the
scalpel into the carcass and said, 'Well, that's lovely.'

She crawled to the window, put her arms on the ledge,
and sucked in the hot, stinking outside air.

Then she stood up, took off the bloody apron and spread
it over the bloody carcass, peeled off her gloves and dropped
them beside it. The rubber sheet was covered with blood and
filth and some had run off onto the linoleum floor.

It ain't any worse than some of the tricks I've turned, she
thought.

She went to the basin and washed her hands, arms and
feet. She took a fresh handkerchief from her bag, saturated
it with perfume, and wiped her bald head, face, neck and
arms, and feet. She remade her face, put on her gray wig
and black straw hat, sat on the bed and put on her shoes
and stockings, put down her skirt, picked up her beaded bag

and parasol, and left the room, locking the door behind her and taking the key along.

The proprietor was coming in from the street as she went out.

'You left your dog,' he said.

'I'm coming back.'

'Will she be quiet while you're gone?'

For the first time in more than thirty years Sister Heavenly felt slightly hysterical.

'She's the quietest dog in the city,' she said.

19

First, Coffin Ed and the youth called Wop had driven out to the Bronx and looked at the remains of Sister Heavenly's house. A police barricade had been thrown about it and experts from the safe and loft squad were still digging in the wreckage. One look had been enough for Coffin Ed.

Afterwards, employing Wop as his guide, he made a junkie's tour of Harlem. Wop was known to all the landprops as Daddy Haddy's runner and had the entree. Coffin Ed had the persuader.

Pushing Wop in front of him to ring the doorbells and give the passwords, with the muzzle of Grave Digger's pistol poking in his spine, he had crashed all the notorious shooting galleries in Harlem, the joints where the addicts met to take their kicks and greet their chicks; where the skinpoppers and the schmeckers (those who used the needle and those who sniffed the powder), the pushers and the weedheads gathered for sex circuses and to listen to the real cool jive.

He had gone in with a long nickel-plated revolver in each hand and homicide in his eyes.

He had flushed famous jazzmen, international blues singers, sophisticated socialites both white and colored, prominent people both men and women, mingling with the racketeers and the gamblers, the whores and the thieves and the dregs of humanity; all being rooked together by the peddlers of the five-colored dreams and the cool dry jags and the hot sex licks.

He had encountered the furtive and the indignant, 'respectable' women who had burst into tears, puffed-up jokers who claimed political pull; those who couldn't care less about being caught and those who figured money would settle it.

His entrance had set off panic, engendered terror, triggered rage. Jokers on the lam had jumped from windows, landprops had threatened to call the police, housewives had hidden under beds, drug-crazed starkers had charged him with stickers.

He had tamed the rambunctious and pacified the pacifists. He was not a narcotics man; he didn't even have a shield. His entrance was illegal and he had no authority. All he had had was muscle, and it hadn't worked.

He had left a trail of hysteria, screaming jeebies, knotty heads and bloody noses. But it hadn't meant a thing. He hadn't gotten any leads, hadn't found out anything he didn't know. Just a blank.

No one had admitted to seeing Pinky all that day. No one had admitted to seeing a yellow-skinned cat-eyed woman in a green suit accompanied by two white mobsters looking for Pinky. No one had ever heard of Sister Heavenly. No one had known anything about anything. He couldn't pull them in and sweat it out.

And yet he knew some of them were lying. He was certain, since talking to Kid Blackie, that Ginny, the janitor's wife, and the two gunmen were making the same tour. They were either in front of him or behind him, or perhaps more than once they had crossed paths. But he hadn't seen a sign of them, nothing to indicate whether they were following him or in front of him. He had doubled back and laid in wait and they hadn't showed.

Now it was eleven o'clock at night. Coffin Ed sat in his parked car with the lights off in the middle of a dark block on St Nicholas Avenue opposite the park. He could feel the trembling body of the youth beside him, even though they were separated by two feet of space. He could hear Wop's teeth chattering in the dark. The youth's jag had worn off and the smell of terror came from him like a sickening miasma.

Coffin Ed reached into the dark and turned on the dashboard radio to catch the eleven o'clock news broadcast.

A mealymouthed male voice came on, imitating some big-name newscaster, and blabbed about domestic politics, the Cold War, what the Africans were doing, the latest on the civil rights front and a fistfight between two motion picture actors in El Morocco.

Coffin Ed wasn't listening but the sound of the voice set his teeth on edge. The top of his head felt like it was coming off. He had long since discarded his goggles but his eyes felt gritty.

He tried to think, but his thoughts didn't make any sense. They were jumping about in his head like buck-and-wing dancers on their last breath. 'Give a little, take a little,' one side of his brain was saying, while the other side was cursing in a blinding rage. He thought for a moment of how he would line the mother-rapers up and shoot them down.

He realized that he was wandering badly and caught himself. 'Ain't no time to blow your top now, son,' he told himself.

They had just one more place to go. It was run by a Harlem society matron, and it wasn't going to be easy to crash. He didn't want to hurry it. If it turned out to be another blank, he'd be up shit alley.

'You said you was going to give me my fare to Chicago,' a choked dry voice stammered from the dark beside him.

'You'll get it,' he said absently, his cluttered thoughts echoing, 'He thinks that's far enough.'

'Kin I get some of my clothes?'

'Why not?' he said automatically, but he didn't even hear the question. The thought of Chicago had got mixed up with the two gunmen he was hunting and he added aloud, 'Mother-rapers better get off the face of the earth.'

Wop shrunk into silence.

The voice from the radio blabbed on: '. . . when Queen

Elizabeth passed over the bridge ...' It sounded to Coffin Ed as though he said 'when Queen Elizabeth *pissed* over the bridge ...' and he wondered vaguely what did she do that for.

'You going to take me by my room?' Wop stammered hesitantly.

'What for?'

'They going be laying for me. They going kill me. You know they going kill me. You promised you'd protect me. You said if I steered you to them cribs wouldn't nobody hurt me. Now you going let 'em—' He began getting hysterical.

Coffin Ed drew back wearily and slapped him across the face.

The voice cut off and the hysteria subsided, followed by snuffling sounds.

Coffin Ed listened to the newscaster report the finding of Daddy Haddy's body by the patrolman on the beat. The words caught in his brain like red-hot rivets: '... died of gunshot wounds received earlier today while investigating a homicide in the basement of an apartment house on Riverside Drive. Jones, known locally in Harlem as Grave Digger, was one of the famous Harlem Detective team, Grave Digger Jones and Coffin Ed Johnson. They were on suspension for assaulting an alleged dope peddler named Jake Kubansky who subsequently died. The assailant, or assailants, are unknown. Reports from the homicide bureau—'

He reached out and turned the radio off. It was a reflex action, without thought. Perhaps from a subconscious desire to reject the knowledge by stopping the voice.

His mind fought against acceptance. He sat without moving, without breathing. But finally it sank in.

'That's it,' he said aloud.

Wop hadn't heard a word of it. His terrified thoughts were concentrated on himself.

'But you're going to take me to the station, ain't you? You going get me safe on the train, ain't you?'

Coffin Ed turned his head slowly and looked at him. The muscles of his face were jumping almost out of control, but his reflexes were like a sleepwalker's.

'You're one of them too,' he said in a constricted voice.

'Give you another month or two and you'll be on junk. You'll have the monkey on your back that you got to feed by stealing and robbing and murdering.'

As the voice hammered him with deadly intensity, Wop cringed in the corner of his seat and got smaller and smaller.

'I ain't robbed nobody,' he whimpered. 'I ain't stole nothing. All I done was just work for Daddy Haddy. I ain't hurt nobody.'

'I'm not going to kill you yet,' Coffin Ed said. 'But I'm going to hang on to you, because you're all I got. And you better hope we turn up something at Madame Cushy's if you don't want to get left. Get out.'

Coffin Ed got out on the street side and when he walked around the front of the car he had a sudden feeling that he was being watched from the park. He stepped onto the sidewalk, made a right turn and wheeled about, drawing from the greased holster in the same motion. His gaze raked the sidewalk, flanked by the low stone wall of the park, and above the rocky brush-spotted terrain rising in a steep hill to Hamilton Terrace.

A few scattered couples strolled along the pavement and old people in their shirtsleeves and cotton dresses still occupied the wooden benches. The heat had not let up with the coming of darkness and people were reluctant to turn indoors, but there was no movement within the dangerous confines of the dark grassless park. He saw no one who looked the least bit suspicious.

'I keep feeling ghosts,' he said as he holstered his revolver and pushed Wop before him toward the glass door of the apartment house.

It was an old elevator house, well-kept, and he knew that Madame Cushy lived on the top floor. But the front door was on the latch. His gaze ranged up the list of names above the push-buttons and settled on one that read: *Dr J. C. Douglas, M.D.*

There was a house intercom beside the row of buttons and when he got the doctor on he said, 'I gotta see you, Doc, I gotta case bad.'

'Let it wait,' the doctor snapped. 'Come in tomorrow morning.'

'Can't wait 'til then. I got a date for tomorrow. It's my money,' he argued roughly.

'Who is this?' the doctor asked.

'Al Thompson,' Coffin Ed said, taking a chance on the name of a pimp.

'I can't cure you overnight, Al,' the doctor said. 'It takes two days at least.'

'Hell, give me all the units at one time, Doc. I been chippie chasing and I'm in trouble. I don't wanna have to kill my whore when she comes back.'

Coffin Ed listened to the doctor's chuckle, and heard him say, 'All right, Al, come on up; we'll see what we can do.'

The latch began to click and Coffin Ed opened the door and pushed Wop into the hall. They rode up to the top floor.

Madame Cushy's was the black enamel door at the front.

'Have you been here before?' Coffin Ed asked Wop.

'Yassuh. Daddy Haddy has sent me with some stuff.' He was trembling as though he were seeing ghosts himself.

'All right, you ring it,' he said.

He flattened himself against the wall while Wop pushed the button.

After a time there was a faint click and a round peep-hole opened outward. Wop looked at the reflection of his own eye.

'What do you want, boy?' a woman's cross and impatient voice came from within.

'I'se Wop; Daddy Haddy sent me,' he stammered.

'No he didn't, he's dead,' the voice said sharply. 'What are you after?'

Coffin Ed knew he had goofed. He stepped out so he could be seen and said, 'I'm with him.'

He was still wearing his beret and it took a moment for the voice to reply, 'Oh! Edward! Well, what the hell do you want?'

'I want to talk to you.'

'Well, why didn't you ring yourself? You ought to know better than to try to front this punk into my house.'

'I know better now,' he said.

'All right, I will let you in, but not as a cop,' she conceded.

'I've been suspended,' he said. 'Didn't you know?'

'Yes, I know,' she said.

There were two locks on the door, both equipped with adjustable cables to hold it at any position, one near the bottom and one near the top; and they worked so silently the door began to open before he knew she had unlocked it.

'This dirty little boy stays out,' she said.

'He's my mascot.'

She eyed Wop distastefully and stepped back so he wouldn't touch her when he passed.

A wide short entrance hall, flanked by two closed doors, ended at glass double doors of a front lounge and a narrow hallway turned off to the left somewhere. Muted male and female voices, along with the sound of jazz, came from the lounge. There was a faint smell of incense in the overplayed atmosphere of respectability.

After closing and locking the front door she stepped past them and opened the door to the right. Coffin Ed pushed Wop before him into a small sitting room that obviously took turns for other purposes. On one side, behind a glass-topped cocktail table littered with an impressive collection of pornographic picture magazines, was a studio couch equipped with as many odd straps as a torture wrack. On the other were two armchairs with suggestive-looking footstools. An air conditioner fitted in the bottom of the window was flanked by a television set and a console radio-phonograph. All manner of obscene figurines filled a three-tiered bookcase in the near corner. Oil nudes of a voluptuous colored woman and a well-equipped colored man faced each other from opposite walls. The air conditioner was turned off and there was the faint sweetish smell of opium in the air.

Madame Cushy followed them in, closed and locked the door, and turned to stare at the demoniacal tic in Coffin Ed's face with impersonal fascination.

She was a buxom Creole-looking mulatto woman with sleepy, brown, bedroom eyes, black hair worn in a bun at the nape of her neck, and a faint black moustache. She wore a red décolleté cotton cocktail dress and high-heeled black net shoes, and her neck, arms and hands gleamed and glittered with jewelry. She looked on the wrong side of forty, but still beautifully preserved and well-sexed. Her voice was a flat contradiction of her looks.

'Well, what is it, Edward? And don't ask me anything about criminals, because I don't know any.'

Coffin Ed said in his constricted voice, 'Just a few questions, and I don't want any mother-raping shit.'

Her face went black with a sudden bloodbursting fury. 'Why, you small-time loudmouthed nigger—' she began, but was cut off by a knock on the door.

A woman's flat unmusical voice from the entrance hall said, 'It's me – Ginny. I may as well go on if you'll let me out.'

'Just a moment, dear,' Madame Cushy forced herself to say, and the next moment she felt her head jerked back by the bun of her hair, a knee in the small of her back, and the sharp edge of a knife blade across her throat.

Coffin Ed had moved so fast during the flicker of her gaze toward the door she hadn't seen it.

'Walk slowly toward the door and open it and tell her to come in,' he whispered in her ear, lowering his knee so she could walk.

She didn't move. Her face was a dull gray-black mask, looking twenty years older than a minute before, and the veins in her temples throbbed like artesian pumps.

'You're going to get yourself killed,' she said in a low tight voice. 'My bodyguard, Spunky, is in the lounge with my husband, and he's wearing a forty-five. There's a sawed-off shot-gun in the bureau drawer. And Detective Ramsey is with them, and he's got his police positive.'

'I always thought he was a crooked dick,' Coffin Ed whispered.

'Now you know.'

'But that won't buy you anything. So help me God, I'll cut your mother-raping throat.'

He motioned with his head to Wop to open the door. But Wop was paralyzed with terror. Huge obsidian eyes looked out in a hypnotized stare from a face gone battleship gray.

'I wouldn't do it,' Madame Cushy said.

'Say good-bye,' Coffin Ed said and his arm tightened.

Madame Cushy looked at Wop's eyes. She raised her voice and said, 'Just one moment, Ginny.'

There was the sound of the lounge door opening and a male voice called, 'What is it, baby?' Then it added in a lower tone as though the face had turned away, 'Go see what's happening, Spunky.'

Coffin Ed transferred Madame Cushy's bun from his left hand to his teeth and drew Grave Digger's pistol from his belt while still holding the knife blade to her throat.

When she moved he moved with her, like a monstrous Siamese twin.

Standing behind the door, she opened it and called out, 'It's nothing, dear. I'm trying to fix a rendezvous.' Then in a voice that sounded normal she added, 'Come on in, Ginny.'

Ginny saw Wop's face and hesitated, then stepped inside.

In one continuous motion Coffin Ed kicked the door shut with the edge of his left foot, spun Madame Cushy out of reach, transferred the knife blade to Ginny's throat and closed her mouth with his left forearm, snapping back her head.

She felt the knife blade on her throat, tasted cloth, and saw the huge nickel-plated revolver gripped in a hard black hand just before her eyes. The strength went out of her knees and her body began to sag.

Madame Cushy stepped quickly to the door, opened it and went into the hall. Spunky was a step away, trying to look into the room. She pulled the door shut behind her and said, 'Let them alone for a while.' Then she turned and called through the closed door, 'Call me when you're ready to leave.'

For a moment there was only the sound of their footsteps going toward the lounge and the closing of a door.

Inside the room the sound of Wop's teeth chattering was as loud as castanets.

'Stand up!' Coffin Ed grated in Ginny's ear.

Her knees straightened and she tried to talk. The movement of her head pressed her long black oily hair into his face.

'Shut up!' he whispered, turning his head to get his face out of the thick, perfumed, rancid, suffocating mass of hair.

The tight, close, abnormal contact of their bodies was aphrodisiacal in a sadistic manner, and both were shaken with an unnatural lust.

'Strip her,' Coffin Ed ordered Wop.

She heard the uncontrollable threads of desire in his voice

and thought she was about to be raped. She shook her head and tried again to talk, mumbling what sounded like, 'You don't have to—'

Wop stared in petrified stupidity. 'Strip her?' he echoed as though he didn't understand the words.

'Take her mother-raping clothes off,' Coffin Ed said through clenched teeth. 'Ain't you never done that?'

Wop moved toward her as though she were a lioness with cubs. She was passive, raising each foot in turn for him to remove her shoes and stockings. No one spoke. Only their heavy breathing and the chattering of Wop's teeth were audible. But he took so long to remove her sheen gabardine suit and chartreuse underclothes the silence became excruciating.

When she was stark naked, Coffin Ed released her.

She turned and saw him for the first time. 'Oh, it's you!' she said in her jarring voice.

'It's me all right.'

She dropped to her knees and clasped his thighs in a tight embrace. 'Just don't hurt me,' she said.

'What the hell!' he said, and grabbed a fistful of her hair and dragged her onto the couch.

Her thick cushiony mouth opened in pain as she sucked in breath, but she didn't dare scream. He rolled her over and carefully examined her for needle marks, but didn't find any.

'Tie her down,' he ordered Wop.

Wop moved like a robot, joints stiff and eyes senseless.

When he had finished, Coffin Ed said, 'Get her compact from her handbag.' Then he leaned over and took her by the hair again. Pulling her head back until her throat was taut, he cut the skin in a thin line six inches across her throat.

She didn't move, didn't breathe. Her eyes were limpid pools of terror set in a fixed stare.

'Give me the mirror,' he said.

He held it before her eyes. 'See your throat.'

A thin line of blood showed where he had cut. She fainted.

He tossed away the compact and said with a choked impotent fury, 'Let anybody's blood flow but their own!'

Then he slapped her until she came to.

He knew that he had gone beyond the line; that he had gone outside of human restraint; he knew that what he was doing was unforgivable. But he didn't want any more lies.

She lay rigid, looking at him with hate and fear.

'Next time I'll cut it to the bone,' he said.

A shudder ran over her body as though a foot had stepped on her grave.

'All right, I'll tell you,' she said. 'I'll tell you how to get it. It's what you want, isn't it?'

He looked at her without answering.

'We'll split it,' she went on. 'We'll cut your partner in too. There's enough for all three of us. You don't want me but you can have me too. You'll want me when you've had me. You won't be able to get enough of me. I can make you scream with joy. I can do it in ways you never dreamed of. You're cops. You'll be safe. They can't hurt you. You can kill them.'

He was caught for a moment in a hurt as terrible as any he had ever known. 'Is everybody crooked on this mother-raping earth?' It came like a cry of agony torn out of him.

Then he said in a voice so tight it was barely audible, 'You think because I'm a cop I've got a price. But you're making a mistake. You've got only one thing I want. The truth. You're going to give me that. Or I'm going to fix you so that no man will ever want anything else you got to give. And I ain't playing.'

'They'll kill me.

'They're going to kill you anyway if I don't kill them first.'

Twenty-three minutes later he had her story. He had no way of knowing whether it was true. Only time would tell.

He looked at his watch. It read 11:57.

He untied her and told her to get up and dress.

He figured he knew as much as he was ever going to know. Before the payoff, anyway. If what she said was true, he had cased it right himself. If it wasn't true, they were all going down together.

While she was dressing he listened to the sound of a

recording coming from the lounge. Other recordings had been playing before, but he hadn't heard them.

It was a saxophone solo by Lester Young. He didn't recognize the tune, but it had the 'Pres' treatment. His stomach tightened. It was like listening to someone laughing their way toward death. It was laughter dripping wet with tears. Colored people's laughter.

His thoughts took him back to the late 1930s – the 'depression' years. When he and Digger had attended a P.S. on 112th Street. They'd heard Lester playing with the Count Basie group at the Apollo, swapping fours and eights with Herschel Evans on their tenor horns.

Pres! He was the greatest, he thought.

'I'm ready,' Ginny said.

'Open the door and call Madame Cushy,' he said.

When Madame Cushy entered the room, he looked her over carefully. Satisfied she was unarmed, he said to Ginny, 'You go out first, I'll follow you,' and then to Wop, 'You come behind me and if you see anybody with a gun, just scream.'

Madame Cushy's lips curled. 'If we were going to hurt you, you'd be dead by now. You won't be hurt around here.'

Silently he sheathed the knife and stuck Grave Digger's pistol back inside his waistband. He looked at her again. 'Digger's dead,' he said, then added, 'And you're living.'

He motioned with his hand and they left in single file.

Madame Cushy held the door open. When Coffin Ed passed her, she said quietly, 'I won't forget you.'

He didn't answer.

He smelled the stink of terror coming from their bodies as they descended in the elevator. He thought bitterly, They're all scared as hell when it's their own lives they're playing around with.

Before crossing the sidewalk to his car, he stood for a moment in the doorway, casing the street, his gun in his hand. He didn't expect any gunplay. If what she had said was true, the gunmen would not be in sight. It was just a precaution. He had learned the hard way not to believe anybody entirely when it's your own life at stake.

He didn't see anyone or anything that looked suspicious.

They walked to the car in the same position as they had left the flat. He got into the front seat from the inside and slid over. The other two came in after him, Ginny in the middle and Wop on the outside.

I wish Digger was here, he thought without thinking.

He didn't think that thought anymore.

20

It took only seven minutes to get there and he didn't hurry. The hurry was off.

He made a U-turn on St Nicholas Avenue, went down the incline to 125th Street, and turned west toward the Hudson River.

For a couple of blocks more, 125th Street was still in the colored section: jukeboxes blared from the neon-lighted bars, loudmouthed people milled up and down the sidewalks, shrill-voiced pansies crowded in front of the Down Beat where the dusky-skinned female impersonators held forth, weedheads jabbered and gesticulated in front of Pop's Billiards Parlor. And then the big new housing project loomed dark and silent.

He turned south on Broadway, west again on 124th Street, and climbed the steep hill of Clermont Avenue behind the high stone wall of International House. Another turn toward the river and he came out into the quiet confines of Riverside Drive beside Riverside Church.

He had kept an eye on the rearview mirror but had seen no indications that he was being followed.

So far so good, he thought.

He parked directly in front of the apartment house and doused his lights; but he sat for a moment casing the street before alighting. Everything looked normal. Nothing was moving for the moment but the cool breeze coming up from the river. Cars parked for the night lined the inside curb despite a city ordinance forbidding it. Nevertheless he had his pistol in his hand when he got out on the street side and walked around the front of the car.

Wop was already getting out on his side and Ginny followed. They crossed the sidewalk in single file and she unlocked the apartment house door with her own key.

Coffin Ed let them both precede him, then said, 'Wait here.'

He went down the hall to the elevator door and brought the elevator to the ground floor. He opened the door and looked inside of it, then closed the door to the elevator itself and stood for a moment studying the outside door to the elevator shaft. There was nothing to be seen. The floor of the elevator was flush with the floor of the hall and the top of the elevator door was flush with the top of the door to the shaft.

He came back and said, 'All right, let's go down,' leading the way.

They came out in the basement corridor and found the night lights turned on as was customary. Coffin Ed stopped them for a moment and made them stand still while he listened. He could see the doors to the janitor's suite, the toolroom, the staircase, the elevator and the laundry, and the one at the back which opened onto the back court. There was not a sound to be heard, not even from outside. His gaze lit for a moment on a short ladder hanging from the inside wall beneath a fire extinguisher. It must have been there before but he hadn't noticed it.

At the end of the corridor, toward the janitor's door, the cheap worn luggage, trunks and household furnishings of the new janitor were stacked against the wall. But the janitor hadn't moved in. There was a police seal on the janitor's door.

Coffin Ed opened his Boy Scout knife and broke the seal. Ginny unlocked the door, stepped inside and switched on the light.

She drew back and cried out, 'God in heaven, what happened?'

It looked the same as when Coffin Ed had seen it last, except the corpse of the African had been removed.

'Your friend got his throat cut,' he said.

She stared in horror at the patches and clots of black dried blood and began trembling violently. Wop's teeth began to chatter again.

'What the hell you so horrified about? It ain't your blood,' Coffin Ed said bitterly, including them both.

Ginny began turning green. He didn't want her sick so he said quickly, 'Just get me the keys.'

She had to pass through the room to the kitchen. She skirted the edge, bracing herself with her hand against the wall, as though traversing the deck of a ship in a storm.

When she returned with the ring of house keys, Coffin Ed said to Wop, 'You stay here.'

Wop looked at the dried blood and the wreckage and turned a shade of light gray that seemed impossible for a person with black skin.

'Do I got to?' he stammered.

'Either that or go home.'

He stayed.

Coffin Ed pushed Ginny into the corridor, closed and locked the door on Wop, then went and bolted the back door that opened onto the rear court. Ginny stood beside the elevator door as thought she were afraid to move.

'Stay put,' Coffin Ed directed when he returned and got into the elevator.

Her face broke out in alarm. 'You're not going to leave me here?'

'No worry,' he said and shut the door in her face.

He heard her protesting as he took the elevator up to the first floor but he paid it no attention.

He left the elevator and started down the stairs and ran head-on into Ginny as she was coming up.

'Whoa, where you going, baby?' he said, heading her off.

'If you think I'm gonna—' she began, but he interrupted, taking her arm:

'You're going to show me how to cut off the power to this thing.'

'Awright, awright, you don't have to be so mother-raping rough every time you open yo' mouth,' she grumbled but she obeyed readily enough.

She showed him a small square key on the ring which

opened the basement door to the elevator shaft. The power switch was inside. 'Just push it,' she said.

He found a button switch and pushed it.

'Anyway, it's not in there,' she said. 'They said they looked in there.' Her voice wasn't loud, but it wasn't lowered.

He looked into a pit of blackness. 'Shut up and give me a light,' he said.

'There's a light inside. Feel down below and you'll find the switch.'

He groped in the dark and found a small switch. A naked bulb at the end of an extension cord lying on the oil-covered floor lit up, showing a six-foot concrete pit at the bottom of the shaft.

A heavy spring bumper supporting a thick steel block rose from the center of the pit. In the back were the cable pulleys and the large electric motor that operated the lift cable. Beside it were a switchboard and adjustment levers.

He lowered himself into the pit, found some greasy cotton waste, and wiped off the instruction plates on the motor and above the levers. One of the levers worked with the motion of a jack handle, and was used to jack the elevator up or down to make it flush with the corridor floors.

He jacked it down as far as it would go, about three feet. Then he climbed out of the pit and, leaving the light on, closed the door to the shaft.

He turned the power back on and brought the elevator down to the basement. Now when he opened the door the floor of the elevator was three feet below the floor of the basement. It was now possible to crawl on top of the elevator from the door of the elevator shaft.

He took the ladder from the wall, propped it against the front of the elevator, and climbed up.

'Do you see it?' she asked breathlessly.

He didn't answer.

He put his head and shoulders through the opening atop the elevator, ascended the ladder as far as he could, then wriggled forward on his belly.

'Have you found it?' she called anxiously.

'Pipe down,' he said, feeling about for the blue canvas utility bag.

When he found it he drew it forward beside his hip, then turned over on his back and drew both revolvers. He checked them in the dim, reflected light coming up the sides of the elevator from the pit. They checked.

He began worming forward on his back, inch by inch, moving the bag forward with his elbow.

'It's not there?' she asked. Her voice was strained to the breaking point and jarred on his nerves.

'Will you shut up and let me look!' he grated.

He kept inching forward until his feet touched the ladder. Only his head and shoulders and his hands holding the revolvers remained unseen. Then he knocked the bag out onto the basement floor.

'He's got it!' she screamed, and dove into the elevator.

There was a slight grunting sound as Coffin Ed jumped and came down like a cat somersaulting in the air.

Simultaneously the hophead gunman leaped into the corridor from the staircase.

Both shot before their feet touched the floor. Coffin Ed shot left-handed with Grave Digger's pistol, shooting from the hip in a manner he despised. The gunman shot right-handed with the silenced derringer across his left shoulder, the police positive dangling from his left hand.

In the tight narrow corridor the very air exploded with the hard heavy thunderclap of the long-barreled .38 revolver, drowning the slight deadly cough of the silenced derringer.

The brass-nosed .38 slug hit the gunman on the pivot of the jaw and scattered bone, blood and teeth into the air, while the .44 slug from the derringer burned a hole through Coffin Ed's left sleeve and seared his flesh like a branding iron.

Landing wide-legged and flat-footed in a half-crouch, Coffin Ed pumped two more slugs into the gunman's body, propelling it into a macabre dance before the fat gunman had cleared the bottom step.

Trying to brake his charge and shoot at the same time, the fat gunman threw two wild shots with his .38 automatic, chipping plaster from the ceiling and puncturing the fire extinguisher; while Coffin Ed blasted with both guns and put two slugs side by side in his bulging belly.

Then Coffin Ed's beret sailed from his head in a forward flight like a missile taking off, and a fraction of a second later a brass-jacketed .45 slug coming from behind hit him on the shoulder blade and knocked him flat on his face.

The third gunman had stepped from the laundry, blasting with a .45-caliber Colt's army automatic. But before he could squeeze the trigger for the third time, plainclothes dicks poured out of the very walls and crevices, and the corridor erupted with the heavy artillerylike booming of several police positives fired in unison. The gunman went down riddled with thirteen slugs.

It was all over in twenty-seven seconds.

The air was blue-gray and suffocating from cordite fumes, and gun-roar still echoed in their ears.

Two gunmen lay dead on the floor. With his guts perforated, his liver punctured and his spleen blown open, the fat gunman lay dying. A detective was trying to get a statement but he wasn't talking.

Another detective dragged Ginny from the elevator and slipped on the cuffs while a third brought Wop from the janitor's flat. There were nine detectives in all, three from the homicide bureau, three from the narcotics squad, and three T-men.

Coffin Ed was gritting his teeth in an agony of bone hurt and trying to push to his feet with his left hand. Two detectives helped him up while another went to the telephone at the end of the corridor and called the precinct station for two police hearses and two ambulances.

'I'm all right,' Coffin Ed said. 'Where's my gun?'

He still had Grave Digger's pistol in his left hand, but he'd been knocked loose from his own by the impact of the .45 slug.

With a grin, a T-man opened his coat and put the pistol into its holster. Coffin Ed stuck the other one back into his waistband. The T-man buttoned the bottom of Coffin Ed's jacket and made a sling for his arm.

The lieutenant from the narcotics squad weighed the blue canvas bag in his hand and looked at Coffin Ed questioningly.

But it was the lieutenant from homicide who asked the question, 'How did you figure it was there?'

The narcotics lieutenant said, 'He didn't. Don't you think we looked there?'

'The hell I didn't,' Coffin Ed said. 'I put it there the first thing I did this afternoon when I left the house.'

'So it's just bait.'

'Yeah. It was the best I could think of.'

For a moment everyone looked at him. His jerking, ugly patch-work face was such a picture of agony, they looked away.

'It gives me an idea,' one of the T-men said. 'If it worked once, it might work twice. We got Benny Mason and his chauffeur staked out down the street, beyond Grant's Tomb. He's watching the entrance here through night field glasses.'

'She said he'd be around somewhere,' Coffin Ed said, nodding toward the woman.

'What's your idea?' the narcotics lieutenant asked.

'Let's send this woman down the street, the other way, carrying this bag. He'll try to get it—'

'Then what? There's nothing in it,' the homicide lieutenant said. 'Nothing to make a charge.'

The T-man smiled. 'We'll put something in it. We were thinking of a trap too, in case we found a way to spring it. So we brought along a little package too, with two kilos of pure heroin. We'll just slip that into the bag—'

'And let him get it?'

'That's the idea. We don't want to disappoint Mister Mason.'

'You'd better hurry,' the homicide lieutenant said. 'In two minutes' time this street will be overrun with prowl cars.'

'That won't make much difference to Mister Mason, as hot as he is after this stuff, but we'll hurry anyway.'

Another T-man produced the package of heroin and they made the substitution and took the handcuffs from Ginny's wrists.

'I won't do it,' she said.

All of them stared at her with those blank looks policemen have when a prisoner defies them.

'What do you have on her?' the T-man asked.

'Conspiracy,' Coffin Ed said.

'We got more than that,' the homicide lieutenant said with a straight face. 'She killed the African.'

'I didn't!' she screamed. 'It's a mother-raping lie!'

'We can prove it,' the homicide lieutenant said in a flat voice.

'You're trying to frame me,' she accused.

'That's the general idea. Of course you can take your chances in court.'

'Dirty mother-rapers!' she fumed.

'Give me thirty seconds alone with her,' Coffin Ed said.

She flicked one glance at his face and her defiance wilted. 'All right, give me the mother-raping bag,' she said.

21

Shadows were framed in dark open windows and the faint distant sound of a siren floated in the silent night when she stepped outside, but no one was in sight.

She turned toward downtown, in the direction of Riverside Church, and began walking fast. She carried the bag as far as possible away from contact with her own flesh, as though it contained a germ bomb that might leak.

Four blocks north, where the drive bends around the sloping green park surrounding Grant's Tomb, a long black Mark II Lincoln, with only its parking lights burning, pulled from the curb. No light emanated from the instrument panel. Only the vague silhouettes of two black-hatted men on the front seat were visible in the dim light coming from the street. The dark aquiline features of the man beside the driver were further obscured by heavy sunglasses. The driver's face was but a round white blur beneath his black chauffeur's cap.

The Lincoln accelerated with incredible speed, but slowed down almost instantly as a prowl car screamed around the far corner by Riverside Church on two wheels, its red light blinking like the eye of hell.

Ginny had seen the Lincoln move and now she welcomed the prowl car as a savior and hastened in its direction. But it was still some distance away. She had started to break into a run when a voice called from the dark entrance of the apartment house next door.

'Honey,' the cracked voice called sweetly.

Her scalp crawled as her head jerked around. Her eyes probed the darkness. She halted on the balls of her feet.

'It's me, Sister Heavenly,' the cracked saccharine voice identified itself.

She stood suspended in flight. 'What the hell do you want?' she demanded viciously.

The prowl car roared past, lighting them briefly with the red spotlight, and dragged to a screaming stop beyond the next-door entrance. It had ignored them.

'Come here, honey, I got something for you,' Sister Heavenly said in what she thought was a sweet cajoling voice.

Ginny realized instantly that Sister Heavenly was after the canvas bag. And I'll give her the mother-raping bag, she decided evilly.

She turned quickly and stepped forward into the dark entrance.

'Here,' Sister Heavenly said sweetly, and plunged the long sharp blade of her knife deep into Ginny's heart.

Ginny slumped without a sound, without so much as a gasp, and Sister Heavenly clutched the bag from her nerveless fingers and hastened down the sidewalk in the same direction.

It went so fast it looked like magic. One moment a young woman in a green suit was carrying a blue canvas bag down the sidewalk; the next moment an old woman in a long black dress and a black straw hat was carrying the same bag in the same direction.

The detectives watching from a black Chrysler sedan parked at the curb up the street didn't know what to make of it.

But Benny Mason's chauffeur said, 'Look, there's been a switch.'

Benny already had his field glasses focused on the bag. 'She gave it to somebody else, that's all,' he said.

The two prowl car cops hit the pavement and charged into the apartment house, obscuring the vision of the watching detectives. For a moment the street looked clear of cops.

The Lincoln accelerated. Behind it the black Chrysler sedan

pulled out from the curb. Far ahead down Riverside Drive was the distant red eye of another prowl car coming fast. And from all directions came the sound of sirens, shattering the night, as unseen cars and ambulances converged on the scene.

'Pull over fast,' Benny said.

The Lincoln lunged to the other side of the street and braked silently just ahead of Sister Heavenly and the driver jumped to the sidewalk with a heavy black sap in his hand.

Sister Heavenly saw the car brake and the man jump out in the same sidewise glance. She was carrying the blue canvas bag along with her own black beaded bag in her left hand. Somewhere along the way she had discarded the parasol and instead was carrying the .38-caliber Owl's Head with the sawed-off barrel wrapped in a black scarf in her right hand.

Without turning her body or slackening her pace, she raised the pistol and pumped four dumdum bullets into the chauffeur's body.

'Jesus Christ!' Benny said, and in a fast smooth motion drew his own P38 Walther automatic and shot twice through the open car door.

One slug caught Sister Heavenly in the left side below the ribs and lodged in the side of her spine; the other went wild. She fell sidewise to the pavement and was powerless to move, but her mind was still active and her vision was clear. She saw Benny Mason slide quickly across the seat, leap to the sidewalk, and aim the pistol at her head.

Well now, ain't this lovely? she thought just before the bullet entered her brain.

Benny Mason snatched the bag from her limp hand and jumped back into the Lincoln beneath the wheel. All around him were the red lights of prowl cars converging in the street. His mind was shattered by the head-splitting screaming of sirens. He couldn't see; the air looked red and his brains seemed to be pouring out of his ears. He began accelerating before closing the car door.

The Lincoln crashed broadside into the Chrysler sedan that had cut across in front of it. T-men poured from the Chrysler and surrounded him. He grabbed the bag and tried to throw it, but a T-man reaching through the open door caught him by the wrist and froze the bag in his hand.

'Son, you're going on a long journey,' the T-man said.

'I want to see my lawyer,' Benny Mason said.

The apartment house basement was filling up with uniformed prowl car cops who couldn't find anything to do.

Coffin Ed had his coat off and his right hand held between the buttons of his shirt in place of a sling. Detectives had cut out the back of his shirt and were using a wad of clean pocket handkerchief to staunch the flow of blood until the ambulance arrived. But he was slowly turning gray from loss of blood.

No one knew what the outcome was outside, and the homicide lieutenant put off interrogating Coffin Ed until his wound had been treated. So they were all just standing about.

But Coffin Ed had a need to talk.

'You guys figured too they'd come back?'

'We didn't figure it,' the homicide lieutenant said. 'We engineered it. We knew you were on the prowl and that they were on your tail. That might have kept up all night. So we had to get you here. We knew they'd come after you, just like you did.'

'You got me here? How was that?'

The homicide lieutenant reddened. 'You know by now that Grave Digger is alive?'

Coffin Ed became rigid. 'Alive? The radio said—'

'That was how we did it. We gave out the story. We knew that after you had heard it you would get them here some way to kill them. You're not sore, are you?'

'Alive!' Coffin Ed hadn't heard the rest of it. Tears were streaming unashamedly from his blood-red eyes. He shook his head. 'Well, I'll be a monkey's uncle.' It felt as though his brains were banging against his skull. But he didn't mind. 'Then he'll never die,' he said.

The lieutenant patted his good shoulder as delicately as though it were made of chocolate icing. 'Only way we could figure to cover you. We don't want to lose our good men.' He smiled a little. 'Of course we didn't expect a theatrical production.'

Coffin Ed grinned. 'I dig you, Jack,' he said. 'But sometimes these minstrel shows play on when grand opera folds.'

Then suddenly and unexpectedly he fainted.

It was past two o'clock in the morning. The prowl cars and ambulances and hearses had gone from the street and only the black inconspicuous sedans of the plainclothesmen remained among the sedate automobiles of the residents. Quiet once again prevailed in this exclusive residential street.

The crew from the Medical Examiner's Office had been and gone and the six corpses had been taken to the morgue. The fat gunman had died before they arrived and had been tagged D.O.A. with the others. He had died without talking. Now there were only the gobs and patches of clotted blood to mark the spots where the six lives had taken exit.

Wop was in jail, safe at last.

But there was still activity in the basement of the apartment house where the interrogations continued and the reports of this fantastic caper were being recorded to shock and horrify what one must hope will be a less violent posterity.

The dining table from the janitor's flat had been set up in the corridor and the two lieutenants and chief of the T-men were sitting in bloodstained chairs about it. A police stenographer sat apart, taking down the words as they were spoken.

Coffin Ed sat facing his interrogators across the table. He had been taken to the Polytechnical Clinic in midtown to have the bullet removed from his shoulder blade and the wound dressed. His guns, sap and hunting knife had been taken from him by the homicide lieutenant, and a detective had accompanied him to the clinic. Technically, he was under arrest for homicide and was being held for the magistrate's court later that morning.

The hospital doctors had tried to put him to bed, but he had insisted on returning to the scene. In lieu of his bloodstained shirt, he now wore a hospital nightshirt tucked into his pants, and his arm was in a black cotton sling. Bandages made a lump on his right shoulder like a deformity.

'It's been a bloody harvest,' the T-man said.

'Gun-killing is the twentieth-century plague,' the homicide lieutenant said.

'Let's get to the story,' the narcotics lieutenant said impatiently. 'This business is not finished yet.'

'All right, Ed, let's hear your side,' the homicide lieutenant said.

'I'll start with the janitor's wife, and just repeat what she told me. You have my statement from before. Maybe you can fit it all together.'

'All right, shoot.'

'According to her, all she knew at first was that Gus had disappeared. He left her and the African in the flat at about eleven-thirty and said he'd be back in an hour. He didn't come back—'

'Where was Pinky during this time?'

'She said she hadn't seen Pinky since late afternoon and hadn't thought about him until we questioned her after the false fire alarm.'

'So he wasn't around?'

'He could have been. She just didn't see him. When she found out he was on the lam and Gus hadn't come back, she began to worry about what to do with the dog. They weren't taking the dog and Gus hadn't made any arrangements for it, and she didn't know about S.P.C.A. And of course if Pinky turned up, there was the rap against him for the false fire alarm, and she intended phoning the police and having him arrested. So along toward morning she sent the African out to drown the dog in the river.

'Digger and I were sitting outside in the old struggle buggy when the African took it away. We thought then he might have drowned it, but it was none of our business and we didn't see anything else suspicious, so we left. If we'd stayed twenty minutes longer we'd have seen Sister Heavenly when she arrived.

'She got here about ten minutes to six and said she was looking for Gus. Ginny, that's the janitor's wife, was suspicious – said she was, anyway – but she couldn't get any more out of Sister Heavenly. Then at six o'clock the front doorbell rang. Ginny had no idea who it was, but suddenly Sister Heavenly drew a pistol from her bag and covered her and the African and ordered her to push the buzzer to release the front door latch; and she made them both keep still. Evidently she expected the caller to come straight to the flat. But instead they took away the trunk and left without knocking. When she finally looked out here in the hall and saw the trunk was gone, she ran out of the house without saying a word. And that was the last Ginny saw of her – so she said.'

'What happened to the trunk finally?' the homicide lieutenant asked.

'She claimed she never found out.'

'All right, we'll get on to the trunk tomorrow.'

'I'm in the dark here,' the T-man said. 'Who was going where?'

'She and Gus – he was the janitor – were going to Ghana. They'd bought a cocoa plantation from the African.'

The T-man whistled. 'Where'd they get that kind of money?'

'She told us – Digger and me – that his first wife died and left him a tobacco farm in North Carolina, and he sold it.'

'We have all that from your first statement,' the homicide lieutenant said impatiently. 'Where did the African fit into this caper?'

'He didn't. He was an innocent bystander. When Gus didn't show up after the trunk was taken, Ginny began getting more and more worried. So the African left the house about a half hour after Sister Heavenly to look for Gus. In the meantime it was getting late and Ginny began to dress. They had to go to the dock to get their luggage on board.'

'The trunk should have been delivered the day before,' the T-man said.

'Yeah, but she didn't know that. All that was worrying her was Gus's continued absence. She was just hoping the African would find him in time for them to make the boat. She never saw the African again. She had just finished dressing when the two white gunmen who shuttled her about Harlem first turned up. They said Gus had sent them to take her to the dock. She left a note for the African telling him where she was going. Then the gunmen picked up her luggage and took her out to their car. When they got in the fat man drove and the hophead sat in the back and covered her with the derringer.

He told her Gus was in trouble and they were taking her to see him.'

'Didn't she wonder about the gun?'

'She said she thought they were detectives.'

The homicide lieutenant reddened.

'They took her to a walkup apartment on West 10th Street in the Village, near the railroad tracks, and bound and gagged her and tied her to the bed. First they went through her luggage. Then they took off the gag and asked her what she had done with the junk. She didn't know what they were talking about. They gagged her again and began torturing her.'

Abruptly the atmosphere changed. Faces took on those bleak expressions of men who come suddenly upon an inhumanity not reckoned for.

'Gentle hearts!' the T-man said.

'The next time they took off her gag she blabbed for her life,' Coffin Ed said. 'She told them Gus had pawned the stuff but when she saw that wasn't the answer she said he took it to Chicago to sell. That must have convinced them she really didn't know about it. One of them went into another room and made a telephone call – to Benny Mason, I suppose – and when he came back they gagged her again and left. I figure they came straight up here and searched the flat.'

'And killed the African.'

'I don't think they killed him then. The way I figure it they must have searched twice. In the meantime they probably went and had a talk with their boss.'

'No doubt he sent them back and told them to find it or else,' the narcotics lieutenant said. 'If it was two kilos of heroin it was worth a lot of money.'

'Yeah. I figure the African must have been here when they returned, or else he came in while they were searching. We'll never know.'

'You think they tried to make him talk?'

'Who knows? Anyway, that's when we ran into them and set off the big chase. If I'd listened to Digger's advice and just laid dead, maybe we'd have never tumbled to the dope angle.'

'Not necessarily,' the narcotics lieutenant said. 'We knew a shipment of H had left France, but we didn't know how or when. The French lost it somewhere between Marseille and Le Havre.'

'But we've been on to it for the past week,' the T-man said. 'Working with the local squad – secretly. We've had the water-front covered from end to end.'

'Yeah, but you'll find out later you didn't cover it far enough,' Coffin Ed said. 'When the hoods returned to the flat in the Village, Benny Mason went with them. The woman became hysterical when they took off the gag. She said Benny sat beside her and comforted her. He sent out for a doctor who came and treated her and put her under sedation—'

'What doctor?'

'She didn't say and I didn't ask her. Benny sent the doctor away and promised her she wouldn't be hurt again if she was co-operative. Anyway, he won her confidence. In the meantime he sent the hoods out of the room and pulled up a chair, straddled it and sat facing her. And he leveled with her—'

'Then he intended to have her killed,' the narcotics lieutenant said.

'Yeah, but she was too square to dig it. Anyway, he told her that he was the boss of the narcotics racket, that he had the shit smuggled into the country and he had used Gus to pick it up sometimes; and that was how Gus got the money to buy this farm in Ghana. That shocked her; she had believed Gus's hype about his wife leaving him a farm down South. He must have figured it would have that effect because he wanted her to start thinking and remember something she hadn't thought was important before. He went on to tell her that he had had Gus thoroughly investigated and he was certain Gus was a square, just greedy for some money. She agreed to that but she didn't know what he was leading to. He told her that Gus had picked up a shipment of heroin at midnight, worth more than a million dollars, and he was supposed to pass it on in the trunk that was picked up at six o'clock.'

'Picked up from who?' the narcotics lieutenant asked.

'He said the heroin was smuggled into the country on a French liner.'

'We know the French liner that docked this week,' the narcotics lieutenant said. 'We've had it under a tight surveillance.'

'Yeah, but you missed the connection. It was dropped overboard to a small motorboat that passed under the bow without stopping at about eleven o'clock night before last.'

'My men were watching that boat through night glasses and there was nothing dropped overboard,' the T-man said.

'Maybe it was already in the water. I'm just repeating what she said Benny told her. Benny had sent a map to Gus by Jake, the pusher – the one Digger and me got suspended for slugging.'

The city detectives looked embarrassed but the T-men missed the connotation.

'The map showed Gus the exact spot where the shipment would be dropped – only a short walk from here. The boat came up the river and delivered the shipment without ever stopping. Benny said he knew that Gus collected it because the connection told him that Gus was waiting when the boat arrived; and furthermore, when the boat returned to the yacht basin in Hoboken the T-men were waiting for it and searched it and they found it clean.'

'By God, I got a report on that boat!' the T-man said. 'It's owned by a taxicab driver named Skelley. He does night fishing.' He turned to one of his men in the background. 'Have Skelley and everyone connected with him picked up.'

The agent went toward the telephone.

'Benny said when his men picked up the trunk the shipment wasn't in it,' Coffin Ed continued. 'She thought maybe Gus had run off with it since it was worth so much. He had gone out before midnight and she hadn't seen or heard of him since, and that wasn't like Gus; he didn't have any friends he could put up with and he didn't have anywhere else to go. Benny said no, he had probably been robbed. They had found Gus and he was hurt and wasn't able to talk and he figured someone had hijacked the shipment—'

'But he left the bundle with Gus for six hours before he sent to pick it up. You think he was that stupid?'

'It was as safe with Gus as anywhere – in fact safer. They had him covered. And since he was actually supposed to sail that day, they figured the trunk dodge would attract less attention than any other. Besides, Benny wasn't taking any chances; he had a lookout posted outside all night. The lookout saw Gus come into the apartment after he had kept the rendezvous and he didn't see anyone leave after then who was carrying anything in which the shipment could have been concealed. The lookout saw Digger and me come and go after the false fire alarm; he saw the African go out with the dog and return without it; he saw Sister Heavenly when she came and left. No, Benny was certain that the shipment hadn't left this house.'

The detectives exchanged glances.

'Then it's still here,' the homicide lieutenant said.

'That's impossible, the way this place has been searched, unless one of the tenants is in on the deal, and we've checked them going and coming and I'd bet my job they're innocent,' the narcotics lieutenant said. 'I personally was with the searching crew when they went through every trunk, every box, every piece of furniture in the storage room; they turned the toolroom inside out, took apart the oil burner, dismantled the washing machines, raked out the incinerator, looked into the sewers, even took two stored automobile tires off the rims; and you saw how the janitor's flat has been searched. We'd have found a signet ring if we'd been looking for it.'

'That's the way Benny figured it. It was too big a bundle to hide, and the only way Gus could have got rid of it was to give it to somebody in this house to hold for him.'

'How big a bundle was it, or did he say?' the T-man asked.

'He told her there were five kilos of eighty-two percent pure heroin in it.'

A cacophony of whistling sounded spontaneously.

'That's one hell of a load,' the homicide lieutenant said.

Calculating rapidly, the T-man said, 'He pays about fifteen thousand dollars per kilo for the junk. Say around seventy-five thousand for the shipment. And after he cuts it down with lactose to about two percent pure, he can retail it for around a half a million dollars a kilo. Say, give or take a little, it's worth two and a half million dollars on the retail market.'

'Now we've got the motive for this massacre,' the homicide lietuenant said.

'But where did the junk disappear to?' the narcotics lieutenant echoed.

'That's the question Benny asked. But she couldn't help

him. She said Gus wasn't on good terms with any of the tenants; in fact his relations were on the bad side.'

'No wonder,' the narcotics lieutenant said. 'He didn't need this job.'

'Then Benny asked her about Pinky. She told him all she knew but he wasn't interested in Pinky's life. He wanted to know if Pinky could have got the stuff from Gus and hidden it somewhere in the house. She said he'd have to wait until Gus could talk and ask him, she hadn't seen either him or Pinky since before midnight. Then he confessed that when they didn't find the shipment in the trunk they had killed Gus and thrown his body in the river.'

'That sounds to me like he was lying,' the T-man said, and turned to the narcotics lieutenant. 'Do you believe that?'

'Hell no! They wouldn't kill Gus, even by accident, as long as the five-kilo bundle of H was missing.'

'That's the way I see it.'

'But where is Gus?'

'Who knows?'

'Maybe he's still somewhere in the house,' the homicide lieutenant ventured.

'No, he's not,' the narcotics lieutenant stated flatly.

'Then maybe Benny was leveling with her.'

'No, he was probably trying to scare her,' the homicide lieutenant said.

'He scared her all right,' Coffin Ed said. 'But right away he offered her five thousand dollars if she would help them find him – Pinky that is.'

'Generous bastard,' the T-man said.

'That's when she got on their side,' Coffin Ed said. 'With Gus dead and five G's in her apron, and now the farm was hers too, she could marry the African. She didn't know he was dead. So she put her mind to it, and then she remembered noticing the night before that the trunk had been moved from the storage room into the hall. And as a rule Pinky did all the heavy moving. So she said maybe Pinky had it with him.

'But Benny discarded that too. He had investigated Pinky along with Gus, and he had him cased as a pure halfwit, incapable of handling that much H; he wouldn't know what to do with it. She argued that Pinky had the habit and maybe he took it for personal use. But Benny's lookout had seen Pinky leave here when he went to put in the false fire alarm, and he couldn't have concealed a handkerchief in the ragged clothes he was wearing. And he hasn't been back here since.

'Then she remembered Sister Heavenly's visit. She told him that Sister Heavenly was Pinky's aunt, and that she sold decks of heroin under the guise of a faith healing racket. Then Benny remembered his lookout reporting that Sister Heavenly had left here shortly after the trunk was picked up. He conceded that maybe she was right, maybe Sister Heavenly was the connection, and maybe Pinky had hijacked the bundle. That would be just like a halfwit.

'They took her down to the car and all of them drove up to the Bronx to look for Sister Heavenly. But by the time they got there the house had been blown up and Sister Heavenly had disappeared. But they found out about Uncle Saint and they saw the Lincoln. It was one of Benny's guards whom Uncle Saint had shot over by the French Line dock and they began putting two and two together.'

'We made a line on that,' the homicide lieutenant said. 'We tied it all together after Sister Heavenly's body was identified by the boy, Wop. And we already had a report on the car from an officer stationed at the Lincoln Tunnel.'

'Yeah. Well, they figured Sister Heavenly had already gotten the bundle and had blown up the house to kill Uncle Saint and destroy her tracks—'

'It was just the old joker trying to crack her safe,' the homicide lieutenant said drily. 'The experts made it.'

'Yeah, it wasn't long before they dug that too. Benny had kept lookouts on this house all day, and one of them remembered Sister Heavenly nosing around here after Digger was shot. So Benny figured by that she hadn't made the connection. After then they concentrated on finding Pinky.'

'We kept a line on all of you after that,' the homicide lieutenant said. 'No need of going into detail now.'

'There's just one question I'd like to ask,' the T-man said. 'How was it they didn't spot you, Ed, when you planted your bag on top of the elevator?'

'They saw me all right, but they didn't make me. You see, I didn't come in here. I went to the second house from here and went up to the roof and crossed over. I dropped the bag from the top access to the elevator shaft. Besides which I was wearing painter's coveralls and carrying the small bag inside of a large paint-smeared bag the last painters had left in my house. And when I went back outside the same house I'd entered, I was carrying the same big bag.'

'All that is well and good and you deserve credit for it,' the narcotics lieutenant said. 'But where in the hell is the junk?'

The T-man said to Coffin Ed, 'You're the only one here who knew Pinky. Do you think he's capable of that?'

'I wouldn't know,' Coffin Ed said. 'I figure him for a halfwit too. But so was Al Capone.'

'All that this proves is one thing,' the narcotics lieutenant said. 'That this case is not finished; not by a damn sight. Not with a fortune in heroin floating around.'

'For us it's just begun,' the T-man said.

'I've got a hunch we'll find it,' Coffin Ed said.

'A hunch? What hunch?' the homicide lieutenant asked.

'If I told you, you'd laugh.'

'Laugh!' the homicide lieutenant exploded angrily. 'Laugh! With eleven people whom we know of already dead from this one caper, and five kilos of pure poison loose in New York City, and we haven't even scratched the bottom of it. Laugh? What the hell's the matter with you? What's your hunch? Let's hear it.'

'I've got a hunch that Gus is coming back and then we'll find out where it's at.'

In the dead silence which followed, the detectives could feel their hackles rise. They stared at him with blank, deadpan expressions.

Finally the T-man said, 'Well, at least no one is laughing.'

23

The dick stationed on the front door came in and said, 'A Railway Express truck just pulled up out front. I think they're delivering something here.'

'Get back and keep out of sight,' the homicide lieutenant said quickly.

'If it's what I think, we ought to clean up here,' Coffin Ed said.

The detectives looked at him curiously, but they did as he suggested. Quickly they moved the table and chairs back into the janitor's flat and then split into two groups. Some remained there and the others rushed to the other end of the corridor and stationed themselves in the laundry.

Ears were pressed to the closed doors, listening for footsteps. But after the faint sounds made by the opening and closing of the front door, the silence was prolonged.

Then they heard a faint rap on the basement floor, followed by a slight scraping sound as though some small object had been placed there stealthily.

Doors were flung open and detectives rushed into the corridor with drawn pistols. They stopped in their tracks as though they had all run into an invisible wall.

A black gaint, so black he looked dark purple in the bright light, the blackest man any of them had ever seen, crouched over a large green steamer trunk that hadn't been there before.

It was the giant who inspired their first amazement. He was dressed in the kind of uniform the Railway Expressmen wear, but it was so small on him the coat wouldn't button, the sleeves ended halfway down the forearms and the pants halfway up the legs. His purple-black feet were encased in blue canvas sneakers, and a uniform cap sat atop kinky hair that was decidedly purple.

Pink eyes darted this way and that from the black-purple face. And then the giant started to run.

'Halt!' several voices cried in unison.

But it was Coffin Ed who stopped him by shouting, 'Give up, Pinky. We got you.'

'Pinky!' the homicide lieutenant exclaimed. 'My God, is this Pinky?'

'He's dyed himself,' Coffin Ed said. 'He's really an albino.'

'Now I've seen everything,' the T-man said.

'Not yet,' Coffin Ed said.

The detectives surrounded Pinky and the homicide lieutenant snapped on the handcuffs.

'Now we'll get to the bottom of this,' he said.

'Let's open the trunk first,' Coffin Ed said. 'Give us the key, Pinky.'

'I ain't got it,' Pinky whined. 'The African's got it.'

'All right, let's break it open.'

A dick got a crowbar from the toolroom and pried open the lock.

When they lifted the lid only a jumble of soiled laundry was at first visible. But after pulling it aside, a corpse was revealed. It was the corpse of a small gray-haired man with a small wrinkled black intelligent-looking face. He wore a suit of spotless clean blue denim coveralls and black hip boots.

Everyone began talking at once.

'It's Gus,' Coffin Ed said.

'His neck's been broken,' the T-man said.

'This makes twelve,' the homicide lieutenant said.

'Maybe the bundle is underneath,' a dick said.

'Don't be silly, Benny Mason's had this trunk,' the narcotics lieutenant said.

'Is this your hunch?' the homicide lieutenant asked Coffin Ed.

'More or less.'

'How did you figure it?'

'You'll see.'

The homicide lieutenant addressed Pinky. 'Why did you kill him?'

'I din kill 'im,' Pinky denied in his high whining voice. 'The African and that woman killed 'im.'

'Why did you bring him back here?' Coffin Ed said.

'So they'd be punished, thass why,' he whined. 'They killed my pa and they got to be punished.'

Coffin Ed turned to the homicide lieutenant. 'That's how I dug it. Why would he put in that false fire alarm if he even knew about the H? He just wants to get Gus's wife and the African charged with murder.'

'They done it,' Pinky insisted. 'I know they done it.'

'Let's skip that for a moment,' the homicide lieutenant said. 'The question is where did you find the trunk?'

'At the dock, where they took it. They was going to take him on the ship and throw him in the ocean so nobody'd ever know what happened to him. But I done beat 'em to him.'

'That's a cunning lick,' the homicide lieutenant said. 'When Benny saw there was only a corpse inside, he had it delivered to the wharf.'

'Let's first find out what he did with the junk,' the T-man said impatiently. 'Every minute counts on that angle.'

'We ought to get to that slowly,' Coffin Ed suggested.

'The African and the woman are dead, Pinky,' the homicide lieutenant said quietly. 'And we know they didn't do it. So that only leaves you.'

'Dead? Is they both dead? Sure enough dead?'

'Dead and gone,' Coffin Ed said.

'So you may as well tell us why you did it,' the homicide lieutenant said.

Pinky looked at the corpse for the first time and tears welled in his pink eyes.

'I didn't go to do it. I didn't go to do it, Pa,' he addressed the corpse.

He looked up first at the homicide lieutenant, then at the circle of blank white faces. Then his gaze came to a rest on the ugly brown face of Coffin Ed. 'He was going 'way to Africa and he wouldn't take me with him. I ast him and I begged him. He was going take that yellow woman and he wouldn't take me, and I'se his real 'dopted son.'

'So you killed him.'

'I din go to kill him. But he made me so mad. I ast him again just 'fore he went out fishing—'

'Fishing?'

Everyone became suddenly alert.

'What time was that?' the homicide lieutenant asked.

''Bout half past 'leven. He put on his high boots and got his line and net and went eel fishing. Thass what made me so mad. He'd ruther go eel fishing in the black dark than lissen to me. So I waited and when he come back I ast him again. And he tole me to go away and leave him alone. He say he was too busy to lissen to foolishness.'

'Had he caught any eels?'

'He caught five big black eels. I don't know how he done

it so fast but he had 'em in his fishnet. He must 'ave caught
'em before and left 'em in the river 'cause they was all
stone dead.'

'How big were they?'

'Big eels. 'Bout two – three pounds, I reckon.'

'Eel skins stuffed with heroin. Waterproof. That's a clever
dodge,' the T-man said. 'Only a Frenchman would think of
it.'

'What was he doing when you talked to him the last time?'
the homicide lieutenant kept hammering gently.

'He were looking in his trunk for somepin. He had it open
looking in and I ast him once more to take me with him and
he tole me to get the hell away from him. I just 'tended to
shake him a little and make him lissen and 'fore I knowed it
his neck broked.'

'And you put his body in the trunk and covered it with
soiled clothes from the laundry and brought it out here in
the hall, then you went and put in the false fire alarm so you
could accuse his wife and the African of his murder.'

'They was guilty in they heart,' Pinky said. 'They was going
to kill 'im for his treasure map if it weren't for the accident. I
heered 'em say they was going to kill 'im. I swear 'fore God.'

'Map! You knew about the map?'

'I seen it just 'fore he went fishing. He tole me it showed
where a big mess of treasure was buried in Africa and made
me promise not to tell nobody 'bout it.'

The detectives looked at one another.

'Did his wife and the African know about it?' the homicide
lieutenant asked.

'Must 'ave. Thass why they was going to kill 'im.'

The homicide lieutenant turned to Coffin Ed. 'Do you
believe that?'

'No, he's making it up to justify something.'

'Let's get back to the eels,' the T-man put in. 'Now just
where were the eels when you talked to him, Pinky?'

'They were on the floor 'side the trunk where he drop 'em
when he come in.'

'What did you do with them?'

'I figure if I left 'em there somebody'd know he'd done
already come back from fishing.'

'Yes, yes. But what did you do with them?'

'Them dead eels? I just threw 'em away.'

'Yes-yes-yes; but threw them away where?'

'Where? I just threw 'em in the 'cinerator. It was full of paper and trash and I just threw 'em in there and set it on fire.'

The T-man became hysterical and had to be beat on the back. 'A three-million-dollar fire!' Tears streamed from his eyes.

Pinky stared at him. 'They weren't nothing but stone-dead eels,' he whined. 'They didn't even look fit to eat.'

The detectives roared with laughter as though that was the funniest thing they had ever heard.

Pinky looked as though his feelings were hurt.

Coffin Ed asked curiously, 'Why wouldn't he take you to Africa with him, Pinky? Was it because of your habit?'

'Twarn't 'cause of my habit. He didn't mind that. He said I was too white. He said all them black Africans wouldn't like colored people white as I is, and they'd kill me.'

'I wonder what the court is going to make of that?' the homicide lieutenant said.

24

Charges were dismissed against Coffin Ed.

After coming from the magistrate's court, he and his wife stopped by the hospital to see Grave Digger. He was out of danger, but he was resting and couldn't be seen.

Leaving the hospital they ran into Lieutenant Anderson, who was on his way to see Grave Digger too.

They told him how he was, and the three of them went to a little French bar over on Broadway in the French section.

Coffin Ed had a couple of cognacs to keep down his high blood pressure. His wife looked at him indulgently. She settled for a Dubonnet while Anderson had a couple of Pernods to keep Coffin Ed company.

Coffin Ed said, 'What hurts me most about this business

is the attitude of the public toward cops like me and Digger. Folks just don't want to believe that what we're trying to do is make a decent peaceful city for people to live in, and we're going about it the best way we know how. People think we enjoy being tough, shooting people and knocking them in the head.'

His wife patted the back of his big calloused hand. 'Don't worry about what people think. Just keep on doing the best you can.'

To change the subject, Anderson said encouragingly, 'It's going to mean something to the commissioner that you helped clean up this case.'

'The thing I'm happiest about,' Coffin Ed said, 'is that Digger is still alive.'

ALSO AVAILABLE FROM PAYBACK PRESS

THE HARLEM CYCLE *VOLUME 1*

A RAGE IN HARLEM, THE REAL COOL KILLERS, THE CRAZY KILL

CHESTER HIMES
WITH AN INTRODUCTION BY
MELVIN VAN PEEBLES

Gathered together for the first time are the first three novels in what came to be known as the Harlem cycle. Combining fantastic plots with blood-soaked realism, Himes produced some of the greatest crime novels ever. This, the first of three compendium volumes, gives a whole generation of new readers the chance to appreciate the black humour, gripping storylines and social awareness that justify his description as the father of black Amercan crime writing.

"A crime writer of Chandlerian subtlety though in a vein of sheer toughness very much his own." *The Times*

"Chester's writing was no third-hand bullshit gleaned from some secondary source...every sentence of every page reeks of authenticity." *Melvin Van Peebles*

The Harlem Cycle is available from all good book shops or alternatively direct from us, postage and packaging free. See back pages for details.